Change is ~~Change~~ good . . . isn't it?

Change. Change. CHANGE.

All over his body, fluctuations in thermo-dynamic potentials, in kinetic reaction rates, hormonal levels. A ferment of cellular renewal, boiling within the changing skin. CHANGE. Liver, spleen, kidneys, prostate, heart, lungs, brain . . . CHANGE. Fires along nerves, flickering lightnings of pain, crashing thunderstorms of sensation, signals flying from reticular network to cerebral cortex to hypothalamus to dorsal ganglia. A clash of arms at the blood-brain barrier . . . CHANGE. SYNTHESIZE. ACCOMMODATE.

. . . And then, suddenly, all voices merging to one voice. And fading, weakening, withdrawing, drifting down in volume. The tide was ebbing. The changes shivered to a halt. The tank tilted and the front cracked open, exposing his skin to cold air.

He walked across the room to a full-length mirror and stared hard at his own reflection. The new skin on his body still bore a babyish sheen, though pale and wrinkled from long immersion. Soon it would smooth and mature to deep ivory.

"And here we are again. But why bother?" Behrooz Wolf spoke very softly to his reflection.

Baen Books by Charles Sheffield

Brother to Dragons
Between the Strokes of Night
The Mind Pool
Dancing with Myself

CHARLES SHEFFIELD

PROTEUS
COMBINED

PROTEUS COMBINED

This is a work of fiction. All the characters and events portrayed in this book are fictional, and any resemblance to real people or incidents is purely coincidental.

Proteus Combined has been published in slightly different form as *Sight of Proteus,* copyright © 1978 by Charles Sheffield and *Proteus Unbound,* copyright © 1988 by Charles Sheffield.

A Baen Books Original

Baen Publishing Enterprises
P.O. Box 1403
Riverdale, N.Y. 10471

ISBN: 0-671-87603-1

Cover art by Barclay Shaw

First combined printing, May 1994

Distributed by
PARAMOUNT PUBLISHING
1230 Avenue of the Americas
New York, N.Y. 10020

Printed in the United States of America

BOOK I

SIGHT OF PROTEUS

To Rachel, Tom, Adam,
Jenny, Daniel, and big and little Emma

PART I

"Have sight of Proteus rising from the sea,
Or hear old Triton blow his wreathed horn."

PART I

CHAPTER 1

The new fall catalog had arrived that morning. Behrooz Wolf, like millions of others, had settled in for an evening of browsing and price comparison. As usual, there were many variations on most of the old forms, plus an intriguing set of new ones that BEC was releasing for the first time. Bey keyed out the catalog displays, studying the images and the prices and occasionally marking a form for future reference.

After about an hour his interest began to fade and his attention wandered. He yawned, put down the catalog, and went to his desk in the corner of the room. He picked up and looked through a couple of texts on form-change theory, then, restless as ever, leafed through his casebook. Finally, he picked up the BEC catalog again. When the phone buzzed, he gave an instinctive mutter of annoyance, but the interruption was a welcome one. He pressed the wrist remote.

"Bey? Put me up on visual, would you," said a voice from the wall screen.

Wolf touched his wrist again, and the cheerful, ruddy face of John Larsen appeared on the wall holo. Larsen looked at the catalog that Bey was holding and smiled.

"I didn't know that was out yet, Bey. Tomorrow's the official release date. I haven't had the chance to see if mine has arrived. Sorry to call you at this hour, but I'm still over here at the office."

"No problem. I couldn't get too interested in this, anyway. It's the same old irritation. The forms that appeal the most need a thousand hours of work with the machines, or else they have a lousy life ratio."

"—or they require a whole mass of computer storage, if they're anything like last spring's releases. How are the prices?"

"Up again, and you're quite right, they need more storage, too. Look at this one, John." He held up the open catalog. "I already have a billion words of primary storage, and I still couldn't begin to handle it. Four billion words, or you shouldn't think of ordering it."

Larsen whistled softly. "That's certainly a new one, though. It's the closest thing I've ever seen to an avian form. What's the life ratio on it? Bad, I'll bet."

Wolf consulted the tables in the catalog and nodded agreement.

"Less than 0.2. You'd be lucky to last ten years with it. You might be all right in low-g, but not otherwise. In fact, there's a footnote that says it can achieve flight in a lunar gravity or less. I suppose they're hoping for USF sales."

He closed the catalog.

"So, what's happening, John? I thought you had a date—why the midnight oil?"

Larsen shrugged. "We've got a mystery on our hands. I'm baffled, and it's the sort of problem you thrive on. Do you feel up to a trip back to the office tonight? You're the boss, but I'd really like to get your opinion."

Wolf hesitated. "I wasn't planning to go out again. Can't we handle it over the holo?"

"I don't think so. But maybe I can show you enough to persuade you to come over here." Larsen held out a sheet so that it could be seen on the holoscreen. "Bey, what do you make of this ID code?"

Wolf studied it carefully, then looked back at Larsen questioningly. "It seems normal enough. Is it somebody I'm supposed to know? Let me just check it through my percomp."

Larsen watched in silence as Wolf entered the digits of the chromosome ID code that had replaced fingerprint, voiceprint, and retinal patterns as the absolute identification method. The link from his personal computer to the central data banks was automatic and almost instantaneous. When the response came, Wolf frowned at it for a moment, then looked in annoyance at John Larsen.

"What's the game, John? There's no such ID in the central files. Is it one that you made up?"

"I wish it were, but it's nothing so simple."

Larsen reached behind him and picked up a printed report.

"I told you, Bey, this is a strange one. I had a call about three hours ago from a medical student. This afternoon, he was over in the transplant ward of Central Hospital when a liver transplant case came in. He's been taking a course in chromosome analysis, and he'd missed one of the lab sessions where they were supposed to try the technique out on a real case. So he had the idea of doing an ID check on a sample from the donor liver—just to see if he had the technique correct."

"That's illegal, John. He can't have the licenses to use that equipment."

"He doesn't. He did it anyway. When he got home, he fed the ID code into central files and asked for donor identification and matching. The files couldn't produce a match."

Bey Wolf looked sceptical—but intrigued. "He must have made a measurement error, John."

"That was my first reaction. But he's an unusual young man. For one thing, he was willing to call us, even though he knew he might get in trouble for doing the ID analysis without proper permission. I told him he must have done something wrong, but he said he'd done it three times, twice the usual way and once with a shortcut method that he wanted to try out. It came out the same each time. He's sure that he handled the technique correctly and didn't make any mistakes."

"But there's no way to fake a chromosome ID, and every human being is listed in the central files. Your student is telling us that he tested a liver that came from a person who never existed."

John Larsen looked pleased. "That's what I wanted to

hear you say. It was my conclusion exactly. Well, Bey? See you over here in an hour or so?"

The evening shower was over, and the streets were once again a wild, colorful chaos. Bey left his apartment and worked his way over to the fastest slideway, threading through the mass of people with practiced ease. With the population over fourteen billion, crowding was normal, night or day, even in the most affluent parts of the city. Wolf, preoccupied with Larsen's problem, scarcely noticed the throng that surrounded him.

How could anyone have escaped the chromosome typing? It was performed at three months, right after the humanity tests—and it had been that way for a century. Could the donor be old, a dying ancient? That was ridiculous. Even if the donor wanted it that way, no one would use a century-old liver for a transplant operation. Bey's thin face was puzzled. Could it be that the donor was an off-worlder? No, that wouldn't explain it either. The IDs for people from the United Space Federation were all separately filed, but they were still in the records at the central data banks. The computer response would have been delayed a little, but that was all.

He was beginning to feel the old mixture, a tingle of excitement modulated by a fear of disappointment. His job in the Office of Form Control was a good one—he didn't know of a better. But although he had been highly successful in it, somehow it was not completely satisfying. Always, he felt that he was waiting for the big challenge, the problem that would stretch his abilities to their limits. Maybe this could be the one. At thirty-four, he should know what he wanted to do with the rest of his life—it was ridiculous still to be full of the heart searching of adolescence.

In an attempt to suppress his illogical sense of anticipation and to prepare his mind for the problem ahead, Bey keyed his communication implant and tuned to the newscast. The familiar beaked nose and sloping brow of Laszlo Dolmetsch appeared, directly stimulated on his optic nerves. The people and the slideways were still faintly visible as a ghostly superimposed image—the laws forbade total exclusion of the direct sensory feeds. The early slideway deaths had taught that lesson.

Dolmetsch, as always, was holding forth on the latest social indicators and making his usual pessimistic prophecies. If the concentration of industry around the Link access points were not lessened, there would be trouble. . . . Bey had heard it all before, and custom had staled the message. Sure, there were instabilities in the social indicators—but that had been the case ever since the indicators were first developed. Bey looked again at Dolmetsch's profile and wondered about the popular rumor. Instead of using form-change to diminish that great beak, the story went, Dolmetsch had increased it—to become an unmistakable figure anywhere on Earth. That he certainly was. Bey could not remember a time when Dolmetsch had not been a prominent prophet of doom. How old was the man now? Eighty, or ninety?

Bey mentally shrugged and switched channels. He had to return to the real world for a moment, to move quickly out of the way of two red-coated medical emergency staff hurtling at top speed along the fastest slideway, then he skipped through the other news channels. Not much there. A mining accident on Horus, so far from most Solar System activities that it would take months for relief to reach it; a promising discovery of kernels out in the Halo, which meant fortune for some lucky prospector and more free energy for the USF; and the perennial rumor of a form-change that would give immortality to the wearer. That one cropped up every couple of years, regular as the seasons. It was a tribute to the continued power of wishful thinking. No one ever had any details— just the vaguest of hearsay. Bey listened scornfully and wondered again how people could pay attention to such a flimsy prospect. He switched back to Dolmetsch—at least the old man's worries were comprehensible and had a solid basis of fact. There was no doubt that the shortages and the violence were barely under control, and the population, despite all efforts, was still creeping upward.

Could it ever hit fifteen billion? Bey remembered when fourteen had seemed intolerable.

The crowds surging along the slideways didn't seem to share Wolf's worries. They looked happy, handsome, young, and healthy. To people living two hundred years earlier they would have seemed models of perfection. Of course, this was the west side, closer to the Link entry point, and that helped. There was plenty of poverty and ugliness elsewhere. But forget for the moment the high prices and the mass of computer storage that was needed. BEC—the Biological Equipment Corporation— could fairly claim to have transformed the world, that part of the world, at least, that could afford to pay. Here on the west side, affluence was the norm and use of the BEC systems a sine qua non.

Only the general coordinators shared Laszlo Dolmetsch's view of the problems in keeping the economic balance of the world. Earth was poised on a knife edge of diminishing resources. Constant subtle adjustments, calculated by application of Dolmetsch's theories, were needed to hold it there. Every week there were corrections for the effects of drought, crop failures, forest fires, epidemics, energy shortages, and mineral supplies. Every week the general coordinators watched the indices for violence, disease, and famine and waited grimly for the time when the corrections would fail and the system would run amok into worldwide slump and economic collapse. In a united world, failure of one system means failure of all. Only the off-Earthers, the three million citizens of the United Space Federation, could cling to their shaky independence—and the USF watched the economic indicators at least as closely and nervously as any Earth-based coordinator.

As he neared his goal, Bey Wolf kept an automatic eye open for illegal forms. Makeup and plastflesh could hide a great deal, but with the Office of Form Control he had been specially trained to see past the outward form, through to the shape of the underlying body structure.

Here, on the public slideways, the chances of running

into an outlawed form were small—but Bey still had occasional nightmares about the feline form he had spotted less than a mile from here two years earlier. That had cost him two months out of action, in the accelerated change and recovery room of the Form Control Hospital unit.

As he made the transitions back to the slowest slideway, he noticed again the large number of rounded Elizabethan foreheads on the people he was passing. That had been a minor special of the spring catalog but had turned out to be a big hit. He wondered what the fall attraction would be—dimples? saber scars? an Egyptian nose?—as he printed into Form Control and went up to Larsen's office on the third floor.

As Bey Wolf was climbing the stairs, a few miles east of him a solitary white-coated figure dialed a vault combination and stepped through into the underground experiment room, four floors below City level. The face and figure would be familiar to any scientist. It was Albert Einstein—Einstein at forty, at the very height of his powers.

The man made his way slowly down the long room, checking the station monitors at each of the great tanks. Most received only a few seconds of attention and the occasional adjustment of a control setting, but at the eleventh station he halted. He examined the outputs closely, grunted, and shook his head. Several minutes passed while he stood motionless, deep in thought. At last he continued his patrol and went on into the general control area at the far end of the room.

Seated at the console, he called out the detailed records for the eleventh station and displayed them on the screen. Then he was again silent for many minutes, twisting around his forefinger a lock of his long, graying hair as he bent over the displays of feed rates, nutrient mixes, and other vital indicators. The program-swapping records occupied him for more long minutes, but finally he was finished. He emerged from his concentration, cleared the screen, and switched to voice recording mode.

"November second. Continued deterioration in tank eleven. Response intensity is down by a further two percent, and there is a renewed instability in the biofeedback loops. Change parameters were recalibrated tonight."

He paused, reluctant to take the next step. At last he went on.

"Prognosis: poor. Unless there is improvement in the next two days, it will be necessary to terminate the experiment."

He sat for a moment longer, visibly shaken. At last he stood up. Moving quickly now through the dimly lit room he reset the monitors at each station and switched on the telltales. He took a final look around the room, locked the vault, and entered the elevator that would take him back to ground level. More than ever now, the face was that of Einstein. Over the warmth, intellect, and humanity was etched the pain and torment of a man who worried and suffered for the whole world.

CHAPTER 2

John Larsen, still fresh-faced and cheerful despite the late hour, looked at Bey closely when he came in.

"Late nights don't seem to agree with you," he said. "You look tired. Been neglecting your conditioning program again?"

Wolf shrugged and involuntarily blinked his eyes several times.

"It shows, does it? I was born a bit myopic, you know. If I don't work out regularly, I get eyestrain. I'll have a full session on the bios—first thing tomorrow."

Larsen raised a sceptical eyebrow. Bey was famous for his "tomorrow" statements. He claimed he had inherited subtlety and shrewdness from his Persian mother, along with tenacity and attention to detail from his German father. But from his Persian side had also apparently come a gift for extreme procrastination. Bey swore that there was no word just like *mañana* in the Persian language—there were a dozen related words, but none of them had that degree of urgency. His tendency to delay didn't seem to extend to his work. He was highly effective there. Dark-haired, dark-complexioned, of medium height and build, he had an uncanny ability to efface himself totally and disappear into any crowd—a useful talent for an investigating agent in the Office of Form Control.

Larsen picked up a typed sheet from his desk and offered it to Wolf.

"There it is. The signed, sworn statement of Luis

11

Rad-Kato—that's the medical student. It has the whole story. Gives the time, tells just what he did, quotes the liver ID, and shows where he filed his results in the data banks."

Wolf took the paper and glanced over it. "I suppose you already pulled the records on this out of Central Data to make sure he filed it the way he said he did?"

"Sure. I did that as soon as I received his report. It was still held in the scratch file. I'll read it out again for you."

He dialed the entry code, and the two men waited as the data search was performed. The wait lengthened. After a minute or so Larsen frowned in perplexity.

"There shouldn't be this much delay. The response last time I checked was almost instantaneous. Maybe I goofed on the access code."

He hit the priority interrupt key and reentered the code. This time the message light blinked on, and the display screen filled: ENTRY CODE DOES NOT CORRESPOND TO ANY RECORD IN FILES. CHECK REFERENCE AND REENTER.

"Damnation. That can't be right, Bey. I used that same code less than an hour ago."

"Let me have a go. I know the supervisor entry codes for that area of central storage."

Wolf, much more at home with computers than Larsen, took over the console. He entered the control language statements that allowed him access to the operating system and began to screen the storage files. After a few minutes work he froze the display.

"This is the area, John. Look at it—talk about bad luck! The data dump shows a hardware malfunction in the medical records section, less than an hour ago. A whole group of records has been lost—including the area where the file we want was stored. They were all erased when the system went down."

Larsen looked miserable. He shook his head in disgust.

"It was a lousy time for it to happen, Bey. Now the whole thing will be a pain to follow up. We'll have to call Central Hospital and ask for a new check on the liver transplant ID. They won't like that, but if we reach Dr. Morris in the Transplant Department, he'll probably arrange to do it for us."

"Tonight?"

"No." Larsen looked apologetic. "It can't be done. It's almost eleven now, and Morris works the day shift. We won't get any action until tomorrow. The best I can do is call and leave a stored request for the morning."

He sat down at the video link and prepared to call the hospital, then paused. "Unless you want to go over in the morning and check it in person? We'd actually get faster action that way."

Wolf shrugged. "Might as well. Tonight's shot anyway. Let's leave it all until tomorrow."

Larsen was still apologetic. "It must have been a million to one chance, losing the record we wanted like that."

"More than that, John. The scratch record is copied into a master file, soon after entry, so that there's always a backup copy. The accident must have happened before they could get the copy for permanent storage. I've never even heard of such a thing before—it must be a one in a billion rarity, maybe one in a trillion."

He wore a thoughtful and dissatisfied expression as they went together into the still-crowded streets.

"I've had no dinner, and I broke a date to follow through on this thing," said Larsen. "Do you know, I haven't been outside the office for a minute since I arrived this morning. What's new on the slideways?"

Wolf looked amused. "If you mean women, as you usually do, I wasn't looking too much on the way over. I saw a couple of new ones this afternoon, though—styles straight from old Persia. Fantastic eyes. It would be nice if they caught on and came into fashion."

They merged into the slidewalkers. Like most members of Form Control, Wolf and Larsen were wearing simple forms, close to those given by nature. Years of form-change training, reinforced by the chilling exposure to the outlawed forms, made form-change for pleasure or entertainment a doubtful attraction to them. It took an intriguing form indeed to tempt them to experiment. The biofeedback machines in the Office of Form Control were used for work and for health, almost never for cosmetics. Before Bey went to bed he took a short program on his own equipment for his myopia, and resolved to take a more complete physical overhaul—tomorrow.

CHAPTER 3

The meeting was running well over its scheduled one hour. That happened often. Every year the list of petitioners grew longer, and every year the committee had to weigh more factors in deciding the new legal forms.

Robert Capman, committee chairman, looked at his watch and called the meeting again to order.

"We're late, ladies and gentlemen. This must be our final decision for today. Turn, if you please, to the description of the twentieth petition. Perhaps I can summarize it for you in the interests of speed.

"The basic form is mammalian aquatic. You will see that fourteen variations are also being applied for in simultaneous petition. The developer of the forms points out that one of these variations has a life ratio a little better than 1—about 1.02, to be more precise. This could translate to an extension of a couple of years on a user's life span. BEC has already stated that they would be willing to handle this form and all its variations as Type 1 Programs, fully certified and supported by BEC warranties. Could I now have your comments, please."

Capman paused. He had a gift—part instinct, part experience—that allowed him to control the pace of the meeting completely. There was a stir at the far end of the long table.

"Yes, Professor Richter. You have a comment?"

Richter cleared his throat. He was a lean, fastidious man with a neat black beard. "A question, really. I notice that the basic form can supposedly be reached with less

than two hundred hours of machine interaction. I know
that the main external change, apart from the skin and
eyes, is just the addition of gills to the human form, but
that interaction time seems to me to be too little. I question its accuracy."

Capman smiled and nodded. "An excellent point,
Jacob. I had the same thought myself when I reread this
petition."

Richter warmed to the praise in Capman's voice.

"However," continued Capman, "I now believe that
the statement is accurate. This petitioner seems to have
achieved a real breakthrough. As you know, a form is
usually reached with less effort when it corresponds to
one somewhere in our own genetic history."

Richter nodded vigorously. "Indeed, yes. I have always
thought that to be the reason why the avian forms have
proved so difficult to realize. Are you suggesting that the
petitioner has developed a form that relates to our own
descent?"

"I believe so. More than that, in his application he
points out a new use of form-change. Since the number
of hours of machine interaction seems to correlate
directly with a form's closeness to human genetic heritage, our own remote history can actually be explored
through systematic form-perturbation. Whenever we suspect that a new form lies close to the line of our own
species development, we should look for the perturbations that decrease machine interaction time. Those
changes will generally take us closer to our evolutionary
path. Thus this petitioner has not only contributed to the
present science of metamorphosis, he has also given us
a new tool to examine our own evolutionary heritage."

There was a stir of excitement around the table. Capman rarely offered personal comment on a petition. He
left it to the committee to make their own evaluation
and recommendation. His praise carried weight. The
approval for the use of the new form was swiftly given,
and the ecstatic petitioner received the formal congratu-
lations of the committee.

He left in a blissful daze—with good reason. Adoption

of his forms by BEC as Type I Programs made him an instant millionaire, in either Earth riyals or in USF new dollars.

As soon as he had gone, Capman called the meeting once more to order.

"That concludes the consideration of petitions for today. There is, however, still one extraordinary item of business that I want to bring to your attention before we leave. We cannot resolve it now, but I urge you to think about it in the weeks until our next meeting."

He motioned to one of the minutes secretaries, who handed him a pile of thin folders, which he distributed to the committee members.

"These contain some details of an unusual petition request that we received last week. It has not been through the conventional screening process, because after a quick look at it I judged that we should consider it directly in this committee. It has a life ratio close to 1.3."

There was a sudden hush. Committee members who had been straightening their papers before leaving stopped and gave Capman their full attention.

"The petitioner does not emphasize this," went on Capman, "but the extensive use of this form could increase the average life expectancy to almost one and a half centuries. The appearance of the form is outwardly normal. The changes are mainly in the medulla oblongata and the endocrine glands."

At the far end of the table, Richter had again raised his hand.

"Mr. Chairman, I urge great caution in discussing this form anywhere outside this committee. We all can guess the public reaction if people see a chance to increase their life spans by thirty percent. It would be chaos."

Capman nodded. "That was going to be my next point. There is still another reason why this form must be handled with special care. As many of you may know, I also serve as consultant and technical adviser to the general coordinators. It is in that role that I am most worried by this petition. The widespread use of any form with a life ratio this high could eventually push the population of Earth up above twenty billion. We could not support such a level. If Dolmetsch is correct, we are already crowding close to the absolute limit of population stability."

He closed his notebook.

"On the other hand, I'm not sure that we have the right to suppress any petition for such arguments. The petitioner presumably knows his legal rights. I would like to get your opinion on this next month, after you have all had time to think about it.

"The meeting is now adjourned."

He smiled his thanks at the participants, gathered his papers, and hurried from the room. After the other committee members had also left, the minutes secretaries remained to clear up and compare notes. The junior of the two skipped through his recording, then compared it with the written transcript.

"I show one clean acceptance," he said, "two conditional acceptances subject to further tests, two more to be continued with sponsored research grants. If my count is right, that leaves us fifteen outright rejections."

"Check. Funny, isn't it, how the percentages seem to run about the same each time, no matter what the petitions are?" The blond girl tried an experimental flutter of her eyelashes and a pout of the lips. Getting the form of the Marilyn variations was fairly easy as far as the outward shape was concerned, but the mannerisms took lots of practice. "There, how was that?"

"Not too bad. You're improving, but you're not there yet. I'll let you know when you have it perfect. Look, do you think we should make any special notes on the rejected forms? There's at least one that might be worth a comment."

"I know. The petitioner who tried to develop the wheeled form? I don't know what we could put in the transcripts. 'Widespread and ill-concealed laughter from the committee members'? They had a hard time controlling themselves, the way he was hopping and rolling all over the room. It's probably better to say nothing. I won-

der why somebody would go to all that trouble to make
a complete fool of himself."

"Come on, Gina, we both know why."

"Oh, I guess you're right. Money will always do it."

Of course.

*. . . would you like to be rich, really rich? Then why
not develop a new form to catch the public fancy? You
will get a royalty from every user. . . .*

It sounded easy, but it was not. All the simple forms
had been explored long before. The change specialists
were driven all the time to more exotic and difficult variations. Any proposal had to pass the stringent require-
ments of the petition board, and only one in a million
hit the jackpot.

*. . . BEC will sell you a low-cost experimental package.
It includes everything that you need to create your very
own form-change program. . . .*

Few of the enthusiasts signing up for form-change
experiments worried about the fine print at the end of
the contract: *. . . BEC takes no responsibility for reduced
life expectancy, physical damage, or unstable physical-
mental feedback resulting from form-change experiments
made with BEC equipment. . . .*

For the one in a million lucky or clever enough to hit
on a really successful form, there was still a hidden catch:
the form would have to be marketed through BEC. The
royalty was factored into BEC's prices, and they made
more than the developer.

The statistics were seldom publicized. Licensed form-
change experimenters: 1.5 million. Living millionaires
from new form inventions: 146. Deaths per year directly
attributed to form-change experiments: 78,000.

Form-change experiment was a risky business.

The minutes secretaries didn't realize it, but in the
final petition board they saw only the cream of the
crop—the ones that could still walk and talk. Less than
one in fifty made it to the board. Many of the failures
finished in the organ banks.

"We should include a summary on the humanity-test
proposal, Gina."

"I guess so. I sketched out a short statement while they were still debating it. How about this? 'The proposal that the humanity test could be conducted at two months instead of three months was tabled pending further test results.'"

"I think it needs a bit more detail than that. Dr. Capman pointed out what an argument the present humanity test caused among the religious groups when it was first introduced. BEC had to show success in a hundred thousand test cases before the council would approve it."

He skimmed rapidly through the record. "Here, why don't we simply use this quote, verbatim, from Capman's remarks? 'The humanity tests remain controversial. Unless an equally large sample is analyzed now, showing that the two- and three-month test results are identical, the proposal cannot be forwarded for consideration.'"

They were both much too young to remember the great humanity debates. What is a human? The answer had evolved slowly and taken many years to articulate clearly, but it was simply enough: an entity is human if and only if it can accomplish purposive form-change using the biofeedback systems. The definition had prevailed over the anguished weeping of millions—billions—of protesting parents.

The age of testing had been slowly pushed back to one year, to six months, to three months. If BEC could prove its case, the age would soon be two months. Failure in the test carried a high penalty—euthanasia—but resistance had slowly faded before remorseless population pressure. Resources to feed babies who could never live a normal human life were simply not available. The banks never lacked for infant organs.

Gina had locked her recorder. She pushed back her blond hair with a rounded forearm and threw a smoldering look at her companion.

"Still not quite right," he said critically. "You should droop your eyelids a bit more and get a better pout on that lower lip."

"Damn. It's *hard*. How will I know when I'm getting it right?"

He picked up his recorder. "Don't worry. I told you before, you'll know from my reaction."

"You know, I ought to try it on Dr. Capman—he'd be the ultimate test, don't you think?"

"Impossible, I would have said. You know he only lives for his work. I don't think he has more than two minutes a day left over from that. But look"—only half joking—"if the hormones are running too high in that form, I might be able to help you out."

Gina's response was not included in the conventional Marilyn data base.

The telltales on the experiment stations glowed softly. The only sounds were the steady hum of air and nutrient circulators and the click of the pressure valves inside the tanks. Seated at the control console, the lonely figure looked again at the records of experiment status.

It had been necessary to abort the failure on the eleventh station—again the pain, the loss of an old friend. How many more? Fortunately, the replacement was going very well. Perhaps he was getting closer, perhaps the dream of half a century could be achieved.

He had not chosen his outward form lightly. It was fitting that the greatest scientist of the twenty-second century should pay homage to the giant of the twentieth. But how had his idol borne the guilt of Hiroshima, of Nagasaki? For that secret, he would have given a great deal.

CHAPTER 4

The unexpected loss of the data set containing the unknown liver ID had nagged all night like a subliminad. By the time Bey Wolf reached the Form Control offices his perplexity was showing visibly on his face. As they set off together for Central Hospital, Larsen mistook Wolf's facial expression for irritation at being called out on a wasted mission the previous night.

"Just another hour or two, Bey," he said, "then we'll have direct evidence."

Wolf was thoughtful for a moment, chewing at his lip.

"Maybe, John," he said at last. "But don't count on it. I don't know why it is, but it seems that whenever I get involved in a really interesting case, something comes along and knocks it away. You remember how it was on the Pleasure Dome case."

Larsen nodded without comment. That had been a tough one, and both men had come close to resigning over it. Illegal form-changes were being carried out in Antarctica as titillation for the jaded sexual appetites of top political figures. Starting from a segment of ophidian skin picked up in Madrid, Wolf and Larsen had followed the trail little by little and had been close to the final revelation when they had suddenly been called off the case by the central office. The whole thing had been hushed up, and left to cool. There must have been some very important players in that particular game.

While the slideways transported them toward the hospital, both men gradually became more subdued. It was a natural response to their surroundings. As the blue glaze of the newer city's shielded walls became less common, the buildings seemed drab and shabby. The inhabitants moved more furtively, and the dirt and the refuse became noticeable. Central Hospital stood at the very edge of Old City, where wealth and success handed over to poverty and failure. Much of the world could not afford the BEC programs and equipment. In the depths of Old City, the old forms of humanity lived side by side with the worst surviving failures of the form-change experiments.

The bulk of the hospital loomed at last before them. Very old, built of gray stone, it stood like a massive fortress protecting the new city from Old City. Inside it, the first BEC developments had been given their practical tests—long ago, before the fall of India—but the importance of the hospital's work lived on, deep in human memory. All moves to tear it down and replace it with a modern structure had failed. Now it seemed almost a monument to the progress of form-change.

Inside the main lobby, the two men paused and looked about them. The hospital ran with the frantic pace and total organization of an ants' nest. The status displays in front of the receptionist flickered all the colors of the rainbow, constantly, like the consoles of a spaceport control center.

The young man seated at the controls seemed able to ignore it completely. He was deep in a thick blue-bound book, his consoles set for audio interrupt should attention be needed. He looked up only when Wolf and Larsen were standing directly in front of him.

"You need assistance?" he asked.

Wolf nodded, then looked at him closely. The face, now that it was no longer turned down to the pages of the book, looked suddenly familiar—oddly familiar, but in an impersonal way. Bey felt as though he had seen him on a holograph without ever seeing the man in person.

"We should have an appointment with Dr. Morris of the Transplant Department," said Larsen. "I called him first thing this morning to arrange some ID tests. He told us to come at ten, but we are a little early."

While Larsen was speaking, Wolf had managed to get a closer look at the book sitting on the desk in front of them. It had been a while since he had seen anyone working from an actual bound volume. He looked at the open pages; very old, from the overall appearance, and probably made of processed wood pulp. Bey read the title word by word, with some difficulty since the page was upside down: *The Tragical History of Doctor Faustus* by Christopher Marlowe. Suddenly, he was able to complete the connection. He looked again at the man behind the desk, who had picked up a location director, keyed it on, and handed it to Larsen.

"Follow the directions on this as they come up. It will take you to Dr. Morris's office. Return it to me when you leave, please. To get back here, all you have to do is press RETURN and it will guide you to the main lobby."

As Larsen took the director, Wolf leaned over the desk and asked, "William Shakespeare?"

The receptionist stared at him in astonishment. "Why, that's quite right. Not one visitor in ten thousand recognizes me, though. How did you know? Are you a poet or a playwright yourself?"

Wolf shook his head. "I'm afraid not. Just a student of history, and very interested in faces and shapes. I assume that you get a positive feedback from that form or you wouldn't be using it. Has it helped a lot?"

The receptionist wrinkled his high forehead in thought, then shrugged. "It's too soon to tell. I'd like to think it's working. I thought it was worth a try, even though I know that the form-change theorists are sceptical. After all, athletes use the body forms of earlier stars for their models, so why shouldn't the same method work just as well for an artist? It was a hassle changing to it, but I've decided to give it at least a year. If I don't see real progress in my work by then, I expect I'll change back to my old form."

Larsen looked puzzled. "Why not stay as you are? The form you have now is a good one. It's—"

He stopped abruptly in response to a quick kick from Bey, below desk level. He stared at Wolf for a second, then looked back at the receptionist.

"I'm sorry," he said. "I seem to be a bit dense this morning."

The receptionist looked back at him with a mixture of amusement and embarrassment. "Don't apologize," he said. "I'm just surprised that either of you could tell. Is it all that obvious?" He looked down ruefully at his body.

Bey waved his hand. "Not at all obvious," he said reassuringly. "Don't forget we're from the Office of Form Control. It's our job; we're supposed to notice forms more than other people do. The only thing that tipped me off was your manner. You still haven't adjusted that totally, and you were behaving toward us more like a woman than a man."

"I guess I'm still not completely used to the male form. It's more difficult than you might think. You can get used to the extra bits and the missing bits in a few weeks, but it's the human relationships that really foul you up. Some day when you have a few hours to spare, I could tell you things about the adjustment in my sex life that other people find hilarious. Even I laugh at it now—mind you, I never saw the humor at the time."

Wolf's own interests extended to anything and everything and quite overshadowed his tact. He found that he couldn't resist a question. "People who've tried both usually say they prefer the female form. Do you agree?"

"So far, I do. I'm still learning to handle the male form properly, but if it doesn't pay off in my writing, I'll be very pleased to change back."

He paused and looked at the panel in front of him, where a cluster of yellow and violet lights had suddenly started a mad blinking.

"I'd like to talk to you about your job sometime, but right now I have to get back to the board. There's a stuck conveyor on the eighth level, and no mechanics there. I'll have to try and borrow a couple of machines from Parthenogenetics two floors down." He began to key in to his controller. "Just go where the location director tells you," he said vaguely, already preoccupied completely with his problem.

"We're on our way. Good luck with the writing," said Wolf.

They went over to the elevators. As they continued up to the fifth floor, Larsen could see a trace of a smile on Wolf's thin face.

"All right, Bey, what is it? You only get that expression when there's a secret joke."

"Oh, it's nothing much," said Wolf, though he continued to look very pleased with himself. "At least, for the sake of our friend back there I hope that it's nothing much. I wonder if he knows that for quite a while there have been theories—strong ones—that although the face he is wearing may have belonged to Shakespeare, all the plays were written by somebody else. Maybe he'd be better off trying to form-change to look like Bacon."

Bey Wolf was a pleasant enough fellow, but to appeal to him a joke had to have a definite twist to it. He was still looking pleased with himself when they reached the office of the director of transplants. One thing he hadn't mentioned to John Larsen was the fact that a number of the theories he had referred to claimed that Shakespeare's works had been written by a woman.

"The liver came from a twenty-year-old female hydroponics worker who had her skull crushed in an industrial accident."

Dr. Morris, lean, intense, and disheveled, removed the reply slip that he had just read from the machine and handed it to John Larsen, who stared at it in disbelief.

"But that's impossible! Only yesterday, the ID tests gave a completely different result for that liver. You must have made a mistake, Doctor."

Morris shook his head firmly. "You saw the whole process yourself. You were there when we did the microbiopsy on the transplanted liver. You saw me prepare the specimen and enter the sample for chromosome analysis. You saw the computer matching I just gave you. Mr. Larsen, there are no other steps or possible sources of error. I think you are right, there has been a mistake all right—but it was made by the medical student who gave you the report."

"But he told me that he did it three separate times."

"Then he probably did it wrong three times. It is no new thing to repeat a mistake. I trust that you are not about to do that yourself."

Larsen was flushed with anger and embarrassment, and Morris, pale and overworked, was clearly resentful at what he thought was a careless waste of his precious time. Wolf stepped in to try to create a less heated atmosphere.

"One thing puzzles me a bit," he said. "Why did you use a transplant, Dr. Morris? Wouldn't it have been easier to redevelop a healthy liver, using the biofeedback machines and a suitable program?"

Morris cooled a little. He did not appear to find it strange that a specialist in form-change work should ask such a naive question.

"Normally you would be quite right, Mr. Wolf. We use transplants for two reasons. Sometimes the original organ has been so suddenly and severely damaged that we do not have time to use the regrowth programs. More often, it is a question of speed and convenience."

"You mean in convalescence time?"

"Certainly. If I were to give you a new liver from a transplant, you would spend maybe a hundred hours, maximum, working with the biofeedback machines. You would need to adjust immune responses and body chemistry balance, and that would be all. With luck, you might be able to get away with as little as fifty hours in interaction. If you wanted to regrow a whole liver, though, and you weren't willing to wait for natural regeneration— which would happen eventually, in the case of the liver— well, you'd probably be faced with at least a thousand hours of work with the machines."

Wolf nodded. "That all makes sense. But didn't you check the ID of this particular liver before you even began the operation?"

"That's not the way the system works." Morris went

over to a wall screen and called out a display of the
hospital operational flow. "You can see it easiest if you
follow it here. When the organs are first taken from their
donors, they are logged in at this point by a human.
Then, as you can see, the computer takes over. It sets
up the tests to determine the ID, checks the main physical features of the donor and the organ, fixes the place
where it will be stored, and so on. All that information
goes to the permanent data banks. Then, when we need
a donor organ, such as a liver, the computer matches
the information about the physical type and condition of
the patient with the data on all the available livers in the
organ bank. It picks out the most suitable one for the
operation. Everything after the original logging in is automatic, so the question of checking the ID never arises."

He came back from the wall displays and looked questioningly at Wolf, whose face was still thoughtful.

"So what you're telling us, Doctor," said Bey, "is that
you never have any organs in the banks which didn't
have an ID check made when they first entered it?"

"Not for adults. Of course, there are many infant
organs that don't have their IDs filed. Anything that fails
the humanity tests is never given an ID—the computer
creates a separate file in the data bank for the information about those organs."

"So it *is* possible for a liver to be in the organ banks
and yet have no ID."

"An infant's liver, from a humanity-test failure. Look,
Mr. Wolf, I see where you're heading, and I can assure
you that it won't work." Morris came to the long table
and sat down facing Wolf and Larsen. He ran his hand
over his long jaw, then looked at his watch. "I have things
that I must do, very soon, but let me point out the reali-
ties of this case. The patient who received the liver, as
you saw for yourself, was a young adult. The liver we
used on her was fully grown, or close to it. I saw it myself
at the time of the operation. It certainly didn't come
from any infant, and we would never use infant organs
except for children's operations."

Wolf shrugged his shoulders resignedly. "That's it,

then. We won't take up any more of your time. I'm sorry
that we've been a nuisance on this, but we have to do
our job."

They rose from the table and turned to leave. Before
they reached the doorway, a gray-haired man entered
and waved casually to Morris.

"Hi, Ernst," he said. "Don't let me interrupt you. I
noticed from the visitors log that you have people in
from Form Control, so I thought I'd stop by and see
what's happening."

"They were just about to leave," said Morris. "Mr.
Wolf and Mr. Larsen, I'd like to introduce you to Robert
Capman, the director of Central Hospital. This is an
unexpected visit. According to the hospital daily sched-
uler, you have a meeting this morning with the Building
and Construction Committee."

"I do. I'm on my way there now." Capman gave Wolf
and Larsen a rapid and penetrating look. "I hope that
you gentlemen were able to get the information that you
wanted."

Wolf smiled and shrugged. "Not quite what we hoped
we'd get. I'm afraid that we ran into a dead end."

"I'm sorry to hear that." Capman smiled also. "If it's
any consolation to you, that happens to us all the time
in our work here."

Again, he gave Wolf and Larsen that cool and curiously
purposeful look. Bey felt a sudden heightening of his
own level of attention. He returned Capman's measured
scrutiny for several seconds, until the latter abruptly nodded at the wall display and waved his hand in farewell.

"I'll have to go. I'm supposed to be making a statement
to the committee in four minutes time."

"Problems?" asked Morris.

"Same old issue. A new proposal to raze Central Hospital and put us all out in the green belt, away from the
tough part of the city. They'll be broadcasting the hear-
ings on closed circuit, if you're interested, Channel
Twenty-three."

He turned and hurried out. Wolf raised his eyebrows.
"Is he always in that much of a hurry?"

Morris nodded. "Always. He's amazing, the work load he tackles. The best combination of theorist and experimenter that I've ever met." He seemed to have calmed down completely from his earlier irritation. "Not only that, but you should see him handle a difficult committee."

"I'd like to." Wolf chose to take him literally. "Provided that you don't mind us staying here to watch the display. One more thing about the liver." His tone was carefully casual. "What about the children who pass the humanity tests but have some sort of physical deformity? You did mention that you use infant organs in children's operations. Are they taken from the ones who fail the tests?"

"Usually. But what of it?"

"Well, don't you sometimes grow the organs you need, in an artificial environment, until they're the size you want for the child?"

"We try to complete any repair work before the children can walk or speak; in fact, we begin work right after the humanity tests are over. But you are quite correct; we do sometimes grow an organ that we need from infant to older size, and we do that from humanity-test reject stock. However, it's all done over in Children's Hospital, out on the west side. They have special child-size feedback machines there. We also prefer to do it there for control reasons. As you very well know, there are heavy penalties for allowing anyone to use a biofeedback machine if they are between two and eighteen years old—except for medical repair work, of course, and that is done under very close scrutiny. We like to get the children away from here completely, to prevent any accidental access here to form-change equipment."

Morris turned to the display screen and lifted the channel selector. "I suppose that I should admire your persistence, Mr. Wolf, but I assure you that it doesn't lead anywhere. Why, may I ask, do you lay all this emphasis on children?"

"There was one other thing in the report from Luis Rad-Kato—the medical student. He says that he not only did an ID check on the liver, he did an age test, too. The age he determined was twelve years."

"Then that proves he doesn't know what he's doing. There are no organs used here from child donors. That work would be done over at Children's Hospital. Your comment to Capman was a good one—you are trying to pursue this whole thing through a dead end. Spend your time on something else, that's my advice."

While he was speaking, the display screen from Channel twenty three came alive. The three men turned to it and fell silent.

"From choice, I wear the form of early middle age."

Capman, in the few minutes since he had left the Transplant Department, had found the time to remove his hospital uniform and don a business suit. The committee members who listened to him were wearing the same colorful apparel and appeared to be composed largely of businessmen.

"However," went on Capman, "I am in fact quite old—older than any of you here. Fortunately, I am of long-lived stock, and I hope that I have at least twenty more productive years ahead of me. I am also fortunate enough to be blessed with a retentive memory, which has made my experiences still vivid. It is the benefit of that experience that I wish to offer to you today."

"On his high horse," said Morris quietly. "He never goes in for that sort of pomposity when he's working in the hospital. He knows his audience."

"My exact age is perhaps irrelevant," continued Capman, "but I can remember the days before 'Lucy's in the Water' was one of the children's nursery songs."

He paused for the predictable stir of surprise from the committee. Larsen turned to Wolf.

"How long ago was that, Bey?"

Wolf's expression mirrored his surprise. "If my memory is correct, it is very close to a century. I know it was well over ninety years ago."

Wolf looked with increased interest at the man on the screen. Capman was *old*. "Lucy's in the Water," like

"Ring-a-Ring-a-Rosy" long before it, told of a real event. Not the Black Death, as in the older children's song, but the Lucy massacre, when the Hallucinogenic Freedom League—the Lucies—had dumped drugs into the water supply lines of major cities. Nearly a billion people had died in the chaos that followed as starvation, exposure, epidemic, and mindless combat walked the cities and exacted their tribute. It was the only occasion in four hundred years when the population had, however briefly, ceased its upward surge.

"I remember the time," went on Capman, "when cosmetic form-change was unknown and medical form-change was still difficult, dangerous, and expensive; when it would take months of hard work to achieve a change that we can manage now in weeks or days; when fingerprint and voiceprint patterns were still in use as a legal form of identification, because the law had yet to accept the elementary fact that a man who can grow a new arm can easily change his larynx or his fingertips."

Wolf frowned. The audience that Capman was addressing seemed to be lapping it up, but he was almost certain that the speaker was indulging in a little artistic license. The first developments Capman was referring to had begun even further in the past than the Lucies. In a sense, they had begun way back in the nineteenth century, with the first experiments on limb regeneration of amphibians. Many lower animals could regrow a lost limb. A man could not. Why?

No one could answer that question until two fields, both mature and well explored in themselves, had come together in a surprising way in the 1990s: biological feedback and real-time computer control.

It was already known in the 1960s that a human could use display feedback devices to influence his own involuntary nervous system, even to the point where the basic electrical wave rhythms of the brain could be modified. At the same time, computer-controlled instrumentation had been developing, permitting electronic feedback of computed signals continuously and in real time. Ergan

Melford had taken those two basic tools and put them to work together.

Success in minor things had come first, with the replacement of lost hair and teeth. From those primitive beginnings, advances had come slowly but steadily. Replacement of lost fingertips was soon followed by programs for the correction of congenital malfunctions, for the treatment of disease, and for the control of the degenerative aspects of aging. That might have been enough for most people, but Ergan Melford had seen far beyond that. At the time that he had founded the Biological Equipment Corporation, he already had his long-term goal defined.

The dam broke on the day Melford released his first general catalog. Programs were listed for sale that would allow a user to apply the biological feedback equipment to modify his appearance—and all the world, as Melford well knew, wanted to be taller, shorter, more beautiful, better proportioned. Suddenly, form-change programs could be purchased to allow men and women to be what they chose to be—and BEC, seventy-five percent owned by Ergan Melford, had a monopoly on the main equipment and programs and held all the patents.

On the screen, Capman continued to build his case. "I remember, even though most of you do not, the strange results of the early days of form-change experiments. That was before the illegal forms had been defined, still less understood. We saw sexual monsters, physical freaks, all the repressions of a generation, released in one great flood.

"You do not remember what it was like before we had an Office of Form Control. I remember it well. It was chaos."

Larsen noticed that Morris was looking across at him. "It's not far from chaos now in the office we're in. We still see the wildest forms you can imagine. I suppose the policy now is to get the chaos off the streets and into the Office of Form Control."

Wolf waved him to silence before he could go into details with office anecdotes. Capman, still on screen, was again building his edifice of logic and persuasion.

He had tremendous presence and conviction. Bey was beginning to understand the basis for the respect and reverence that showed through when Morris and others at the hospital spoke about their director.

"All these things I remember, *personally*—not by secondhand reporting. Perhaps you, as members of this committee, wonder what all this has to do with the proposal to tear down Central Hospital and build a new facility outside the city. It has a great deal to do with it. In *every one* of the events that I have referred to, this hospital—Central Hospital, this unique structure—has played a key and crucial role. To most people, this building is a tangible monument to the past of form-change development. Much of that past has been disturbing and frightening, but we must remember it. If we forget history, we may be obliged to repeat it. What better reminder of our difficult past could there be than the continued presence of this building as an active, working center? What better assurance can we have that form-change is under control and is being handled with real care?"

Capman paused for a long moment and looked around the committee, meeting each man or woman eye to eye as though willing their support.

"I should finish by saying one more thing to you," he said. "To me, the idea of removing such a monument to human progress is unthinkable. I do not relish the idea of working, myself, in any other facility. Thank you."

Capman had swept up his papers, nodded to the committee, and was already on his way out of the room before the applause could begin.

"That was the clincher," said Morris. He looked ready to applaud, himself. "I wondered if he'd say that last point. The committee is terrified of the idea that he might resign if they go too far. They'd get so much grief from everybody else, they won't press the point."

He had clearly lost all signs of his earlier irritation with Wolf and Larsen. As they prepared to leave the hospital, he even assured Wolf of his continued cooperation, should anything new be discovered. They said polite farewells inside the hospital, but once outside they felt free to let their own feelings show.

"*Tokhmir*! Where do we go from here, John? That got us absolutely nowhere."

"I know. I guess we'll have to give it up. Rad-Kato made a mistake, and we've chased it into the ground. Isn't that the way it seems to you?"

"Almost. The one thing I still can't swallow is the loss of those data records last night. The timing on that was just too bad to be true. I'll admit that coincidences are inevitable, but I want to look at each one good and hard before I'll accept that there's only chance at work. Let's give it one more try. Let's call Rad-Kato again when we get back to the office."

CHAPTER 5

"I am quite sure, Mr. Larsen." The medical student was young and obviously a little uncomfortable, but his holo-image showed a firm jaw and a positive look in his eyes. "Despite what you heard from Dr. Morris, and I think I can guess his views, I assure you that I did *not* make a mistake. The ID that I gave to you yesterday was correctly determined. More than that, I can prove it."

Larsen pursed his lips and looked across at Wolf, standing beside him. "I'm sorry, Luis, but we went through all that already, in detail. The liver for the patient who received the transplant was given a microbiopsy for us today. We were there, and we watched every stage of the process. We found a different ID, one that's in the central data bank files."

Rad-Kato was clearly surprised, but he looked stubborn.

"Then perhaps they got the wrong patient, or perhaps they made a mistake in their testing."

"Impossible, Luis." Larsen shook his head. "I tell you, we watched the whole thing."

"Even so, I can prove my point. You see, I didn't mention this last night, because I didn't think it was relevant, but I wanted to run a full enzyme analysis on the sample that I took as well as doing the chromosome ID. I didn't have time to do all the work last night. So I stored a part of the sample in the deep freeze over at the hospital. I was going to do the rest of the work tonight."

Wolf clapped his hands together exultantly. "That's it,

John! It's time we had a break. We've had nothing but
bad luck so far on this. Look"—to Rad Kato—"can you
stay right where you are until we get over there? We
need part of that sample."

"Sure. I'm in Fertility. I'll ask the receptionist to send
you to this department when you arrive."

"*No*—that's just what you *don't* do. Don't tell *anybody*,
not even your own mother, that you have that sample.
Don't do anything to suggest that Form Control is interested in it. We'll have someone over in twenty minutes."

Wolf cut the connection and turned to Larsen. "John,
can you get over there at once and pick up the tissue
sample? Bring Rad-Kato with you and do the test with
him in our own ID matching facilities. I would go with
you, but I'm beginning to get ideas on what may be
going on in this business. I need to get to a terminal and
work with the computers. If I'm right, we've seen some
very fast footwork in the past twenty-four hours. I want
to find out who's doing it."

Before Larsen had even left the room, Wolf had
turned to the terminal and begun to call out data files.
It was going to be a long, tedious business, even if he
was right—especially if he was right. He was still feeling
his way through the intricacies of the software that protected files from outside interference when Larsen
returned with the results of their own test of the liver
sample. Rad-Kato had been right. He had made no mistake in his previous analysis; the liver ID corresponded
to nothing in the central data bank files. Wolf nodded
his satisfaction at the results, waved Larsen away, and
carried on with his slow, painstaking search.

In the eighteen hours that followed Wolf moved only
once from his chair, to find the bathroom drug cabinet
and swallow enough cortamine to keep him awake and
alert through the long night. It wasn't going to be too
bad. The old tingle of excitement and anticipation was
back. That would help more than drugs.

In the hidden underground lab three miles from
Wolf's office, two red telltales in the central control sec-

tion began to blink and a soft, intermittent buzzer was sounding. When the solitary man at the console called out the monitor messages, the inference was easy. Certain strings of interrogators were being used to question the central medical data files. His software that looked for such queries was more than five years old and had never before been called upon. He thanked his foresight.

One more tactic was available, but it would probably be only a delayer, and not much of that. The white-coated figure sighed and canceled the monitor messages. It was the time he had planned for, the point where the phaseout had to begin and the next phase be initiated. He needed to place a call to Tycho City and accelerate the transition. Fortunately, the man he wanted was back on the Moon.

"Sit down, John. When you hear this you'll need some support."

Wolf was unshaven, fidgety, and black under the eyes. His shoes were off, and he was surrounded by untidy heaps of output listings. Larsen squeezed himself into one of the few clear spots next to the terminal.

"You look as though you need some support yourself. My God, Bey, what have you been doing here? You look as though you haven't had any sleep for a week. Did you work right through?"

"Not quite that bad. A day." Wolf leaned back, exhausted but satisfied. "John, what did you think when you found out that Rad-Kato was right?"

"I was off on another case all yesterday and this morning, so I haven't been worrying too much about it. I thought for a while that Morris must have done something like palming the sample and substituting another one for it. The more I thought about that, the more ridiculous it seemed."

Wolf nodded. "Don't be too hard on yourself. That was the sort of thing that was going through my head, too. We were both watching him, so it was difficult to see how he could have done it—or why he would want to. That's when I began trying to think of some other way that it could have happened. I began worrying again about the computer failure and the loss of the records that we wanted the first night on the case. Two days ago, was it?"

Wolf leaned back again in his chair. "It feels more like two weeks. Anyway, I used the terminal here to ask for the statistics on the loss of medical records due to hardware failure, similar to the one that happened to us. That was my first surprise. There were *eighty* examples. It meant that the loss of medical data was averaging *ten times* higher than other data types."

"You mean that the medical data bank hardware is less reliable than average, Bey? That doesn't sound plausible."

"I agree, but that's what the statistics seemed to be telling me. I couldn't believe it, either. So I asked for the medical statistics, year by year, working backward. There was high data loss every year in the medical records, until I got back to a time twenty-seven years ago. Then, suddenly, the rate of data loss for medical information dropped to about the same level as everything else."

Wolf had risen from his chair and begun to pace the cluttered office.

"So where did that leave me? It looked as though some medical records were being destroyed *intentionally*. I went back to the terminal to ask for a listing of the specific data areas that had been lost in the medical records, year by year. The problem was, by definition, that the information about the missing areas had to be incomplete. Anyway, I got all I could, then I tried to deduce what it was that the lost data files must have contained."

Larsen was shaking his head doubtfully. "Bey, it doesn't sound like a method that we can place much reliance on. There's no way that you could check what you deduce. That would need a copy of the missing files, and they are gone forever."

"I know. Take my advice, John, and don't ever try it. It's like trying to tell what a man is thinking from the shape of his hat. It's damned near hopeless, and I could only get generalities. I squeezed out four key references with twenty-two hours of effort."

He stopped and took a deep breath. "Well, here's something for you to chew on, John. Did you ever hear— or can you suggest any possible meaning—of research projects with these names: Proteus, Lungfish, Janus, and Timeset?"

Larsen grimaced and shook his head. "I don't know about the possible meanings, but I can tell you right now that I've never heard of any of them."

"Well, that's no surprise, I'm in the same position. I got those names by going to the index files that define the contents of data areas, then querying for the missing files. Apart from the names I came up with, I found out only one other thing. All the four have one common feature—the same key medical investigator."

"Morris?"

"I wouldn't have been surprised if it had been that, John. But it goes higher: Capman. I think that Robert Capman has been purging the data files of certain records and faking it to make it look as though the loss is the result of a hardware failure. I told you you'd need a seat."

Larsen was shaking his head firmly. "No way, Bey. No way. You're out of your mind. Look, Capman's the director of the hospital—you'd *expect* his name to show up all over the medical references."

"Sure I would. But he isn't just the overall administrator of those projects, John, he's the single, key investigator."

"Even so, Bey, I can't buy it. Capman's supposed to be one of the best minds of the century—of any century. Right? He's a consultant to the general coordinators. He's a technical adviser to the USF. You'll have to offer a motive. Why would he *want* to destroy data, even if he could? Can you give me one reason?"

Wolf sighed. "That's the real hell of it. I can't give you a single unarguable reason. All I can do is give you a whole series of things that seems to tie in to Capman. If you believe in the idea of convergence of evidence, it makes a pretty persuasive picture.

"One." He began to check off the points on his fingers. "Capman is a computer expert—most medical people are not. He knows the hardware and the software that's used in Central Hospital better than anyone else. I asked you how we could get the wrong liver ID when Morris did the test. I can think of only one way. Morris put the sample in correctly—we saw him do it—but the data search procedures that handle the ID matching had been tampered with. Somebody put in a software patch that reported back to us with the wrong ID. Morris had nothing to do with it. Now, I'll admit that doesn't really do one thing to link us to Capman—it's wild conjecture.

"Two. Capman has been at the hospital, in a high position, for a long time. Whatever is going on there began at least twenty-seven years ago."

"Bey," broke in Larsen impatiently, "you can't accuse a man just because he's been in a job for a long time. I'm telling you, if you tried to present this to anyone else, they'd laugh you out of their offices. You don't have one scrap of *evidence*."

"Not that I could offer in a court of law, John. But let me keep going for a while. It builds up."

Wolf had on his face a look that John Larsen had learned to respect, an inward conviction that only followed a long period of hard, analytical thought.

"Three. Capman has full access to the transplant organ banks. He would have no trouble in placing organs into them, or in getting them out if he wanted to. He could have disposed of unwanted organs there, and the chance that he would be found out would be very small. It would need a freakish accident—such as the test that Luis Rad-Kato did the other night, by sheer chance.

"A couple more points, then I'll let you have your say. According to the records, Robert Capman personally does the final review of the humanity-test results that are carried out at Central Hospital. If those results were being tampered with, Capman is the one person who could get away with it safely—anybody else would run the risk of discovery by Capman himself. Last point: Look at the hospital organization chart. All the activities I've mentioned lead to Capman."

Wolf flashed a chart onto the display screen, with added red lines to show the links to Capman. Larsen looked at it with stony scepticism.

"So what, Bey? Of course they all lead to him. Damn it, he's the director, they *have* to lead to him. He's ultimately responsible for everything that's done there."

Wolf shook his head wearily. "We're going around in circles. Those lines I added end with Capman, sure—but not in his capacity as director. They end far below that, at a project level. It looks as though he chose to take a direct and personal interest in those selected activities. Why just those?

"There are a couple more things that I haven't had the time to explore yet. One of them would need a trip back to the hospital. Capman apparently has a private lab on the first floor of the place, next to his living quarters. No one knows what he does there, and the lab is unattended except for the robo-cleaners. Capman's an insomniac who gets by on two or three hours sleep a night, so he usually works in the lab, alone, to three or four in the morning. What does he do there?"

Wolf looked at his notes. "That's about it, except for a couple of points that are less tangible."

"*Less* tangible!" Larsen snorted in disgust, but Wolf was not about to stop.

"Didn't you find it peculiar, John, the way that Capman 'dropped in' on our meeting with Morris? He had no reason to—unless he wanted to get his own feel for what we were doing on the investigation. I don't know how aware of it you were, but he looked at the two of us as though he had us under a microscope. I've never had such a feeling before of being weighed and measured by someone.

"One final point, then I'm done. Capman has had absolute control of that hospital for forty years. Everybody there knows he's a genius, and they do whatever he wants without questioning it much. If I know anything at all about human psychology, he probably thinks by this time that he's above the ordinary laws."

Larsen was looking at him quizzically. "That's all very nice, Bey. Now give me some real evidence. You have a lot of circumstantial points. With one piece of solid fact about the case, I'd even be convinced. But everything you've said is still guesswork and intuition. I'll be the first to admit that you're rarely wrong on this sort of hunch, but—"

He was interrupted by the soft buzz of the intercom. Wolf keyed his wrist remote and fell silent for a few seconds, listening to the private line accessing his phone implant. Then he cut the connection and turned to Larsen.

"Real evidence, John? Here's your solid fact, as hard a one as you could ask for. That was Steuben himself on the phone, and he was relaying a message from two levels higher up yet. There is a request for our services—the two of us, specifically, by name—to help investigate a form-change problem for the USF on Tycho Base."

"When?"

"At once. We have orders to drop any other cases that we're working on—Steuben didn't say what they were, and I doubt if he even knows—and leave tomorrow for the Moon. Apparently the request came direct from the office of the general coordinators. When does coincidence get to be past believing?"

"I don't know anybody at all in the general coordinators' office, Bey, and I'm pretty sure they don't know me. Do you know people there?"

"Not a soul. But somebody there—or one of their special consultants, such as you know who—seems to want us off the case we're on now. So somebody knows us and what we're doing. Like to take a bet?"

Larsen's face had begun to flush red. He looked again at the display of the Central Hospital organization, with its glowing lines leading to Capman, and swore softly.

"Bey, I won't take that twice. The business with Pleasure Dome was the last time I'll let them call me off. But they've got us trapped on this. We can't refuse a valid assignment—and for all we know the Tycho Base job is a real one. If only we had more time here. What can we do in one day?"

Wolf looked pale, but he was ready for a fight. He rose to his feet. "We can do at least one thing, John, before they can stop us. We can take a look at Capman's private lab."

"But we'd need a search warrant from head office before we can do that."

"Leave that to me. It reveals exactly what we're doing, but that can't be helped. We have to get over there this afternoon, while Morris is still on duty. I don't know how far we'll get, but we may need some assistance."

"What are you expecting to find, Bey?"

"If I could tell you that, we wouldn't need to go. I feel the same as you do—I'm not willing to be pulled off a case so easily this time, no matter where the order comes from. I want to know how those projects in the missing files—Proteus and the rest of them—tie in to that unidentifiable liver in the Transplant Department. We don't have much time. Let's plan to get out of here half an hour from now."

CHAPTER 6

On the way to the hospital, Larsen became silent and uncommunicative. Wolf noticed that he was listening intently to his phone implant and guessed at the reason.

"Any change in the situation at home, John?" he asked when Larsen finally cut the connection. He thought he could guess the answer.

Larsen looked somber. "Only the change you might expect. My grandfather's still with her. She's going down fast, and she knows it. It won't be more than another day or two. Damn it, Bey, she's a hundred and six years old—what can you expect? She's still using the machines, but it's not doing any good."

He drew a deep breath. "We love grandmother, but what can we say to her? How do you tell someone you love that the right thing now is to go gracefully?"

Wolf could not give him an answer. It was a problem that every family dreaded. Just as BEC's work had provided an answer to the old question of defining humanity, it also provided a definition of old age. Life expectancy was still about a century for most people; fertile, healthy, years spent in peak physical condition. Then one day the brain lost its power to follow the profile of the biofeedback regimes. Rapid physical and mental decline followed, each reinforcing the other. Most people chose to visit the Euth Club as soon as they realized what was happening. An unfortunate few, afraid of the unknowns of death, rode the roller coaster all the way down.

Larsen finally broke the silence. "You know, Bey, I've

never seen old age before. Can you imagine what it must have been like when half the world was old? Losing hair and teeth and eyesight and hearing." He shuddered. "A couple of hundred years ago, I suppose it was all like that. How could they stand it? Why didn't they become insane?"

Wolf looked at him closely. With a difficult time coming at Central Hospital, he had to be sure that Larsen was up to it.

"They had a different attitude in those days, John," he said. "Aging used to be considered as normal, not as a degenerative disease. In fact, some of the signs used to be thought of as assets—proof of experience. Imagine living a couple of hundred years before *that*, if you really want to scare yourself. Life expectancy in the thirties— and no anesthetics, no decent painkillers, and no decent surgery."

"Sure, but somehow you *can't* really think of it. You only really know it when you see it for yourself. It's like being told that in the old days people lived their whole lives blind, or with a congenital heart defect, or missing a limb. You don't question it, but you can't imagine what it must have been like."

They moved on, and finally Wolf spoke again.

"Not just physical problems, either. If your body and appearance were fixed at birth, think how many emotional and sexual problems you might have."

The outline of Central Hospital was looming again before them. They left the slideways and stood together in front of the massive granite columns bordering the main entrance. Each time they entered, it seemed that old fears were stirred. Both men had taken the humanity tests here, although of course they had been too young to have any memory of it. This time it was Larsen who finally took Wolf by the arm and moved them forward.

"Come on, Bey," he said, "They won't test us again. But I'm not sure you'd pass if they did. A lot of people in Form Control say part of you isn't human. Where did you get the knack of sniffing out the forbidden forms the way you do? They all ask me, and I never have a good answer."

Wolf looked hard at Larsen before he at last relaxed and laughed. "They could do it as well as I can if they used the same methods and worked at it as hard. I look for peculiarities—in the way people look or the way they sound and dress and move and smell—anything that doesn't fit. After a few years it gets to be subconscious evaluation. I sometimes couldn't tell you what the give-away was on a forbidden form. I'd have to give it a lot of thought, after the fact."

They were through the great studded doors. The same receptionist was on duty. He greeted them cheerfully.

"You two seem to have caught Dr. Capman's fancy. He gave me this code for you. You can use it anywhere in the hospital—he said you would need it when you got here."

He smiled and handed an eight-digit dial code to Wolf, who looked at Larsen in surprise.

"John, did you call and say we were coming?"

"No. Did you?"

"Of course not. So how the devil did he—"

Wolf broke off and walked quickly to a wall query point. He entered the code, and a brief message at once flashed onto the viewing screen. MR. WOLF AND MR. LARSEN ARE TO BE GIVEN ACCESS TO ALL UNITS OF THE HOSPITAL. ALL STAFF ARE REQUESTED TO COOPERATE FULLY WITH OFFICE OF FORM CONTROL INVESTIGATIONS. BY ORDER OF THE DIRECTOR, ROBERT CAPMAN.

Larsen frowned in bewilderment. "He can't have known we'd be here. We only decided it half an hour ago."

Wolf was already walking toward the elevator. "Believe it or not, John, he knew. We'll find out how some other time. Come on."

As they were about to enter the elevator, they were met by Dr. Morris, who burst at once into excited speech. "What's going on here? Capman canceled all his appointments for today, just half an hour ago. He told me to wait here for you. It's completely unprecedented."

Wolf's eyes were restless and troubled. "We don't have time to explain now, but we need help. Where is Capman's private lab? It's somewhere on this floor, right?"

"It is, along this corridor. But Mr. Wolf, you can't go in there. The director has strict orders that he is not to be disturbed. It is a standard—"

He broke off when Wolf slid open the door, to reveal an empty study. The other two followed him as he went in and looked around. Wolf turned again to Morris.

"Where's the private lab?"

"Through here." He led the way into an adjoining room that was equipped as a small but sophisticated laboratory. It too was empty. They quickly examined both rooms, until Larsen discovered an elevator in a corner closet of the lab.

"Doctor, where does this lead?" asked Wolf.

"Why—I don't know. I didn't even know it was there. It must have been left over from the time before the new lift tubes were installed. But that's over thirty years ago."

The elevator had only one working button. Larsen pressed it, and the three men descended in silence. Morris was counting to himself. When they stopped, he thought for a moment and nodded.

"We're four floors underground now, if I counted them correctly. I don't know of any hospital facilities this deep under the building. It has to be very old—before my time here."

The room they stepped out into, however, showed no signs of age. It was dust-free and newly painted. At its far end stood a large vault door with a combination lock built into the face. Wolf looked at it for a few seconds, then turned to Larsen.

"We don't have too many options. Good thing it's not a new model. Think you can handle it, John?"

Larsen walked up to the vault door and studied it quietly for a few minutes, then nodded. He began to move the jeweled key settings delicately, pausing at each one. After twenty minutes of intense work, with frequent checks on his percomp, he drew a deep breath and carefully keyed in a full combination. He pulled, and following a moment's hesitation the great door swung open. They walked forward into a long, dimly lit room.

Morris pointed at once to the line of great sealed tanks that ran along both walls of the room.

"Those shouldn't be here! They're special form-change tanks. They are like the ones we use for infants with birth defects, but these are ten times the size. There shouldn't be units like this anywhere in this hospital."

He moved swiftly along the room, inspecting each tank and examining its monitors. Then he came back to Wolf and Larsen, eyes wide.

"Twenty units, and fourteen of them occupied." His voice was shaking. "I don't know who is inside them, but I am quite certain that this whole unit is not part of the hospital facilities. It's a completely unauthorized form-change lab."

Wolf looked at Larsen with grim satisfaction. He turned again to Morris.

"Can you tell us just what change work is going on in here?"

Morris thought for a moment, then replied. "If this is the usual layout, there has to be a control room somewhere. All the work records on the changes should be there—computer software, experimental designs, everything. It's not at this end."

They hurried together along the length of the room. Morris muttered to himself in satisfaction when he saw the control room there. He went to the console and at once began to call out records for each of the experiment stations in turn. As he worked, his face grew paler and his brow was beaded with sweat. At last he spoke, slowly and in hushed tones.

"There are missing records, but I can already tell you something terrible—and highly illegal—has been going on here. There are humans in fourteen of those tanks. They are being programmed to adapt to prespecified forms, built into the control software. And I can tell you one other thing. The subjects in the tanks are definitely of an illegal age for form-change work—my rough estimate puts them between two years old and sixteen years old, all of them."

It took a few seconds for that to sink in. Then Larsen said quietly: "You are telling us that there are human *children* in those tanks. That's monstrous. How can a child assess the risks that go with form-change?"

"They can't. In this case, the question of knowing the risk does not arise. The arrangement is a very special one, never used legally. We've known how to apply it, in principle, for many years. The stimulus to achieve a programmed form-change is being applied directly to the pleasure centers of their brains. In effect, they have no choice at all. These children are being forced to strive for the programmed changes by the strongest possible stimulus."

He leaned back in the control console chair and put both hands to his perspiring forehead. When he finally spoke again, his voice was slurred and weary.

"I can't believe it. I simply can't believe it, even though I see it. In Central Hospital, and with Capman involved. He's been my idol ever since I left medical school. He seemed more concerned for individuals, and for humanity as a whole, than anyone I ever met. Never cared for money or possessions. Now he's mixed up in this. It makes no sense. . . ."

His voice cracked, and he sat hunched and motionless in his chair. After a few seconds, Wolf intruded on his troubled reverie.

"Doctor, is there any way that you can tell us what form-changes were being used here?"

Morris roused himself a little and shook his head. "Not without the missing records. Capman must have kept those separately somewhere. I can get the computer listings through the display here, but it would be a terrible job to deduce the program purpose from the object listings. Even short subroutines can take hours to understand. There's a piece of code here, for example, that occurs over and over in two of the experiments. But its use is obscure."

"What do you think it is, Doctor?" asked Bey. "I know

you can't tell us exactly, but can you get even a rough idea?"

Morris looked dubious. "I'll be reading it out of context, of course. It looks like a straightforward delay loop. The effect is to make each program instruction execute for a preset number of times before moving on to the next one. So everything would be slowed down by that same factor, set by the user."

"But what would it do?"

"Heaven knows. These programs are all real-time and interactive, so it would be nonsensical to slow them all down." He paused for a second, then added, "But remember, these programs were presumably designed by Robert Capman. He's a genius of the first rank, and I'm not. The fact that I can't understand what is being done here means nothing. We need Capman's own notes and experimental design before we can really tell what he was doing."

Wolf was pacing the control room, eyes unfocused and manner intent.

"That's not going to be easy. Capman has left the hospital, I'll bet my brains on it. Why else would he have given us free run of the place? I don't understand why he did that, even if he knew we were on to him. Somehow he must have tracked what we were doing and decided he couldn't stop us. But unless we do trace him, we may never know what he was doing here."

He turned to Larsen in sudden decision, "John, go and get a trace sensor. It's my bet that Capman has been here, in this room, in the past hour. We have to try and go after him, even if it's only for his own protection. Can you imagine the public reaction if people found out he had been stealing human babies for form-change experiments? They'd tear him apart. He must have taken the children by faking the results of the humanity tests. That's why their IDs aren't on file."

Larsen hurried out of the vault. As he left, Morris suddenly looked hopeful.

"Wait a minute," he said. "Suppose that Capman was

working with subjects that had *failed* the humanity tests. That wouldn't be as bad as using human babies."

Wolf shook his head. "I had that thought, too. But it can't work. Remember, the whole point of the humanity test is that nonhumans *can't* perform purposive form-change. So they must be humans he's using, by definition. Not only that, remember that the liver we found came from a twelve-year-old. Capman didn't just have experiments, he had *failed* experiments, too. The organ banks were a convenient way of disposing of those, with small risk of discovery."

He continued to pace the room impatiently, while Morris sat slumped in silent shock and despair.

"God, I wish John would hurry up," said Wolf at last. "We need the tracer. Unless we can get a quick idea where Capman went, we're stuck."

He continued his pacing, looking at the fittings of the control room. The communicator set next to the control console looked like a special purpose unit, one of the old models. All the response codes for setting up messages had changed since they were used—which meant any dial code might key different responses. Bey thought for a moment, then entered the eight-digit dial code that had been left for him by Capman at the main lobby. This time, instead of the earlier message requesting cooperation with Form Control, a much longer message scrolled steadily into the viewer. Bey read it with steadily increasing amazement.

DEAR MR. WOLF. SINCE YOU ARE READING THIS, YOU ARE IN THE PRIVATE VAULT AND HAVE, AS I FEARED AFTER OUR FIRST MEETING, DEDUCED THE NATURE OF MY WORK HERE. I HAVE KNOWN FOR MANY YEARS THAT THIS DAY MUST COME EVENTUALLY, AND I HAVE RESIGNED MYSELF TO THE FACT THAT THIS WORK WILL PROBABLY NOT BE COMPLETED UNDER MY DIRECTION. MR. WOLF, YOU MAY NOT KNOW IT YET, BUT YOU AND I ARE TWO SPECIMENS OF A VERY RARE BREED. IT WAS APPARENT TO ME VERY QUICKLY THAT THIS WORK WOULD PROBABLY END WITH YOUR INVESTIGATION. I REGRET IT, BUT ACCEPT IT.

LONG AGO, I DECIDED THAT I WOULD PREFER TO LIVE

OUT MY LIFE IN QUIET ANONYMITY, SHOULD THIS WORK BE DISCOVERED, RATHER THAN ENDURE THE EXTENSIVE AND WELL-MEANING REHABILITATION PROGRAM THAT WOULD BE INFLICTED ON ME AS PUNISHMENT FOR MY CRIMINAL ACTS. TO MOST, THESE DEEDS MUST APPEAR UNSPEAKABLE. TO YOU, LET ME SAY THAT MY WORK HAS ALWAYS HAD AS ITS OBJECTIVE THE BENEFIT OF HUMANITY. TO THAT END, A SMALL NUMBER OF HUMAN LIVES HAVE UNFORTUNATELY BEEN SACRIFICED. I FULLY BELIEVE THAT IN THIS CASE THE END JUSTIFIES THE MEANS.

IN ORDER TO ACHIEVE THE ANONYMITY I DESIRE, IT WILL BE NECESSARY FOR ROBERT CAPMAN TO VANISH FROM THE EARTH. IT IS UNLIKELY THAT WE WILL MEET AGAIN. THE RISK FOR ME WOULD BE TOO GREAT, SINCE I SUSPECT THAT YOU AND I WOULD ALWAYS RECOGNIZE EACH OTHER. AS HOMER REMARKS, SUCH KNOW EACH OTHER ALWAYS. MR. WOLF, LEARN MORE FORM-CHANGE THEORY. YOUR GIFT FOR THE PRACTICAL IS ASTONISHING, BUT ITS TRUE POTENTIAL WILL BE WASTED UNTIL YOU MASTER THE THEORETICAL ALSO. DO THAT, AND NOTHING WILL BE BEYOND YOU.

THIS MORNING I COMPLETED ALL THE NECESSARY PLANS FOR MY DEPARTURE, AND NOW I MUST LEAVE. BELIEVE ME, THERE IS A POINT WHERE FAME IS A BURDEN, AND A QUIET LIFE AMONG MY RECORDINGS AND HOLOTAPES IS DEVOUTLY TO BE WISHED. I HAVE REACHED THAT POINT. SINCERELY, ROBERT CAPMAN.

That was the end. Wolf and Morris watched the screen intently, but nothing further appeared.

"I'm beginning to understand why you people in the hospital regard him as omniscient," said Wolf at last. "But I'm sure you realize that I can't let him get away. If I can track him down, I have to do it. As soon as John Larsen gets here, we'll try and follow him—no matter where he's gone."

Morris did not reply. He seemed to have had more shocks than he could take in one day. He remained at the seat of the control console, slack-jawed and limp, until Larsen appeared at last through the great vault door.

"Sorry that took so long, Bey," he said. "I thought I'd

better go by Capman's apartment and train the sensor on a couple of his clothing samples. It should be pretty well tuned now to his body chemistry. We can go any time, as soon as we get a faint scent. The sensor kept pointing this way, so somehow he must have been able to exit from here. See any signs of a concealed way out?"

The two men began to search the wall areas carefully, while Morris looked on listlessly and uncomprehendingly. Finally, John Larsen found the loose wall panel behind an air-conditioning unit. Working together, they lifted it aside and found that beyond it lay a long, narrow corridor, faintly lit with green fluorescence. Larsen held the trace sensor in the opening, and the monitor light glowed a bright red. The trace arrow swung slowly to point along the corridor.

"That's the way he went, Bey," said Larsen. He turned to Morris. "Where will this lead?"

Morris pulled himself together and looked around him. "I'll have to think. The elevator was in the west corner of the study. So that would mean you are facing just about due east."

Bey Wolf pinched thoughtfully at his lower lip. "Just about what I expected," he said. "Where else?" He turned to Larsen. "That's the way we'll have to go, John, if we want to catch Capman. See where we'll be heading?—straight into the heart of Old City."

CHAPTER 7

Take the toughest and seediest of the twentieth-century urban ghettos. Age it for two hundred years and season it with a random hodgepodge of over- and underground structures. Populate it with the poorest of the poor and throw in for good measure the worst failures of the form-change experiments. You have Old City, where the law walked cautiously by day and seldom by night. Bey Wolf and John Larsen, armed with cold lights, stun guns, and trace sensor, emerged from the long underground corridor just as first dusk was falling. They looked around them cautiously, then began to follow the steady arrow of the tracer, deeper into Old City.

The evidence of poverty was all around, in the cracked, garbage-strewn pavements, the neglected buildings, and the complete absence of slideways. Travel was on foot, or in ancient wheeled vehicles without automatic controls or safety mechanisms.

"Let's agree on one thing, John," said Wolf, peering about him with great interest. "While we're hunting Cap-man, we'll not be worrying too much about the usual forbidden forms. For one thing, I expect we'll see more of them here than we've ever seen before. Look there, for example."

He pointed down the side alley they were passing. Larsen saw a hulking ursine form standing next to a tiny, rounded man no more than two feet tall. They had a reel of monofilament thread, which they were carefully unwinding and attaching to a frame of metal bars. Wolf kept walking.

"Run into that," he said, "and it would shear you in two before you knew you'd been cut. They're obviously setting a trap. It's not for us, but we'd better watch how we go in here."

Larsen needed no reminding of that fact. His eyes tried to move in all directions at once, and he kept his hand close to his stun gun.

"They don't look much like failed attempts at the usual commercial forms, Bey," he said. "I suppose that's what happens when some poor devil who's really twisted in the head gets hold of a form-change machine."

Wolf nodded. "They probably try and fight against taking those forms with their conscious minds, but something underneath dictates their shapes. Maybe in another hundred years we'll understand what makes them do it."

As he spoke, Wolf was coolly assessing all that he saw and storing it away for future reference. Old City was off-limits for all but real emergencies, and he was making the most of a rare opportunity. They hurried on through the darkening streets, becoming aware for the first time of the absence of streetlights. Soon, it was necessary to use the cold lights to show their path. The tracer arrow held its steady direction. As night fell, the inhabitants of Old City who shunned the day began to appear. Larsen held tighter to the handle of his gun as the sights and sounds around them became more alien.

They finally reached a long, inclined ramp, leading them again below ground level. Larsen checked the tracer, and they continued slowly downward. Their lights lip up the tunnel for ten yards or so, and beyond that was total blackness. A gray reptilian form with a musty odor slid away from them down a side passage, and ahead of them they heard a chitinous scratching and scuttling as something hurried away into the deeper shadows. Wolf stopped, startled.

"That's one to tell them about back at the office. Unless I'm going mad, we've just seen someone who has developed an exoskeleton. I wonder if he has kept a vertebrate structure with it?"

Larsen did not reply. He lacked Wolf's clinical attitude, and he was becoming increasingly uncomfortable with their quest. They moved on, and the surroundings became damp and glistening as the ramp narrowed to an earth-walled tunnel with a dirt floor. Ahead of them, a slender figure mewled faintly and slithered away with a serpentine motion down another side passage.

Wolf suddenly stopped and fingered the metal shaft of the tracer he was holding. "Damn it, John, is it my imagination or is this thing getting hot?"

"Could be. I think the same thing is happening to the gun and the flashlight. I noticed it a few yards back."

"We must have run into an induction field. If it gets any stronger, we won't be able to carry metal with us. Let's keep going for a few more meters."

They moved on slowly, but it was soon apparent that the field was strengthening. They backed up again for a council of war.

"The tracer signal is really strong now, John," said Wolf. "Capman can't be far ahead of us. Let's leave all the metal objects here and scout ahead for another fifty meters. If we don't spot him after that, we'll have to give up."

Both men were feeling the strain. In good light, Wolf would have seen the reaction that his suggestion had produced in Larsen. As it was, he heard a very faint assent, and leaving guns, lights, and trace sensor behind, they went on into the darkness, meter by cautious meter.

Suddenly, Larsen stopped. "Bey." His voice was a faint whisper. "Can you hear something up ahead?"

Wolf strained his ears. He could hear nothing.

"It sounded like a groan, Bey. There, again. Now do you hear it?"

"I think so. Quietly now, and carefully. It's only a few yards in front of us."

They crept on through the musty darkness. They heard another low groan, then heavy and painful breathing. Suddenly, a weak voice reached them through the gloom.

"Who's there? Stay where you are and for God's sake don't come any closer."

"Capman? This is Wolf and Larsen. Where are you?"

"Down here, in the pit. Be careful where you tread. Wait a second. I'll show you where it's safe to go."

A thin beam of light appeared, coming from the floor in front of them. They moved hesitantly forward and found themselves standing at the edge of a twelve-foot drop. At the base of it they could see Capman lying helpless, limbs contorted. He was holding a small flashlight and shining it toward them.

"This pit wasn't here a couple of days ago," he said faintly. "It must have been dug by one of the modified forms that live in these tunnels. A big one, I think. It came this way a few minutes ago, then went away again. That way."

He shone the flashlight along the bottom of the pit. They could see a large tunnel running away from the base of it. Capman seemed weak and obviously in pain, but he was still perfectly rational and composed.

"If it survives down here, it's probably carnivorous," he said, "I wonder what the basic form is."

Wolf was astonished to hear a note of genuine intellectual curiosity in Capman's tone. He advanced closer to the edge and tried to see farther along the tunnel in the pit.

"I don't know what you can do to help me," went on Capman calmly. "If you can't get me out, it's vital that I give my records to you. I should have left them at the hospital. They are a crucial part of the description of the work I've been doing. Make sure they get into the right hands."

He broke off suddenly and swung the light back along the wall of the pit. "I think it's coming back. Here, I'm going to try to throw this spool up to you. Step nearer to the edge. I'm not sure how well I can throw from this position."

Capman shone the flashlight on the wall of the pit to give a diffuse light above and threw a small spool awkwardly upward. Reaching far out, almost to the point of overbalancing, Larsen managed to make a snatching one-handed catch. Capman sighed with relief and pain and sank back to the dirt floor. They could hear a deep grunting, and a scrambling noise was approaching along the pit tunnel. While they watched in horror, Capman remained astonishingly cool.

"Whatever happens here," he said, "remember that your first duty is to get those records back to the hospital. Don't waste any time."

He turned the flashlight again into the pit. In the uncertain light, Wolf and Larsen had an impression of an enormous simian shape moving toward Capman. Before they could gain a clear view of it, the light fell to the floor and was suddenly extinguished. There was a grinding noise and a bubbling cough from the pit, then silence.

Wolf and Larsen were seized suddenly with an understanding of their own defenseless position. Without another word or a wasted moment, both men turned and sped back through the tunnel. They picked up guns, lights, and tracer and continued at full speed through the dark ways of Old City. Not until they were once more in the elevator, rising through Central Hospital to Capman's laboratory, did Larsen finally break the silence.

"I don't know what Capman did in that vault, but whatever it was he paid for it tonight."

Wolf, unusually subdued, could do no more than nod agreement and add, "Requiescat in pace."

They went at once to the Transplant Department, where Morris received the precious spool of microfilm. At Wolf's urging, he agreed to have a team assigned to an immediate analysis of it, while they told him of the strange circumstance of its passage to them.

CHAPTER 8

An hour before sunrise, Wolf and Larsen were break-
fasting in the visitors' section of the highest floor of Central Hospital. At Morris's insistence they had taken three
hours of deep sleep and spent another hour in programmed stress release. Both men were feeling rested
and fit and had accepted a substantial meal from the
robo-servers. Before they had finished, Morris came bustling in again. It was clear from his appearance that he
had not slept, but his eyes were bright with excitement.
He waved a handful of listings and sat down opposite
them.

"Fantastic," he said. "There's no other word for it. It
will take us years to get all the details on this. Capman
has gone further in form-change than we dreamed. Every
form in that underground lab explores new ground in
form-change experiment."

He began to leaf through the listings. "Here's an
anaerobic form," he said. "It can breathe air, as usual,
but if necessary it can also break down a variety of other
chemicals for life support. It could operate under the
sea, or in a vacuum, or almost anywhere. Here's another
one, with a thick and insensitive epidermis—it should be
very tolerant of extreme conditions of heat and radiation.

"Then there's this one." Morris waved the listing excitedly. He was unable to remain seated and began to pace
up and down in front of the window, where a pale gleam
of false dawn was appearing. "Look, he has a complete
photosynthetic system, with chlorophyll pouches on his

chest, arms, and back. He could survive quite happily in a semidormant state on traces of minerals, water, and carbon dioxide. Or he can live quite well as a normal human form, eating normal food.

"Here we have miniaturized forms, only ten inches high when fully adult. They have a normal life expectancy and a normal chromosome and gene structure. They can breed back to full-sized children in a couple of generations."

Wolf was struck by a sudden memory. "Do these forms have any special project names with them?" he asked.

"They do. They are all shown in Capman's general work notes under the heading of Project Proteus, except for one form—and that one has us baffled at the moment. It's the one we were talking about in the lab last night."

He riffled through the listings and came up with one that seemed much more voluminous than the others. "It's the one with the delay loop that occurs all over the program. We have made several efforts to revive the subject, but we can't do it. He seems to be in some kind of catatonic trance, and when we try and calculate the life ratio on the computer, we get overflow."

Wolf looked at Morris and thought of Capman's note to him in the underground vault. Perhaps Capman was right and Wolf did think in the same way. There was no doubt that he found the intention of the new form obvious, while it had Morris and Larsen baffled.

"Doctor," he said. "Did Capman ever talk to you about the future of the human race—where we will be in a hundred years, for instance?"

"Not to me personally. But his views were well known. He leaned very much toward Laszlo Dolmetsch's views— society is unstable, and without new frontiers we will stagnate and revert to a lower civilization. The United Space Federation can't prevent that; they are too thinly spread and have too fragile a hold on the environment."

Wolf leaned back and looked at the ceiling. "So doesn't it seem clear what Capman's plan was? We need new frontiers. The USF can't provide them unless it has assistance. Capman has been working towards a single, well-defined objective—to provide forms that are adapted to space exploration. The forms you've been describing are ideal for working out in space, or on the Moon or Mars—or for terraforming work on Venus."

Morris looked blank. "You're right. But what about the small ones, or this catatonic one?"

"He's not catatonic. He's asleep. All his vital processes have been slowed down by some preset amount. I don't know how much, but you should be able to find out if you look at the delay factor in the biofeedback program. Capman set up that delay loop so the software could interact with the form-change experiment in its own 'real time.'"

Morris looked again at the listings in his hand. "Twelve hundred," he said at last. "My God, it's set now for *twelve hundred*. That means that . . ."

His voice trailed off.

"It means that he will sleep for one of his 'nights,'" said Wolf. "That will be equal to twelve hundred of ours. I expect his life expectancy will be in proportion—twelve hundred times as long. That makes it about a hundred and twenty thousand years. Of course, that's not his *sub-jective* life expectancy—that will probably be about the same as ours."

"But how do we communicate with him?"

"The same way as Capman did in his form-change programs. You'll have to slow all the stimuli down by a factor of twelve hundred. Feed him information at the same rate as he's programmed to receive it."

"But what's the point of it?" asked Morris. "He can't work in space if he's incapable of communicating with the rest of us."

"New frontiers," said Wolf. "We want new frontiers, right? Don't you see you've got an ideal form there for interstellar exploration? A trip of a century would only seem about a month to him. He'll live for more than a hundred thousand Earth years. If you put a form-change machine on the ship with him, he could be brought back to a normal pace when he got there, for the observation work. Combine him with the miniaturized forms you found, and you've got people who can explore the stars with the present ships and technology."

"The delay factor is set in the program," said Morris. "There's no reason to think twelve hundred is a limit. I'll have to check and see how high it could go. Do you think it's possible that the programs would allow him to run *faster* than normal?"

"That's much harder. I don't see how you could speed up nerve signals. But I'm no expert on that, you need to look at it yourself. You can see now why your computer hit an overflow situation when you tried to compute a life ratio. In subjective terms it's still unity, but in terms of an outside observer it's twelve hundred. We need a new definition of life ratio."

Morris was still pacing the room excitedly, listings crumpled in his hands. "There's so much that's new. We'll be years evaluating it without Capman. You have no idea what we lost with his death. I'll have to get back and help the others in the analysis, but none of us has his grasp of fundamentals. It's a gap that can't be filled."

He seemed to have recovered from his earlier shock at discovering that Capman was using human subjects. The potential of the new forms drove all else from his mind. As he turned to leave, Wolf asked him a final question.

"Did the catatonic experiment have any special project name?"

Morris nodded. "Project Timeset—of course, that makes perfect sense now. I must check how big the delay factor can become. I see no reason why it couldn't be ten thousand or more. Can you imagine a man who could live for a million years?"

He hurried out, and his departure took the energy and excitement from the room. After a few seconds, Wolf stood up and went over to the window. It faced out across Old City, toward the coming dawn. He looked at the dark, sprawling bulk of the city beneath him in silence.

"Cheer up, Bey," said Larsen after a couple of

minutes. "Capman's death is still eating you up, isn't it? We couldn't have done a thing to help him. And I don't think we should judge him. That's for the future. He did a terrible thing, but now he's paid for it with his life. It's no good you brooding on it, too."

Bey turned slowly from the window, his eyes reflective and introspective. "That's not what's worrying me, John," he replied. "I'm troubled by something a lot less abstract. It's hard for me to believe that a man could be as smart as Capman and yet die so stupidly."

Larsen shrugged. "Everybody has their blind spots, Bey. Nobody's all smart."

"But Capman told us that he knew he might be discovered all along. He didn't know when it might be, but he had to allow for it. He set up elaborate checks to see if anyone was about to discover what he was doing, and when he found we were on to him, he got ready to disappear."

"That's just what he did," agreed Larsen. "He was all set to disappear, but he didn't allow for that monster's trap over in Old City."

Wolf was shaking his head. "John, Robert Capman allowed for *everything*. I don't believe he'd fall into a trap like that. We are the ones who fell into the trap. Don't you see, everything that happened was designed to draw us to pursue him? He knew we would try and follow him—we had to. All that talk about disappearance and a quiet life was nonsense. He *expected* to be followed."

"Maybe he did, Bey. But he didn't expect that illegal form in the tunnel."

"Didn't he, John? He wanted the trail followed while it was hot—just the two of us, without a lot of special equipment and with no preparation. So like a pair of dumb heroes, we rushed in."

Wolf looked down at the streets of Old City, where a phosphorescent green trail of light was slowly spreading; the street scavengers were off on their last predawn search for pickings.

"We should have been suspicious," he continued, "as

soon as we ran into that induction field. Who would have set up such a thing—and why? Somebody wanted us to get to Capman without lights or guns. So, sure enough, Larsen and Wolf arrive on the scene without lights and guns."

"But we saw the monster form, Bey, and we saw Capman killed. Are you saying that was all part of the plan?"

Wolf looked at Larsen sceptically. "Did we see it? Did we really? What did we actually *see*? A big, vague form, then Capman dropped the flashlight and the place went dark. We ran. We didn't really see one thing that proved that Capman died down there. When was the last time you ran away from something in a blind panic?"

Larsen nodded. "I'm not proud of that, Bey. I haven't run from anything for a long time. I don't know what got hold of us."

"I think I do. We ran away, but we had a little assistance. I'll bet there was a subsonic projector and a few other items near that pit—all set up to scare the hell out of us as soon as we had the spool of microfilm. Capman even told us, twice, that we had to get the film back to the hospital—so we could justify it to ourselves that we were right to run away. Capman said he 'forgot' to leave it at the hospital, but it would have needed a separate conscious act for him to have taken it from the hospital in the first place—and all the people here say that he never forgot *anything*, no matter how small a detail."

Wolf sighed and peered out through the window. "John, it was a setup. We were moved around down there like a couple of puppets. Capman is no more dead than we are."

Larsen was silent for a couple of minutes, digesting what Wolf had told him. Finally he too came to the window and looked out.

"So you think he is alive somewhere down there. How can we prove it?"

Wolf looked at his own reflection in the smooth glass. He saw a man with a worried frown and a thin, unsmiling mouth. Morris's satisfaction and enthusiasm at Capman's discoveries had not proved infectious.

"That's the hellish part of it, John," he said. "We can't prove it. No one would believe the bits and pieces that I've told you. If we report the facts, and we have to, then Capman will be declared dead. There will be no more pursuit. He will be free in a way that he could never have been if we hadn't followed him."

Larsen too was frowning. "Part of what you say is still hard to accept, Bey. Capman lived for his work; we've heard that from many people here. Now that's gone from him. What would he do with his life?"

Bey Wolf looked back at him questioningly. "Has it gone from him, John? Remember, there are twenty tanks in that vault, and only fourteen of them were occupied. What happened to the experiments that were in the other six? We know now what the code words in the index file, Proteus and Timeset, were referring to. But I found two others there, too. What about Project Janus and Project Lungfish? We don't know what they were, and we don't know what happened to them.

"I think that Robert Capman has another laboratory somewhere. He has those other six experiments with him, and he's still working on them. You can bet that those are the six most interesting forms, too."

"You mean he has a lab out there in Old City, Bey?"

"Maybe, but I think not. If we wanted to, we could follow him to Old City. He told the Building Committee that he hoped to have twenty more working years. I think that he would look for a place where he can work quietly, without danger of interruption. Would you like to speculate on the forms that he might create in twenty years? I don't think Old City could hold them."

"Even if he's not there, Bey, we ought to check it out and make sure." Larsen turned away from the window. "Let me go and file a report on this—I assume that we won't be going to the Moon today, the way Steuben is expecting us to. I'll request that we send a search party back along the way that we went last night. Maybe we can pick up some clues there."

He left, leaving Wolf alone in the long room. On impulse, Bey went and switched off all the lights, then

returned to the window overlooking the eastern side of
the city.

Search if you want, John, he thought. *I'm pretty sure
you won't find any signs of Robert Capman. What was
it his message to me said? "It will be necessary for Robert
Capman to vanish from the Earth." I'm inclined to take
that literally.*

Wolf began to feel the old sense of letdown and disappointment. After the excitement of discovery and pursuit,
there was only another blind alley, another trail that
ended in criminality and futility.

Or did it? Something didn't feel quite right. Bey
frowned out on the darkened city, allowing his instinct
to direct his thinking.

*If Capman is what I think he is—and if I am what he
thinks I am—then I must also assume that he expected
me to see through his 'death.' So what does he expect me
to do now? Pursue him. Then he must also know he has
a hiding place where I cannot follow him.*

It was another dead end. All that was left was Capman's instruction: Learn more form-change theory.
There must have been a reason for that. Capman was
not a man to provide vague general advice.

And there was still the great inconsistency. On the one
hand, Capman was performing monstrous experiments
on human children; on the other, he was a great humani-
tarian who cared about humans more than anyone. Those
two statements could not be reconciled. Which left the
question, what was Capman *really* doing in his
experiments?

Wolf did not know, and Capman did not want to tell—
not yet. But if the time for explanations ever did arrive,
Bey wanted to be ready to understand. Could *that* be
the point of Capman's message?

Project Janus. Project Lungfish. Something there was
just beyond reach. Wolf felt like a man who had been
given a glimpse of the promised land, then seen it
snatched away. He had to go back to the Office of Form
Control now, when what he'd like to be doing was work-

ing with Capman, wherever he was. He sensed a new world out there, a whole unknown world of changes.

Wolf's thoughts ran on, drifting, speculating on when he would next meet with Robert Capman. The first rays of the coming dawn were striking through the window, high in the hospital. Below, still hidden in darkness, lay the forbidding mass of Old City. Behrooz Wolf watched in silence until the new day had advanced into the streets below, then he turned and left the room. Capman had disappeared, but the data banks still had some questions to answer. Wolf was ready to ask them.

CHAPTER 9

Sunshine Setting,
Mail Code 127/128/009
Free Colony.

Dear Mr. Wolf,

First off, let me say how sorry I am that I took so long to reply to you. I had your inquiry, then I mislaid it among some of my other things, and I only found it again two days ago. I was going to send you back a spoken answer, but these days they tell me that I tend to ramble on and repeat myself, so I thought that this way would be better. Say what you like about the feedback programs, when you get older they don't let you keep the memory you once had. Just last week, I couldn't find my implant plug for a long time, and then finally one of my friends here reminded me that I had sent it off for service. So I thought it would be better if I sent you a written answer.

Well, one thing is certain. I certainly remember Robert Capman all right, maybe because I met him so long

69

ago. Most of the things that you mentioned in your letter are true, and I
was a little surprised that you
couldn't rely on what the public
records said for the facts on his life.
Maybe you are like me, though, and have
trouble with the computer call-up
sequences.

I'll never forget Capman, and I even
remember quite clearly the first time
we ever met. We went to study at Hopkins
the same year, and we arrived there on
the same day—in the fall of '05. It was
before they had introduced all that
chromosome ID nonsense, and we had to
sign in the book together when we
arrived. He signed before me, and I
looked at his name as he was picking up
his case, and I said, joking, ''Well, we
ought to get on well together, we cover
the whole range between us.'' What I
meant was, with his name being Capman
and my name being Sole, we had the whole
body, from head to toe, between us. Then
I said, ''Better let me help you with
that case,'' because he was just a little shrimp compared to me. I mean, he
was nearly ten years younger than I was.
I was twenty-five, and he hadn't quite
reached sixteen and was small for his
age. I didn't know it at first, but I
should have guessed that he was something special—that was the year they
put the year for college entrance up to
twenty-six, and I was squeaking in
myself under the legal limit. He had
taken the entrance tests and left his
age mark blank, so they didn't find out
how old he was until after they had
already read his exam papers. By then,

they were ready to do something outside the rule book to let him into the college.

You know how it is when you are in a strange place; any friendship seems bigger than usual. After that first introduction, we hung around together for the first week or so, and when it came to the time to assign quarters we agreed that we would share, at least for the first few months. As it turned out, we eventually shared for over two years, until he went off for an advanced study program.

In a way, I suppose that we might have seen even more of each other than we did if we *hadn't* shared quarters. As it was, one of us had to be on the night shift for using the bed (Hopkins was even tighter for accommodation in those days than they are now) and the other had to take a daytime sleep period. Robert took the day sleep period—not that he ever did much sleeping. He never seemed to need it. Many times I've seen him, when I'd be coming home from one of my classes. He'd be still sitting at the desk after working all day on some problem that interested him, and he didn't seem to be in the least bit worried that he'd had no sleep. ''I'll just nap for half an hour,'' he'd say, and he'd do that and then be ready to go off to his classes, perfectly awake again.

You ask what he studied. Well, he was doing biochemistry, same as I was, but he was the very devil for theory. Things that nobody else would worry about—that weren't ever on any examination—he'd tear away at. I used to hear the teachers

talking to each other, and they weren't
sure whether they were very pleased to
have him as a student or just plain nervous about it. You see, with him they
could never get away with a glib answer,
and they found that out pretty quickly.
He'd be back the next day with chapter
and verse on the most obscure points if
they didn't give him good answers.

I'm not sure how much more description
you want. Certainly, the basic facts
that you quoted are correct. He was at
Hopkins from '05 to '09, to my personal
knowledge, and then he went off to one
of the European colleges—I think it was
Cambridge—for two years, and then he
came back again to serve as a research
assistant to the Melford Foundation.
That's where he became famous, a few
years later, when he published the taxonomy of permissible forms. It didn't
start then, of course. He was developing the theory long before, in his
first years at Hopkins. He would come
over to the rest of us with these long
lists of symbols on big sheets and try
and explain them to me and the other bio
students. I don't know about the rest of
them, but I didn't have any idea what he
was talking about.

As for close relationships, he didn't
have many at Hopkins, and I suppose of
all the people he knew I must have been
the closest to him. He didn't show much
sexual interest in men or women, and I
don't think he ever formed any sort of
bond in the time that I knew him. The
nearest he ever got to a contract bond
was with Betha Melford, when he was
working for the Melford Foundation. She

was quite a few years older than he was, but they were very close. The two of them, along with a group of others, who lived in different places around the world, formed a sort of society. They called it the Lunar Society, but I guess that was some sort of joke, because it had nothing at all to do with the Moon. There were some pretty important people in that group, either important then or important later, but I don't think any of them had a close physical relationship that lasted more than a few weeks. We thought they were a bunch of cold characters.

I wouldn't want that last comment to be misunderstood. Robert Capman was a fine man, a man that I would trust with my life. I say that, although we haven't seen each other in the flesh for about forty years. I heard all that talk up from Earth, about his killing people in experiments, but I don't believe it. It's the usual sensation mongering; the news services will say anything for an effect. As I always say, they are not just holo-people, they are hollow people. I don't think that you can believe what they say now, any more than you could believe what they said about Yifter's disappearance, back in '90. I remember that well, too.

Of course, all these things are a long time ago, but I remember them all very clearly, the way you do remember things that happen when you are very young. Nowadays, I don't find things so memorable, but I'll be having my hundred and ninth birthday next week, and I'm enjoying good health, so I mustn't

grumble. I'm sorry to have taken so long
to get this off to you, but I thought it
would probably be better to give you a
written answer. You said that you were
asking a number of Robert's friends
about him, and I wanted to mention that
if any of them want to get in touch with
me I hope that you will give them my
address. It would be nice to see some of
them again, and talk about old times
with people who lived through them. Of
course, I can't go to any place that has
a high-gravity environment, but maybe
some of them could visit me up here.
  I hope this letter will be useful to
you, and I hope that the rumors about
Robert Capman can be stopped.
                    Ludwig Plato Sole, D.P.S.

Bey read the letter through to the end, then placed it
on top of the stack. It was the last reply to his inquiries,
and he'd been lucky to get it. Attached to it was a brief
note from the chief physician at Free Colony, pointing
out that Ludwig Sole was rapidly losing the ability to use
the biofeedback machines, and thus the information in
the letter came from a man of failing faculties. No further information was likely to come from Sunshine Setting. Fortunately, thought Bey, no more was needed.
Sole's letter covered much the same ground as some of
the others, though he had been closer than anyone during the Hopkins years.
  In the eight months since the disappearance, Wolf had
painstakingly located forty-seven surviving acquaintances
and close contemporaries of Capman. The oldest was one
hundred and ten, the youngest almost ninety.
  The summary before him, culled from all the replies
to his inquiries, was complete but baffling. Nowhere
could Bey read any signs of cruelty or megalomania in
their descriptions of Capman. Oddness, yes, but oddness
that hinted at the solitary mental voyaging of a Newton

or an Archimedes, at the lonely life of a genius. Had some chance event, twenty-seven years ago, tipped the balance? "Great wits are sure to madness near allied," no denying it—but Robert Capman wouldn't fit the pattern.

Bey turned to the yellowed sheet that was pinned to the back of Sole's letter. It was faded and almost unreadable, a relic of an earlier age, and it would need special treatment before it could be fully deciphered. It seemed to be an old transcript of Capman's academic records, and it was curious that Sole had made no reference to it in his letter. Bey increased the strength of the illumination on the sheet and varied the frequency composition of the light sources until he had the best conditions for reading the thin blue print.

Robert Samuel Capman. Born: June 26th, 2090.

Date of entry: September 5th, 2105.

Category: BIO/CH/PHY/MAT.

Bey bent closer to the page. Below the general biographical data a long list of numbers was faintly visible. He hadn't seen anything quite like it, but it looked like a psych profile output, one in a different format. He linked through to the Form Control central computer and added an optical character reader as a peripheral. The scanner had trouble with the page that Bey placed beneath it, but after a few iterations, with help and corrections from Bey for doubtful characters, it flashed a confirming message and performed the final scan.

Bey called for character enhancement. He waited impatiently while the computer performed its whirl of silent introspection. The months since Capman's discovery and flight had not lessened the eagerness to trace him; in fact, if anything Bey's determination had strengthened. He was resigned to the fact that it would probably take years. All the evidence suggested that Capman was nowhere on Earth, and it was not practical to pursue him across the Solar System—even if the USF were to cooperate, which they showed little wish to do. Meanwhile, there was form-change theory. It was more evident every day how appropriate Capman's advice had been. New vistas were opening to Bey as he advanced, and there was evidence that he was still in the foothills. At least he had begun to learn how—and how well— Capman's mind worked.

The computer was finally satisfied with its work on character recognition. While Bey looked on impatiently, the screen slowly filled with the final interpretation of the transcript. It was all there, in a slightly different format from the modern displays but quite recognizable. Intelligence, aptitudes, mechanical skills, associative ability, subconscious/conscious ratios, paralogic, nonlinear linkages—they were all listed, with numerical measures for each one.

Bey looked through them quickly at first, puzzled by the low scores in some areas. About halfway through, he began to see a familiar pattern. He stopped, suddenly dizzy with the implications. He knew the overall profile very well. It was different in detail, as any two people were different, but there were points of resemblance to a psych profile that Bey Wolf knew by heart, as well as he knew his own face in the mirror.

Wolf was still sitting motionless in front of the screen when Larsen returned from the central troubleshooting area upstairs. He ignored Bey's pensive attitude and broke out at once into excited speech.

"It's happened, we've had a break on the salamander form. The Victoria office uncovered a group of them, still coupled. If we leave at once we can get the Link entry that Transport is holding for us. Come on, don't just sit there, let's go."

Bey roused himself and stood up. As always, work demanded first priority. He looked unhappily at the display that still filled the screen and then followed John Larsen from the room.

PART II

"Beware, beware, his flashing eyes, his floating hair."

PART II

CHAPTER 10

The monsters first came to public attention off the coast of Guam. They stood quietly on the seabed, three of them abreast, facing west toward the Guam shore. Behind them, plunging away rapidly to the abyssal depths, lay the Mariana Trench. Faintest sunlight fled about their shadowy sides as they stirred slowly in the cold, steady upwelling.

To the startled eyes of Lin Maro as he cruised along in his new gilled form, they seemed to be moving forward, slowly and purposively breasting the lip of the coastal shelf and gliding steadily from the black deeps to the distant shore. Forgetting his long months of training and feedback control, Lin gasped and pulled a pint of warm seawater into his surprised lungs. Coughing and spluttering, gills working overtime, he surged 150 feet to the surface and struck out wildly for the shore and safety. A quick look back convinced him that they were pursuing him. His glance caught the large, luminous eyes and the ropy tendrils of thick floating hair that framed the broad faces. He was in too much of a hurry to notice the steel weights that held them firmly and remorselessly on the seabed.

The reaction onshore was somewhere between amusement and apathy. It had been Lin's first time out in a real environment with his new gilled form. Everybody knew there was a big difference between the simulations and the real thing. A little temporary hallucination, a minor *trompe l'oeil* from the central nervous system, that

79

wasn't hard to believe on the first time out with a new BEC form. After all, the guarantees were on physical malfunction, not on sensory oddities. It took long, hard arguing before Maro could get anyone to show even polite interest. The local newsman who finally agreed to go out and take a look did so as much from boredom as from belief. The next day they swam out, Maro in his gills, the reporter in a rented scuba outfit.

The monsters were still there, all right. When the two men swam cautiously down to take a look at them, it became clear that Lin had been fleeing from three corpses. They swam around them in the clear water, marveling at the wrinkled gray skin, massive torsos, and great dark eyes.

When the story went out over the comlink connections, it was still a long way down the news lists. For three hundred years, writers had imagined monsters of the deep emerging from the Mariana Trench and tackling human civilization in a variety of nasty ways. Silly season reports helped to provide some light relief from the social indicators, the famines and the real crises, but they received scant interest from the professionals. Nobody reported panic along the coast or fled to the high ground.

The three monsters got the most interest from the Guam aquarium and vivarium. A group of marine biologists took a day off from plankton culture and went for a party offshore. They inspected the bodies on the seabed, then lifted them—shackles and all—to the surface, quick-froze them, and whipped them back to shore on the institute's hover-craft for a real inspection. The first lab examination showed immediate anomalies. They were land animals, not marine forms. Lung breathers with tough outer skins and massive bone structure. As a matter of routine, the usual tissue microtome samples were taken and the chromosome ID run for matches with known species.

The ID patterns were transmitted to the central data banks back at Madrid. At that point every attention light on the planet went on, the whistles blew, and the buzzers

buzzed. The computer response was prompt and unam-
biguous. The chromosome patterns were human.

The information that moves ceaselessly over the surface of the Earth, by cable, by ComSat link, by Martin
Link, by laser, and by microwave, is focused and redis-
tributed through a small number of nodes. Bey Wolf,
after much effort, had finally arranged that the Office of
Form Control should be one of them. His recent
appointment as head of Form Control entitled him to a
complete interaction terminal in his office, and it was
his peculiar pleasure to sit at this, delicately feeling the
disturbances and vibrations in the normal pattern that
flowed in the strands of the information web. John
Larsen had suggested that Bey sat there like a fat spider,
waiting for prey, and the analogy rather pleased him. His
was, Bey would point out, only one of many webs, all
interlocking, and not by any means the most important
one. Population, Food, and Energy all had much bigger
staffs and bigger budgets. But he would argue that his
problems called for the shortest response times and
needed a reaction time that some of the other systems
could manage without.

Bey was sitting at the terminal, studying a type of
omnivorous form that promised to be truly an omni-
vore—plants, animals, or minerals. He was oblivious to
the unscheduled fierce snowstorm that was raging outside the building, and when the priority override interrupted his data link with news of the Mariana Monsters
(the press's dubbing of the Guam discovery), his first
reaction was one of annoyance. As the details came in,
however, his interest grew. It looked very much as
though some new group had been using the form-change
equipment in unsuccessful experiments, and the results
were nothing like any previous line of work.

Although he was fairly sure of the answers, Bey ran
the routine checks. Were the experiments authorized as
medical research? Were the forms already on the forbidden list? Negative answers, as he expected, came from
the data banks. Was quick action needed to stop the

appearance of a potentially dangerous form? The answer to that was much harder. The computer pleaded shortage of data—which meant that the decision would have to be made by human judgment, and the human in this case was Bey Wolf.

He sighed a sigh of hidden pleasure and opened the circuits for more data. The physical parameters began to flow in. The cell tests were strange in both chemistry and structure, with a mixture of haploid and diploid forms. The lungs were modified, showing changes in alveolar patterns. A note added to the analysis pointed out the resemblance to animals that were adapted to life at high pressure. Strangest of all, the big eyes were most sensitive in the near infrared—but another added note pointed out that this wavelength region is cut out almost completely underwater.

Bey began to gather printed output. He liked to approach a job by asking very basic questions. What was the objective of a new form? Where was it designed to operate most effectively? Most important of all, what was the probable motive of the developer? With answers to those questions, the next step in the form-change sequence could usually be guessed.

The trouble was, it wasn't working. Bey swore softly and leaned back in his chair. The Mariana Monsters were breaking the rules. After looking at the physical variables of the forms for a couple of hours, it seemed to Bey that they were not adapting to any environment that he could imagine.

It was time to drop that line and try another attack. All right, how had the forms reached their position on the seabed? Certainly they had not placed themselves there. And how had they died? There was information on that in the medical records. They had been asphyxiated. It was a fair guess that they had been weighted with steel after they were dead, then dropped to the seabed. From a surface vessel, by the looks of it—the reporters mentioned no sign of skin contusions.

Where had they come from? Bey pulled out the list. He had a complete catalog of the world's form-change centers, especially the ones elaborate enough to include the special life-support systems the new forms would have needed. He was reading steadily through the list of sites, correlating them with the physical changes noted for the Mariana forms, when Larsen returned from a routine meeting on the certification of new BEC releases.

He halted in the doorway.

"How do you do it, Bey? You've only been in this office for a month, and it looks like a rubbish heap."

Bey looked around him in surprise at the masses of new listings and form-change tabulations that cluttered the office.

"They are accumulating a bit. I think they reproduce at night. Come in, John, and look at this. I assume you didn't get too much excitement out of your review meeting?"

Larsen dropped into a chair, pushing aside a pile of listings. As always, he marveled at Bey's ability to operate clearly and logically in the middle of such a mess of documents and equipment.

"It was better than usual," he replied. "There were a couple of good ones. C-forms, both of them, adapted for long periods in low gravity. They'll revolutionize asteroid work, but there were the usual protests from the Belter representatives."

"Naturally—there'll always be Luddites." Bey still had a weakness for outmoded historical references, even though his audience rarely understood them. "The law will change in a couple of years. The C-forms are so much better than the old ones that there's no real competition. I'm telling you, Capman has changed space exploration methods forever. I know the Belters claim they are losing jobs to the new forms, but they are on the wrong side of the argument. Unmodified forms are an anachronism for free space work."

He switched on a recall display and pulled a set of documents from one of the heaps.

"Get your mind reset and let me tell you about the latest headache. It has the Capman touch. If I weren't convinced that he's not on Earth, I'd be inclined to label it as his work."

Bey ran rapidly over the background to the Mariana discoveries, finishing with the question of where they had come from.

"I suspect that they came into the general area of the Marianas through one of the Mattin Links," he concluded. "The question is, which one? We have twenty to choose from. I don't believe there is any way they could have come in from an off-Earth origin, otherwise I'd have thought they were aliens."

"With human chromosome IDs? That would take some explaining, Bey."

John Larsen went over to the wall display, which Bey had tuned to show the locations of the Mattin Link entry points.

"No, I agree with you, Bey; they've come from a lab here on Earth. If they came through the Links, we can rule out a few of them—they're open ocean, and they only act as transfer points. Have you correlated the big form-change labs with the Mattin Link entry points?"

"I started to do it, but it's a big job. I'm waiting for more output on that to come back from the computer. I'm still waiting for the full identification of the three bodies, too. I don't know why it's all taking so long. I slapped a top priority code on the inquiry."

He joined Larsen over at the wall screen. Working together, they reviewed the locations of the Mattin Links that formed the pivot points for Earth's global transportation system. They were deep in the middle of their work when the communicator beeped for attention. Larsen went over to it, leaving Wolf to record the analysis of the wall outputs. As the first words of the message scrolled onto the communicator display, Larsen whistled softly to himself.

"Come over here and get a look at this, Bey," he called. "There's the reason that Central Records took so long to get you an answer. Are you still as sure that the forms didn't come from off-Earth?"

The message began, ID SEARCH COMPLETED AND IDEN-

TIFICATION MADE. INDIVIDUALS OF INQUIRY ARE AS FOL-
LOWS: JAMES PEARSON MANAUR, AGE 34, NATIONALITY USF;
CAPERTA LAFERTE, AGE 25, NATIONALITY USF; LAO SARNA
PREK, AGE 40, NATIONALITY USF. BIOGRAPHICAL DETAILS
FOLLOW. CONTINUE/HALT?

Wolf pressed CONTINUE, and the detailed ID records
appeared: education, work history, family, credit ratings.
Bey noted with surprise that all three of the men had
spectacular credit, up in the multimillionaire class, but
his mind was still mainly occupied with the first item of
background. The three men were all members of the
USF, and that made for a real mystery. Since the USF
had declared its sovereignty fifty years earlier, in 2142,
its citizens had always been a relative rarity down on
Earth. Surely the disappearance of three of them should
have roused a loud outcry long before their bodies had
been found off the Guam shore.

The two men looked at each other. Larsen nodded in
response to Wolf's raised eyebrows.

"I agree. It makes no sense at all. The USF still have
their ban on form-change experiments. If they won't
accept the C-forms, I doubt if they'd be playing with
completely new forms, even as part of their defense programs. And it's still harder to believe that they'd bring
their failures down to Earth."

"Even if they could get them here—you know how
tight quarantine is since the Purcell spores." Wolf shook
his head. "Well, we don't have much choice about what
to do next. We have to get a USF man in on this—it's
too sensitive for us to handle on our own."

He had a reason to look gloomy. The investigation had
just grown two orders of magnitude in complexity. To
go further without USF concurrence would create an
interplanetary incident.

"I'll put a request in," said Larsen. "The less we can
get away with telling them at this point, the better. I'll
shove the bare facts at them and let them decide who
they want to send down from Tycho City. I hope they
send somebody who at least knows how to spell 'form
change.'"

While they talked, the communicator continued to pump out the information in display and hard copy form. It had reached the point where the requested correlation between Link entry points and form-change labs was being presented—Bey had almost forgotten that he had asked for it. The day promised to be a long and confusing one.

Not surprisingly, BEC was getting into the act as well. An incoming news release set out their official position:

> Biological Equipment Corporation (BEC) today released a formal statement denying all knowledge of the human bodies discovered recently in the Pacific. A BEC representative informed us that the bodies had clearly been subjected to form-change, but that no BEC program developments, past or present, could lead to forms anything like those which have been found. In an unusual procedure, BEC has agreed to release records showing forms now under development in the company. They have also invited government inspection of their facilities.

"That's a new one," said Bey. "They must really be running scared. I've been waiting for them to plead innocent or guilty. I've never known BEC to release their new form secrets before. They must be losing their old commercial instinct."

"Not quite." Larsen pointed at the final words of the message. "I wonder what it cost them to get that tagged on to the end of the news release."

The display continued.

> BEC is the pioneer in and world's largest manufacturer of purposive form-change equipment utilizing biological feedback control methods. The release of BEC proprietary information to assist in this investigation is voluntary and purely in the public interest.

"There we go," said Bey. "That's more like the old BEC. Old Melford died a long time ago, but I'll bet his skeleton is grinning in the grave."

CHAPTER 11

Third-generation USF men, like top kanu players, are usually on the small skinny side, built for mobility rather than strength. It was a surprise to greet a giant, more than two meters tall and muscled like a wrestler, and find that he was the USF man assigned to work with the Office of Form Control on the Guam form-change case. Bey Wolf looked up at the tall figure and bit back the question on the tip of his tongue.

It made no difference. Park Green was regarding him knowingly, a sly smile on his big baby face.

"Go on, Mr. Wolf," he said. "Ask me. You'll do it eventually anyway."

Bey smiled back. "All right. Do you use form-change equipment? I thought it was banned for everything but repair work in the USF."

"It is, and I don't. I came this way, and it's all natural. You can guess how hard it is, acting as a USF representative and looking just as though you've been dabbling with the machines."

Wolf nodded appreciatively. "I'm not used to being read so easily."

"On that question, I've had lots of practice. I thought we ought to get rid of that distraction before we get down to work. What's new on the Guam case? I've had orders to send a report back to Tycho City tonight, and at the moment I have no idea what I'm going to say. Did you get a time and cause of death yet from the path lab?"

"Three days ago, and they all died within a few hours of each other. They were asphyxiated, but here's the strange part. Their lungs were full of normal air—no gaseous poisons, no contaminants. They choked to death on the same stuff that you and I are breathing right now."

Park Green sniffed and looked perplexed. "They changed to something that found air poisonous. I don't like that one. How about the way they got to the seabed?"

"They were dropped off twenty-four hours or less after they died. It must have been done at night, or we'd have had reports of sightings. That part of the coast is full of fishing herdsmen during the day. My guess is that they died a long way from there."

"Excuse my ignorance, but I don't follow your logic."

"Well, I'm conjecturing, but I think they were intended for the bottom of the Mariana Trench. Five miles down, they'd never have been found. So they were accidentally dropped a few miles too far west, and that suggests it was done by somebody who didn't know the local geography too well. Whoever did it was in a hurry, too, or they would have been more careful. That suggests it was an accident, with no time for detailed advance planning. Somebody was keen to hide the evidence, as far away and as fast as they could. You don't look very surprised at any of that," added Wolf as Green slowly nodded agreement. "Do you know something they haven't bothered to tell me?"

The big man had squeezed himself into a chair and was slowly rubbing his chin with an eleven-inch hand.

"It fits with some of the things I know about the dead men," he replied. "What else have you been able to find out about them?"

"Not much," said Wolf. "Just what I got from the data bank biographies. They were Belters, the three of them, all off the same ship—the *Jason*. They arrived here on Earth three weeks ago, rolling in money, and went out of sight. Nobody has any records of them again until they were found dead off Guam. We had no reason to follow them once they had cleared quarantine. They had no trouble there, by the way, which seems to rule out anything like the Purcell spores or any other known disease. They were in the middle of a form-change when they died."

"That's right, as far as it goes," agreed Green, "but you're missing a few facts that make a big difference. First off, you said they were Belters, and technically you're right. They worked the Belt. But in USF terms, they were really Grabbers—prospectors, out combing the Belt for transuranics. They'd been looking for over two years when their monitors finally sniffed Old Loge. Maybe you don't realize it back here on Earth, but the only natural source of transuranics in the Inner System is fragments of Loge that drift back in as long-period comets. The Grabbers sit out there and monitor using deep radar. One good find and they're made for life."

"And the *Jason* hit a good one, I assume," said Wolf. "I couldn't believe their credit when I saw the records."

"A real big one," agreed Green. "They hit about three months ago, and it was packed with Asfanium and Polkium, elements 112 and 114. They crunched the fragment for the transuranics and came in to Tycho City a month ago, all as rich as Karkov and Melford. They started to celebrate, and three weeks ago they came down to Earth to keep up the fun. We lost touch with them then and don't know what they did. We didn't worry. No Belter would live on Earth, and we knew they'd be back when the flesh-pots palled. You can probably guess what they did next."

Wolf nodded. "I think I can, but I'd like to see where you are heading. Keep going."

"They came to Earth," continued Green. "Now, I saw them in Gippo's bar a couple of days before they left the Moon. They looked terrible. You can imagine it, a couple of years of hardship in space, then a celebration you wouldn't believe when they reached Tycho City. If you came to Earth in that condition, wouldn't you find it tempting to hook up for a superfast conditioning session with a biofeedback machine? It's not very illegal, and it would get you back to tip-top physical condition faster than anything else. Costs a bit, but they were rolling in money."

"And easy to arrange," said Wolf. "I know a thousand places where you could do it. They don't have fancy form-change equipment there, but you're talking about something rather trivial. It makes good sense—but it wouldn't explain the forms they were in when they were found off Guam. You couldn't get to those without a fully equipped change center. Now let me tie in our side of it, and see what you think."

He pressed the interoffice communicator and asked Larsen to join them.

"I'm going to ask you this cold, John," he said when Larsen entered the room. "Is Robert Capman dead?"

"I thought he was four years ago," replied Larsen. He sighed and shrugged his shoulders. "Now, I'm not so sure." He turned to the USF man. "Bey has always been convinced that it was a setup, and he has me halfway persuaded. I must admit it had the makings of one, but he hasn't been heard of for four years, ever since he disappeared. I agree with Bey on one thing, though; the Guam forms have just the right look to be a Capman product."

"They certainly do," said Bey. He turned to Park Green, who was looking very puzzled. "How much do you know about Capman and what he did?"

Green thought for a moment before he replied, his high forehead wrinkling in thought.

"All I can really tell you is what we hear in Tycho City," he said at last. "Capman was a great man here on Earth, a genius who invented the C-forms, the ones that are adapted for life in space. According to the stories, though, he did it by using human children in his experiments. A bunch of them died, and finally Capman was found out. He tried to escape and died himself as he was trying to get away. Are you telling me there's more to it than that?"

"I think there is," said Bey. "For one thing, it was John and I who handled that case and found out what

Capman was doing. Do you have strong personal feelings against him?"

"How could I? I never knew him, and all the things I've heard are not things I know about personally. If he was really using children, of course I have to be against that. Look, what's it got to do with me?"

"That's a fair question." Wolf paced about in front of Park Green's seated figure, his head scarcely higher than Green's despite their different postures. "You have to see how my thoughts have been running. Earth's greatest-ever expert on form-change, maybe still alive, maybe in hiding. Along comes a set of changes that seem to defy all logic, that don't conform to any known models. It could be Capman, up to his old tricks again. But even if it *isn't*, Capman would be the ideal man to work with on this. I should have added one other thing; neither John nor I ever met a man, before or since, who impressed us as much with his sheer brainpower."

Green wriggled uneasily in his seat, still uncomfortable in the higher gravity. "I know you're selling me something, but I haven't figured out what it is. What are you leading up to?"

"Just this." Wolf halted directly in front of Park Green. "I want to find Robert Capman—for several reasons. We think he's not down here on Earth—hasn't been for the past four years. Will you help me reach him? I don't know if he's on the Moon, out in the Belt, or somewhere further out. I do know that I can't get messages broadcast to the rest of the Solar System unless I have USF assistance."

Green nodded understandingly. "I can't give you an instant answer," he replied. "You're asking for a healthy chunk of communication assist, and that costs money."

"Charge it to this office. My budget can stand it."

"And I'll have to check it out on a policy level with Ambassador Brodin. He's down in Paraguay, and you know Brodin, he won't agree to *anything* unless you ask favors in person." He stood up, stretched, and inflated his sixty-inch chest with a deep, yawning breath. "I'd better get to it before I fall asleep—we're on a different clock in Tycho City. What's the best way to travel to Paraguay?"

"Through the Mattin Link. There's an exit point in Argentina, then you'll go the rest of the way by local flier. We can be at the Madrid link in ten minutes, and you'll be to Argentina in two jumps. Come on, John and I will get you to the entry point."

"I'd appreciate that. I've really had trouble getting used to the complexity of your system down here. We only have four entry points for the whole Moon, and you have twenty. Is it true that you'll have more in a few years?"

It was not true, and it never would be. The Mattin Link system offered direct and instantaneous transmission between any adjacent pair of entry points, but the number and placing of them was very rigid. With perfect symmetry required for any entry point with respect to *all* others, the configuration of the system had to correspond to the vertices of one of the five regular solids. Plato would have loved it.

The dodecahedral arrangement, with its twenty vertices on the surface of the Earth, was the biggest single system that could ever be made. The Lunar system was the simplest, with just four entry points set at the vertices of a regular tetrahedron. The intermediate arrangements, with cubic, octahedral, and icosahedral symmetry, had never been used. Mattin Links away from the planetary surfaces were immensely attractive for transportation, but they were impractical close to a star or planet because of constantly changing orbital distances.

Gerald Mattin, the embittered genius who had dreamed of a system for instantaneous energy-free transfer between any two points anywhere, had died during the first successful tests of the concept. The system that came from his work was far from energy-free—because Earth was not a homogeneous sphere and because space-time was slightly curved near its surface. Mattin had derived an energy-free solution defined for an exact

geometry in a flat space-time, and no one had yet succeeded in generalizing his analysis to other useful cases.

Mattin's death came twenty years before the decision
to build the first Mattin Link system on the surface of a
planet, twenty-five years before the first university was
named after him, thirty years before the first statue.

CHAPTER 12

"We have a go-ahead now, but I had to bargain my soul away to squeeze it out of the ambassador. I don't want to waste all that work. Where do we go from here?"

Park Green was back in Wolf's office, shoes off, long legs stretched out. The general confusion of the place had worsened. Computer listings, empty food trays, and maps were scattered on every flat surface. Wolf and Larsen were again standing by the wall display, plotting the Mattin Link access from both the Mariana Trench entry point and the spaceport entry point in Australia. Wolf read off the results before he replied to Green's question.

"North Australia direct to the Marianas—so they could have gone there direct from the spaceport, except that we know they didn't. The Mariana entry point connects direct to North China, Hawaii, and back of course to North Australia. None of those are promising. There's no big form-change lab anywhere near any of them. What do you think, John?"

Larsen scratched his head thoughtfully. "Two possibilities. Either your hunch about the use of the Link system is all wrong, or the people who moved the Mariana Monsters to Guam did more than one jump in the system. Where do we get with two jumps?"

Wolf read out the connections and shook his head.

"That takes us a lot further afield. With two jumps you can get almost anywhere from a Marianas starting point. Up to the North Pole, down to Cap City at the South Pole, into India, up to North America—it's a mess."

Wolf put down the display control and came over to where Park Green was sitting.

"I'm more convinced than ever that we need Robert Capman's help," he said. "We still don't know what was happening when they died. They started on some form-change program, and somewhere along the line it went wrong. I wish I could ask Capman how."

"You never answered my question, you know," said Green. "What do we do next? Where do we go from here? Advertising for Capman won't solve your problem—he'll be regarded as a mass murderer if he ever does show up on Earth."

"I think I can produce a message that he will recognize and be intrigued by, but other people won't understand," answered Wolf. "As for protecting him if he does show up, I'm not worried about that. I feel sure that he'll have found ways to cover himself in the past four years. I've got another worry of my own. I have no way of knowing how urgent this thing is. It could be a once-in-a-lifetime accident that will never happen again, or it could be the beginning of some kind of general plague. We think it isn't contagious, but we have no proof of it. Until we know what we're dealing with, I have to assume the worst. Let me take a crack at that message."

The final announcement was short and simple. It went out on a general broadcast over all media to the fourteen billion on Earth and by boosted transmission to the scattered citizens of the United Space Federation. The signal would be picked up all the way out past Neptune, and a repeater station would even make it accessible to parts of the outer system Halo.

To R.S.C. I badly need the talents that caused me to pursue you four years ago through the byways of Old City. I promise you a problem worthy of your powers. Behrooz Wolf.

Troubles were mounting. Bey spent many hours with a representative of BEC, who insisted on presenting more confidential records to prove that the company had no connection with the monster forms. The central coordinators' office sent him a terse message, asking if there would be other deaths of the same type, and if so, when, where, and how many. Park Green was getting the same sort of pressure from the USF. Unlike Bey Wolf, he had little experience of that kind of needling. He spent a good part of his time sitting in Bey's office, gloomily biting his nails and trying to construct positively worded replies with no information content.

Two days of vagueness brought a stronger response from Tycho City. Bey arrived in his office early and found a small, neatly dressed man standing by the communicator. His clothes were USF style, and he was calling out personnel records for the three crew members of the *Jason*. He turned around quickly as Bey entered, but there was no sign of embarrassment at being discovered using Bey's office without invitation.

He looked at Bey closely before he spoke.

"Mr. Green?" The voice was like the person, small and precise, and offered more of a statement than a question.

"No, he'll be in later. I'm Behrooz Wolf, and I'm head of the Office of Form Control. What can I do for you?" Bey was suddenly conscious of his own casual appearance and uncombed hair.

The little man drew himself up to his full height.

"I am Karl Ling, special assistant to the USF Cabinet." The tone of his voice was peppery and irascible. "I have been sent here to get some real answers about the deaths of three of our citizens here on Earth. I must say at the outset that we regard the explanations offered so far by your office and by Mr. Green as profoundly unsatisfactory."

Arrogant bastard, thought Bey. He looked at his visitor closely while he sought a suitably conciliatory answer, and felt a sudden sense of recognition.

"We have been doing our best to provide you with all the facts, Mr. Ling," he said at last. "We all thought it was unwise to present theories until we have some definite way of verifying them. I'm sure you realize that this case is a complex one and has a number of factors that we haven't encountered before."

"Apparently it does." Ling had taken a seat by the communicator and was tapping his thigh irritably with a well-manicured left hand. "For example, I see that the cause of death is stated as asphyxiation. But the postmortem shows that the dead men had only normal air in their lungs, with no poisonous constituents. Perhaps you would be willing to present your theory on that to me—there is no need to wait for a full verification."

Ling's tone was sceptical and definitely insulting. Bey felt a sudden doubt about his own intuitive reaction to Ling's presence. In the past, dealing with officious government representatives, Bey had found an effective method of removing their fangs. He thought of it as his saturation technique. The trick was to flood the nuisance with so many facts, figures, reports, graphs, tables, and analyses that he was inundated and never seen again. The average bureaucrat was unwilling to admit he had not read what he was given. Bey went over to his desk and took out a black record tablet.

"This is a private interlock for the terminal in this office. It has in it the data entry codes that will allow you to pull all the records on this case. They are rather voluminous, so analysis will take time. I suggest that you use my office here and feel free to use my communicator as the output display device for Central Files. Nothing will be hidden from you. This machine has a full access code."

Bey felt rather self-conscious about his own pompous manner, but it was the right action, whether or not his first intuitive response to Ling had been correct.

The little man stood up, his eyes gleaming. They were a curious brownish yellow in color, with flecks of gold. He rubbed his hands together.

"Excellent. Please arrange it so that I am not disturbed. However, I do wish to see Mr. Green immediately when he arrives."

Far from being subdued, Karl Ling was clearly

delighted at the prospect of a flood of information. Bey left him to it and went to give the news to Park Green.

"Karl Ling?" Green looked impressed. "Sure I know him—or know of him. I've never met him myself, but I know his reputation. He's supposed to be one of the inner circle at top levels of the USF. He's also something of an expert on Loge and the Belt. He did a whole series of holovision programs a few years ago, and he used part of one of them in tracing the history of the discovery of Loge. It was a popular program, and he did a good job. He began way back, hundreds of years ago. . . ."

(Cameras move from the illuminated model and back to Ling, standing.)

"School capsules give the 1970s as the first date in Loge's history. Actually, we can find traces of him much further back than that. The best starting point is probably 1766. A few years before the French and American revolutions, a German astronomer came up with a formula that seemed to give the relative distances of the planets from the Sun. His name was Johann Titius. His work didn't become famous until it was picked up a few years later by another German, Johann Bode, and the relation he discovered is usually called the Titius-Bode law, or just Bode's law."

(Cut to framed lithograph of Bode, then to the table of planetary distances. Zoom in on blank spot in the table showing question mark.)

"Bode pointed out that there was a curious gap in the distance formula. Mercury, Venus, Earth, Mars, Jupiter, and Saturn fitted it—and that is all the planets they knew of at the time—but there seemed to be one missing. There ought to be a planet between Mars and Jupiter, to make the formula really fit the Solar System. Then William Herschel, in 1781, discovered another planet, farther from the Sun than Saturn."

(Cut to high-resolution color image of Uranus, rings in close-up, image of Herschel as insert on the upper left. Cut back to Ling.)

"It fitted Bode's law, all right, but it wasn't in the right place to fill the spot between Mars and Jupiter. The search for a missing planet began, and finally in 1800 the asteroid Ceres was discovered at the correct distance from the Sun. Soon after, other asteroids were found at about the same distance as Ceres. The first pieces of Loge had appeared."

(Cut to image of Ceres, zoom in for high-resolution shot of Ceres City and greenhouse system. Cut to diagram showing planetary distances, with multiple entry between Mars and Jupiter, then back to Ling.)

"There now seemed to be too many planets. As more and more asteroids were found, the theory grew that they were all fragments of a single planet. It was a speculation without hard evidence for a long time, until in 1972 the Canadian astronomer Ovenden provided the first solid proof. Using the rates of change in the orbits of the planets as his starting point, he was able to show they were all consistent with the disappearance from the Solar System of a body of planetary mass roughly sixteen million years ago. He was also able to estimate the mass as about ninety times the mass of the Earth. Loge was beginning to take on a definite shape."

(Cut to image of Ovenden, then to artist's impression of the size and appearance of Loge, next to an image of Earth at the same scale.)

"The next part of the story came just a few years later, in 1975. Van Flandern in the United States of America integrated the orbits of long-period comets backward through time. He found that many of them had periods of about sixteen million years—and they had left from a particular region of the Solar System, between Mars and Jupiter. Parts of Loge were paying their first return visit, after a long absence."

(Cut to animated view of cometary orbits, showing their intersection with a diagram of the system. Run animation backward, to show all orbits coming together at a single point between Mars and Jupiter.)

"This led to the first modern ideas of Loge: a large planet, a gas giant of ninety Earth masses, almost the same size as Saturn. It disintegrated about sixteen million years ago in a cataclysm beyond our imagining. The explosion blew most of Loge out of the system forever. A few parts of the planetary core remain as the asteroids. Other fragments, from the outer crust of Loge, drop back into the Solar System from time to time as long-period comets."

(Move in to close-up of Ling, head and shoulders.)

"That looked like the full story, until we were able to go out and take a close look at the long-period cometary fragments. We found that some of them are packed with transuranic elements. The mystery of Loge had returned, bigger than ever. Why should parts of Loge's outer crust, alone of all the Solar System, contain transuranic elements? Their half-lives are less than twenty million years, in a system that is many billions of years old. They should have decayed long ago. Were they formed somehow in the explosion of Loge? If so, why are they found only in the outer crust, not in the asteroids that came from Loge's core? *How* were they formed? To all these questions, we still have no satisfactory answers."

(Cut to image of Loge again, feed in beginning of fade-out music, at low volume.)

"One final and tantalizing fact. Sixteen million years is nothing; it is like yesterday on the cosmic scale. When Loge disintegrated there were already primates on the Earth. Did our early ancestors look into the sky one night and behold the fearful sight of Loge's explosion? Is it conceivable that another planet might suffer a similar fate?"

(Fade-out as image of Loge begins to swell, changes color, breaks asunder. Final music crescendo for the ending.)

"It still puzzles me why Ling should be appointed to this investigation. He writes his own ticket, of course. Maybe he knew one of the dead Grabbers—he seemed to know everything there was to know about the Belt and the Belters." Green shook his head unhappily. "I suppose I'll have to get in and meet the man and find out what he wants me to do now that he's here. I hope he's not going to try and demote me to being a messenger boy."

Together, Green and Wolf walked back to Bey's office. Karl Ling did not look up as they entered. He was oblivious to his surroundings, deeply engrossed in his review of the autopsy records on the three dead crew members of the *Jason*. Wolf's saturation techniques apparently didn't work on Ling. He became aware of them only when Wolf stepped in front of him and spoke.

"As soon as you want it, Mr. Ling, we are ready to give you a briefing on our findings. This is Park Green, who is representing the USF here at Form Control."

Ling looked up briefly, then returned his attention to the medical records. His glance had taken in the two other men for only a fraction of a second, but Bey had the feeling they had both been scanned and tucked away in memory.

"Very good," said Ling, eyes still fixed on the output screen. "For a start, why don't you answer the most basic question for me. The three dead men had clearly been involved in a form-change process. Where are the bio-feedback machines located that were used on them?"

Wolf grimaced at Park Green. "We don't have that answer for you yet, sir," he replied. "Though of course we recognize its importance, and we are working on it."

Ling looked up again. This time, his gaze locked on to Wolf. For some reason, it seemed to have been the answer he was expecting, even hoping for.

"No answer yet, Mr. Wolf? I thought that might be the case. Would you perhaps like me to enlighten you?"

Bey stifled the sudden impulse to go over and choke Ling and managed a cool reply. "If you can, certainly. I must say that it is hard for me to imagine that you could have reached a rational conclusion on such a brief inspection of our records."

"I did not. I knew it before I left the Moon." Ling smiled for the first time and stood up from his seat. "You see, Mr. Wolf, I have no doubt that you and your fellow workers here in Form Control are proficient in your work. In fact, I took pains to verify your excellent reputation before I left the Moon. That is not the issue. The particular situation we have here requires something that by definition you and Mr. Larsen do not have: the ability to think like a USF citizen. For example, if you were suddenly a millionaire because you had struck it rich out in the Belt, where on Earth would you choose to go for your entertainment? Remember, you may choose freely without thought of cost."

"Probably to the Great Barrier Reef, in a gilled form."

"Very good." Karl Ling turned to Park Green. "Now let me ask you the same question. You are a Belter, and suddenly a millionaire. Where on all of Earth would you want to go? What is the Belter's dream of a place for all the most exotic delights?"

Green rubbed thoughtfully at his chin. "Why, I guess it would be Pleasure Dome. I've never been there, and I don't know what it offers, but that's the place we all hear about."

"Right. And of course you haven't been there—neither has anybody else who is not extremely rich. Just the same, it's the USF idea of paradise, especially for people who live out in the Belt. Part of the reason you would *want* to go there would be to prove how rich you are."

He went over to the large map display on the far wall and called out a South Polar projection.

"Now let's take this a little further. Look at the geography. The crew of the *Jason* landed at the North Australian spaceport. That's within easy transport distance of the Australian Mattin Link entry point. One transfer gets them to New Zealand; a second one puts them at Cap City in Antarctica. Pleasure Dome, as I am sure that you know, Mr. Wolf, though Mr. Green may not, lies directly beneath Cap City in the Antarctic ice cap. Total travel time from the spaceport: an hour or less."

Park Green was nodding slowly in agreement. "I guess so. I'm not used yet to the number of Link entry points that you have here on earth. I don't see where your analysis gets us, though. We need to find a place that has sophisticated form-change equipment. I saw the list

of labs that Mr. Wolf has, and I'm sure that Cap City
and Pleasure Dome weren't anywhere on it."

Karl Ling smiled ironically. "I feel sure they were not.
You saw the legal list." He turned to Bey, who realized
what was coming and felt a steadily rising excitement.
"Pleasure Dome offers *all* pleasures, does it not, Mr.
Wolf? Even the most exotic. Would it not be logical to
assume that a number of those recreations involve the
use of form-change equipment?"

"It certainly would. That's rather a sore point with me,
as a matter of fact. We know that there are illegal form-
changes going on there, to cater to some of the more
debauched physical tastes. But we have orders to keep
out of there. I must say, we usually have no trouble with
them. They are very discreet, and since the last trouble,
a few years ago, we've had a sort of informal truce with
them. I would be surprised to find they have equipment
complex enough to handle the Mariana changes, but I
wouldn't rule it out. There's plenty of money there, and
they could get the equipment if they wanted it. You can
probably guess how much power the managers of Pleasure Dome have when it comes to influence in high
places. There are rumors about a number of Central
Coordinators who go there fairly often."

Ling touched the map controls, and a new image
appeared on the display.

"Then this must be our next stop: Cap City, and Pleasure Dome. We still do not have the answer to the basic
question: How did those three men become three dead
monsters?

"Mr. Green, you should remain here and be available
to answer inquiries from Earth and Moon authorities."

Green could not resist a snort of disgust. His view of
Ling's order showed clearly on his face.

"Please make travel arrangements for Mr. Wolf and
myself," went on Ling calmly. "Take the highest-priority
links and the fastest interchanges. Don't worry about
finance, Mr. Wolf," he said, seeing Bey's questioning
look. "That is not an issue. I can call on the complete

financial resources of the USF if necessary to pursue this inquiry."

"That wasn't why I was frowning, Mr. Ling. I was wondering why the Mariana Trench was chosen to dispose of the bodies. Can you explain that also?"

"I have a speculation," said Ling, "and I rather think it is the same one that you have. I even think I know what you are trying to gain by asking it, but that's another matter."

There was a hint of humor deep in his tawny eyes. "Let us indulge our imaginations. The crew of the *Jason* died in Pleasure Dome. The proprietors of that facility looked at their identifications and knew at once that they were all in trouble. They know that the USF looks after its own. They decided that they had to get the bodies off-Earth, and they took them to Australia through the Mattin Link. Unfortunately for their plans, they did not realize how tight the security regulations have become since the Purcell spores found their way in. There was no way to smuggle three bodies into space, so that plan was dropped and they were obliged to improvise another one. Deep water looked attractive. One further transfer through the Link took them to the Marianas. But hasty planning, and inadequate knowledge of the local geography, led to a botching of the disposal job. We know the rest."

Ling looked questioningly at Bey. "Plausible? It is, I admit, no more than a deductive argument, but I think it has a high probability of being right.

"Now, quickly, have preparations made and let us be on our way."

Green hurried out, but Wolf lingered for a moment. During Ling's last exposition, he had been listening intently, studying the manner of the speaker. Ling raised his eyebrows as Wolf showed no sign of leaving.

"You have further business, Mr. Wolf? There is still a great deal of work to be done on the records, and little time to do it."

"I want to make one comment," said Bey. "I've spent my life studying form-change, and I believe that I understand it pretty well. One man is my master in the theory, but when it comes to seeing through exterior changes I will match myself against anyone. I am sure that we have met before, Mr. Ling, and it was under very different circumstances. The problem we have here is an urgent one, and I want to tell you that I do not propose to do anything about my ideas. But I want you to know that I can tell the lion by his paw."

Karl Ling's acid look seemed to soften briefly. There was a hint of a smile again on his lips.

"Mr. Wolf, I really have no idea what you are talking about, and I must get on with this biological work. Perhaps you would like to stay here and help me with it. I have a high regard for your insights. Let's get to work quickly. I want to be in Cap City four hours from now."

After Bey Wolf and Karl Ling had left, Park Green and John Larsen went off together for a stimulant and a sharing of their dissatisfaction. By the third round Larsen had become morose and militant.

"Just our luck," he said. "Those two go off to sample Pleasure Dome, and they leave us here to handle the brainless bureaucrats. It's always the same; we get all the dog work, and those two get all the excitement."

He had never met or even heard of Karl Ling until that day, but fine points of logic were beneath him.

"I'd like to show those two," he went on, sniffing again at the dispenser. "I'd like to show them what we can do without them. Solve the whole thing while they're gone." He slid a little lower in his seat. "That would show them."

Green and Larsen had been matching round for round, but with twice the body mass Green was in much better shape. He watched Larsen sink lower yet, his chin almost down to the level of the table.

"Come on," he said, "if we're going to do it at all, it had better be while you're still capable of it." He lifted Larsen's limp figure easily to a standing position and held him there one-handed while he paid their bill.

"Just let's get a couple of shots of detoxer in you and

you'll be as good as new. Once we're all set, let's go over the full records again and see if we can come up with something. We've got Ling's comments to help us. We never had that when we were working before." He walked an unsteady Larsen from the room. "It would do me a lot of good to beat that smarmy supercilious midget to the answer."

Fifteen minutes later they were both cold sober and deep into the case records. There was a long period of sifting before Larsen sat back, snapped his fingers, and said, "Question: What is there about the crew of the *Jason* that made them different from everybody else who was undergoing form-change here on Earth?"

Park Green looked at him and shrugged. "Grabbers? Belters? Super-rich?"

Larsen shook his head. "No. Answer: They had recently been handling large quantities of transuranic elements and probably experiencing high levels of radioactivity. So here's my second question. Did the autopsies look for Asfanium and Polkium in the bodies? Did they even test for a high radioactivity? My bet is that they didn't."

"It shouldn't make any difference, John. We know that the crew didn't die from chemical poisoning, and they didn't die from radioactive dose."

"Of course they didn't—but form-change depends on the condition of the central nervous system. So, final question: What do the transuranics do to that system? I doubt if anyone really knows. It might throw off the fine tuning, and that might make them behave strangely in form-change. What do you think?"

Green shrugged. "It's certainly a long shot, but we should check out the transuranics content of the bodies. Do you know where they went after the postmortem?"

"Sure. They're in the Form Control cold storage center in Manila."

Green stood up. "Come on, then. We'll need authorization for another postmortem, and we'd better find a pathologist to take along with us."

CHAPTER 13

The exit point from the Mattin Link system was in the upper levels of Cap City, almost at the polar surface. Bey Wolf and Karl Ling emerged from the final chamber and looked about them for the elevators that would take them down to Pleasure Dome, four thousand feet below in the polar ice. Above them, the howling winds of an Antarctic July tore at the surface, carrying the groan of protesting surface structures all the way down to the Link exit point. It was not a congenial spot, and they were keen to move downward. As they stood there a soft voice spoke suddenly in their ears.

"Come to Pleasure Dome, satisfy your heart's desires."

Ling looked at Wolf and smiled ruefully. "An omniprojector. What an abuse of a technology. That system would be worth millions to us in Tycho or out in the Halo."

The soft voice continued. "In Pleasure Dome, you can shed the cares of the world and feel free again, free to fulfill your wildest imaginings. Visit the lustrous Caves of Ice or swim in the Pool of Lethe. Win a world in the great Xanadu Casino or spend an unforgettable day as a shuttle in the Coupling Loom. Be free, be with us in Pleasure Dome."

"Free, at a price," said Bey.

Ling smiled. "These aren't really advertisements, you know. Any message given here is only heard by people who are already on their way to the Dome, so it's preaching to the converted. People just want a reassurance that they are about to spend their money on something really exciting."

The omniadvertising went on, and finally they received a useful comment, "Follow the blue lights to the Temple of Earthly Delights."

Moving along the chain of blue lights as directed, they were soon in an elevator, dropping steadily and swiftly down deep into the polar cap. The entrance to Pleasure Dome was a great sparkling chamber, lined with perfect mirrors, like the inside of a giant multifaceted diamond. The effect was shattering. Walls, floors, ceilings, all were perfectly reflecting. Bey could see images of himself and Ling marching off to infinity in every direction. He struggled to orient himself, to find a view that did not extend indefinitely away from him.

"You'll get used to it in a few minutes," remarked Ling coolly. He seemed quite unaffected by his surroundings. "Pleasure Dome is all like this."

"I didn't realize that you had been here before."

"A couple of times, long ago. These reflecting walls are a necessity, not a luxury, you know—though of course the owners here to do their best to turn the situation to a special feature of the place." He glanced around him with interest. "They've come a long way. When they first cut this city beneath the ice cap, thirty years ago, the big problem was the heat. People produce heat, all the time, from themselves and their equipment. There's nothing you can do about that, but without a special system the ice walls would have melted in no time. You can see the solution. All the walls have been coated with passivine, perfectly reflecting and with a very low coefficient of thermal conductivity."

He reached out his hand and held it close to the wall.

"See, you can feel the reflected heat on your skin. A tiny amount of heat passes through to the ice walls underneath, and a modest refrigeration unit connecting to the polar surface takes care of that very easily."

Bey was looking on ironically. "I must say, Mr. Ling, for a man who is from off-Earth, you have a quite astonishing knowledge of Earth affairs."

"The lunar nights are long. We have plenty of time for reading." Ling's formal reply carried definite hints of humor. Before Bey could comment further, a third person had joined them, moving smoothly and silently across the polished floor.

"Welcome to Pleasure Dome, sirs."

She was tall and slim, dressed in a long white gown. Her skin was pale and flawless, her hair a fine white cloud. Even her lips looked faded and bloodless. She looked at them quietly, with cool gray eyes as expressionless as clouded crystal. A Snow Queen. Bey wondered how much of it was natural and how much she owed to the form-change equipment.

"I am your hostess. I will help you to arrange your pleasures. Do not be afraid to ask, whatever your tastes. There are few wishes that we cannot accommodate.

"Before we begin, there are a few formalities."

"You want our identifications?" asked Bey.

"Only if you choose to give them, sirs. They are not necessary. We do need proof of adequate means, but that can be cash or any other method you prefer."

"We are together," said Ling. "My credit will serve for both of us. Do you have a bank connection?"

"Here, sir." The Snow Queen produced a small silver plate from within her gown. Ling placed his right index finger on it, and they waited as the ID was established and the central bank returned a credit rating. As she read the credit, her expression changed. Previously she had been remote and self-possessed, a being without sex or emotion. Now she suddenly lost her composure and for the first time became a young woman. Bey realized that Ling's credit was probably that of the entire USF.

"What is your pleasure, sirs?" A pink tongue licked nervously at the pale lips. Even her voice had changed, become uncertain, tremulous, almost childish. With that much credit available, Bey suspected that there was nothing, literally nothing, that could not be bought at Pleasure Dome. The goods on sale included the body and soul of their hostess, and she knew it. It was dangerous for her to be in contact with such financial power. She could never know when one of Ling's whims might include her as a purchased pleasure.

Ling had read her uneasiness and divined the reason for it.

"We want none of the conventional pleasures," he said. "We want to talk to the men who control the form-change tanks at Pleasure Dome. The men who recently handled three off-Earthers. Don't worry if you do not know what I am referring to—the men we seek will understand fully."

She hesitated. It was odd how her vulnerability had suddenly cracked the glacial shell. There were wrinkles of worry on that perfect brow, and animation in those clouded gray eyes. Ling's request fell far outside the usual list of fancies, and the decision as to how to proceed made her uncomfortable.

"Sirs, I must consult others on this matter. It will take me a few minutes. If you would wait here"—she led them to another, octagonal room—"I will return as quickly as possible. It is a viewing room, as you will see. The scenes change every two minutes, unless you wish to cancel and advance to another before that. The control button is on the seats."

"And this?" said Ling, pointing to the metal cylinder that stood above each seat.

"Don't worry about it. It is a sensor that will monitor your responses and move to others that should have increasing appeal to your particular tastes."

As she left them, the room grew dark, then slowly lightened. They were in the middle of a holo-setting, surrounded by the filtered emerald light of a submarine reef. Across from them, winnowing the green gloom with giant questing tentacles, floated a huge octopus. The great eyes fixed on them, lambent and unblinking.

"An illegal form, I assume?" asked Ling quietly.

"Very much so," said Bey, staring in fascination at the slowly moving arms. "All the cephalopods are illegal. There is at least a five percent chance that reversion would be impossible in that form. I am surprised that anyone would pay huge sums of money to take such a stupid risk."

"*De gustibus* . . ." said Ling. He shrugged, and the room again grew dim. When it lightened, Bey at first thought that they were again in an underwater setting. The light was again a dappled green. He looked up to the fronded leaves far above them. The scene was over-canopied by a continuous growth of vegetation. In front of them, blending perfectly into the broken patches of light and dark, crouched the silent form of a tiger. As they watched, the great muscles bunched beneath the smooth coat, and the beast sprang. The unsheathed claws ripped at a boar's throat at the same time that the other forepaw made a mighty swipe at the exposed backbone. The boar moved its head quickly, intercepting the extended forelimb with a razor-sharp set of long tusks.

"If you don't mind . . ." said Ling quietly, and pressed the button to change the scene. "I hope that is not an accurate reflection of your taste or my own," he said as the light again dimmed.

"I'm not even sure which form we were offered there, the boar or the tiger," replied Bey. "Both of them, I expect."

The light grew brighter, then brighter yet. The man standing in front of them was imperious and command-ing. He stood, arms folded, in the blazing light of an Egyptian noon, watching the groaning timber as it moved slowly over the wooden rollers. Heavy ropes held the great block of stone securely on the flat support, and the forms of the long lines of slaves who hauled it slowly across the desert were smeared with sweat and dust. In the distance ahead of them, the long, rising ramp led to the unfinished shape of the looming pyramid.

"A real power kick," said Ling.

Bey nodded. "No man has had that much absolute power for thousands of years. I don't think we really know much about Cheops, but I'll bet that the Pleasure Dome artists have made a creditable shot at the times."

They looked in silence for a few moments at the glaring,

empty sky and the tall, white-robed figure standing rock-steady in the paralyzing heat.

"I don't think too much of the power of that monitor to read our tastes," said Bey. "Unless that man is Imhotep rather than Cheops."

The scene was shifting again, the bright white light of an Egyptian morning fading to a flickering red glare. It took time for their eyes to adjust to the smoky firelight. The groan of timber and the sighs of hard-working slaves had given way to the creak of pulleys and the hiss of a bellows-driven furnace. The men moving around the long table were naked except for their black hoods and leather aprons, and the sweat trickled down their muscular bodies. The man on the table was silent, mouth gaping. His limbs were bound at wrist and ankle with wrappings of cloth and rope, spread-eagled and strained.

A black-cowled figure was approaching the table, brand glowing orange-red in his hand. Bey pressed the button hurriedly.

"Who could want that?" said Ling. Even he seemed moved from his ironic detachment. "I should have guessed it; there is nothing here for people like us."

"How does the machine see us—victims or torturers?" asked Bey.

The scene this time was pastoral and quiet. A young man was sitting alone by a great oak tree, his face calm and thoughtful. The sun was shining, but it was the soft green of a European summer rather than the harsh browns and ochers of Egypt. The birds flew about the garden, and there was the muted sound of distant running water. The man did not move. He was dressed in the shirt and woolen breeches of the seventeenth century. Wolf and Ling looked at each other, both puzzled.

"Do you understand it?" asked Ling.

Bey peered more closely at the man's hands, at the wedge of glass that he was holding. He felt a sudden thrill of recognition.

"Newton," he said softly to Ling. "Look at the hands."

"What?" Ling stared hard. After a moment he made a curious sound, half grunt, half groan. "It is, it's Newton at Woolsthorpe. See, he's holding a prism." His voice was changed from a cynical amused tone to one of fascinated longing. "God, can you imagine what it would be like? To see the world through Newton's eyes, in those years. His *annus mirabilis*, the plague years—he discovered all the basics of modern science, the laws of motion, optics, calculus, gravity. All during those two years when he was at Woolsthorpe to avoid the plague."

Ling leaned forward further, his eyes alight with interest. Wolf, no less intrigued, was wondering how long the scene would remain for their inspection.

"Well, sirs, I am sorry to have taken such a long time."

The soft voice behind them broke the spell. The scene faded. Ling looked at the helmet above his head with respect.

"I would have sworn that there was nothing that Pleasure Dome could offer me with real appeal. Now I know I am wrong," he said ruefully.

He turned to the woman behind him, who had with her an equally striking blond-haired man, also dressed all in white.

"Who programmed this viewing section?" asked Ling.

The man smiled. "It is not the policy of Pleasure Dome to reveal our working secrets. Just be assured, everything we offer is done as well as history permits. The psychology, if we use the form of a real person, is as accurate as modern methods allow. You are interested in one of the worlds we offer?"

Ling sighed. "All too interested. But we have other business. You have seen the credit I control. We need help. If we don't get it, we can close down the form-changing services here completely. I hope that will not prove necessary."

The man nodded. "Sirs, your credit is enough to purchase any pleasure. However, you must appreciate that certain things in Pleasure Dome are not available at any price. The detail of our operations is one. Please state your wishes again so that we can see if we are able to accommodate them."

"We have no wish to cause trouble here," said Ling.

"If we wished to, there is no doubt that we could. This is Behrooz Wolf, the head of the Office of Form Control on Earth. I am Karl Ling, special assistant to the USF Cabinet. I tell you this so that you will know we are not trying to trick you. Check our credentials if you wish to."

The man smiled. "That was done as you arrived. Pleasure Dome takes certain precautions, although it does not advertise them. We seek an ID if anyone makes an unusual request—otherwise, the anonymity is total."

Ling nodded. "Good. That saves time. All we are looking for is information. Three men died recently during form-change. We believe that they died here. We want to speak to the men who were in charge of that operation, and we want to see the full records of the monitors that were recording and supervising the form-changes."

The man made no attempt to deny the charge. He was silent for a few moments, then asked, "If we cooperate, you will take our involvement no further, here or elsewhere."

"You have our word."

"Then come with me." The blond man smiled. "You should be flattered. You are obtaining a service free of charge. To my knowledge, that has never happened before since Pleasure Dome was first created."

The three men walked quickly through a maze of ice caves, fairy grottoes lit by lights of different colors. They came at last to a door that led to an ordinary office, with paneled walls and a functional-looking desk.

The man motioned to Wolf and Ling to sit down on the hard chairs.

"I will return in a moment. This, by the way, is our idea of luxury. Normal walls, furniture, and privacy. We all aspire to it, but our lives here rarely permit us the chance."

He left, to return a few minutes later with his identical twin. Bey felt that his question about the use of form-change equipment on the staff had been answered. The ultimate bondage: someone else dictated the exact shape of their bodies.

The newcomer was distinctly ill at ease. The idea of

talking about his work to an outsider clearly disturbed him. Bey was able to see a new side of Karl Ling in action as he soothed and coaxed the man to become more relaxed and talkative. After a few minutes of introductory chatting, the real interview began.

"All those three wanted was a full-speed reconditioning program," the Pleasure Dome controller said. Once started, it promised to be a torrent of words. "The only thing we did for them that is in any way illegal was the speed. We used the biofeedback machines twenty-four hours a day and provided the nutrients intravenously. It looked like a completely straightforward job, and we didn't give them any special monitoring, the way we would if a customer was to come in and ask for a special change. We can do some pretty fancy things here, though of course we can't compete with the big BEC labs for change experiment. The program that the three of them had asked for takes about a hundred and fifty hours, nearly a week of changing if you run it continuously. I know there are versions that will do the same thing in a third of the time, but believe it or not we take all the precautions we can. I prefer to run the slower version; it's less strain on the people taking it."

"You've run this course many times before, I assume?" asked Ling. The speaker seemed in need of a chance to breathe—all the information had come out as one burst.

"Often, especially for off-worlders. It wasn't my job to ask their origins, of course, but I can make a good guess from their clothes and their speech. If anybody had thought to ask me at the beginning, I'd have told them the three we had weren't Earthers."

He looked at the other blond man, with a hint of a dispute that still rankled.

"Ever since Capman's work on the changes," he went on, "a straightforward program like this one has been completely automatic. The tanks have automatic monitors that control air and nutrient supplies, and the pace of the process is all regulated from the computer. Of course, the subject has to be conscious at some level, because it's purposive form-change that's involved. You understand what I mean, do you, or shall I explain it more?"

He looked at Ling, taking Wolf's understanding for granted.

"Enough," said Ling. He glared at Bey, who was looking smug. "Keep on going."

"Well, the unit is completely self-contained. There's no viewing panel on the tanks, so the only way we know what's happening inside is by looking at the monitors and telltales on the outside."

"How often do you do that?"

"In a simple case like this, once a day. Even that shouldn't be necessary. We never have anything to do, but we check anyway. The three off-worlders had all checked in together and started the program at the same time, so one look a day was enough to monitor all of them. They all had the same reconditioning program. Needed it, too. They looked done in when they arrived—I don't know what they'd been up to."

He paused for a moment. Bey wondered what the staff of Pleasure Dome did for their own entertainment—what would appeal to the men and women who had seen everything, who had provided for every possible taste? Probably something very simple. The chefs of the most expensive restaurants seemed to dine on the most basic fare.

"The evening of the third day," the man finally continued, "I took my usual routine look at the telltales. All three men were dead. I couldn't believe it. At first I thought there had to be something wrong with the telltales, or maybe a programming error for the displays. Then we opened the tanks."

He paused again, reliving the memory.

"It was awful. God, it was like a nightmare. They had changed; they weren't men anymore. They were monsters, with great big glowing eyes and wrinkled skin—just like a horror holo. We checked that they were all dead, then looked at their IDs. I knew, even without that, we had three off-worlders on our hands. Everybody around here really panicked. We thought we might be able to get them off-Earth, but it isn't as easy as it used to be. When we found we couldn't do that, we decided the safest thing would be to put them deep at sea. But apparently that didn't work, either."

There was a long silence. Ling was too engrossed even to give Bey a look of triumph at his reconstruction of events. He was bound in a spell of concentration so intense that he looked blind, his eyes unblinking and focused on infinity.

"Did you do any chemical analysis of the bodies?" he asked at last.

"God, no. We wanted to get them out of here. We weren't about to waste time with tests. There should be records of all the chemistry, though, as it was measured during the biofeedback work. It will all be in the files, still, along with the monitor and telltale records. Blood chemistry and cell chemistry should be recorded continuously."

"Right. I want to examine those now. Bring them here or take us to them."

"I'll get them. But they'll be in raw form. Only a form-change expert would be able to read them."

Ling caught Bey's glance. "Bring them in. We'll manage somehow," he said. "It's a skill you never lose once you've mastered it completely."

John Larsen looked at the spectrograph output, then at Park Green.

"It's far less than I expected," he said. "There are traces of Asfanium in all the bodies, but the amount is very small. There's a tiny trace of radioactivity because of that, but it's not enough to make a big physical effect, even if form-change amplifies it. I wonder if it could be a subtle *chemical* effect? Trace elements, even in microscopic amounts, do funny things to the biochemical balance. We still don't know too much about the chemical properties of the transuranics in the island of stability around 114."

"Well," began Green doubtfully, "we don't know all that much. But we've found no strange properties for

Asfanium or Polkium in our work on the Moon. I think it's something different. The crew of the *Jason* never encountered form-change before. They weren't experienced. I wonder if they somehow let things get out of control—they ran into something new, like a trace of Asfanium, and they didn't have the form-change experience to know how to handle it."

Larsen slapped the spectrograph output sheet against his thigh.

"Park, I bet you're on to something. Experience *is* important in form-change work. With inexperienced people, something could go wrong."

"So can we test it?"

"I think so. We already know that Asfanium concentrates in the thymus gland. We can take an extract from one of the bodies and conduct a controlled test to see if funny things happen when you use a form-change program."

Green frowned. "It's a nice idea, but where could you get a test animal? I thought the whole point of form-change was that only humans could do it. After all, that's the basis for the humanity tests."

Larsen laughed confidently. "Exactly right. You want to see the test animal? Here it is." He tapped his chest. "Now, don't get the wrong idea," he added as he saw Park Green begin a horrified protest. "One of the things that we get in Form Control is many years of training in form-control methods. If anything starts to happen, I'll have no trouble at all in stopping and reversing it. That's the difference between me and the three Grabbers—experience."

He stood up. "Don't forget, it's a *purposive* process. It only changes you because there is a desire to change. Come on, let's get a thymus extract made here and then go back to the form-change tanks at Form Control headquarters. We'll really have something to show Bey Wolf and your boss when they get back from their jaunt to Pleasure Dome."

CHAPTER 14

The "jaunt" to Pleasure Dome was becoming a grind. The staff employees looked on in amazement as Wolf and Ling worked their way through the monitor records at express speed, reading raw data, swapping comments and shared analyses as they went. They had to deal with a mixture of body physical parameters such as temperature, pulse rate, and skin conductivity, and system variables such as nutrient rates, ambient temperatures, and electrical stimuli. Programs in use as they were swapped in and out of the computer, plus chemical readings and brain activity indices, were all recorded in parallel in the same files. Reading the outputs required many years of experience, plus a full understanding of the processes—mental and physical—of the human body. Ling was tireless, and Bey was determined not to be outdone.

"Who is he?" whispered the Pleasure Dome form-change supervisor to Bey during one of their brief halts to await more data. "I know who you are, you're Head of Form Control; but where did *he* learn all this?"

Bey looked across at Ling, who was deep in thought and oblivious to comments, whispered or otherwise.

"Maybe you should ask him yourself, I've already had that conversation once."

The arrival of more data pushed the question aside.

After thirty-six hours of intense work, the basic analysis was complete. They had an incredible array of facts available to them, but one dominated all others: The crew of the *Jason* had died long, long before their form-change

119

was complete. They had died because the forms they were adopting were unable to live and breathe in normal air. The final forms remained unknown. There were other mysteries. Why were they changing to those forms, under the control of a simple reconditioning program that had been used a thousand times before with never a hint of trouble?

Karl Ling sat motionless, as he had for the past two hours. From time to time he would ask Bey a question or look again at a piece of data. Rather than disturb him with general questions, Bey decided that he would go into another room and try to reach Form Control headquarters. He wanted to check with John Larsen on the general situation. Ling was voyaging on strange seas of thought, alone, and Bey Wolf had developed a profound respect for that man's mind.

It was Park Green who answered the communicator instead of Larsen. He looked very uneasy.

"Where's John?"

"He's in a form-change tank, Mr. Wolf. He went in yesterday morning."

"Well, that's one way to keep the bureaucracy off your back."

To Green's great relief, Bey Wolf didn't seem at all concerned. Even when he explained the whole thing to him, Bey just laughed.

"John's been around form-change equipment almost as much as I have. He knows how to handle it as well as anyone on earth. But honestly, Park, I'm sceptical about your theory. Those Belters have probably all had use of form-change equipment before. When they use it for injury repairs, it's called regeneration equipment, but it's just the same principle. The only thing the USF is down on is form-change for cosmetics or inessentials."

Park Green looked as though a big weight had been lifted off him.

"Thank heaven for that. I've been worried ever since he gave himself that thymus injection. I thought he might have talked me into letting him do something where he had a big risk. I didn't know enough about all this stuff to argue with him."

Bey smiled at the big man's obvious concern. "Go over to the tank and keep an eye on him if you're at all worried," he said, and signed off the connection. He strolled back to join Karl Ling, who had now come out of his trance and accepted a cup of syncaff, "compliments of Pleasure Dome." Having broken their standard policy by letting them in free of charge, the staff of Pleasure Dome had apparently decided to adopt them. Ling had just politely refused a Snow Queen's offer of an age-old technique to relax him after all his hard work. He looked rather pleased at her suggestion and quite annoyed when she made the same offer to Bey.

"I think I have the answers, Mr. Wolf, and they are fascinating ones. More than I dreamed. If I am right, this is a special day in our history." Ling sat back, relishing the moment.

"Well, Park Green and John Larsen think they have the answers, too," said Bey. "I've just been in video contact with them."

"They do? Without the evidence that we have available to us here?" Ling's eyebrows were raised. "I can't believe it. What do they think we are dealing with?"

Bey sketched out Larsen and Green's theory. It sounded much thinner than it had when he had first heard it. He summarized the situation back in headquarters and finally mentioned that Larsen was now putting the idea to a practical test.

"He injected an extract from one of the dead men and put himself into a form-change tank?" Ling's self-possession failed him. He turned as white as one of the Snow Queens. "He's a dead man. My God, why didn't they consult us before they began?"

He sprang to his feet, hurled the records aside, and grabbed for his loose jacket.

"Come on, Mr. Wolf. We must get back as fast as we possibly can. If there is any chance to save John Larsen's life, it depends on our efforts."

He ran out of the room. Bey, bewildered and alarmed,

followed him at top speed. When Karl Ling lost his dignity so completely, it was time to worry.

In the elevator, on the Mattin Link transfers, and through the ground transit system, Ling rapidly explained the basics of his discoveries to Bey Wolf. By the time they reached the Office of Form Control it was hard to say which man was the more frantic. They went at once to the form-change tanks.

Park Green, alerted as they traveled, was waiting for them there. He looked at Ling as though expecting an outburst of insult and accusation. It did not come. Ling went at once to the tank containing John Larsen and began to read the telltales. After a few minutes he relaxed a little and gave a grunt of satisfaction.

"Everything's still stable. That's good. If he follows the same pattern as the other three, we have about twenty-four hours to do something for him. The one thing I daren't do is stop this process in the middle. We'll have to let it run its course, try to keep him alive while it happens, and worry afterward about reversing it. Bring me the tank schematics. I need to know exactly how the circuits work that control the nutrients and the air supply."

Wolf went for them and was back in less than a minute. Park Green was still standing by the tank, looking totally bewildered. When Ling had the schematics, Green took Bey to one side.

"Mr. Wolf, does he know what he's doing? He's an expert on the Belt, I realize that. But he doesn't know about this stuff, does he? Are we risking John's life by letting him do this?"

Wolf put his hand up to Green's massive shoulder. "Believe me, Park, he knows what he's doing. If anyone can help John now, he can do it. We have to give all the help we can and save the questions until later. I'll tell you my views on this when it's all over."

Ling interrupted their conversation. His voice had a reassuring ring of certainty and authority.

"One of you come over here and make a note of the

equipment changes that will have to be made. I'll read off the settings as I find them on the charts. The other one of you, call BEC. I want their top specialist on interactive form-change programs. Maria Sun, if she's available, the best they can offer if she isn't. Tell them it's code word circuits, if that will move them faster."

Wolf nodded. "I can get Maria." He hurried out.

The equipment modifications began. At every stage Ling rechecked the telltales. Maria Sun arrived, took one look at the monitors, and settled in by Ling's side. She swore continuously, but it did nothing to lessen her effectiveness as they sweated over the tank. Larsen's condition inside remained stable, but there were big changes occurring. His pulse rate was way down, and there was heavy demand on calcium, nitrogen, and sodium in the nutrient feeds. Skin properties were changing drastically.

"They could have noticed all this in Pleasure Dome if they'd only bothered to look," grunted Ling. "Give them their due, they had no reason to expect anything peculiar. But take a look at that body mass indicator."

Maria Sun swore a string of oaths. "It's up to a hundred and twenty kilos. What's his usual weight?"

"Eighty," said Bey, absorbed in watching the indicators. He longed to see inside the tank, but there was no provision for that in the system.

The work went on. After many hours of equipment change and work on program modification with Maria Sun, Ling finally declared that he had done all that he could. The real test would come in a few hours time. That was when the records from the crew of the *Jason* had begun to go wild. It remained to be seen if the equipment changes could keep Larsen's condition stable as the change proceeded further. The time of watching and waiting began.

As Ling made his final checks on the telltales, Bey realized the mental anguish that Park Green must be going through. He looked at the big man's unhappy face.

"Mr. Ling, have we done all that can be done here?" Bey asked.

"For the moment. The rest is waiting."

"Then, if you will, would you explain all this to us, from the beginning. I got a quick overview on the way here, but Park Green is still in the dark completely, and I'm sure Maria is just as curious."

Ling looked at the three of them as though seeing them for the first time. Finally, he nodded sympathetically.

"You deserve that, even if I'm wrong. From the beginning, eh? That's a long story. I'll have to tell it to you the way that I imagine it. Whether it's true is another matter."

He sat down, leaned back, and put his hands behind his head.

"I have to begin it sixteen million years ago, and not on Earth. On the planet Loge. Loge was a giant, about ninety Earth masses, and it was going to explode. Now for something speculative, something you may find hard to believe. Loge was inhabited. It had living on it a race of intelligent beings. Maybe they were too intelligent. We know that their planet blew up, and we don't know why. Maybe they were to blame for that. I doubt if we'll ever know. The race had nuclear energy, but not spaceflight."

"Come on now." Maris Sun was looking at Ling sceptically. "You can't possibly know that. I'll buy your Logians, maybe, but you just said we'll never know much about them."

"I know that much, all the same. How do I know it?" Ling was almost pleased by the questioning. "Well, I know that they had nuclear energy because they made transuranic elements. Any *natural* source of transuranics would have decayed by natural processes since the formation of the planet. The only possible way we could find a source of transuranics on Loge—and only on Loge—would be if they were created there, by nuclear synthesis. We don't know how to do that efficiently ourselves, so there's good reason to think that the Logians had a more advanced nuclear technology than we do."

"All right." Maria nodded her dark head. She had changed her appearance since Bey had last seen her and was now wearing the form of an exquisite Oriental. The terrible streams of swearing that came out of that petal mouth when she was hard at work made a strange effect that she was probably quite unaware of. "So, they had nuclear energy. But how could you possibly know they *didn't* have spaceflight?"

"Elementary, my dear Maria." Ling was too engrossed in his explanation to note Bey's quiet reaction to that evidence of prior acquaintance. "They couldn't escape from Loge, not any of them, even when they found that it was going to disintegrate. They must have had some years of warning, some time to plan—but no one got away, not one of them."

Ling rose from his seat. "Wait one moment, I must check the status." He went to the tank, nodded as he inspected the telltales, and returned. "It is still all stable, and the change is accelerating. The next hour or two is crucial."

"We'll stay here," said Bey. "So they could not get off Loge," he prompted.

"That is correct." Ling resumed his relaxed posture, eyes far away. "They had time to plan, so I imagine it was not a nuclear war. Perhaps they had found a way of making large-scale interior adjustments to the planet and lost control. That would be relatively slow.

"What could they do? They looked around them in the Solar System. They knew they were going to die, but was there any way that their race might survive? To a Logian, the natural place for that survival would be Jupiter, or best of all Saturn. They probably never even considered Earth—a tiny planet, by their standards, too hot, oxygen atmosphere, a metal ball crouched close to the Sun. No, it would have been Jupiter or Saturn, that was their hope. That's where they turned those big, luminous eyes—adapted for seeing well in a murky, methane-heavy atmosphere."

Bey suddenly thought of the great, glowing eyes of the Mariana Monsters as they stood guarding the deeps off Guam. The Grabbers could never have imagined such a fate as they touched down in triumph on the gray surface of Tycho.

"The crew of the *Jason*," he said.

"You are running ahead of me, Mr. Wolf," said Ling, smiling. "Let me keep the story going, true or false—as I said, all this is pure conjecture. Their scientists calculated the force of the explosion for Loge, and they gave a grim report. No life form, even single-celled ones, could survive it. Parts of Loge would be thrown in all directions. Some would leave the Solar System forever. Some would land in the Sun. And some would undoubtedly hit Jupiter, Saturn, and the other planets—including Earth. Was it possible that anything could survive that explosion and long transit?"

Park Green spoke for the first time. "If single-celled creatures couldn't survive, it would have to be something very primitive. How about a virus? That's just a chunk of DNA, without any wrapping."

Ling was looking at Green with an expression of surprise. "That's it exactly. A virus has no 'life-support system' of its own. To grow and multiply, it must have a host cell. The Logians took a chance and packed their genetic material as a viral form."

"And it worked?" asked Maria Sun.

"Not as they expected it to," said Ling. "Or maybe it did. We've never had a ship down to the surface of Jupiter or Saturn, and we don't know what's there. Maybe there are Logians down there, with viral growth of their genetic materials in host bodies.

"Some of their viral material was on fragments of Loge that were blown way out of the Solar System and became part of the long-period comets. That didn't matter. A virus lasts indefinitely. Sixteen million years later, some of the fragments that fell back into the Solar System under the Sun's gravitational pull were mined by men—not for their Loge DNA, not at all. For their transuranic elements."

"And the Loge DNA began to grow in them?" said Green, his face puzzled. "Wait a minute, that wouldn't work. If that were possible, *every* Grabber would be ..."

Ling nodded approvingly. "Very good, Mr. Green. You are quite right. Humans are very poor hosts for Logian development. The Loge virus could get into the human body easily enough, and it could even take up residence in the central nervous system. But it couldn't thrive in those unfamiliar surroundings. Wrong atmosphere, wrong chemical balance, wrong shape."

Ling paused and looked at the other three. His manner had changed. He had become the great scientist, lecturing on his own field to an interested audience.

"You know, I knew there was a Logian civilization before I ever came to Earth for this investigation. The transuranics proved it, beyond doubt. Otherwise I would never have been led so quickly to this train of thought.

"I think you can now complete the story yourselves. The crew of the *Jason* picked up Logian DNA in viral form from the fragment that they were crunching for its Asfanium and Polkium. It got into their bodies, and nothing at all happened. They went and had their great celebration in Tycho City, and still nothing happened. But finally they came to Earth—and they got into the form-change machines. At last, the virus could begin to act. It stimulated their central nervous systems, and the purposive form-change process began. It was creating a form that was optimal *for Logians*, not for Earthmen. When that change had proceeded to the point where the changed form could not survive in the atmosphere of Earth, the creatures died. Asphyxiated, in normal air."

Park was looking at the tank containing John Larsen. He had at last realized the full implications of Ling's words.

"You mean that is happening to John, too?"

"It would have happened, and it would have killed him," replied Ling. "He injected himself with Logian DNA along with the Asfanium he took from the bodies. The work we've been doing this past day has been to modify the life-support system of the tank so that it follows the needs of the organism inside it. If you go and look at the telltales now, you'll find that the nutrients and the atmosphere would be lethal to a human being."

Park Green hurried over to the tank. He looked at the monitors and came quickly back.

"Body mass, two hundred kilos. Oxygen down below eight percent, and ammonia way up. Mr. Ling, will John live?"

Ling stood up and went over to the tank. He looked carefully at each of the readouts. "I believe he will," he said at last. "The rates of change are down, and everything is very stable. I don't know if we will be able to return him to his former shape. If we can do it, I think it will not be for some time."

Ling came back to the other three. He looked at Bey Wolf and caught the reflection of his own excitement.

"Look on the positive side," he said. "We've dreamed for centuries about our first meeting with an alien race." He nodded toward the great tank. "The first representative will be in there, ready to meet with us, a day or two from now."

PART III

"Let the Great World spin forever, down the ringing grooves of change."

CHAPTER 15

The external lights had dimmed to their late-night glow. Wolf was sitting by the great tank, half-asleep, musing over the social indicators. His weariness showed in the stiff shoulders, the bowed head, and the slack posture. In front of him, the screen display of the global map revealed concentric circles of change spreading out from the Link entry points. He could visualize the frantic activity in the general coordinators' offices as they sought to stabilize Earth's economic system. Even the long-term indicators—fertility, births, deaths, and change rates—would soon be affected unless the new controls produced better results.

"Sorry to be so 'ong, Bey." The sibilant words from the wall speakers broke suddenly into his drifting thoughts. "The BEC peop'e wanted to test more of my visua' responses. Apparent'y I can see everything from near u'tra-vio'et out through the therma' infrared. Rough'y three-tenths of a micron out to fifteen microns. No wonder I've noticed the wor'd is 'ooking strange these days."

Wolf shook his head, took a deep breath, and sat up straighter in his chair. He turned to look into the tank through its transparent side panels. Inside, John Larsen raised a massive, triple-jointed arm and gestured in greeting. His torso was massive, wrinkled and umbonated, with a smooth oval area immediately above the central boss that housed the secondary motor nerve center. The broad skull was dominated by the great jeweled eyes and

131

the wide fringed mouth beneath it. Larsen moved his head forward in the movement that Bey had come to recognize as the Logian smile.

"We had a 'ong session," he said, "but at 'east the doctors seem to think I've kept my sanity through a' this—yesterday they didn't sound too sure of that."

As he spoke, forming the words slowly and carefully, the smooth oval area on his chest modulated in color, from a uniform pale pink, to brown, to soft green, following his words like a sound-sensitive visual display.

Wolf smiled wearily. "That's an improvement, then—you never showed much sign of sanity before the change. Ultraviolet through thermal infrared, eh? More than five octaves on the electromagnetic spectrum, and we see less than one. Can you cover all that range on the chest display?"

"Sure I can. Watch this. Therma' first, then I wi' gradua'y shorten the wave'ength a' the way down. Here we go."

Larsen hooded the nictitating membrane over his prominent eyes and pointed to the smooth area on his chest. Wolf watched in silence. For a while the oval remained gray, then it finally glowed a deep red. Almost imperceptibly, it moved gradually to yellow, then to green, and on to a pale violet-blue before it faded.

Wolf shook his head. "I'll just have to take your word for it, John. I didn't get anything except the usual visual spectrum. You know, you're the ultimate chameleon. When you get through all the tests here, you and I ought to go on a tour. There's been nothing like this in the history of form-change—and we've seen some pretty strange stuff between the two of us."

"I wi' do it, Bey, if you can find a good way of moving me around. You'd have to dup'icate this who'e area." He indicated the inside of the great tank with a wave of a massive forearm. "How much did it cost to set this up so I cou'd 'ive in it? It's comfortab'e, but I'm g'ad it didn't have to come out of my sa'ary."

"I don't know what it cost," said Wolf. "Ling set up the credit and made all the physical arrangements before he disappeared again. I guess it all comes out of some USF budget. He certainly had enough credit to impress the proprietors of Pleasure Dome, and we know that's not easy. I still have no word on him, no idea how he got away from here, where he went—anything."

Larsen nodded his broad, wrinkled head, with its wreath of ropy hair. "You won't hear from him again unti' he wants you to, if you ask me. I found out a'ot about him in those few weeks that he was working with me, making sure I cou'd survive a' right in this form. I'm sure you were right in what you said. 'ing is Capman, no doubt of it. He seems to have found ways to move on and off Earth, and round the So'ar System, that we can't even track."

"I know." Wolf rubbed at his chest, his habitual gesture of frustration. "Losing him once was something that I learned to live with. Losing him the second time is unforgivable—especially when I *knew* he was Capman, knew it in my bones, long before he took off again. He once said he and I would recognize each other anywhere, regardless of disguise, and I believe him. As soon as you're ready for a reverse change, we'll go and have another look for him. I'm more convinced than ever now that we didn't really understand most of what was going on at Central Hospital."

"I don't know what he did there, Bey, but there's no doubt that he saved my skin."

"How long before you can go back to your old form, John? BEC should be getting close to plotting out all the steps. I'm keen to find out the details, but I know they want to find out how to go both ways before they start the reversal."

Larsen laughed, and it came as a harsh, glassy noise over the speakers. "Don't rush me, Bey. First of a', now that I fee' sure I *can* reverse when I want to, I am in 'ess of a hurry. According to BEC, it wi' need a fu' four weeks in a form-change tank, and you know what a bore that wi' be. Anyway, I am not sure that I even want to change back."

Wolf looked at him in surprise.

"I mean it, Bey," Larsen went on. "You know, when I 'ook back on it I know I was not too smart in the human form of John 'arsen. I can remember what a strugg'e I used to have to try and fo'ow your thought processes—and often I cou'd not do it. Now it is easy for me. I used to forget things, now everything I hear or see is waiting to be reca'ed."

He leaned back in the sturdy supporting chair, resting his three hundred kilograms of body mass.

"And there is something e'se. We on'y found out about it during the tests today. I suspected I had it, but I had no idea how we' deve'oped it is. Do you remember the troub'e I had with math? Even with ordinary arithmetic, even with an imp'ant?"

Bey sighed. "It would be hard to forget it, even without total recall. You were practically famous for it. 'Doughhead Larsen,' Smith used to call you in the theory courses."

"You don't know how often I wished he would form-change to a toad—it was his natura' shape. Anyway, ask me something that ought to be hard for me, something beyond John 'arsen's grasp."

Wolf frowned. He scratched his dark head thoughtfully. "John, almost *everything* was. How about special functions? I seem to recall that they were your big hate, whenever they came up in the form-change theories. Do you remember anything at all about the gamma function?"

"How many figures would you 'ike? Suppose I give you six digits and step the argument in interva's of a hundredth? 'ike this. Gamma of 1.01 is 0.994326, gamma of 1.02 is 0.988844, gamma of 1.03 is 0.983550, gamma—"

"Hold it, John." Bey held up his hand in protest. "I don't want the whole table—even if you know it. What happened, did Capman fix you up with a calculator implant when he was working with you in the first couple of weeks?"

"No imp'ant." Larsen laughed again, and Wolf winced at the noise like shattering glass. "It is bui't in, comes free with the form if you are a 'ogian. I don't even know if it is ca'cu'ation or memory—a' I know is, when I want them the numbers and the formu'ae are there waiting. Do you see now why I am in no hurry to change back?"

The glass panel that separated them was thin, but it had to withstand a pressure difference of almost three atmospheres. Wolf was reluctant to lean against it, even though he was sure it would take the extra load with no trouble. He came close to it, and peered through at the alien form.

"Bottom, thou are translated. Much more of this, and I'll feel like a moron. I'm not sure my ego will be able to stand it unless you get started on that reverse-change."

" 'et me give it one more b'ow, then." Larsen learned forward, scratching at his side, where the great, gray torso framed the oval central display in his chest. "You have been trying to trace Robert Capman for four years, and you have not succeeded. Now he has disappeared again, and you do not know where you might find him— but do you rea'ize that you have more information now than you ever had before?"

He scratched the other side of his chest. "I think I wi' comp'ain about this skin, it does not fit right."

"More information?" Wolf had lost the last trace of sleepiness. "I don't see how I have more. We know that Ling is Capman, and I've tried to pursue that. I get no cooperation at all from the USF people. Either they don't want Capman extradited to Earth or they don't care either way. I put a call through to Park Green this morning in Tycho City, and he has been told to get back to his other work and not waste time looking for Capman. So where's the new information supposed to come from?"

Larsen had stopped scratching and picked up a green wedge of fibrous sponge. "I have to eat this stuff to keep me a'ive, but I fee' sure it was never the standard 'ogian diet. It tastes 'ike the outf'ow from the chemica' factory." He touched it to the delicate fringes of his mouth, which served as both taste and smell organs. The expression on his face changed. He closed his eyes briefly, then placed the spongy mass down again on the rack by his side. "Now I know how they must fee' in the famine areas when they get their rations of five-cyc'ed pap. Maybe I wi' reverse-change now. It is ages since I had any decent food, I think I am beginning to forget what it tastes 'ike."

"New information, John," prompted Wolf impatiently. "I know you're doing it to annoy, and I know you're sitting there luxuriating in the thought that now you're three times as smart as I am. You ought to realize that anything about Capman puts me on to full alert."

Larsen moved his head forward in a self-satisfied Logian smile but did not speak.

"*How* do we have new information?" went on Wolf. "We haven't had anything useful from the USF, and if you learned something during the weeks you were working with him around the clock, getting adjusted to the Logian form, this is the first time you've mentioned it. So, what's new?"

"'A' right, Bey, no more sta'ing. 'et us app'y simp'e 'ogic, and see what we can deduce. First, think back to your origina' idea that Capman was somehow *responsib'e* for the 'ogian forms that were found in the Mariana Trench. That turned out to be wrong. So, it wou'd be natura' to assume that Capman shou'd have had no interest in 'oge before the arriva' of the unknown forms. On the other hand, Capman—*as Kar' 'ing*— was a 'eading expert on 'oge, and everything to do with it, years ago. 'ong before the forms appeared on the scene. Where does that idea take you?"

Wolf peered into the poisonous atmosphere inside the tank. "*Tokhmir*, John, I hate these conversations in separate rooms. It's worse than a video link."

"Now who is sta'ing? You can come in if you want to, Bey, the air is fine—once you get used to it. Now, answer my question."

Wolf nodded. "It's a good question, and it's an obvious one. I must have been a lot more tired than I realized in the past few weeks. It's been hectic out here since you began to change. All right, let me think."

He sat down and leaned his head forward on his hands.

"Capman became Ling. So, either he knew about the Logian forms before we called him in to help or he had some other reason for being interested in Loge. I find I can't believe he knew about the forms before we went to Pleasure Dome—he really was working it all out for the first time there. That leaves only the other alternative: an interest in Loge, but one that was nothing to do with the Logian forms. That sounds improbable to me."

"Improbab'e or not, it is the on'y reasonab'e conc'usion. So now"—Larsen's voice rose in pitch, and the color of his oval breastplate glowed more intensely—"carry the thought to its end point. What is the next step for you to take?"

Bey was nodding, his head still bowed. "All right. You've got something. The added piece is one simple fact: Capman's prior interest in Loge. Now I guess I have to trace the background on that. I think I know the best way to do it. Park Green has access to all the USF data, and he should be able to trace Ling's movements and background." He looked up. "Maybe I should get into one of the tanks myself and switch to a Logian form. I could use the boost in brains."

Larsen nodded seriously, head and trunk moving together. "You may think you are joking, Bey, but it is an idea that you ought to be taking more serious'y. I can't describe how it fee's to be smarter than I was, but I 'ike the sensation. When we get a' the reverse-change p'otted out, there wi' be a 'ot of peop'e who wi' want to try this form."

Larsen opened his mouth wide, revealing the bony processes inside and the rolled, mottled tongue. "Excuse me, Bey. The 'ogian yawn is a 'itt'e disgusting, if I can be'ieve the mirror. If you are going to ca' Park Green, I think I wi' go back to the s'eeping quarters and try and get some rest. We sti' haven't pinned it yet, but the BEC peop'e now think I am on a seventeen-hour cyc'e. A' these tests are wearing me out. Ten hours so far, just on my eyes! At 'east I know what the first reverse-change step wi' be—I want to be ab'e to say my own name."

He stood up. "Say hi to Park from me—you know I cannot say he'o to him."

When Wolf had left for the comlink center, Larsen turned and walked heavily through to the inner room that contained the sleep area. His movement was silent but ponderous, gliding along on the round padded feet that ended the bulky lower limbs. In the screened inner area, he went at once to the communications panel that had been built into one of the walls. The thick rubbery pads on his digits were awkward for the comlink's small keys, but he managed to dial a scrambled connection for an off-Earth link. When the circuit was established, Larsen at once began transmission.

Expressions on a Logian face were not easily read by any human, but perhaps some of the BEC specialists who had been working with Larsen for the past few weeks would have seen the satisfaction on his countenance as he began his message. The comlink coded it and hurled it on its way as a tightly focused beam, up to the relay by the Moon, then far on beyond to its remote destination.

CHAPTER 16

The social parameters were tabulated on color displays all around the offices of the general coordinators. Eighteen key indicators in a stylized map format dominated the central office, and summaries in cued form were given by each chart. Next to the ninety-day history was the current ninety-day forecast, showing trends and rate of change of trends.

In the center of the room the six chief planners had gathered, grim-faced, around the circular table. The picture was clear. The perturbations to the usual stable pattern were unmistakable, and they were growing steadily in spite of all attempts to stabilize them. A certain level of statistical variation was tolerable—indeed, was inevitable—but perturbations beyond a certain size, according to Dolmetsch doctrine, would force a major change. The new steady state of the system was difficult to calculate, and there was not a general agreement on it. One school of theorists predicted a partial social collapse, with new homeostasis establishing itself for a reduced Earth population of about four billion. That was the optimist view. Others, including Dolmetsch himself, thought there could be no new steady state solution derived continuously from the old one. Civilization must collapse completely before any new order could arise from the ruins.

None of the planners was a theoretician. For practical people, it was hard to distinguish between theoretical alternatives, where one meant the death of ten billion and the other the death of fourteen billion. Both were

139

unimaginable, but the indicator profile was not encouraging.

The group leader finally picked up his pointer again and shook his head in disgust.

"I can't tell if we're even touching it. There are improvements here——he gestured at the area centered on the Link entry point in Western North America—"but everything is going to hell again in the China region. Look at that violence index. I haven't looked at the computer output, but I'll bet the death rate from unnatural causes has tripled."

The woman next to him looked at the area indicated. "That's my hometown, right at the trouble center," she said quietly. "Even if we don't know the best course, we have to keep on trying."

"I know that—but remember the rules when you leave today. No public comments unless they're optimistic ones, and no release of anything longer than the sixty-day forecast. God knows, though, that's bad enough all by itself."

They stood up.

"How long do we have, Jed, before we're past a point of no return?" she asked.

"I don't know. Three months? Six months? It could go very fast once it starts; we've all seen the snowball effect—on paper." He shrugged. "We can't say we haven't worried about something like this before. Half the papers on social stability in the past twenty years have predicted trouble at better than the fifty percent level. Well, there are a few positive things we can do in the next day or two."

He turned to the woman next to him. "Greta, I'll need a summary of the whole situation to send to the USF headquarters. Dolmetsch is up there now, and he can do the briefing. Sammy, I want you to see how the USF reacts to the idea of lending us an energy kernel for a few months and orbiting it above Quito in synchronous station. If we beam the power down, it will help the local energy problem in South America for the next month or two. Ewig, I need the latest data from Europe. I have to brief the council in an hour, and Pastore is sure to ask what's happening in Northern Italy. I'll be back to pick up the material in twenty minutes—I need time to study it before I go in there."

He hurried out. The noise level in the big room rose rapidly as the planners redoubled their efforts to stabilize the world economy. One hope sustained them all: it was not the first crisis of the past half century. They had always managed to find the right combination of restorative measures to arrest the oscillations in the social indicators. But this one looked bad. Like a shore community bracing for the arrival of a hurricane, the planners prepared for a long, hard struggle.

Park Green, seated in the Permanent Records Center six kilometers beneath the surface, completed the listing he wanted. He looked at his watch, whistled, stored the output he had generated into his percomp, and signed off the computer terminal. He sat in silence for a few minutes, reviewing everything he had found, then looked again at his watch. Bey would still be up, even though he was on Central Time instead of U.T., but if he didn't call him now he would have to wait another ten hours. Park decided to delay his return to the living sections and put in a request for a comlink to Earth.

The connection was almost instantaneous—at this hour, traffic was light. When Wolf's image appeared on the holoscreen, sleepy-looking and irritated, Park decided he must have made a slight error in his time calculation. He concluded that it was no time for the conventional greetings.

"It's a mystery, Bey," he began. "A complete mystery. The records here look as though they are intact, with full data on Ling—personal data—going back for fifty years. I agree with you that Ling is Capman, but how can he be if he has full records like this?"

Bey rubbed his eyes and came more fully awake. "Full records, eh? For most people, that couldn't be faked. But we had evidence a few years ago that proved Capman is a master at manipulating computer software. Stored data isn't safe when he's around. There's a good chance that most of Ling's 'history' is a *constructed* background, made up and inserted into the records by Capman. He must have had some cooperation to do that, though. There must be some leaders in the USF who are helping him—an ordinary Earth citizen would have no way to get started. Somebody up there with you helped Capman get access to your data banks."

"I don't see how they'd do that." Green looked at the computer terminal next to him. "Most of the files here are read-only memory. How could he affect those?"

"Most read-only memory is software protected—it's not special-purpose hardware."

"But how would he know which type he had to deal with? Well, I'll leave that one to you. I've been trying to trace Ling, and all I can really find out is that he isn't on the Moon, right now. According to the records, he's supposed to be down there on Earth. Are you sure he's not there?"

Wolf nodded. "Medium sure—you can't be all that certain with Capman about anything. According to me, though, he's off-Earth. I checked every manifest, coming and going, and every mass record for lift-off. Unless he's found a new wrinkle, we've lost him again from the Earth-Moon system. Did you check the Libration Colonies?"

"Yes. They're easy, because they have no hiding places. He's not there."

"Well, keep looking on the Moon. I won't even guess what form he's wearing now—probably not either Ling or Capman."

Green stood up and leaned against the console. He looked depressed. "Well, Bey, what do you want me to do now? I'm dead-ended here, and you seem to be getting nowhere there. Any ideas?"

Wolf was silent for a minute, recalling his own experiences four years earlier, when he was first hunting for Capman's hidden tracks.

"I can only suggest one thing, Park," he said. "Capman gives this impression that he's infallible, but he's not.

Last time I tangled with him I found there are limits to what he can do to change the data banks."

"He seems to have done pretty well here."

"Maybe not. He can change his own records, if he can get access to the protected files, but he couldn't change all the cross-reference files that might mention his name or his actions. That was the way we got a trace on him before, when I went through the medical records from Central Hospital. For some reason, Capman won't destroy other people's records. That's his weakness."

"So what are you suggesting, Bey?"

"We have to try the same method here. We have to track him from the *indirect* references—other people's records that somehow refer to him."

Green had a very dubious look on his face. "I know what you're telling me, Bey. But honestly, I wouldn't know how to begin a thing like that. I'm no computer hot-shot. How would I know *who* would be likely to have a reference to Capman or Ling in his file? There are three million people here in the USF. I can't go through three million personnel records, but that's what you seem to be suggesting."

"There are other ways, if you know how to handle sorts and merges." Wolf hesitated. "Park, is there any way that you could get me a direct hookup to interface with the USF Permanent Data Bank? From here, in my office? It would be enough if you get me a read-only link—I don't propose to try and change any of the files, only to analyze their contents."

"I don't see why not. After all, we have a full cooperative exchange program between the USF and Earth computer banks. Doesn't work too well sometimes, but this shouldn't be hard to do."

"If you can arrange it, I'll take a shot at the analysis myself, from here. If I find anything, I probably won't be able to follow up—but you could help on that, if you're willing."

"I'll be glad to. My trouble has been finding any lead to follow up. Bey, let me check this out and call you back. Tomorrow," he added hastily, noticing again Wolf's rumpled hair and appearance of broken sleep.

"No. Call me tonight if you get approval."

"All right. One other thing I need from you though—a charge code. The comlink hookup will be expensive. Do you have a budget that will cover it?"

Wolf nodded. "No problem." He keyed a fourteen-digit code for transmission to the Tycho City accounting bank. "One thing about the Office of Form Control, it may run out of toilet paper but they never stint you on comlink costs. One other thing, if you can get access for me but not remote access, take that. I'll make a trip up there if I have to and work from your terminal. It would be better from here, though, so I can keep my eye on John."

Green nodded. "I saw him yesterday, being interviewed on holovision. Do you know, I think he's enjoying himself. He looks strange, but that doesn't seem to bother him. He was there in his tank, and they had a couple of Indian philosophers on the program with him. They started to debate whether John is human. He tied them in logical knots. By the end of the program he used their own arguments and had them deciding that *they* weren't human."

"I didn't see it, but I can imagine it. I wouldn't like to get into an argument with him now—he's smarter than he ever was. If all the Logians had that caliber of mental equipment, it's lucky for us they aren't still around. They'd have us all doing whatever they wanted, and convinced that it was all for our own benefit."

Wolf yawned, and stretched luxuriously. "But you're right, Park. John is enjoying himself—he was a good deal less happy before we were sure that a reverse-change would be possible."

"I'll believe that." Green nodded, and reached out his hand to cut off the connection. "As a matter of fact, I wouldn't mind total recall and increased brain power myself. I never seem to really know what's going on here these days. With Dolmetsch in Tycho City, there are council meetings going on around the clock. The news takes a while to filter down to my level, but there must be trouble somewhere. I'll call you back as soon as I have an answer on your question—that shouldn't take more than an hour or two."

CHAPTER 17

CHAPTER 17

Four years earlier, Bey Wolf had sworn that once was enough; he would never attempt it again. Now he was in much the same situation, but he was faced with something even harder. Instead of sorting through the structure of Central Hospital's medical records, he was working with the data of the whole of the USF. The planetary information file was a maze, and he was in the middle of it, looking for signs of Karl Ling's early work. The path he was following in the records crossed and recrossed itself. First it appeared to be leading to something promising, then it petered out or led him to a restricted record area that only the USF leaders could access. It was a labyrinth without an Ariadne.

Bey plowed doggedly on from his office in Form Control, fourteen and sixteen hours a day. It was almost a week before he had the smell of a lead, another week before he had enough to make it worth discussing with anyone. When he finally dumped his output and cut the connection to Tycho City, he was ready to talk it over with John Larsen. He went again to the viewing panel that connected to the Logian living quarters.

Larsen was not alone. Maria Sun was standing by the viewing panel, along with three other engineers from BEC. Maria, after the help she had given in modifying Larsen's form-change tank when the Logian change had first begun, felt a proprietary interest in the progress of her delivery. Now, however, she was not pleased. She turned to Wolf in exasperation as he approached them.

"Bey, give us your opinion, will you? Who will own the rights to the form-change programs that were involved when John changed? I want to get all the details, but nobody will even tell me who I ought to be talking to. All we get at BEC are hearsay and wild stories about Karl Ling, and the monster here won't tell me a thing."

Bey looked in through the viewing panel to the big living area, where Larsen was sitting comfortably on his specially built chair with its accommodation for the double knee. He gave Bey a nodding of the head that no doubt was the Logian version of an irritating smile.

Wolf could not resist a quick wink at Larsen, which he hoped went unobserved by the BEC group.

"It's only my opinion, Maria," he said, "but I'd say John owns the rights himself, by default. He and Karl Ling are the only ones who know the whole story on the programs that they used, and if you're going to track down Ling, I wish you luck. I've been trying that myself for the past month. It's not easy. I want to talk to John about it."

Maria Sun stepped away from the panel and shook her head in disgust. "I'll come back later, when you've finished." She looked again at Larsen. "According to the outputs I've seen, the life ratio for that form is more than three. I'm really interested in his body."

"—You should have taken me when you had the chance," said Larsen.

She glared at him. "I don't know how much fun it would be to wear a Logian form, but he"—she gestured with her thumb at the inside of the tank—"seems in no hurry to get out of it. If it's comfortable, and if it really lets you live that long, a lot of people will be interested in it even if you have to live in a tank to get the benefit. The fellows back at BEC are talking already of building more big tanks. It could be the hottest thing in next year's research budget."

She gave Larsen another scowl. He lifted his great arm and waved at her without speaking. Accompanied by her three companions, Maria swept out.

"She wi' be back," said Larsen as soon as she had gone. "Maria never gives up on a new form."

"I know," replied Bey, pulling a chair close to the observation panel. "Be nice to your girlfriend, John. She did more than anybody else to pull you through when the changes first began—more than I ever could. Well, let's get down to business. This may feel like old times to both of us—tracking Robert Capman through the data banks."

"Except this time, Bey, I intend to understand what you are doing. 'ast time it was a mystery to me. I've had the opportunity to 'ook at the computer system in the past few weeks, and I suspect that I grasp the concepts proper'y for the first time in my 'ife." Larsen rubbed at the ropy hair on his rounded skull with a bony protuberance that projected from the second joint of his left upper limb. "I hope, though, that this time you do not want to drag me through O'd City—I wou'd have some prob'ems carrying my 'ife-support packages with me."

"If I'm right, we'll have to go a lot further than that," said Wolf calmly. He settled his percomp on his knee and began to call out displays. "Let's start at the very beginning. That means going back more than ten years."

"Wait a minute, 'ing was sti' Capman ten years ago," protested Larsen.

"He was both. I thought that if Ling was an expert on the Solar System, he'd have had to write papers on it— real papers—and that meant that others would have referred in *their* papers to his work. I began by scanning the citation index in the Tycho City reference files. It wasn't easy. I suspect that a lot of references to Ling's work have been deleted, but I managed to trace him. I even obtained a display of an actual paper, published nearly ten years ago. So his interest in Loge—that was discussed in the paper—is real, and it goes back long before Capman was forced to disappear. Any deduction that you'd care to make based on that, John?"

Larsen made a gesture like a shrug, a rippling upward movement of his upper body. "I can make the obvious one. Capman had known for a 'ong time that he might get caught one day. He knew he'd have to prepare his retreat in advance. Somehow, he estab'ished the character of 'ing, and his interest in 'oge was something that he had to deve'op for his own convenience, probab'y because it was important to his continued experiments."

"That's my conclusion exactly." Wolf entered a confirming note to his file. "So then I took a closer look at Ling's publications. That's when I found something a little different from the way that Park Green had described it to us. Ling was an expert on Loge, that's true—but if you look at his publications, the ones that he tried to cover up in the literature, you find that Loge is the minor part of it."

Larsen nodded. "This is no surprise. It is hard to re'ate his interest in form-change to any simp'e interest in 'oge."

"He's interested in the Asteroid Belt. He wrote a series of papers about its formation—and he did a really big series of papers on some specific asteroids. If you catalog all his work, only a few deal with Loge, and most of them concern one group of asteroids. Did you ever hear of the Egyptian Cluster?"

Larsen nodded. "Yes. If you had asked me that a month ago, I'd have to say no, but I can absorb information faster now, and I have had a 'ot of time to spend with the termina' here. Most of the free hours when you were not giving me tests, I have been catching up on my reading."

He leaned back and closed his lustrous eyes. "The Egyptian C'uster. I think I can quote the re'evant texts verbatim for you. 'A group of about one hundred asteroids, with orbits that are different from a' others in the Be't. They 'ie in an orbit p'ane a'most sixty degrees from the ec'iptic.' 'et me see, what e'se?"

Larsen opened his eyes again for a moment. "Excuse me, whi'e I scan my interna' fi'es." He was silent for a few seconds, then nodded. "Here we are. What are you interested in? Members of the C'uster, masses, orbits?"

"How about history."

"No." Larsen grimaced, new wrinkles appearing in the

gray skin. "That is an area of the fi'es that I have not read yet."

"That's a relief. I was beginning to think that you knew everything." Wolf consulted his output displays. "Store this away. The cluster was discovered by accident, in 2086, during a deep radar search program. They were surveying the Halo, looking for power kernels. First visited during the Outer System search. According to the Ling paper that I found, all the asteroids in the cluster were formed out of one piece of Loge, after the main explosion of the planet. Most of them are small, five kilometers or less, but there are a few bigger ones."

"That much I know. The data bank 'ists a' the main members. Five of them are bigger than eight ki'ometers in mean diameter—Thoth, Osiris, Bast, Set, and Anubis. No transuranics on any of them. They must have been formed from a piece of 'oge's core. There is a mining sett'ement on Isis, and another on Horus, main'y for the rare earths. No permanent sett'ement on any of them. They seem 'ike a very du' group. Why the big interest in them?"

"I'm getting to that," said Wolf. "You're right, they are a remote lot. It's not the distance, but they're so far out of the ecliptic that it takes a fair amount of fuel to match orbits with them. That's why they aren't a good commercial prospect, even though the lodes of minerals are rich, especially on Horus. The one I'm interested in isn't one you've mentioned. What do you know about Pearl? Anything in your head on that one?"

"Hm. I think I need to go back to my references and dig deeper. I have a 'itt'e information, but there must be more. Pear' used to be ca'ed *Atmu*. That fits in with the idea that it is part of the Egyptian C'uster, but I don't know why it was renamed."

"That's because you've never seen a picture of it. You're quite right; it was named Atmu when it was first discovered. A good name for one of the cluster, oldest of the Egyptian gods. But the first expedition there, forty years ago, changed the name. Other factors seemed more important than the mythology. Pearl is quite small, less than two kilometers across—but it's an odd shape; a perfect sphere of white, fused glass."

"Wait a moment, Bey." Larsen was shaking his great head. "That sounds wrong to me. If it is made of g'ass, it must have been part of the outer crust of 'oge, near enough to the surface to be fu' of si'icates."

Wolf looked up from his records and shook his head admiringly. "It took me a while to come to that conclusion, John. You're getting too smart for your own good. I finally decided it was part of the outer core, deep enough to be very hot and near enough the surface to have the silicates. It's a very small piece of Loge. The diameter is listed as 1.83 kilometers. Now, do your records include a mass figure for it?"

Larsen's broad skull and upper torso dipped forward in a nod. "I show a mass of about one bi'ion tons. That means—" He paused and looked up at the ceiling of the tank. "That can't possib'y be right. Un'ess . . ."

Wolf was nodding. "Go on, John, let the calculator run free for a moment. You're heading in the right direction."

Larsen shrugged his heavy shoulders, again the upward rippling movement of the body. "With that diameter, it must have a density of 'ess than thirty-five ki'os per cubic meter. Fused si'ica g'asses mass at 'east two tons per cubic meter. So . . . *it must be ho'ow.*"

"Quite right." Bey was nodding his agreement. "It's as thin as an eggshell. The references give the inner diameter as about 1.7 kilometers. Pearl is nothing more than a big, delicate glass bubble, blown by trapped gases inside the fragment when Loge exploded. It's classified now as one of the protected asteroids. The USF declared it one of the natural wonders of the system. No one is allowed to land on it—but I think that rule is being broken."

Wolf paused. He felt that there had been an inconsistency in Larsen's replies, but he couldn't put his finger on it. After a few moments, he went on. Larsen continued to sit there motionless, his luminous eyes unblinking.

"Let me give you one more fact, John, then you can tell me what you make of all this. Nine years ago, Karl

Ling wrote twelve separate papers on the structure, formation, and stability of Pearl. All references to those papers have been deleted—I had to dig out the information by indirect references. Do you recognize the pattern? It's the one that we saw with Capman's medical records back in Central Hospital."

Larsen nodded calmly. "I see where you are heading. You think that Pear' ho'ds some specia' secret, something that keys you to find Capman. It is p'ausib'e, Bey, but I see one prob'em. You are suggesting that Capman managed to create the person of 'ing, at the same time as he was the director of Centra' Hospita'. How cou'd he do that?"

Wolf stood up and began to pace up and down in front of the viewing panel. His manner was tense and nervous. "I checked that, too. All Ling's early papers show an *Earth* address. His other records show him living on Earth until six years ago, then moving to the Moon. That's the USF files—but the Earth ID files don't show anything for him at all. I suspect that the USF chromosome ID they have is faked. One more thing, then I'm done. Capman's travel records at Central Hospital for the final two years before he was forced to run for it show that he was off-Earth far more than ever before. He always seemed to have a good reason for it—hospital business—but he would have had no trouble making up a reason; he was the boss."

Larsen was nodding his head and trunk slowly, eyes unblinking.

"And so, your conc'usion, Bey? What do you propose to do next?"

Wolf stopped his pacing. His manner was resolute. "First, I'm heading for the Moon. I have to know more about Pearl, and I have to know why Capman was interested in it. I'll be leaving tomorrow. I don't like to leave you out of it, but you're in good hands here. Maria will do all that you need if you want to begin reversion."

"Of course, that is no prob'em. But one thing before you go, Bey." Larsen was looking directly at Wolf, his gaze steady and penetrating. "You ought to ask yourse'f one other question. *Why* do you pursue Robert Capman

with such zea'? Even if you think he is a monster, why
is he so important to you?"

Wolf, who was turning to leave, was stopped in mid-
stride. He swung quickly round to face Larsen through
the viewing panel. "*Tokhmir!* You know that, John. There
were two other projects in Capman's background at the
hospital. We only traced two of them, Proteus and
Timeset. What about the others? I want to know what
Lungfish and Janus are. They're still complete mysteries.
That's what fascinates me about Capman."

His tone was defensive, not quite steady. Larsen
looked at him quietly for a few moments.

"Ca'm down, Bey. They are mysteries, I agree. But is
that sufficient reason? I don't think so. We've had
unso'ved mysteries before in the Office of Form Contro'.
You managed to 'eave them a'one after a whi'e, didn't
you? Remember when we were ba'ked on the form
changes in Antarctica? We were pu'ed off that, and we
hated it—but you managed to 'ive with it after a month
or two. This has chased you, and you've chased Capman,
for more than four years. Think about it, Bey. Do you
have to keep up the hunt?"

Wolf's eyes were introspective and thoughtful. He
rubbed his fingers absently along the seam of his loose
jacket.

"It's hard to explain, John. Do you remember the first
time that we met Capman, back in Central Hospital? I
had a feeling, even then, that he was an important figure
in my life. I still have that feeling." He paused, then
shrugged. "I don't know. I'm not a believer in paralogic,
and I don't find my own words very convincing. All the
same, I have to go. I'm going to tell Park Green that I'll
be up there in a couple of days."

He hurried out. It was John Larsen's turn to become
thoughtful. The hulking alien figure sat in silence for a
few minutes, then went through to the inner living quarters. He seated himself before the comscreen and
opened the high data-rate circuits. When the ready light
appeared and the array of sensors was ready, he keyed

in the destination. The prompter waited until the link was complete.

Larsen looked at the face that had appeared on the screen.

"Burst mode," he said softly.

The other nodded and activated a switch to his left. Larsen closed his eyes and leaned back in his chair. The smooth gray oval of skin on his broad chest turned to a pale rose-pink, then swiftly became a dazzling kaleidoscope of shifting colors. The area now contained a multitude of separate point elements, each changing color as fast as the eye could follow. Larsen sat rigid in his chair, but after twenty seconds he began to draw in shallow, pained breaths. The brilliant display on his chest flickered on, a bright, changing rainbow shimmering like a winter aurora. The great body was motionless, racked by an unknown tension as the patterns fed into the communicator screen.

Eight thousand miles away, at the global communications center in the South Pacific, the com monitors began to flash red. There was an unexpectedly heavy load on the planetary com circuits. Auxiliary channels automatically cut in. Through a thousand output displays, the worldwide network complained to its controllers at the sudden excess message burden. The load ended as suddenly as it had started. In his tank, Larsen lolled back in his seat, too drained to sign off with his distant receiver.

CHAPTER 18

The journey to Tycho City was supposed to be routine. Wolf had gone by aircar to the nearest Mattin connection, linked twice to get to the Australian exit, and taken a ground car to the North Australian spaceport. After a rigorous USF inspection and certification—no wonder, thought Bey, the staff of Pleasure Dome had given up on the idea of getting the *Jason*'s crew off Earth—a scheduled shuttle took him up to equatorial parking orbit. The lunar connection was due in three hours.

On the journey to the spaceport, and up to orbit, Wolf was preoccupied with Larsen's last question to him and with the simple practical details of his departure. Then, waiting for the lunar transport, he was surprised by an urgent call from Earth. He went along the corridor to the main communications center.

There was a brief delay in establishing the video link. When the channel was available, Maria Sun's image appeared on the tiny utility screen. Her china-doll face looked grim and suspicious.

"All right, Bey," she began. "You don't have to be nice to us at BEC, I know that. But just let me remind you that if I hadn't helped you, you might not have been able to save John Larsen. So—*what have you done with him?* The USF people at the Australian spaceport swear that he's not with you, and none of the other manifests show any extra people or equipment."

It took Wolf a second or two to grasp her meaning.

"I've not done a thing with him," he said. "You're

155

telling me he's gone, but he ought to still be in the living quarters at Form Control. There's no other place with a life-support system for him. Did you check—"

He stopped. Maria was shaking her head firmly. "We've looked everywhere in Form Control. One thing I'm quite sure of, he's not here. Bey, that system Ling and I fixed up for John is really fancy. If he doesn't have a special environment, he'll die within hours. Are you telling me that you didn't arrange this between the two of you?"

"Maria, I'm as surprised as you are. Damn it, I was with John yesterday, talking about my trip to Tycho City. He didn't give any sign that he wasn't going to stay just where he was. I agree with you; he *had* to stay put, he wouldn't last a minute without that special atmosphere."

Maria bit at her full upper lip. She shook her head in perplexity. "I believe you, Bey, if you swear that's the truth. But then what is going on?"

Bey looked past the viewing screen. He was beginning to feel a prickling sensation at the nape of his neck. A number of small factors from his discussion with Larsen began to sum in his subconscious. The curious arrangement of Larsen's living quarters, the elaborate comlink that Ling had arranged—ostensibly for tuition purposes of the new form—the way that Larsen had steered the conversation, all was coming together. Bey needed to think it out in detail.

"Maria," he said at last. "I told you I didn't know what happened, and I was telling you the truth. But all of a sudden I'm getting suspicions. Let me call you back later. I know John couldn't live without his special equipment, but I don't think we should be too worried about that. Give me a couple of hours to do some thinking and let me call you back."

Without waiting for her reply, Wolf pushed himself away from the console and drifted slowly back through the ship to the transit area. He settled himself in one corner, lay back, and let his thoughts roam freely back over the past few weeks, picking out the anomalies.

They were there. Strange that he hadn't noticed them

before. Even so, it was disturbing to realize that he could be led so easily, even by someone he trusted completely. For the future, he would have to remember that he was dealing now with a new Larsen, one whose mind was quicker, clearer, and more subtle than it had ever been in the past. Look at the tuition circuit that Ling had installed. Larsen needed to be able to acquire information from scattered data sources all around Earth. True enough. But why had he needed an off-planet capability, why a complete two-way link, why a circuit rated at many thousands of voice-grade lines?

Wolf's thoughts were suddenly interrupted by a flicker of movement at the port. He looked up in surprise. A crewman was staring in through the panel, held securely against the outer hull by the magnetic subcutaneous layer on wrist and inner ankle. Just above them were the suction cups that provided a grip during the air-breathing elements of shuttle ascent. The crewman was checking part of the antenna. Wolf couldn't resist a closer look. It was the first time he had seen a C-form development in its space environment.

The crewman's skin was thick and toughened, and his eyes were coated with a thick transparent layer of protective mucus. He wore no air tank or protective suit. The modified lungs, structurally modeled after the deep-diving whales, could store enough oxygen, under pressure, to work outside in comfort for several hours. The scaly skin was an effective seal against loss of fluids to the hard vacuum surrounding it. The hard ultraviolet was screened out by abundant melanin surrogates in the epidermis.

Wolf watched as the crewman moved off easily along the hull, quite at home there. He sighed as his thoughts came back to his own stupidity. Larsen had led him, coaxed him easily along, to find out more about Ling, more about Pearl. So Capman wanted him to be aware of that connection, wanted him interested in the Egyptian Cluster—there was no doubt now that Larsen and Capman had been in regular communication ever since Capman/Ling's disappearance a few weeks earlier. Larsen had moved Bey steadily along in his thinking, to the point where Bey had made his decision to set off for the Moon. With that accomplished, Larsen had promptly disappeared. He couldn't have done it without help, but it was quite clear where the help had been coming from. Capman, with resources available to him that Bey could still only guess at, had removed Larsen from the Form Control offices and sent him—where?

Bey was getting ideas on that question, too. Although it was only ten minutes to ship separation, he hurried back to the communications center and placed a quick call to Tycho City. When Park Green appeared on the screen, the first buzzer had already sounded to tell Bey to get back to his seat.

"Park, I'm on my way and don't have time to say much." It was Wolf's turn to dispense with formal greetings. "Check if there's a ship available with enough fuel capacity to make a trip right out of the ecliptic, up to the Egyptian Cluster. If there is, charter it. Use my name, with Form Control on Earth as surety. Don't say where I want to go with it. I'll see you in twenty-four hours. Tell you everything then."

The purser, his face red-veined with vacuum blossom, was motioning to him urgently. Wolf cut the connection, swung hastily back to his seat, and strapped in.

"Cutting it fine," said the purser gruffly.

Wolf nodded. "Urgent call," he said. "You know, I just saw a C-form working outside the ship. I thought they were still forbidden for USF work."

The purser's expression became more friendly, and he smiled.

"They are. There's a little game being played here. The C-forms aren't USF men at all. They're part of a student exchange program—Earth gets a few specialists in power kernels, the USF gets a few C-forms."

"What do you think of them?"

"The best thing to hit space since the cheap vacuum still. It's only the unions who are holding things up. Job worries." He looked at the readout at his wrist. "Hold on now, we're cutting ties."

As the ship began the slow spiral away from parking orbit, Wolf switched on the small news screen set above the couch. Movement about the cabins would be restricted during the high-impulse phase of the next hour. He turned to the news channel.

The media had picked up from somewhere a surmise that John Larsen was missing. It was a small item, far down on the news priorities. More to the public interest were the latest statements on the social indicators. They were still oscillating, with swings of increasing amplitude. Even with the power kernel beaming down to Quito, energy was still desperately short in South America. The famine deaths were rising rapidly in Northern Europe. Compared with the mounting crisis that faced the general coordinators, Bey realized that his own preoccupations were a tiny detail. But he could not rid his mind of Larsen's question. Given all this, why was Capman as much on his mind now as he had been four years before?

From where he was lying, Wolf could see ahead into the pilot's station. The computer could handle most things, but the man preferred to operate in manual mode for the beginning of the trip. It was another C-form, added proof that events were moving faster than the union wished. The pilot, hands and prehensile feet delicate masses of divided digits, was manipulating sixty controls simultaneously. Bey watched in fascination while his thoughts continued to revolve around the same old issues.

After the first surprising moonquake, the second construction of Tycho City had placed the living quarters deep underground. Bey, vacuum-suited, rode the high-speed elevator down through the Horstmann Fissure, toward the main city more than three kilometers below. He left it at the optional exit point, halfway down, and walked over to the edge of the ledge. The preserved body of Horstmann, still sealed in his spacesuit, hung from the old pitons fixed in the fissure wall. Wolf looked at the Geiger counter next to the suited figure. The rapid chatter carried clearly to him through the hard rock surface. The half-life of the nuclides was less than ten years, but Horstmann would be too hot to touch for at least another century. The radioactivity could have been lessened more quickly by stimulated nuclear transitions, as was done with the usual reactor wastes, but the lunar authorities were against that idea. Bey read the commemorative metal plaque again, then continued his descent through the fissure.

Park Green had managed to pull strings with Immigration and Customs. The reception formalities were smooth and very brief. Green's grinning face, towering a good foot above the other waiting USF citizens, greeted Wolf as he emerged from the third and final interlock.

"Bey, you don't know the trouble you caused me," he began as he engulfed Wolf's hand in his own. "I didn't know how well known you are. As soon as our people who've been working on regeneration methods found out that you were heading for Tycho City, they started to flood me with calls. They all want to know how long you'll be staying, what you'll be doing, the whole bit. I had a hard time stalling them. They want to meet you and talk about the work that you began a couple of years ago on transitional forms."

Wolf was a little startled. "They know about that work up here? I didn't think it was particularly surprising. All I did was follow up some of the clues that were buried in Capman's work. He had the idea."

"People up here don't seem to agree. If the clues were there, they must have been well hidden. Are you willing to spend some time with them? All they—"

"Look, Park, in other circumstances I'd be glad to," broke in Bey, "but we have no time for that now. Did you get the ship?"

"I think so—it will be a few hours before I know for certain. I've had a problem with that, too. All the forms I've filled out require an actual destination before you can get clearance for any trip longer than a couple of hundred hours. I checked your license, so at least that seemed all right."

"What did you tell them for a destination? Nothing specific, right?"

"I think that should be easy enough. I booked for the Grand Tour, all the way through the Inner, Middle, and Outer System, right out to the Halo. Once that's approved, there'll be enough fuel and supplies on her to take her anywhere in the Solar System. One thing you ought to know, I charged it all to you—I don't have the credit for it."

"How much?"

Wolf winced at the figure.

"If all this works out," he said, "I'll get everything back. Otherwise, I'll be a slave to the USF for the rest of my life. Well, let's worry about that later."

As they spoke, Green led the way through the long corridor that led to the final clearing section before the main living quarters. He was sliding along in the fast, economical lope that all USF people acquired in early childhood. Wolf, not too successfully, tried to imitate it. The floor of fused rock felt slippery beneath his feet, and he had the curious feeling that the lunar gravity was a little lower than it had been on his last trip to Tycho City, many years before.

"No," said Green in answer to his question. "I think that physics here may be a little ahead of anywhere else in the system, but we still don't have an efficient generator. Gravity's one thing we haven't tamed so far. McAndrew came up with a method a long time ago for using shielded kernels for local gravity adjustments, and that's as far as anyone has been able to go. Nobody's willing to try even that much, down on a planetary surface. What you're feeling is a change in oxygen content. We put it a fraction of a percent higher about three years ago. You'll find that you get used to it in a couple of days."

"A couple of days! Park, I have no intention of *being* here in a couple of days. I want to be well on the way to the cluster. When can the ship leave? I hope it's today."

Green stopped and looked at Wolf quizzically. "Bey, you're dreaming. You just don't know the problems. First, there's no way they can get a ship ready in less than seventy-two hours. Damn it, it has to be equipped to support the two of us on a two-year trip—that's how long the Grand Tour can take. I know we're not really going on that, but they're getting her ready for it. Second—"

"What do you mean, support the two of us? Park, I'm not dragging you on this trip. It's a risky game that far out of the usual system ship routes, and it may all be a complete waste of time. I'm going solo."

Green listened calmly, towering way above Wolf. He shook his head.

"Bey, you're a real expert on form-change, I'll be the first to admit that. But you're a baby when it comes to space operations. Oh, don't say it—I know very well that you have your license. That's just the beginning. It means you're toilet trained in space—not that you're ready to hare off around the system on your own. I'm telling you, no matter how confident you feel about your ability to look after yourself, the owners wouldn't agree. There's no way they'd even let you get *near* that ship unless I go with you—not once around the Moon, never mind the Grand Tour. It's got to be me, or you'll find they push some other USF pilot on to you—somebody you don't even know."

Wolf looked at Green's calm confidence. It was obvious that the big man was telling the truth. He shrugged and resigned himself to the inevitable.

"It wasn't what I had in mind, Park. I wasn't proposing to drag you into all this when I asked you to help in checking Ling's records up here."

Green smiled slightly and shook his head. "Bey, you still don't understand it, do you? I'm not going along because I'm a kind-hearted martyr. I'm going along because I *want* to. Damn it, don't you realize that I've been itching to know what's been going on with John back on Earth since the minute that I set out to come back to Tycho City? You could almost say that it was my fault that John ever got changed to a Logian form. If I'd been a bit smarter and known what was happening, I might have been able to talk him out of injecting Logian

DNA into himself. Get rid of the idea that I'm going along for *your* sake."

Wolf was staring up at the other's earnest face. "Sorry, Park," he said in a subdued voice. "I let my own compulsions blind me to everybody else's. You deserve to come along. I still wish we could beat that figure of seventy-two hours. I didn't plan on spending anything near that long here in Tycho City."

Green was smiling again. "You'll need that much time to prepare. And you still owe me some explanations. Your message from the ship set a new high for being cryptic. We're getting ready to go right out of the System and you still haven't told me why. I heard that John had disappeared, and I know the two things are connected."

"We're not going out of the System, Park, just to the Egyptian Cluster."

"Same thing, to a USF-er. Technically, you're right, of course. The System goes all the way out to the long-period comet aphelia. But so far as anybody in the USF is concerned, when you go to an orbit plane that far off the plane of the ecliptic, you might as well be right out of the System. The delta-v you need is so big, and there are so few things of interest up there. We just don't bother to do it very often. Do you know, I've never even *met* anybody who has been to a member of the Egyptian Cluster. I've been looking up the facts on it ever since you called me from the ship. I still can't imagine why you want to go there."

They were approaching the big hemispherical chamber that marked the city edge. Beyond it, slideways led to the separate centers for manufacturing, maintenance, utilities, and habitation. Agriculture and power were located back up on the surface, 3,500 meters above their heads.

"I'll brief you on all the background as soon as we're settled in here," said Bey. "That won't take me more than a few hours. I don't know what plans you have to spend the rest of the time before we can leave, but I'd like to have another go at the data banks. There may still be things in there that I missed last time on Capman's activities here as Karl Ling."

"You'll have time for that. There will be other things, too." Green pointed ahead of them to where a small group of men and women was standing by a wall terminal. "There's your fan club. I'm sorry, Bey, but I couldn't stop it. Those are the Tycho City experts on regeneration methods. They want to hold a reception later in your honor, and nothing I've said has managed to dissuade them. You see the price of fame? Now, are you too tired, or shall we be nice to them while you're here?"

CHAPTER 19

The *Explanatory Supplement to the Ephemeris, 2190 Edition* lists the mean orbital inclination for the asteroids of the Egyptian Cluster as fifty-eight degrees and forty-seven minutes to the plane of the ecliptic. The cluster's physical data are given at the very end of the reference section, a fair measure of its relative importance in the planetary scheme of things. All cluster members have perihelion distances of about three hundred million kilometers, strongly supporting the idea of a common origin even though any clustering in a purely spatial sense has long since been dissipated. Pearl, with an almost circular orbit, crosses the ecliptic near the first point of Aries. Unfortunately she was riding high, far south of that, when Wolf and Green finally set out.

"Nearly a hundred and thirty million kilometers, Bey," grumbled Green, hunched over the displays. "It will take more fuel to get us there than it would to take us to Neptune. I hope you're right in all those guesses."

Wolf was prowling restlessly through the ship, savoring the half-g acceleration and inspecting everything as he went.

"You say it would take just as much fuel, Park, if Pearl were heading through the ecliptic right now. All we would save is a little time. If I'm wrong on the rest of it, we'll have wasted a few weeks each."

He paused by the radiation-shielded enclosure, eyeing it speculatively.

"It's a pity that doesn't have a form-change tank inside

it," he went on. "This ship is plenty big enough to carry the equipment, if there were a suitable tank."

Green looked up briefly. "Remember, Bey, C-forms are still illegal here."

"I know. I was just thinking that we could really use one now to slow down our metabolisms a few times. The Timeset form would do us nicely. How's the fuel supply look? Any problem?"

"No. We could do this twice if we had to. I told the provisioners that we might want to do some unusual out-of-ecliptic maneuvers during the trip. They gave us the biggest reserves the ship can hold."

Green finished his final checking of the trajectory and straightened up. He looked at Wolf, who was still eyeing the closed compartment.

"Eyes off, Bey. You know the USF is ultracautious on the use of C-form experiments. Really, you can't blame us. People are precious out here. We don't have a few billion to spare, the way that you do down on Earth. We'll let you do the wild experiments. It will be a few years before we're ready to play with the form Capman developed in Project Timeset. Meanwhile, we've got our own methods. Did you take a good look yet at the sleeping quarters?"

"A quick look. They're tolerable. I was going there next to look at a few bits of equipment that I didn't recognize. The place looked very cluttered. Why not use one compartment and save on space?"

"That's what I mean, Bey." Green switched off the display and swung the seat around. The legroom at the trajectory monitor had been meant for someone two feet shorter. He stretched his long limbs straight out in front of him.

"You see," he went on, "back on Earth you've been forced to develop methods that let people live on top of each other, millions of you where naturally there should only be thousands. Well, we have a different problem here in the USF. We have a lot of space and not many people, but we've still had to worry about the situation where a small number of people live for a long time in very close contact—in a ship, or a mining colony, or an Outer System settlement. It's even worse than Earth, because there's no chance to vary the company you keep. You have to be able to live for months or years without murdering each other."

Green swiveled his chair around to face Wolf and looked at him with a strange expression. "Bey, answer me honestly. Just what do you think of me?"

Wolf, puzzled by the sudden change in subject, pulled up in midprowl. He looked at Green thoughtfully for a moment before he replied. "I think I know where you're heading, Park, but I'll play the game. An honest answer, eh? All right. You're good-natured. You're a bit of a worrier. You're not stupid—in fact, you're pretty shrewd—but you're also a little bit lazy. You bore easily, and you hate things that are too theoretical and abstract for your taste. We're off to a devil of a beginning here for a long trip together, but you did ask me."

"Right." Green sniffed. "I have trouble with that evaluation—it all rings much too true. Now, let me tell you what you're like. You're as smart as Satan, but you're a bit of a cold fish, and that sometimes throws off your judgment when it comes to people. In fact, you prefer ideas to people. You really love puzzles. You're stubborn, too. Once you get started on something, there's no way of shaking you off it. You're obsessive—but not about the usual human frailties. I'll hazard a guess, but I suspect that you've never formed a permanent link of any kind with either man or woman."

Bey had winced at the accuracy of some of the comments, but he was smiling at the end.

"Park, I didn't realize that you knew me so well—better in some ways than I know myself. So what's the punch line? I presume that you are not proposing that we spend the next few weeks exchanging character assessments. If so, I'm not impressed with your USF ideas on the way to pass the time on a long trip."

Green stood up carefully, looking with annoyance at the low ceiling. "Not at all. Here, Bey, follow me." He started forward, stooped over. "This ship wasn't built for somebody my size. You should have no trouble, but watch your head anyway. I want to show you a few features of this ship that you weren't aware of on your first inspection. We just exchanged character comments, Bey, and we weren't complimentary. But we're still behaving in a civilized way toward each other—even though I'm sure neither one of us greatly enjoys having some of our defects pointed out, even though we know them well enough for ourselves.

"Let me assure you, though, what would happen if you and I were to be cooped up together for six months or a year with no outside contacts and no one else to speak to without a half-hour light-time delay. You may not believe me, but the USF has a couple of hundred years experience on this one. Things would change. Little things about me that you don't like would seem to get bigger and bigger. After three months I'd strike you as impossibly soft and stupid, incredibly big and clumsy, unendurably lazy. And in my eyes you'd be a cold monster, an untrustworthy, calculating madman. Do you find that hard to swallow?"

"Not really." Wolf followed Green through into the separate sleeping quarters, quite large but full of odd pieces of equipment. "I've read about the effects of prolonged small-group contacts, particularly where the people are short of real work to do. Are you telling me that the USF has developed a solution to that?"

"Three solutions. In my personal opinion, none of them is as good as use of the C-forms. Here's the first."

Green reached up above one of the bunks and carefully took down a large padded headgear from its recessed storage area.

"See the contact points, here and here? You attach them to the skin and put the cups over your eyes. It looks similar to the equipment they used in the early form-change work, doesn't it?"

"Close to it." Bey stepped forward and peered at the microelectrodes in the interior of the cap. "It won't permit real biofeedback, though—there's no adaptive control here."

"It's not intended for that. All it does is monitor purpose and wish, just the same as the form-change equipment. But instead of providing form-change feedback, it gives sensation feedback. It's connected to the computer, and that profiles a sensation response for you, maximized for relaxation and peace of mind."

"What!" Wolf was looking at the headgear in disgust. "Park, I don't know if you realize it, but you've just described a Dream Machine. They're illegal on Earth. Once you get hooked on one of these, it takes years of therapy to get you back to a normal life."

"I know. Don't get excited, Bey. This only gets used as a last resort, when somebody realizes that they're going over the edge mentally." Green's voice was grim. "Which would you rather do, Bey? Go under one of these when you start to crack and take a chance that they will get you back to normal—or be like Maniello on the first Iapetus expedition, flaying his partner and using Parker's skin to re-cover the seat of the control chair? I'm telling you, the ship environment does funny things to people. Are you beginning to see why there's more to flying the System than a pilot's license?"

Wolf was looking chastened. "Sorry, Park. One of the problems of living down on Earth—we tend to get the idea that the USF is still a bit backward. For some things it's just the other way around. What else have you worked out here to help you keep sane?"

"These others are the ones that we prefer to use. The first one I showed you is strictly for desperate cases." Green pulled a large blue plastic cover, shaped like a man, from a panel under the bunk. "This one is an inferior version of a Timeset C-form. It's called a hibernator. We inject a combination of drugs to lower body temperature. It kills you, if you want to sound melodramatic about it. The suit holds you in a stable condition at about five degrees above freezing. The effective rate of aging is about a quarter of normal. You can go into it for about a week at a time, then you have to be revived. The suit does that automatically, too. See the monitors on the inside? After four or five days to get the muscle tone back up, you can go under again."

"I don't like the sound of that. You lose a week out of four, completely, while you're in there. Why not use a cryo-womb and make it really cold?"

Green shrugged. "This is safer. The fail rate on cryo-revivals is up near two percent."

"More like one percent, with the latest systems."

"All right, one percent. This thing is just about fool-proof. I admit, it's the poor man's version of a Timeset C-form. I expect we'll be using that in a few years. Meanwhile . . ." Green shrugged.

Bey slid open the suit fasteners and looked at the array of sensors running along the whole inside. "Any reason why we shouldn't both use it on this trip? We could cut the subjective time down more if we were both under at once."

Green coughed. "Well, when I said just about fool-proof, I only meant that. I would rather that we weren't both under at once. Once in every few thousand times there's a problem with the revivication process. It's nice to have somebody who's awake, waiting around to see if the suit does its job properly and helping out if it doesn't. With both of us under, there's a very small chance that we'd find ourselves on a much longer trajectory than we're planning. Unless we apply the correct thrusts when we get to Pearl, we'll drop back into the Solar System in about seven hundred thousand years. I'd rather not rely on whoever is around at that time to come along and get us out of our suits."

Wolf looked at him closely and decided that Green was only half joking. He looked at the suit, then began to fold it up. "What else do you have? So far I'm not too enthusiastic."

Green shrugged. "I told you, none of these methods is as good as a working C-form." He reached up again into the recess above the bunk and pulled down another helmet, this one smaller and lighter than the first. "This has similar connections to your 'Dream Machine,' but it has a different working principle."

He turned it over. "See these leads? They link to the computer and also to the helmet in the other sleeping area. It still provides a sensation feedback, but in this one it's modulated by what the other person in the system is thinking and dreaming. The computer is programmed to modify those thoughts, before the feedback, to make our impressions of each other more favorable. All the time that we have the helmets on, we are sharing each other's thoughts and emotions. It would be much harder for us—so the theory goes—to develop any hatred for each other. It would almost be like hating yourself."

"I do that anyway, sometimes." Wolf was looking at the helmet with a good deal of distaste. "Speaking personally, Park, I find this device disgusting. It's no reflection on you, but I don't like the idea of somebody else sneaking in on my dreams. Some of the things I think just don't bear to be shared. Whoever thought up this one had a diseased mind—worse than mine."

Green nodded sympathetically. "It's odd that you should say that. Most people don't seem to mind the idea, but I have an instinctive dislike of it. It must feel like a two-way computerized seduction, creeping into each other's hidden territories. Anyway, which one do you want to use on this trip—or would you rather not try any of them?"

Bey looked at the helmet he was holding. "It's not much of a choice, is it? I suppose the hibernator is least bad. I don't mind sleeping for a week, provided we don't feel too bad afterward."

"All right. We'll take it in turns to go under. Really, though, for this trip we don't have to use these things at all. They're not even recommended for trips under a month, and they don't become mandatory until you're going to be six months between stops. Want to skip it completely?"

"Let's see if we get bored at all. You know, Park, I wish the USF was more broad-minded about form-change work. For a start, I feel sure I could set up a system that would work with somebody in the hibernator and use biofeedback to keep good muscle tone. That has to be easy. In fact"—Bey was beginning to sound enthusiastic—"I'll be willing to make a bet with you. I'll wager that I can take a Dream Machine helmet and a hibernator and make a system from them that will do just what I said—and I'll have it finished before we get to Pearl. What's the capacity of the on-board computer?"

"Ten to the tenth directly addressable. About a hundred times that as low-speed backup."

"That's ample. Even if we don't find what I'm looking for, maybe we can take something back with us that will interest the USF."

Green looked at Bey warily and shook his head. "Experiment as much as you like. There's a spare set of helmets and a spare hibernator. But I don't like that mad-scientist look in your eye. I'm telling you now, you don't have a volunteer as a test subject if you think you have it working. When I hear you talk, I sometimes think you're as bad as Capman must be—form-change is the most important thing in the world to both of you." He was silent for a moment, then he sighed. "I only hope I still have a job when I get back. The USF government doesn't take kindly to sudden extended absences without a real explanation. But I'll tell you one thing, Bey, your obsession with Robert Capman seems to be infectious. I just can't wait to get to Pearl."

CHAPTER 20

More than ninety-nine percent of all the mass in the Solar System lies close to the plane of the ecliptic. Of the remainder, the Halo of kernels accounts for all but the tiniest fraction, and that Halo is at the very outer edge of the system, never visible from Earth or Moon with even the most powerful optical devices. For all practical purposes, Pearl and her sisters of the Egyptian Cluster swim in a totally empty void, deserted even by comparison with the sparse population of the Outer System.

The ship climbed steadily and laboriously up, away from the plane of the ecliptic. Finally, the parallax was sufficient to move the planets from their usual apparent positions. Mars, Earth, Venus, and Jupiter all sat in constellations that were no part of the familiar zodiac. Mercury was cowering close to the Sun. Saturn alone, swinging out at the far end of her orbit, seemed right as seen from the ship. Bey Wolf, picking out their positions through a viewport, wondered idly how the astrologers would cope with such a situation. Mars seemed to be in the House of Andromeda, and Venus in the House of Cygnus. It would take an unusually talented practitioner to interpret those relationships and cast a horoscope for the success of this enterprise.

Bey turned the telescope again to scan the sky ahead of them, seeking any point of light that could be separated from the unmoving star field. It was no good. Even though the computer told him exactly where to look and

assured him that rendezvous would be in less than an
hour, he could see nothing. He was tempted to turn on
the electronic magnifiers, but that was cheating as he
had been playing the game.

"Any sign of her yet?" said Green, emerging from the
sleeping area.

"No. We should be pretty close, but I can't see anything. Did you pick up your newscast?"

"Just finished watching it. It was a terrible picture,
though, the signal-to-noise ratio was so bad. I don't
understand how they can pick up those broadcasts all the
way out to Uranus with a receiving antenna no bigger
than the one we have. We're only a tenth of that distance, but the signals seem to be right at the limit of
reception."

"We're just picking up one of the power side lobes,
Park. Nearly all the real power in the signal is beamed
out along the main lobe, in the ecliptic. It's surprising in
a way that we can pick up anything at all here. Anyway,
what's in the news?"

"What I heard didn't sound good." Green's voice was
worried, and he didn't want to meet Bey's eye. "It's
Earth again. All the social indicators are still pointing
down. I know old Dolmetsch is a prize pessimist, but
I've never heard him sound so bleak before. He was
being interviewed in Lisbon, and he's projecting everything going to hell before the general coordinators can
damp out the swings in the social parameters. He looked
as though he was going to say more and tell us the swings
couldn't be damped at all, but the interview was cut off
short at that point."

Wolf looked out of the viewing port, back to the brilliant blue-white point of light that was Earth. "It's hard
to make yourself accept that there are fourteen billion
people back there on that little speck. Did you catch any
hard facts?"

"Some—but I'm sure they are censoring heavily. Tremendous riots in South America, with the biggest death
rate in Argentina. Power blackouts all over. Hints at
something really bad in China. It sounded like wide-

spread cannibalism. The general coordinators are even talking of putting a kernel down onto Earth's surface; that gives us a good idea how bad the energy shortage must be."

"It does." Bey looked back at Earth as though expecting to see it wink out of existence like a snuffed candle. "If they lost the shields on a kernel, it would be worse than any bomb in the stockpile. All the Kerr-Newman holes they're using in kernels radiate at better than fifty gigawatts. They'd be mad to take one down to the surface."

"Mad, or desperate. Maybe Dolmetsch has a right to be a pessimist—after all, he invented the whole business. The famine in South Africa is getting worse, too. They are talking now about cutting off all supplies there and using them where people may be salvageable."

Green had joined Bey Wolf at the port, and they were gazing together at the star patterns, each seeing his own personal specter. They stood in silence for several minutes, until Green frowned and looked about him.

"Bey, we're turning. It's not enough to feel yet, but look, part of the star field seems to be rotating. The computer must be turning us for final rendezvous. Do you remember the setting?"

Bey nodded. "One kilometer surface distance, exact velocity match. I thought we ought to take a look from close in before we get any ideas about a landing on Pearl." He swung the viewer into position and switched on the screen.

"Well, there she is, Park. We've come a long way to see that."

The asteroid appeared on the screen as a small, perfect circle. It glowed softly, but not with the highlights of a reflection from a polished glass surface. Instead, there was a diffuse uniform glow, a pearly gleam with a hint of green in the white. Green frowned and turned the gain up higher. The image seemed to swell on the screen.

"Bey, that's not the way I expected it to look. It's scattering and absorbing a lot more light than it should.

It really looks like a pearl, not a hollow glass ball. Why isn't it just reflecting the sunlight?"

"I don't know, Park. Look at the left-hand side, there. See it? There's something different there, a dark spot."

The image on the screen was still growing steadily larger and clearer as the ship neared rendezvous. It was difficult for Wolf and Green to suppress their impatience as the asteroid's milky surface slowly became more visible. Soon it was obvious that the dark spot was more than a patch of different reflectance, and there were other faint mottlings and markings on the smooth surface, tinged with a cloudy green.

"It's some kind of a pit, Bey." Green hunched closer to the screen. "Maybe a tunnel. See where it angles down into the surface? I don't remember anything like that in any of the descriptions of Pearl."

Bey was nodding his head in satisfaction.

"It's not a natural formation. Somebody's been doing heavy engineering there. See how sharp those edges are? I'll bet that was cut with a big materials laser. Park, there's no way that Capman—or anybody else—could have done all that without a lot of assistance and equipment. You know what that means? Somebody in the USF has been helping him—and whoever it was has lots of resources to play with."

The computer interrupted his final words with a soft whistle. The orbit match was complete. They stared hard at the nearby asteroid. From a distance of one kilometer, Pearl filled a quarter of the sky. The whole surface shone with a pale, satiny gleam. It was smooth and unbroken, without any irregularity except for the exact, circular hole thirty meters in diameter that showed its black disk near the left side of the image.

They studied it in silence for a few minutes. Finally Bey moved over to the computer console.

"It's no good, Park," he said. "We can't learn much from here. There's nothing to see on the surface. We have to get a look at the inside. I'll bet that tunnel runs right through to the interior. We'll need suits."

"Both of us?"

"Unless you're willing to stay behind here. I know I didn't come all this way to watch. The computer has everything under control on the ship. I think it's safe enough to go in close and jump the gap wearing our suits. Take us in to fifty meters, and let's go."

The two men, fully suited, drifted across from ship to surface. The gravity of Pearl was too small to be noticed. They hovered a few feet from the planetoid and looked at it more closely. It was clear why Pearl shone so softly. Through the many millennia since Loge's explosion, the impact of micrometeorites had pitted the surface, to develop a matte, frosted coating that caught and diffused the light from the distant Sun. Pure white alternated with greenish clouds in a patchwork over the sphere. The two men drifted slowly toward the tunnel. Near the edge, Wolf shone a hand torch downward. Deep channels had been scored in the smooth glass by heavy equipment. The hole narrowed as it descended, ending about fifteen meters down in a smooth plate of black metal.

Wolf whistled to himself, the sound thin and eerie over the suit radios. "That disposes of the idea that nobody's allowed to land on Pearl. Why would anybody put in an air lock down there if it's just an empty shell?" He looked down the steep-sided hole. "Ready to go down, Park? All we need now is the White Rabbit."

They floated together downward to the big portal, untagged the outer door, and went inside. Green took hold of the port, then hesitated for a moment.

"Should I close it, Bey? We don't know what we may be getting into. There could be anything inside."

"I don't see that we have much choice. Either we go in or we go back. I'm expecting to find Capman behind the door and John Larsen with him. If you want to stand guard outside, that's fine—but I'm going in."

Green did not answer, but he pulled the outer door firmly shut and dogged it with the clamps. There was at once a hissing of air.

"Don't assume that it will be breathable," warned Wolf as the inner door swung open. "John should be here, and the atmosphere may be his idea of nice fresh air."

Green snorted. "Bey, give a USF man some credit. Anybody who grew up off-Earth would no more try and breathe untested air than want to live back down on Earth and breathe your soup. Look at the second display panel in the helmet inset. It's registering 6-S. That means it's safe to breathe and a little less than half Earth-normal for pressure. All the same, I'm going to keep my suit closed. I suggest you should do the same."

The inner door was slowly irising open. A pale green light filtered into the lock from the interior of the plane-toid. With the port open to its full thirty-meter diameter, the whole of the inside of Pearl became visible. In complete silence the two men drifted forward together, looking about them.

The inner wall of Pearl had a smooth, shiny finish that had been missing on the exterior. No meteorites had marred its perfection. The inner surface was a perfect globe, a little more than a mile in diameter. In the center of the vast, arching chamber, tethered to the wall by long, glittering struts and cables, hung two great metal structures. The nearer was itself another bright sphere of steel or aluminum. Bey, eyeing it thoughtfully, wondered at the source of the materials that had been used in its construction. Certainly they had not come from Pearl itself. Considering the energy needed to transport materials from the main system, it seemed certain that the ball must have been built from metals mined on one of the sister asteroids of the Egyptian Cluster. Bey estimated that the sphere was a hundred meters across. A long tubular cable led from the port where they had entered to another lock on the sphere's smooth face.

The second structure could only be a ship. That made no sense. Bey looked around him again. There appeared to be no way that the vessel, forty meters across at the widest point, could have reached the interior of Pearl— or, once there, could ever leave it. His eyes followed the guide cables that led from the ship to a slightly darker section of the inner wall, directly opposite to the point where they had entered. It had to be a concealed exit. Other cables, running to empty areas in the interior, hinted at the sometime presence of other ships, moored to the inner surface in the same way.

The surface of Pearl, with its wall of translucent glass, provided an efficient conversion of incident solar radiation. The suit thermometers indicated an ambient temperature quite comfortable for human habitation. The inside was lit with the faint sunlight that had been transmitted through the outer walls and suffused about the interior. There were no shadows except those thrown by the torches that Wolf and Green were carrying.

At first Pearl seemed completely silent, a dead world. As their ears adjusted, Wolf and Green became aware of a deep, muffled pulsing, felt more than heard, filling the interior. It came from the metal sphere at the center of the asteroid, regular and slow, like the working of air or nutrient circulators or the beating of a vast heart. Nowhere through the great space of the central bubble was there any other sound or sign of life.

Park Green finally broke the spell. "I'm beginning to think I don't know anything at all about the USF. There's no way this place can exist. That ship up there must be unregistered, and if Capman came here in it I can't even guess where he could have started out from. Not Tycho, that's for sure."

Wolf grunted his agreement. His instincts told him that something was very wrong. He had come to Pearl convinced that he would find Capman and Larsen there. If that were true, surely there should be some sign of their presence. He looked again at the metal sphere ahead of them. Without speaking both men moved to the great hollow cable that led there from the entry port.

As they started along it, the sheer size of Pearl came home to Bey. The far wall looked close at hand, but the vaulted interior of the asteroid could easily have contained tens of millions of Earth dwelling units. They progressed along the cable until their entry lock behind them had shrunk to a small black dot. They both felt more comfortable when they had finally reached the sphere and entered the lock on its shining face.

The first rooms were clearly living quarters. The furnishings were simple, but there was expensive automated equipment to handle all routine chores. Bey, seeing the food delivery system, realized how long it had been since they had eaten. He looked at Green.

"What do you think, Park? Assuming that's in good working order, are you ready to risk the air in here?"

Green was looking hungrily at the dials of the robo-chef. He nodded. "I think we're safe enough, as long as we don't go through any air locks. This area is a standard USF automat life support, with a few VIP luxuries thrown in. Take a good look at that menu. I'll bet you don't eat like that back on poor old Earth."

Unsuited, they felt a good deal of the tension evaporate. There was still no sign of life, and by the time they were ready to continue their exploration, Bey had become convinced that the whole sphere was uninhabited. After the living quarters came three rooms crammed with monitors and control consoles, exactly like the general control room for a form-change lab—similar, and yet dissimilar. It was bigger than anything Bey had ever seen, bigger even than the research center facility at BEC.

"The tanks should be behind that wall," he said, explaining to Park Green what they had found. "But I don't think we'll find John there. Somewhere, I missed the point. I was sure I was right, then—"

He shrugged and looked about him. Four years earlier he had thought he knew what Capman was doing—only to find that he had been outthought every step of the way. It could happen twice. Capman had *expected* him to unravel the skein that led to Pearl. If necessary, John Larsen could provide a little prompting, since it was clear that he had been in constant communication with Capman ever since the change to a Logian form. Once he knew that Bey was on the way, Larsen had promptly disappeared.

It all sounded so logical—but so unlikely. Bey wasn't sure that he could explain to Park Green just how they had been guided here like a couple of puppets.

While Wolf stood there in silence, Green had been looking closely at the control panel.

"Bey, I know I'm no expert on this stuff, but look at the readouts. They all seem to be from one tank. Could all these be from one form-change station?"

Wolf came forward also. He studied the panels for a few seconds, his face puzzled. "It looks like it, I admit. But there are far too many monitors for one subject. There have to be three hundred of them. I've never seen anything nearly as complicated for one experiment. I wonder if it could be . . ."

He stood, unwilling to state his own belief.

"You and your companion are quite correct, Mr. Wolf," said the speaker grille above the console. "This is indeed all one experiment."

CHAPTER 21

"Capman?" Wolf swung around swiftly to face the grille.

"No, I am not Robert Capman. I am an old friend of his. In fact"—there was a hint of amusement in the light, musical tone—"I could fairly say that I'm a very old friend. Welcome to Pearl. I have heard a great deal about you from both Robert Capman and John Larsen."

Green was looking around him in confusion. "Where are you? The only way out of here looks as though it leads to the tanks."

"Correct. I am in the tank area. It is quite safe for you to proceed through at the moment. I am maintaining the atmosphere at the same level as in the rest of Pearl."

"Should we come through?" asked Wolf.

"Come through by all means, but be ready for a shock. You perhaps consider that you are past surprise, Mr. Wolf, but I am not sure that the same is true for Mr. Green."

"But where are Capman and Larsen?"

"Far from here. Mr. Wolf, the conversion of John Larsen to an alien form was completely unexpected. It added a new dimension to an activity that was already vastly complex. But it also provided great benefits. Part of the explanation of our activities is not mine to give, and you must hear it from Capman. Part, however, I can tell you. Come through into the tank."

Wolf and Green looked at each other, and finally Bey shrugged. "I'll go first. I don't think there will be any danger. I don't know what we're going to see, but I've

182

had a close look at most things in the years with Form Control."

The chamber that they entered was enormous. It occupied at least half of the whole metal sphere. Bey looked around him in vain for the familiar tank fittings. At first he could see nothing that he recognized. Then, suddenly, what he was looking at made sense. He gasped. It *was* a tank, but the proportions on the service modules were unbelievable. Nutrient feeds and circulators were massive pipes, each two meters in diameter, and the neural connectors were heavy clusters of wave guides and thick fiber-optic bundles. Bey looked around for the origin of the voice, but it was all a complex series of interlocking vats, each one large enough to hold several men. He could see nothing to tell him where to focus his attention.

"Where are you?" he said at last. "Are you in one of the vats?"

"Yes and no." The voice now seemed to come from all sides, and again there was a hint of detached amusement in the tone. "I am in *all* the vats, Mr. Wolf. This experiment has been going on here for a long time. My total body mass must be well above a hundred tons by now, but of course it is distributed over a large volume."

Green, mouth gaping open, was goggling around him like a startled frog. Bey felt that his own expression must be much the same. "Are you human, or some kind of biological computer?" he said at last.

"A good question indeed, and one that has exercised my mind more than a little over the past few years. I am tempted to say simply, yes."

"You're both? But then where is your brain located?" asked Green.

"The organic part is in the large tank straight in front of you, at the rear of the chamber. You can pick it out easily by the number of sensor leads that feed into it. The inorganic part—the computer—is in a distributed network extending through most of the sphere. As you will gather, Robert Capman has shown that the idea of man-machine interaction can go a good deal further than a computational implant."

"But how do you . . ." Wolf paused. His mind was seeing a hundred new possibilities and a hundred new problems to go along with them.

"If there is no one else here," he went on, "how can you get the nutrient supply that you need? And how can you ever change back? I assume that you began as a human form." Another disturbing possibility suddenly suggested itself. "How did you get to be like this? Was it voluntary or were you forced to take this form?"

"Questions, questions." The voice sighed. "Some of them, I have promised not to answer. Their replies, if you want them, must come from Robert Capman himself. One thing I can guarantee, a reverse form-change would be very difficult. On the other hand, by the time I expect to be interested in such a thing, I feel sure that the capability will be well established—perhaps even forgotten. Enough of that. If you would please turn around. . . ."

The voice, for all its bizarre origin, sounded cheerful and rational, even amused. As Wolf and Green turned to look behind them, a screen flashed into color on the nearer wall of the tank.

"How do I obtain my nutrients, you ask. Very efficiently. My whole life-support system is completely self-contained. Look at the screen and let me take you on a brief tour of Pearl. We are leaving now and heading out to the inner surface."

The screen showed the output of a mobile vidicon that was moving steadily out along one of the connecting cables that led to the inside wall of the asteroid. Seen close up, it was clear that many of the cables were much more than simple supporting members for the sphere. They included tubes, communication guides, and flexible connection points onto which other cables could easily be joined. As the vidicon came closer to the wall, it was again obvious that the image of the screen showed something more complex than the smooth, glassy surface that appeared from a distance. Some patches were lighter than the background and transmitted a light distinctly greener in color.

"Algal tanks!" said Park Green suddenly. "Just like the ones in the Libration Colonies. But these must be cut into the surface of Pearl. See how green the light looks."

"Quite right," said the disembodied voice. "You can see what a great convenience it is to have an asteroid that was almost designed by nature for our purpose. The algae are the source of both my air and my nutrients. We are one closed system, including all the circulation equipment. The thermal gradients do all the work. It is no longer necessary for Capman—or anyone else—to be here to provide services to me. That control console you saw outside is no longer needed here. In fact, I control it myself, through the computer network. The whole of Pearl is a single self-contained environment."

Long experience had inured Bey to just about every conceivable form, but Park Green was much less comfortable with what he was seeing and hearing. He seemed horrified by the implications of the conversation.

"Capman did this to you, did he?" he finally burst out. "Surely he knew what he was creating. You can't move from here, you're tied to Pearl, and you can't do a reverse form-change. You don't even have anyone here to talk to or relate to. You, whatever you once were, don't you see what he's done to you? Didn't you know he's a murderer? How can you stand it?"

"Still more questions." For the first time, the voice sounded irritated. "My name, for what it matters, is Mestel. I need pity from no one. For your other remarks, perhaps I should point out that you are completely captive in your body, at least as much as I am in mine. Who is not? And I possess a degree of control over my own movement, care, and protection that you certainly are lacking. How can *you* stand it?"

"Movement?" Bey picked up on the word. "You mean vicarious movement, through the remote sensors?"

"No—though I have that too. I mean physical movement, as a whole. Wait and see, Mr. Wolf. I admit that I am bound to Pearl for an indefinite period. But why should that be considered a disadvantage? If I can believe the newscasts that I have picked up in the past few weeks, Pearl may soon be the only place left with a decent level of civilization. Or has old Laszlo become even more of a pessimist than usual?

"Perhaps that is enough talk." Mestel's voice became sharper in tone. "I suppose that I do miss the opportunity for conversations without light-time delays. Now I have another duty to perform. Your arrival here was expected, but it was not clear *when* you might come or how many of you there would be. I thought you would arrive alone, Mr. Wolf. Robert Capman believed that Mr. Green would arrive also, and John Larsen insisted on it." A curious amplified noise came from the speaker. Mestel had sniffed. "Whatever it is that makes up the Logian form, there is formidable intellect there. With all the computer assistance that is built into me, I expect to outthink anyone except Capman. Others abide the question, but he is outside normal experience. Now it seems that Larsen can think rings around both of us."

"That's my feeling, too," said Bey. "I knew John very well before the change, and it's not being unkind to say that he was no great intellect. Now he's something special. Robert Capman has always been something special."

"I know you think that. Now let me ask a question that you alone can answer. You have pursued Capman steadily since your first meeting, down the nights and down the days, down the arches of the years. If you wish to pursue him further, there will now be a significant risk to you. You will also be away from Earth for many months. Do you want to proceed on those terms?"

"Wait a minute," said Green. "What about me? I've been in on this from the beginning, at least as far as the Logian forms are concerned. I'm not going to be left out of things now."

"You will not be left out, Mr. Green. You and I, for our sins, will be embarking on a different mission. It is a crucial and a demanding one, but it does not include a meeting with Robert Capman. That encounter is not necessary for us. But there are reasons why Behrooz Wolf needs one more meeting with Larsen and Capman."

Wolf was listening very closely. He was intrigued by
the intonation in Mestel's voice and by the slightly old-
fashioned and formal manner of phrasing and address.
He looked around him again at the tank. Apart from the
sheer size, it showed an individual taste in the layout, a
little different from the standard arrangement.

"Mestel," he said at last. "Is the layout of this place
your work, or did Capman do it for you?"

"Capman and a work crew arranged for the physical
labor. That was before I had full control of the remote
handling equipment, so I still needed help. Now I could
do the whole thing with my waldos. I did all the specifications, though—Robert never did care at all what his
surroundings looked like; he lived inside his head."

Wolf was nodding in satisfaction. "Then I'd like to ask
you a couple more questions. How old are you, and are
you male or female?"

Green looked at Wolf in astonishment. But Mestel was
laughing heartily, a musical gale of sound that swept out
of a hundred speakers inside the great tank.

"Male or female? Come, Mr. Wolf, is it not apparent
that the question is now purely academic? I presume you
mean, was my original form male or female? Full marks.
My name is Betha Mestel, and I was for many years a
female—but never, I'm glad to say, a lady. Robert Capman told me that you have an unmatched talent for reading through an exterior form. I see he did not exaggerate.
Can you go further? On the basis of what I have already
said, would you like to attempt further deduction?"

Bey was nodding thoughtfully, dark eyes hooded by
the half-closed lids. "Betha is not a name much used
now. It had a big vogue a hundred and twenty years ago,
and you said you are an old friend of Capman." He
paused. "I think I am beginning to see a whole lot of
things that should have been obvious to me a long time
ago. Is it possible that you—"

"Never, as they said in the old days, ask a woman her
age." Beneath the flirtatious tone of Betha Mestel's voice
there was an undercurrent that was anything but casual.
"As you surmise, the answer would take us far afield. I

must return to my question and ask again: Mr. Wolf, are you willing to take the risk that a meeting with Robert Capman would entail?"

"Definitely." Wolf's voice was firm, his resolution increased by the implications of Betha Mestel's words. "How do I get to him?"

Wolf paused. The far side of the room was suddenly indistinct, a blur of color in front of his eyes.

"I will get you to him. Mr. Green and I will not go with you; we have our own duties to perform back in the Inner System." The voice was fainter, farther away. "Let me apologize to you for what is about to happen. There are good reasons for this, also. Relax, both of you."

Neither Park Green nor Bey Wolf had heard Mestel's final sentence. Two of the handling waldos came forward and gently carried the two unconscious forms back toward the control room.

One hundred million kilometers above the ecliptic, there is an isolation that is more complete than anything found in the plane of the planets. There were no observers to watch Pearl as the asteroid moved steadily on its three-year circuit around the Sun. The nearest inhabited object was Horus, with its fifty-man mining outpost. That group was far too busy to spend any of their time heavens-watching. In any case, at thirty million kilometers distance, Pearl was at the resolution limit of their best telescopes.

No one saw the great lock in the side of Pearl iris open, and the ship emerge from it like a small, bright minnow darting from the shelter of a hollow rock. The ship fell freely for a while, until it was a safe distance from the asteroid. Then the fusion drive went on. The ship began to move out and down, dipping toward the ecliptic on a trajectory that headed farther from the Sun. The single passenger knew nothing of the motion. He was cocooned deep within the form-change tank at the ship's center.

Soon afterward, the mechanical handlers emerged from Pearl's smaller lock. They went across to the ship that Bey Wolf and Park Green had arrived in. It had remained close to Pearl's surface, with the auxiliary thrusters making the tiny adjustments necessary to hold it at a precise fifty meters from the asteroid. The handlers moved it gently toward the lock, electronically overriding the command sequence that held the ship's position. Once moved inside, the ship was secured firmly by supporting cables that threaded the faintly lit interior.

The currents began to flow through superconducting struts and cables. The interior configuration of Pearl became rigid, constrained by the intense electromagnetic fields within. When the fields had stabilized, the main lock opened again to reveal a power kernel shielded and held in position by the same powerful controls.

The propulsion unit went on. Plasma was injected into the ergosphere of the kernel, picked up energy, and emerged as a highly relativistic particle stream. Little by little, the orbit of Pearl responded to the continuing thrust. It began to change, to shift inclination and semimajor axis.

Betha Mestel was moving house.

CHAPTER 22

It had been added to the air of the room. Asfanil, probably, judging from the lack of general side effects. There was no headache or uneasiness in the stomach. And yet . . .

Bey Wolf frowned. Something didn't feel quite right. He ran his tongue cautiously over his upper lip. There was a faint taste there. No, not a taste, a feeling, like a slight stickiness. He breathed deeper, and the air felt oddly different, hot in his lungs. At last he ventured to open his eyes.

—and was suddenly completely awake. He was still sitting in the form-change tank, but he knew from long experience that the process had already run its course. The change was complete. The monitors were still, the electrodes inactive against his skin.

Full of a sudden alarming notion, Bey reached out a hand in front of him. He looked at it closely. Normal, except for the color, and that was an effect of the lighting. He breathed again, half relief, half disappointment, and looked up at the odd, blue-tinted lamps above his head.

He was no longer on Pearl. That was obvious as soon as he emerged from the tank. He was on board a ship. It could be the vessel they had seen in Pearl's interior, but the backdrop outside the viewports was of open space, not the gleaming inner surface of the asteroid.

Not on Pearl, and form-changed. But to what?

Bey inventoried his body and could find no change there. He sat down by the viewport to think things through. His body was the same, but his senses felt subtly different. The noise of the ship's engines was wrong, a high-pitched scream of power up at the limit of his hearing. It sounded quite different from the familiar drone of a fusion drive. He looked aft. The equipment was conventional enough, and he could not believe that Capman and Betha Mestel had invented a completely new propulsion system.

Wolf stared out of the port, his face vacant with concentration. Where was he? Where were Pearl, Betha Mestel, Park Green?

He switched on the other viewing screens and tried to gain an idea of the direction in which he was being carried. The Sun was the first reference point. It lay far astern, much reduced in size and brilliance. Its color was changed to a peculiarly intense violent-blue. He peered at it in perplexity. Was it the Sun? It seemed more like a strange star, alien and remote.

Bey looked for other information. Through one of the side screens, a brilliant planet was visible, quite close to the ship. Surely that had to be Jupiter—but it too was the wrong color. The ship was swinging past it, using the planet's gravitational field to pick up free momentum, and the planet itself was only a few million kilometers away. Bey turned up the magnification of the screen with strangely uncoordinated hands, focusing on the satellites that orbited the brilliant primary.

It was Jupiter all right. There were the four Galilean satellites, all clearly visible, and there was the red spot, itself changed to a peculiar lime-green color. He watched in silence for a few minutes. Io was close to occultation by the great mass of the planet. The satellite's angular separation from the main body was steadily decreasing as he looked on. Just before Io vanished, Bey sat up straight in his seat. He looked again at the Sun and at the lamps inside the ship. Suddenly he understood exactly what had happened. He swore to himself. It should have been obvious to him long before. He looked at the plotter set by the display screen. He had a suspicion what he would find as the end point of the calculated trajectory.

Farside watch tended to be quiet. No parties, no people, not even VIP inspections to provide an irritating relief from tedium. Tem Grad and Alfeo Masti had pulled it three times in four months, and they were beginning to suspect that the random duty selector was loaded against them. Once the big antennae had been recalibrated at the beginning of the residence period, there was nothing to do for the next fourteen days except an occasional personal message from a friend in the Outer System when, as now, Nearside was facing the Sun.

They had run through the usual pastimes left by former duty officers the first couple of times they had been assigned to Farside. Those were few enough, and not too enthralling at that. Now they had retired to opposite ends of the main monitor room, Tem to listen to music and Alfeo to play bridge with the computer. Even that wasn't much fun as far as Alfeo was concerned. He was getting very annoyed with the machine. It was supposed to adjust its game so that the three hands that it was playing represented players with roughly Alfeo's level of skill. Instead, he was being slaughtered, and he couldn't even curse his partner with any pleasure. After two hours, he was looking darkly at the screen and wondering if the random hands that the computer was supposed to be generating were as open to suspicion as the selection procedure for Farside watch assignments.

It was a surprise and a positive relief when the communications monitor began its soft call for attention. A ship was approaching Farside, asking for trajectory confirmation as it neared the Moon. At this time of the month, it had to be coming from Mars or beyond. Alfeo hit the button that canceled his latest losing hand and activated the display screen. The computer uttered a low whir of changing peripherals, like a mutter of protest at Alfeo's poor sportsmanship for quitting when he was behind.

It took a few seconds to get a visual fix on the ship. The computer took range-rate information from the Doppler shift in the communications band signals, used that to compute a relative position, and finally pointed the biggest telescope to line up on the approaching ship.

When the image of a gleaming white sphere finally appeared on the screen in front of him, Alfeo looked at it with interest. It didn't seem to be one of the usual freighters. He glanced automatically at the display beneath the image giving the ship's distance. Then he frowned, gasped, and looked again at the image on the screen.

"Tem," he said urgently. "Get over here. We've got a ship approaching, and according to these readouts she's a real monster. The screen shows her subtending over six seconds of arc at the station, and she's still more than sixty thousand kilometers out. See if you can find her in the register."

Tem Grad unhurriedly uncoiled his long frame from the chair and sauntered over to the screen.

"You're star sick, Alf. Six seconds at sixty kay would mean something a couple of thousand meters across. The biggest ship in Lloyd's Register is only three hundred meters. You must be reading the display wrong."

Alfeo did not deign to answer. He merely jerked his thumb at the screen by his side. Grad looked at it, then the numerical displays. He looked again. His expression changed abruptly.

"See if she has a voice channel active, Alf. I think we may have an alien out there."

His voice was excited. Earth, the USF, and the whole Solar System had been pulsing with rumor and talk of aliens ever since the first guarded and cryptic announcements had come from the Office of Form Control on Earth regarding John Larsen's metamorphosis. Speculation had been wild. With so little being said officially, the news media had gone back to the stories of the Mariana Monsters, combing sources in Guam for anything suggestive.

As the voice and video link was completed, Tem

hooked in the communicator channel. A chubby, boyish face suddenly appeared on the screen in front of them.

"Hey, I know him," said Alfeo. "I was in school with him, for tertiary vacuum survival. You remember, the courses over in Hipparchus. He's no alien."

Tem gestured him to silence. The voice circuit had corrected for Doppler shift and was now tuned correctly to the sending frequency of the ship.

"This is *Pearl*, requesting approach trajectory approval and parking orbit assignment, Earth equatorial," said Green's holo. "Repeat, this is *Pearl*. Farside, please acknowledge signal and confirm orbit."

Alfeo threw in the second circuit, permitting the computer to provide a message acceptance and a video link of Alfeo and Tem as they worked at the console.

"Acceptance received," said Green after a moment's pause. Then he blinked and leaned forward in his chair, obviously looking at his own screen. "Is that Alf—what was it?—Massey? What are you doing on Farside duty?"

"I'm not sure. Penance, maybe," said Alfeo. "And it's Masti, not Massey. And you're Park, right? Park Green. A better question is, what are you doing in that ship? She's not listed in Lloyd's, and she's very peculiar-looking."

"Watch those comments, sonny," broke in a new voice on the circuit. "Remember, handsome is as handsome does. Look, you and Park can socialize later. We need the highest-priority circuit you can give us to Laszlo Dolmetsch. Is he on Earth or on the Moon?"

Grad held back his questions, responding to the note of authority and urgency in the unknown voice.

"Last thing I heard, he was on Earth," he replied. "That was a week or so ago. I'll try and track him. Meanwhile, I'm giving you a slot that will take you to LEO, eight hundred kilometers perigee, zero inclination. I don't know if you'll be able to get landing permission. With the emergency down there, we've got a ban on everything except top-priority traffic down to the surface."

"We've heard that things are getting bad. The news-

casts on the way in were full of it." The four-tenths of a
second round-trip delay between *Pearl* and Farside Station was decreasing steadily as the ship flew closer on
her lunar flyby. "Anyway, there's no way that Betha could
land on Earth. She's not right for it."

"What's the problem?" said Alfeo. "Need a special
suit? They can fly one out to you from the Libration
Colonies if you're willing to wait a day for it. Where is
Betha, anyway?" He stared hard at the screen. "All we're
picking up is a picture of you, Park."

"I'd need a special suit, all right," said Mestel. "But
I'll guarantee they don't have one that would fit me. How
are you doing on the circuit to Dolmetsch? Do you have
it yet?"

Alfeo glanced across at the computer output. "We
know just where he is now. He's down on Earth meeting
with a group from the General Coordinators. I don't have
the priority codes that will let me interrupt a session
there. I can get a short message to him, that's about all.
There's no way that I can give you a two-way unless he
wants to initiate it from that end."

"Fine. Send him this message," said the invisible voice.
"It's short enough. Tell him that it's Lungfish Project,
Phase Two, calling."

"Lungfish Project," said Tem, keying in a second connection. "Right. But what about a message for him?"

"That's all you need. He'll be on the circuit fast, unless
the shock knocks him flat."

"But who are you?" persisted Tem. His own curiosity
was thoroughly aroused. "Don't you even want to give
him your name? You must be a friend of his."

"I was a friend of his long before you two were cutting
teeth. But I haven't seen him for a long time, and I've
changed a little since then. If you can send a video with
the message, give him a shot of *Pearl*. There's no point
in sending him the video signal that we're sending you."

"You mean give him a picture of the ship?" Alfeo
looked dubious. "You don't look like any ship in the register. I thought I knew every type, but there's nothing
that's anything like your size and shape. What sort of

drive units do you have? They must be something special."

"They're kernels," said Park Green, "with McAndrew plasma feeds. The same as the Titan freighters, but the bracing is all done internally instead of externally. *Pearl* started out as a natural formation. It was an asteroid in the Egyptian Cluster."

The two men on Farside duty looked again at the image on the screen, then at each other.

"I guess that makes sense," said Tem Grad. "That way, Alf, she'd be in the natural feature listings, not in Lloyd's. Even so, I've never seen an asteroid that looked anything like that." He turned back to the screen. "You know, you should have applied for a reclassification, the way they did when they put drives on Icarus for the solar scoop. You should be classified now as interplanetary passenger."

"Not quite," said Betha Mestel's voice. "For one thing, there's only one passenger—I count as crew. For another thing, as soon as I can get old Laszlo and be sure he'll act on what we're going to tell him, *Pearl*'s status will change again. She'll be *interstellar*, not interplanetary."

"What the devil is all this?" broke in an impatient voice on the incoming circuit. "If this is a hoax, you'd better be ready to answer to the General Coordinators. Who sent that message about Project Lungfish?"

Alfeo turned nervously to the screen, where Dolmetsch's angry face glared out at them. "This is Farside Station, sir. We have a direct video link with *Pearl*, former asteroid of the Egyptian Cluster, now an interplanetary—inter*stellar*—ship." He choked a little at the words and looked at the other screen for moral support. "They requested a priority link to you at GCHQ and asked that that specific message be sent to you."

There was a perceptible pause as the messages went from Farside, through lunar low orbit relay, down to Earth via L-5 relay, then all the way back. Dolmetsch's face was a study as he saw the gleaming sphere appear on his screen. Confusion, alarm, and finally excitement showed there in turn before he finally spoke again.

"Is that Betha? Where are you? The picture that I'm getting can't be from the Cluster; it's much too clear."

"I moved, Laszlo. You know, we were planning to do it anyway in a year or two. We felt we had to advance it. You may be able to guess why—the situation down on Earth, with the economic breakdown, and then the Logian changes to John Larsen. I'm flying *Pearl* around the Moon at this moment, piloting her down to low Earth orbit."

Dolmetsch was nodding his head gloomily. With his great beaked nose, he seemed like some bird of prey ready to dive on its victim. "You're quite right about the situation here," he said. He sighed. "It's getting worse by the hour. We've even stopped trying to keep it secret. We are trying every empirical correction I know, but it's like a sand heap against a tidal wave. Is Robert there with you?"

"No. He has already started on the other mission. Look, Laszlo, you know I can't come down to Earth. All the changes are still going well, and I'm ready to begin Phase Two. We've picked out the target star. There's no way I can approach a planetary surface in this form. But both Robert and I felt that my appearance here might be the only way we could persuade you to act on the information that we want to give you."

"Who's Robert?" said Alfeo to Tem in a low voice. "Weren't you telling me just a few hours ago that nothing interesting ever happens on Farside watch?"

"Come up and match us in orbit," went on Betha Mestel. "Then come over into *Pearl*. Bring the General Coordinators with you, as many as you can. They have to be persuaded even more than you do. The man who is with me, Park Green, will go back to Earth with you. He has all the materials that Robert left here—and he will have the general theory of stabilization with him."

The pause before the answer came back was much longer than usual. When Dolmetsch spoke, his voice sounded guarded and suspicious.

"Betha, we've known each other too long to lie, but I think you may be very mistaken. You know how long and hard we've looked for a general theory. I've said it before, many times but let me say it again. The work I've done has been useful, no denying it. But at best I've been a Kepler or a Faraday. We're still waiting for our Newton and our Maxwell, to explain all my empirics with a few fundamentals—mathematical laws that underpin everything. Now you're telling me we have it, just when we most need it. I find it hard to accept any coincidence that big. Are you trying to tell me that this fellow, Green, worked out the general theory just like that?"

"No. He's not an economic theorist; he doesn't know even the basics Laszlo, I've learned something in the past month or two, and you'll have to learn it too. There is now an intellect present in the Solar System that makes you and Robert look like two children. Beginning with what he already knew of your work, he saw how to move to the underlying laws. It took him just a few weeks to do it."

"Weeks!" Dolmetsch sounded even more sceptical. "And we've been working on it for many years. I'd like to meet your superman—and I'll want to see that theory, in detail, before I'll accept or use any of it."

"You've met him already, but you won't be able to meet him now. I'll show you the theory when you get here. It's carried through far enough to define a set of corrective measures that you need to stop the economic oscillations."

"Betha, that's *impossible*, general theory or no general theory. Don't you see, you have to treat the cause, not the symptoms. We have to know what it was that triggered the new oscillations."

"I know. You'll understand too when you see the formal evidence. We can tell you what started it, and you can check it for yourself. The root cause of the problems began the day of the first rumor that we had been contacted by aliens. In other words, the very day that John Larsen completed his change to a Logian form."

Dolmetsch looked thoughtful. "The timing's right," he said grudgingly. "That's when it began, and since then things have become steadily worse. Go on, Betha."

"You can do it for yourself. What's the most likely cause for the instabilities?"

"Psychological perturbation." Dolmetsch frowned in concentration. "We've always suspected that a basic change in attitudes would be the most likely starting point for widespread instability. You're saying that the rumors about Larsen were the beginning? Maybe. People would change their views of many things if they thought aliens were here. Xenophobia is always a powerful force, and there are rumors about immortality and superintelligence already running wild down here on Earth."

He shook his head. "Betha, I'd love to believe you—but doesn't it just sound too unlikely, for the general theory to come along as a solution exactly when we need it?"

"It would be, if the two events were independent. They're not. They are really one and the same. The Logian form produced the instability and also created the intelligence that could understand it and develop a countermeasure. Not coincidence, *consequence*. There was one basic cause for both events—the Logian form-change."

As the conversation proceeded, Pearl was swinging further around Moon on her approach path to Earth orbit. When the geometry permitted it, the comlink to Earth was automatically rerouted through an alternate path by L-5 relay, and the reception of the signals at Farside began to fade. Tem and Alfeo bent over the screen, straining their ears for the weakening voices.

"I'll be up there by the time you arrive," said Dolmetsch. His voice was firm, and he seemed to have made up his mind. "You don't know how bad it is down here. If I wait longer before we begin new corrections, we may be too late to do any good. Can you begin sending me something here, as you fly in, so that I can get something going even before I get up there to meet you in orbit?"

"No problem. We'll begin sending on a separate data circuit as soon as you can open one for us."

The distortion in the signal received at Farside was

growing rapidly. Alfeo had turned the gain to maximum, but the voices were fading in and out as the transmission to the Farside antenna was intercepted by the lunar horizon.

"And where is Robert Capman now?" asked Laszlo Dolmetsch, his voice a faint wisp of sound among the background.

Tem and Alfeo crouched by the console, waiting for Mestel's reply.

"What did she say?" whispered Tem.

Alfeo shook his head. All they could hear was the amplified hiss of interplanetary static, seething and crackling with the noise from suns and planets. Betha Mestel's reply was gone forever, lost in the universal sea of radio emissions.

Farside watch, when it wasn't simply boring, could be most irritating.

CHAPTER 23

Outside the orbit of Jupiter, the Solar System displays a different tempo, a new breadth of time and space. The pulse of Saturn, only fifteen million kilometers ahead of the ship but almost one and a half billion from the Sun, beats thirty times as slowly as Earth's in its majestic revolution about the solar primary. The great planet, even at that distance, looked four times as big as the Moon seen from Earth. From the angle of Bey's approach, the rings made the planet seem almost twice its solid width.

Bey looked at the display that marked the time to rendezvous. Just a few ship-days to go, and he wasn't sure of the speed of the reverse-change process. He suspected that it would be fast—the sophistication of all the form-change equipment on the ship was an order of magnitude better than that of most commercial installations, and many of the programs in the change library were unfamiliar. Even so, it would be better to go into the tank a little early rather than a little late.

Capman would wait for him—that wasn't the issue. Bey didn't want to wait any longer than he had to, to hear Capman's explanations and to confirm the ideas that had been fermenting in his mind ever since his departure from Earth. Longer than that, really. Bey thought back to his own first reaction, years earlier, when John Larsen had told him of the liver without an ID.

The data bank on the ship, primed by Betha Mestel, had informed him of *Pearl*'s mission, bearing back to Earth the precious stabilization equations. It had told

201

him nothing about his own mission. Bey sighed. He would know soon enough.

He took a last look at the ringed planet, growing steadily ahead of him, and at the Sun—still the wrong color—shrunk to a fiery pinpoint, far behind. With a little reluctance, knowing that a boring time was ahead in the tank, Bey set all the ship controls to automatic. He climbed slowly into the form-change tank in the central part of the ship, called out the necessary program, and began the change.

By luck or skill, his timing had been good. When he emerged from the tank, the vast bulk of Saturn was filling the sky ahead like a mottled and striated balloon. The trajectory maintenance system was already operating. The ship was past the outer satellites, moving from Enceladus to Mimas, then beyond, heading for a bound orbit inside the innermost ring of the planet.

Bey looked back at the Sun. It was only a hundredth of its familiar area, but now it was the usual yellow orb, with all traces of blue-violet gone. The tackiness had gone from his lips. When he reached out to touch the control panel, his coordination already felt better. On the panel, the attention light was blinking steadily like an insistent emerald lightning bug.

Bey had no nerves at all—or so he claimed. The tremor in his hand as he reached out to press the connect button had to be, he told himself, a lingering aftereffect of the form-change procedure. He hesitated, swallowed, and finally pressed.

The display gave him an immediate estimate of the direction and range of the signal being beamed to him. The other ship was less than ten thousand kilometers ahead of him, in a decaying orbit that would spiral it slowly and steadily down toward the upper atmosphere of Saturn. When the video signal appeared on the screen, Bey could examine the fittings of the other ship's interior. They were unfamiliar, neither form-change tank nor conventional living quarters. But the figure who crouched over the computer console was very familiar. There could be no mistaking that massive torso and wrinkled gray hide. Bey watched in silence for a few seconds and finally realized that the other was unaware of his surveillance. The monitor must be on a different part of the console.

"Well, John," said Bey at last. "Last time I saw you, I certainly didn't expect we would ever meet here. We've come a long way from the Form Control office, haven't we?"

The Logian figure swung around to face the video camera and looked at Bey quietly through huge, luminous eyes.

"Come on, John," said Bey as the silence lengthened. "At least you might say hello to me."

The broad face was inscrutable, but finally the head and upper body nodded and the fringed mouth opened.

"A natural mistake on your part, but my fault. Not John Larsen, Mr. Wolf. Robert Capman. Welcome to our company."

While Bey was still struggling to grasp the implications of what he had heard, the other spoke again.

"I am pleased to see that you are none the worse for the form-change that you went through on the way here. May I ask, how long did it take you to realize what had been done to you?"

"How long?" Bey thought for a few moments. "Well, I knew I'd been changed as soon as I became conscious in the tank, and I knew it had to be something that affected the senses the moment I saw the Sun. It looked as though it had been Doppler-shifted toward the blue, by a big factor—and I knew that couldn't be real. The ship was heading away from the Sun, not toward it, and in any case it wasn't going that fast. I didn't catch on then, though, and I still didn't catch on when I noticed that the sound of the ship's engines seemed to be at the wrong frequency. Not too smart. But when I saw Jupiter as we swung by, Io was going into occultation. As I was watching it, I realized that it looked to be happening *fast*, much faster than it ought to. Physical laws are pretty inflexible. So, it had to be me. It was a subjective change in speed. I had been slowed down."

The Logian form of Capman was nodding slowly. "So just when did you understand what had happened?"

"Oh, I suppose it was about ten minutes after I came out of the tank. I should have caught it sooner—after all, I already knew all about Project Timeset. Ever since we found your underground lab, I've been expecting to meet forms that have been rate-changed the way that I was. I can't have been thinking too well when I first came through the form-change."

The Logian was nodding his head now in a different rhythm, one that Bey had learned was the alien smile. "You may be interested to know, Mr. Wolf, that I made a small wager with Betha Mestel before I left Pearl. She asserted that you would take a long time to realize what had been done to you. She thought you would understand it only when you read it out of the data banks that had been loaded on the ship. I disagreed. I said that you would achieve that realization for yourself, and I bet her that it would happen within two hours of your leaving the form-change tank."

Capman rubbed at the swollen boss below his chest with a tri-digit paw. "The only thing we did not resolve, now that I look back on it, is any mechanism by which I might collect the results of the wager. It is three months now since Betha Mestel passed on to Dolmetsch the stabilization equations. She is well on her way out of the system and should not be back for several centuries. She could afford to make her bet with impunity."

The appearance and structural changes were irrelevant. It was still the same Robert Capman. Bey was convinced of it and realized again the insight of Capman's remark soon after their first meeting: the two of them would recognize each other through any external changes.

Before Bey could speak again, a vivid flash of color lit up the screen in front of the console on the other ship.

"One moment," said Capman. He faced the transmission screen and held his body quite still. For a brief second, the panel on his chest became a bewildering pointillism of colored light. It ended as suddenly as it had begun, returning to a uniform gray. Capman turned back to face Bey.

"Sorry to cut off like that. I had to give John Larsen an update on what has been happening here. He wanted to know if you had arrived yet. He's very busy there, getting ready for atmospheric entry, but he wants to set up a standard voice and video link and talk to you."

"What sort of link do you have with him? I saw John change the color of his chest panel, but always one color at a time. You did it with a whole lot of different color elements."

Capman nodded, head and trunk together. "That was for rapid transfer of information. I didn't want to take much time to explain to John what we are doing. Burst mode, we've been calling it. We found out about it soon after John changed, but I wanted to use it as a special method of communicating with him, so we kept quiet about it. It handles information thousands of times faster than conventional methods."

"Are you being literal or exaggerating the rate?" asked Bey, unable to imagine an information transfer rate of hundreds of thousands of words a minute.

"I'm not exaggerating. If anything, I'm understating. I suspect that this is the usual way that Logians communicated—they only used speech when they were in a situation where they could not see each other's chest panels. It's a question of simple efficiency of data transfer. The Logian chest panel can produce an individual, well-defined spot of color about three millimeters on a side, like this."

On Capman's chest panel, an orange point of light suddenly appeared, then next to it a green one.

"I can make that any color, from ultraviolet through infrared. The Logian eye can easily resolve that single spot from a distance of a couple of meters. That was probably the natural distance apart for typical Logian conversation. Each spot can modulate its color independently, so."

The pair of points changed color, then for a moment

the whole panel swirled with a shifting, iridescent pattern of colors. It returned quickly to the uniform gray tone.

"I ran the color changes near to top speed there. It's very tiring to do that for more than a few seconds, though John has held it for several minutes when he had a real mass of information to get to me quickly. Now, you can do the arithmetic. The panel on my chest is about forty-five centimeters by thirty-five. That lets me use roughly sixteen thousand spots there as independent message transmitters. If he were here, John could read all those in directly. His eyes and central nervous system can handle that data load. If we were in a *real* hurry, he'd come closer, and I could decrease the spot size to about a millimeter on a side—just about the limit. The number of channels goes up to over a hundred thousand, and each one can handle about the same load as a voice circuit. That would be hard work for both of us, but we've tried it to see what the limits are."

Bey was shaking his head sadly. "I knew there had to be something strange about the com system that you put in the tank back on Earth—there was no reason for it to have such a big capacity. But I never thought of anything like this."

"You would have if we had used it much. It was one of the things that worried me when John was using that mode to send me information when I was on Pearl: Would somebody notice the comlink load and start to investigate it? I don't think anyone did, but as you well know there is really no such thing as a completely secret operation. You always need to send and store data, and sometime that will give you away. John tried to be careful, but it was still a danger."

Bey sat down on the bench next to the communicator screen. "I don't know who could have discovered you. I tried to guess what was happening, and I think I know a part of it—but it's only a part. I assume that John knows the whole story."

"He deduced it for himself within a couple of days after assuming the Logian form. His powers of logic had increased so much that I couldn't believe it at first. Now, I have observed it in myself also."

There was another flicker of light from the screen in front of Capman.

"John will be in voice communication in a couple of minutes," he said. "He's very busy making the last minute checks on the ship."

"I heard you say he would be making atmospheric entry. Surely he can't survive on Saturn. The form he is in was designed for Loge, and I assume that he's still in that."

"He is—but don't worry. The ship he's in has some special features, as does this one. You can see his ship from here if you look ahead of you. He's already in the upper atmosphere, and the fusion drive is on."

Bey looked at the forward screen. A streak of phosphorescence was moving steadily across the upper atmosphere of the planet. As he watched, it brightened appreciably. The ship was moving deeper into the tenuous gases high above Saturn's surface. In a few minutes more, ionization would begin to interfere with radio communications. Bey felt a sense of relief when the second channel light went on and a second image screen became active.

The two Logian forms were very similar, too similar for Bey to distinguish by a rapid inspection. However, there were other factors that made identification easy. The second figure was festooned with intravenous injectors and electronic condition monitors. It raised one arm in greeting.

"Sorry I couldn't stay up there to greet you, Bey," said John Larsen. "We're working on a very tight entry window. I want to descend as near as possible to one place on the planet. We've calculated the optimum location for low winds and turbulence."

"John. You can't survive down there."

"I think I can. We have no intention of committing suicide. This ship has been modified past anything you've ever seen before. It will monitor the outside conditions and keep the form-change programs going that will let me adapt to them. The rate of descent can be controlled, so that I can go down very slowly if necessary." John Larsen's Logian form sounded confident and cheerful. "Well, Bey, you've had a while to think on the way out here. How much of it have you been able to deduce?"

Bey looked at the two forms, each on their separate screens. "The basic facts about what's been going on for the past forty years. Those are fairly clear to me now. But I don't have any real idea of motives. I assume you know those too, John."

"I do. But if it's any consolation to you, I had to be told them, I don't think they are amenable to pure logic."

"I agree," cut in Capman. "You would have to know some of Earth's hidden history before you can understand why I would rather be thought of as a murderer than have the truth known about the experiments. I am curious to see how far your own logic has taken you. What do you know about my work?"

"I know you're not a murderer—but it took me long enough to realize it. I understand all four of your projects now. Proteus was the basic spacegoing forms, and Timeset was the form that allows a change of rate for the life process. I knew about them four years ago. I assume that Lungfish is Betha Mestel. She's about to go out into a new living environment—interstellar space. How long will she be away?"

Capman shrugged. "We are not sure. Perhaps two of three hundred years. She was always an independent spirit. She will return when she feels that it is useful for her to do so. *Pearl* was arranged to be completely self-contained. Fusion-powered internal lighting takes care of the illumination for the algal tanks when sunlight is too weak for growth—and Betha has a supply of the Logian virus in case she becomes bored with the potential of her present form and wants to try a change."

"I hope I'm around to see her come back," said Bey. "I now think that's a real possibility. You know, John, I didn't follow my first instincts when you told me about that liver in Central Hospital. My first thought was that it must have come from a very old person, one so old that he had not been given the chromosome ID. That would have made him over a hundred, and I decided that no one would use a hundred-year-old liver for a transplant. Then we got an age estimate from Morris in the Transplant Department, and that showed a young liver. That seemed to be the end of the original thought. But it wasn't. Correct?"

"It was not." Capman nodded. "As usual, your instincts were good."

"The only project we haven't accounted for was Project Janus," went on Bey. "I should have realized that you gave your projects names that told something about the work you were doing. And Janus was the two-faced god, the one who could look both ways. You had developed a form-change program that could 'look both ways' in time. It could advance or reverse the aging process. The liver we found was from a very old person who had undergone age reversal as a result of your work. Right?"

Capman's big eyes were hooded by their heavy lids. He was reliving another period of his life, rocking slowly backward and forward in his seat. He nodded. "It was from an old person. Worse than that, it was from an old friend. I could not prevent some of those experiments ending in failure."

Bey was looking on sympathetically. "You can't blame yourself for the failures. Not everything can succeed. I assume that *all* the people who were used in those experiments were your old friends? But they knew the risks, and they had nothing at all to lose."

Capman nodded again. "They had all reached a point where the feedback machines could not maintain a healthy condition. They had a choice. A conventional and rapid death or the chance to risk what remained of their lives in the experiments. As you know, the compulsions we used to achieve form-change were extreme, but even so they did not always work. Let me assure you, the knowledge that their deaths were inevitable did not lessen the loss. When someone died in the experiments, I had killed an old friend. There was no escape from that feeling."

"I can understand that. What I can't follow is your reluctance to share the burden. No one who understood your work would have blamed you for what you were doing. Your friends were volunteers. This is the piece I can't follow. Why did you choose to keep everything a secret—even after your first discovery? Why was it necessary to have a hidden lab, away from the Earth?"

Capman was still nodding slowly and thoughtfully. He sighed. "As you say, Mr. Wolf, that is the key question. In a real sense, I did not make that decision. I am known to the system as a mass murderer, the monster of the century. It is not a role I sought; it was forced upon me. I could even argue that the real villains are Laszlo Dolmetsch and Betha Melford. But I don't believe it."

"Betha Melford? You mean Betha Mestel?"

"The same person. I tend to call her by the name she had before her bond with Mestel."

"What did you think of her, Bey?" broke in Larsen. "You must have met her on Pearl."

"I did. I think she's marvelous, and I can't help wondering what she looked like before the form-changes. Betha Melford. Is she related to *the* Melfords?"

"She is Ergan Melford's only surviving heir. Every form-change royalty that BEC collects contributes two percent to Betha." Capman paused again, briefly carried into the past. "The merger with the Mestel fortunes made her the single most influential person on Earth, but she always knew the importance of keeping that hidden."

"And now she has given all that up?" asked Bey.

"She did that a number of years ago. Betha is almost a hundred and thirty years old, and when we embarked on the age-reversal experiments she had no way of knowing if she would survive them. Her financial interests are managed by a small group of people on earth and in the USF."

"Including you?"

Capman nodded. "Including me—and also including Dolmetsch. I told you there are pieces of history that you need before you can hope to know what has been going on. None of this has ever been written down.

"My own involvement began when I was still a student, soon after I came back from studies in Europe. I went to work at the Melford Foundation and met Betha. Bey Wolf, if you thought she was marvelous on Pearl, you should have seen her in her prime. She was tall, and elegantly dressed, and sophisticated enough to put a cocky young man who thought he knew everything in his place with one nod of her coiffured gray head."

"She did that to *you*?" exclaimed Bey.

"Actually, I was thinking more of Laszlo Dolmetsch." The head nodded in that smiling gesture. "But I suppose it applied equally well to me. She made a special point of bringing the two of us together at one of her parties. She insisted that I take a drink—as a defense mechanism, she said, until I learned what to do with my hands—and introduced me to half the wealth on the planet. Then, when I was softened up, she took me outside onto the terrace. Laszlo Dolmetsch was sitting there, alone.

" 'Laszlo,' Betha said to him. 'This is Robert Capman. You two will hate each other at first, but you have to get to know each other.'

"Dolmetsch looked no different then than he does now—same big, jutting nose, same sunken eyes. I don't know how I looked at him, but he lifted his head in the air and scowled superciliously at me along his nose.

"Betha Melford shook her head. 'You two deserve each other,' she said. 'Neither of you has the faintest idea of the social graces. Oh well, you'll learn. I'm going back inside now. Come and look for me when you can't stand each other's company any longer. And not before.'

"It took a while before we could talk to teach other. We couldn't get started, but I think we were both scared to go back in and face Betha. She had that effect on you. So Dolmetsch asked me if I knew anything about econometric models. I didn't. And I asked him what he knew about form-change theory. Not a thing, he said. It wasn't until we somehow stumbled on to talking about catastrophe theory that we hit common ground. I had been using it for form-change bifurcations; he had built it into his theory of the effects of technology on social systems. After that we couldn't stop. We went on to representation theory, and stability, and the final limits of technology. It was long after dawn when Betha came back to us. She listened for maybe two minutes—we didn't really take much notice of her—then she said, 'All right, you two, I'm going to bed. Everyone else left hours ago. There's a hot breakfast in the west wing dining room, when you can tear yourselves away. Tomorrow, remind me to tell you about the Lunar Club.'

"That was the beginning." The broad, alien face somehow carried the message that Robert Capman was still staring far back across the years. "We realized after that first night that we *had* to work together. What we were doing was going to change history, one way or another. Betha made sure that we never had any problem with money. And as soon as I had the form-change ideas into a suitable form, we began to feed them into Dolmetsch's programs that modeled the Earth and USF economies. The results were depressing. Most of the changes that I wanted·to explore were destabilizing, and some of them were completely catastrophic. The worst one of all was the age-reversal change. A few people might get to live a lot longer, but as soon as the news got out, the economy would blow up."

"But you did the experiments anyway," said Bey.

Capman nodded. "We both believed that there were two conflicting needs. Earth had to be stabilized, if we could do it. But we also had to have a new frontier, off Earth—more than the USF could offer. You know what we did. With Betha's help, we went underground. She financed the operations, and we had help from the rest of the Lunar Club. They were a small group of influential people who shared a common worry about the future. They were modeled on the Lunar Club that flourished in England in the second half of the eighteenth century. Most of them are dead now. Many of them died in the experiments. They were all willing volunteers for the work, as soon as they knew that a natural death was close."

He fell silent for a while. Larsen spoke softly to Bey,

switching in a voice circuit that would not include Capman's ship.

"He's lived with this for eighty years, Bey, one way or another, and yet it still gets to him, the death of the people who'd been age-reversed in the form-change tanks. I'll be in atmospheric entry in a few minutes, and out of contact. He needs to get all this off his chest."

"I don't understand how it could be eighty years, John," said Bey. "We only saw evidence that it went back thirty."

"That's when they moved the main base of operations to Pearl. Capman moved what was left into the facility under Central Hospital. Dolmetsch thought that was an acceptable danger, even if it was discovered. He calculated a limited social effect, one that he thought he could compensate for."

"John, how much of all this do you understand now? Will the general theory of stabilization really work?"

"Within limits. We still can't let people know that age reversal is possible. I understand most of this—I helped Capman when he was working out the theory, in the past few months. Make no mistake, Bey. You know how I've changed mentally since I became a Logian form—but Capman has changed just as much, and you know where he started from. I still can't follow his thinking. I can't describe the way this form feels. You should take the change yourself and know it firsthand."

Larsen stopped speaking and looked across at the display screen in his control cabin. "I'm close to entry. We'll lose radio contact very soon. I should be able to reestablish it in a few hours." He switched back to a circuit that connected him also with Capman's ship. "Sixty seconds to signal blackout."

"John," said Bey rapidly. "I still don't know why you're going down there. There must be a big risk."

"Some. Less than you think, as we have calculated it. Why are we going down there? Come on, Bey, use your imagination. We think there's life down there, and we think humans in Logian form can live there. It's our second beachhead, an area ninety times as big as Earth.

If the collapse comes—and we hope it won't—we need some other options, off-Earth."

The quality of the voice transmission was rapidly deteriorating as Larsen's ship dug deeper into Saturn's atmosphere. Larsen obviously knew it too. He raised one heavy arm and spoke his last words rapidly. "See you soon, Bey. Come on in, the water's fine."

Bey looked through the forward screen, watching the trail of ionized gases that glowed from Saturn's face behind Larsen's plunging ship. The entry was a daunting prospect. Saturn's surface gravity was almost the same as Earth's, but with an escape velocity more than three times as high, movement to and from low orbit was a difficult feat for any vessel.

"Don't worry, Mr. Wolf." Capman had come out of his reverie and read the expression on Bey's face. "This has all been calculated very closely. Unless there are unknown forces at work in Saturn's lower atmosphere, the danger to John Larsen is very small."

"And you are intending to follow him down?" asked Bey.

"Perhaps. Let me answer the question behind the question. Obviously, we could have exchanged all the information between us by radio link. Why did I think it necessary to bring you all the way to Saturn in order to talk to each other? After all, in my present form it is obvious that we cannot meet in person, even if there were reason to do so."

"That will do," said Bey. "I might have chosen different ent words, but the meaning is the same."

"Then since I asked your question, would you care to attempt to give my answer?"

Bey smiled. "There is one obvious answer. You want me to join you in this experiment. To change to the Logian form and descend to the surface of Saturn."

"And then?"

"As I said, that is the obvious answer. Unless I am losing my ability to read a little deeper, it is not the whole answer. I can't provide the rest of it."

Capman was sitting perfectly still in his chair, big eyes

unblinking. "It is not simple," he said. "Like many things, it involves a choice. Tell me, in your investigation of my background, did you ever see a psychological profile?"

Bey nodded. "An old one. When you were still in your teens."

"That would do. Did you notice anything peculiar about it?"

"You're joking, of course. As you know very well, it was similar to mine—more similar than I would have thought possible. I must say, I found it very encouraging in some ways. You showed low scores on some of the same things as I did—intelligence, for instance. Until I saw your profile, mine had always worried me a little."

"We don't fit well on the standard charts, either of us," said Capman with the nodding smile of the Logians. "I doubt if I would fit them at all in this form. But we are a little different—not a lot, but enough to worry me that some people like us are failing the humanity tests. You may be interested to know that *you* just squeaked through. Well, that is irrelevant at the moment. Shortage of people, even of people like oneself, is not Earth's current problem. Let me get to the point. I brought you here to offer you a choice. It is one that I would not make to anyone else. I can do it in your case only because we have that curious affinity of mind. Both branches call for self-sacrifice of a sort."

Bey began to feel again a rise of tension, a suspicion coming from the base of his brain. "To change to the Logian form and explore Saturn . . ."

Capman nodded. "Or else?"

"To return to Earth and continue the work on the control of form-changes? Laszlo Dolmetsch and the others need advice from somebody who really knows form-change theory. If I choose Saturn, you will return to Earth yourself."

"That is correct. If that is your choice, to remain here, I will borrow your outward appearance and go back to Earth. One of us must be there. No one would question Behrooz Wolf's return, or knowledge of form-change."

"It must be quite obvious to you that I would prefer

to stay here. The mental advantages alone of the Logian form are enough to make me want to choose that alternative."

"I know." Capman sighed. "That cannot be denied. All I can say is that the return to Earth, and all its problems, would not be permanent. When Earth's troubles lessen, or become hopeless, or you find and train your own successor, the Saturn experiment will still be here. There will be other work to do—Betha was the first of the Lungfish series, not the last. But it is your decision as to the next step. I am prepared for either role."

"How much further can form-change be carried? Betha Mestel suggests that we are only at the beginning."

"We are." Capman bowed his head. "I am beginning to suspect that the boundary that we impose between the animate and the inanimate is an artificial one. If that is true, form-change has no real limits. We can conceive of a conscious, reasoning being as big as a planet, or as big as a star. It would have to be a mixture of organic and inorganic components, just as Betha is; but that presents no logical problems. I have a more fundamental question: At what point would the result cease to be human? If our tests for humanity are valid, any human— or alien—and machine combination that can achieve purposive form-change should be considered human. I can think of worse definitions. Tell me, have you made your decision?"

Bey was silent for several minutes, watching the clouded face of Saturn speeding by below the ship. "Tell *me*," he said at last. "Do you remember the time that we were in Pleasure Dome, waiting for the decision as to whether they would let us talk to the people who were in charge of the form-change operations?"

"Very well. Why do you ask?"

"Just before they showed us Newton, in the garden at Woolsthorpe, there was a scene of a torture chamber. If the Snow Queen was telling the truth, that scene showed something that one of us wanted. Would you agree that we were the victim, not the tormentor?"

"I believe so."

"Then *who* was the victim, Behrooz Wolf or Robert Capman?"

Capman sighed. "I have wondered that, too. I do not think the machine would tune to an interest that was not common to both of us. We were both the victim."

Bey nodded, his face intense. There was a lengthening silence as the two forms, man and Logian, watched the brown and crimson thunderclouds of the planet rear and clash beneath their ships.

EPILOG

"The music stopped and I stood still, and found myself outside the hill."

CHAPTER 24

It couldn't happen again, but of course it had. Tem Grad and Alfeo Masti had been picked out for Farside watch. The two men landed the runabout that they had flown over from Nearside next to the group of domes and went slowly over to the main entrance lock. They went inside and looked miserably about them.

"You know the problem, Tem?" said Alfeo, walking through from the main room into the sleeping quarters. "This horrible place is beginning to feel like home. Another two tours of duty here and I'll be afraid to go back to Nearside."

"I know." Tem dropped his case on the bunk and patted it. "Well, this time I'm ready for anything. I brought a natural features listing to supplement the Lloyd's Register. If somebody puts a drive on Jupiter and brings it past here, I'll be able to slap the correct ID right on it."

"This might be your chance," said Alfeo. "Isn't that the com monitor over in the main area? Somebody's trying to call us. Want to grab it?"

Grad ran quickly back to the main communications room and was gone for a few minutes. When he returned he looked puzzled.

"Jupiter?" asked Alfeo.

"No such luck. It was a standard one. Long trip, though. She'd flown in all the way from Saturn orbit. It was one of the ships in the Melford fleet, requesting Earth approach orbit."

"That sounds routine enough. Why the frowns?"

"There was one thing about it I didn't understand—not the ship, the pilot. After he'd given me the ship's ID, I asked him to identify himself for our records."

"Was he somebody special?"

"Not really; I'd never heard of him. It was the way he put it, as though it was somehow supposed to be a joke."

"You never did have much of a sense of humor, Tem. Did he sound amused?"

"Not at all. Sort of sad, if anything."

"So what did he actually say?"

"He said, 'This is the *real* Behrooz Wolf, returning to Earth duty.' "

BOOK II

PROTEUS UNBOUND

Part I

'S=k.log W'
—epitaph of Ludwig Boltzmann (1844-1906),
carved on his tombstone in Vienna.

Part 1

CHAPTER 1

*"When change itself can give no more
'Tis easy to be true."*

—Sir Charles Sedley

They found Behrooz Wolf on the lowest levels of Old City, in a filthy room whose better days were far in the past.

In the doorway, Leo Manx paused. He looked at the sweating, mouldy walls and cobwebbed ceiling, gagged at the rank smell, and retreated a step. The floor of the room was covered with old wrappers and scraps of food. The man behind pushed on through. He was grinning for the first time since they had met. "There's a breath of Old Earth for you. Still sure you want him?"

"I have to have him, Colonel. Orders from the top." Manx tried to breathe shallowly as he moved forward. He knew Hamming was goading him, as everyone had done since he arrived on Earth and explained what he wanted. He ignored Hamming; the mission was too important to let small issues get in the way.

The furnishings were minimal: a single bed, a food tap, a sanitary unit, and one padded chair. As Manx moved farther inside the stink became stronger; it was definitely coming from the man slumped in that chair. Bald, sunken-eyed, and filthy, he stared straight ahead at the life-size holograph of a smiling blonde woman that covered most of one spotted and water-stained wall. The lower part of the holograph displayed a verse of poetry, in letters six centimeters high.

Ignoring both the man and the 'graph, Colonel Hamming crouched to inspect a little metal box on the floor next to the chair. Plaited braids of multi-coloured wires ran from the box to the electrodes on the seated man's scalp. Hamming peered at the settings, his nose just a few centimeters away from the control knobs.

"You're in luck. It's so-so, a medium setting."

Manx stared at the seated man's lined, grimy neck. "Meaning what?"

"Meaning he's been emptying his bladder and his bowels when he needs to, and maybe he ate something now and again, so he shouldn't need surgery or emergency care. But he won't have bothered with much else."

"So I see." Leo Manx examined the man with more disgust than curiosity, knowing that in a couple more minutes he might have to touch that greasy, mottled skin. "I thought Dream Machines were illegal."

"Yeah. So's cheating on taxes. All right, Doc, tell me when you're ready. When I turn this off, he may get nasty. Violent. Losing all his nice dream reinforcement. I've got a shot ready."

"Don't you want to check that we have the right man before we begin? I mean, I've seen pictures of Behrooz Wolf, and this . . . he's . . . well . . ."

The security man was grinning again. "Not quite up to your expectations? Don't forget Wolf is seventy-three years old. You've probably only seen pictures when he's on a conditioning program. We'll check the chromosome ID if you like, but I'll vouch for him without that. It's not the first time, you know. He did this three other times, before he was kicked out as Head of the Office of Form Control. He always comes here, and he always looks pretty much like this. Never quite so far gone before. When he still had his official position, we came and got him earlier. Can't let a government bureaucrat die on the job."

"You mean this time, if I hadn't asked to find him . . . ?"

"You, or someone else," Hamming shrugged. "I don't know how you Cloudlanders do it"—contempt in the voice—"but here on Earth a free citizen can die any damn way he chooses. Get ready, now, I'm pulling the plug. We'll go cold turkey."

Manx hovered impotently near as the security officer flipped four switches in quick succession, then ripped taped electrodes from the bald scalp. There was no sound from the bio-feedback unit, but the man in the chair shivered, gasped, and suddenly sat upright. He stared wildly around him.

"Wolf. Behrooz Wolf," said Manx urgently. "I must talk——"

"Grab his other arm," rapped Hamming. "He's going to pop."

The man was already on his feet, glaring about him with bloodshot eyes. Before Leo Manx could act, Behrooz Wolf had spun around to pull free and was feebly reaching for him with scrawny, taloned hands. The security officer was ready. He fired the injection instantly into Wolf's neck, and watched calmly as the scarecrow figure froze in its tracks. Hamming waved a hand in front of Wolf's face and nodded as the eyes moved to follow it.

"Good enough. He's still conscious. But he has no volition, he'll do what we tell him." Hamming was already turning to pack away the cables in the compact biofeedback kit. "Let's get him aloft, and dump him into his own form-control tank before he starts to get lively again."

Manx could not take his eyes away from the frozen tormented face. Behrooz Wolf was still glaring at the holograph, not interested in anything else. "Do you think that the form-control unit will work? He has to *want* it to. He seems to want to die."

"We'll have to wait and see. Hell, you can't *make* somebody want to live. You'll know in a few hours. Carry the feedback unit, would you?" Hamming took Wolf's arm and began to walk him towards the door. "Oops. Mustn't forget her. It's the first thing he'll want if he makes it through the form-control operation." He detoured to the wall and pointed to the verse. "That's the way Wolf was feeling. And here"—he poked the projection of the woman in her bare navel—"is the reason for it."

Manx read the verse below the picture.

> *My thoughts hold mortal strife; I do detest my life,*
> *And with lamenting cries, peace to my soul to bring,*
> *Oft call that prince which here doth monarchise,*
> *But he, grim-grinning king,*
> *Who caitiffs scorns, and doth the blest surprise,*
> *Late having decked with beauty's rose his tomb,*
> *Disdains to crop a weed, and will not come.*

"Gloomy thoughts. What does it mean?"

"Damned if I know. Wolf was always a nut for old-fashioned things—poetry, plays, history, useless crap like that. He must have thought the poem applied to him."

"That's terrible. He must have loved her very much, to break down like this when he lost her."

"Yeah." Hamming had switched off the projection unit and put the cube into his pocket. He shrugged. "It's odd. I knew her, and she wasn't much of a looker. Good in bed, I guess."

"How long ago did she die?"

"Die? You mean Mary there?" Hamming had taken hold of Wolf's arm again, and was leading him firmly out of the room. He gave a coarse, loud laugh. "Who mentioned *dying*? Mary Walton is alive and well. Didn't you know? She dumped him! Buggered off to Cloudland with one of your lot, some guy she met on a Lunar Cruise. Me, I'd have said good riddance to her, but he took it different. Come on, let's get Wolf up to his tank. I've had enough stink for today."

CHAPTER 2

"A message is not a message until the rules for interpreting it are in the hands of the receiver."

Apollo Belvedere Smith

They would not go away. There was nothing to see, nothing to hear, nothing to taste, to touch, to feel. Nothing. And yet there were the voices, whispering, prompting, nudging, cajoling, commanding.

That way. A generalised murmur. *That's where you are going.*

"No. I don't want to change." He struggled, unable to move or speak as he tried to identify the source of the sounds. The argument had been going on inside him forever, and now he was losing. The voices were invading him, micrometer by micrometer.

This way. This way. Change. They were ignoring his wish to rest, pulling him, pushing him, twisting him, turning him inside out. He could feel them now in every cell, stronger and more confident. *Change.* A trillion voices merged. The rush of blood through clogged arteries, organic detergents washing the dry, inelastic skin, the weak, flabby muscles, the old, tired sinews. *Change.* Liver and spleen and kidneys and testicles, ion balances on a roller-coaster, local temperatures anomalously high or low. *(Too high, too low. He was dying.) Change.* The delicate balance of endocrine glands, testes and thyroid and adrenals and pancreas and pituitary. All disturbed, homeostasis lost, desperately seeking a new equilibrium. *Change. Change. CHANGE.*

He cried out, a silent scream. LEAVE ME ALONE. The intruders ran wild in every cell. He was helpless, fainting, fading before the assault of a chemical army.

CHANGE. All over his body, fluctuations in thermodynamic potentials, in kinetic reaction rates, hormonal levels, energy rushing to dormant follicles, sloughing old tissues, redefining organic functions, thrusting along capillaries. A ferment of cellular renewal, boiling within the changing skin. *CHANGE.* Solvents along sluggish veins and arteries, the sluice of plaquey deposits, the whirl of fats and cholesterol. *CHANGE.* Liver, spleen, kidneys, prostate, heart, lungs, brain ... *CHANGE.* Fires along nerves, synapses sparking erratically, spasms of motor control, floods of neurotransmitters, flickering lightnings of pain, crashing thunderstorms of sensation, signals flying from reticular network to cerebral cortex to hypothalamus to dorsal ganglia. A clash of arms at the blood-brain barrier ... *CHANGE, SYNTHESIZE. ACCOMMODATE.*

... And then, suddenly, all voices merging to one voice. And fading, weakening, withdrawing, drifting down in volume. He could hear it clearly. He listened to the murmur of that dying voice, and at last recognised it. Knew it. Knew it exactly. It was the mechanical echo of his own soul, whispering final commands through the computer link. His physical profile, amplified a billionfold, transformed in the bio-feedback equipment to a set of chemical and physiological instructions, and fed back as final commands.

The tide was ebbing. The changes shivered to a halt. In that moment, senses returned. He heard the surge of external pumps and felt the wash of amniotic fluids as they drained from his naked body. The tank tilted and the front cracked open, exposing his skin to cold air. There was a sting of withdrawn catheters at groin and nape of neck, and a slackening of restraining straps.

He felt a growing pain in his chest, a terrible need for air. As the pertussive reflex took over he coughed violently, expelling gelatinous fluid from his lungs and taking in a first ecstatic, agonizing breath. Its cold burn inside him was simultaneous with the sudden full opening of the tank. Harsh white light hit his unready retinas.

He shivered, threw up his forearm to protect his eyes, and sagged back in the padded seat. For five minutes he moved only to lean forward and cough up residual sputum. Finally he summoned his strength, stood up, and stepped out of the tank. He staggered forward two steps, caught his balance, and stood swaying. As soon as he was sure of his own stability he reached for the towel that hung ready by the tank, wrapped it around his waist, and turned back to the form-change tank itself. Another moment to gather his will, then he gripped the door and swung it firmly closed.

It was a final, ritual step; his first choice, after the unspoken decision to live. He was rejecting the idea of tranquillizing drugs to ease the rigors of transition. Instead he walked across the room to a full-length mirror and stared hard at his own reflection.

The glass showed a near-naked man about thirty years old, dark-haired and dark-eyed, of medium height and build. The new skin on his body still bore a babyish sheen, though pale and wrinkled from long immersion. Soon it would smooth and mature to deep ivory. The face that peered back at him was thin-nosed and thin-mouthed, with a cynical downward turn to the red lips, and thoughtful, cautious eyes.

He examined himself critically, working his jaw, lifting an eyelid with a forefinger to inspect the clear, healthy white around the brown iris, peering inside his mouth at his teeth and tongue, and finally rubbing his fingers along his renewed hairline. He flexed his shoulders, inflated his chest to the full, moved his neck in an experimental roll back and forth, and sighed.

"And here we are again. But why bother?" He spoke very softly to his reflection. " 'What a piece of work is a man. How noble in reason, how infinite in faculty. In form, in moving, how express and admirable. In action, how like an angel, in apprehension how like a god. The beauty of the world, the paragon of animals.'"

"Very good, Mr Wolf," said a silky and precise voice from the communications device in the corner of the room. "The Bard wrote it, and perhaps he believed it. But do you?"

Bey Wolf turned, slowly and cautiously. The unit was showing no visual signal. He stepped across and turned on its video and recorder. "You did not let me finish that quotation. It goes on, "Man delights me not, no, nor woman neither." And let me point out that this is my private apartment. Who are you, and how the devil did you get my personal comcode?"

"I brought you here." The voice was unembarrassed. "I helped to carry you up out of Old City—for that, you may thank me or curse me. I set you up in that form-change tank. And I stayed, long enough to turn on your communications unit and note its access code." The screen flickered, and a man's image appeared. "I do not want to intrude on your privacy, and you will note that I was not receiving visual signals until you just activated that channel. I am sure you are still feeling fragile, but I must talk with you as soon as you are recovered. My name is Leo Manx. I am a member of the Outer System Federation."

"I can tell that much by looking at you. What do you want?"

"That cannot be discussed over public channels. If I could return to your apartment, or if you would agree to visit me at the Embassy . . . my time is yours. I came all the way from the Outer Cloud, specifically to seek you. Perhaps you could join me for dinner—if you feel able to eat, so soon after so full a treatment."

Behrooz Wolf stared at the other man. Leo Manx had the piebald look of the fourth-generation Cloudlander, brown freckles on a chalk-white hairless skin. His build was thin and angular, with overlong arms and bowed, skinny legs. "I can eat," he said at last. "Provided it's Earth food—none of your rotten Cloud synthetics."

"Very well," Manx replied without hesitation, but there was a sudden half-humorous twist of the mouth and the flicker of an eyelid. Like any Cloudlander, Manx was disgusted by the thought of food made from anything beyond single-celled organisms. Bey Wolf had insisted on an Earth meal more to gauge Manx's seriousness of purpose than anything else. But now, on the basis of the flimsiest of evidence, he decided that he rather liked Leo Manx. (Nobody could be all bad who recognised Shakespeare.)

"Why not?" he said. "I'll come and see you. I've nothing better to do, and I haven't been outside for a long time."

"Then I await your convenience." Manx nodded and disappeared from the screen.

Wolf consulted his internal clock. Until that moment he had no idea what time it was—nor what day or month. Midafternoon. If he left in the next half-hour he could be at the Embassy before the evening shower. He skimmed his accumulated mail and messages. Nothing worth worrying about. Better face it, since he was fired by Form Control he had become a nonentity. He dressed quickly and dropped ten floors to street level. There he worked his way over to the fastest slideway, threading a path easily through the crowds and staring around him as he went.

A Biological Equipment Corporation catalog must have been issued since he had fled underground in Old City. The new forms were already appearing on the streets, squarer shoulders, more prominent genitals, and deeper-set eyes for the men, a fuller-bosomed, long-waisted look in the women. As usual, BEC had chosen the styles with great care. They were different enough to be noticeable, but close enough to last year's fashions for the form-change programs to be (just) within the average person's price range.

As Head of the Office of Form Control (*former* Head, he reminded himself) Bey Wolf considered himself above the whims of fashion. He wore his natural form, with minor remedial changes. That made him a rarity. More and more, the people on the slideways all looked the same as each other. It was—soothing? No. Boring. After a few minutes he keyed in his implant to receive the communication channels.

He had a lot of news to catch up on. With his retreat to Old City and his subsequent spell in the form-change tank, he had missed a minor political battle over optimal population levels, the BEC release of a spectacular new avian form, a revised Species Preservation Act that applied to all of Earth, impeachment of the Head of the United Space Federation on charges of corruption, and a heated new exchange of insults between the governments of the Inner System and the Outer System concerning energy rights in the Kernel Ring.

He had also, though this was not news, missed seventy-five days of a perfect summer. But why count time, when he no longer had a job? The purposive feedback process could do no more than respond to his will, so there was no doubt that he *wanted* to live, deep inside. But for what?

How weary, stale, flat, and unprofitable . . . And at that very moment, before the familiar words could complete themselves in his mind, the madness began again. The slideways and the scene from the news broadcasts darkened as another image was overlaid on them.

The Dancing Man. He was back. Dressed in a scarlet, skin-tight suit, he came capering across Bey's field of vision. He danced backwards, with jerky, doll-like movements of his arms and legs. There was curious music in the background, atonal yet tonal, and the man was singing, in a tuneful, alien manner that sounded like Chinese. In the middle of the overlain field of view he paused and grinned out directly at Bey. His teeth were black, and filed to points, and his face was as red as his suit. He spoke again, seeming to ask a question, then waved, turned, and danced backwards out of the field of view.

Bey shivered and put his hand to his head. He had heard Manning's words underneath Old City, but the Colonel had been wrong. Mary's loss had been desperately painful; he thought of her every day, and he would carry her holograph with him always. But something else had driven him over the edge, to seek the solace of the Dream Machine: conviction of his own growing insanity.

Since the Dancing Man had first appeared, he had checked every possible source of the signal. No one else could see it—even when they were viewing the same channel as Bey. Every test for outside signal had proved negative. He had mimicked the Dancing Man's speech, all that he could remember of it, and been told by specialists in linguistics and semiotics that it corresponded to no known language. Worst of all, when Bey went into recording mode the signal vanished. It was never there to be played back. Physicians and psychiatrists were unanimous: the signal was generated within Bey's own head. He was suffering "perceptual disturbance" of a "severe and progressive form, intractable and with a strong negative prognosis."

In other words, he was going crazy. And no one could do a damned thing about it. And it was getting worse. At first no more than a scarlet spot on the scene's horizon, the Dancing Man was getting steadily closer.

And the ultimate irony: as long as he and Mary had lived together, he had been concerned with *her* sanity, *her* mental stability! He was the impervious rock, against which the tides of insanity would break in vain.

Bey saw that he had reached his destination, the deep-delved Embassy of the Outer System. He fled for the express elevators (". . . *then will I headlong run into the Earth; Earth gape. Oh, no, it will not harbor me . . .*") and plunged down, down, down, rejecting his own frantic thoughts and seeking the cool caverns of underground sanctuary.

CHAPTER 3

"I fled him down the nights and down the days,
I fled him down the arches of the years.
I fled him down the labyrinthine ways
Of my own mind . . ."

Francis Thompson

The average surface temperature of real estate in the Outer System is minus 214 degrees Celsius: fifty-nine degrees above absolute zero, where oxygen is a liquid and nitrogen a solid. The mean surface gravity of that same real estate is one four-hundredth of a gee. Mean solar radiation is 1.2 microwatts per square metre, weaker than starlight, a billionth as intense as the Sun's energy received by the Earth.

Faced with those facts, the designers of the Earth Embassy for the Outer System had a choice: should they locate the Embassy off-Earth, and face extensive transportation costs to and from the surface for all Embassy interactions? Or should they accept an Earth environment uncomfortable and highly unnatural to the Ambassador and staff? Since the designers were unlikely to visit Earth themselves, they naturally took the cheaper option. The Embassy that Bey Wolf was visiting sat two hundred meters underground, where temperature, noise and radiation could all be controlled.

Gravity was another matter. He dropped with

stomach-wrenching suddenness through the upper levels. As he did so his surroundings became darker, quieter, and colder. Every surface was soundproofed. At about a hundred and thirty meters the hush became so unnatural and disturbing that Bey found himself listening hard to nothing. He decided he did not like it. Humans make noise, humans clatter and bang and yell. Total silence was inhuman.

Leo Manx was waiting for him in a room so cold that Bey could see his own breath in the air. The Cloudlander remained upright long enough to shake Bey's hand and gesture him to a seat, then sank with a sigh of relief into the depths of a water-chair that folded itself around his thin body. The head that was left sticking out smiled apologetically. "I used a form-change program to adapt me to Earth gravity before I left the Outer System." His shrug emerged as a ripple of the chair's black outer plastic. "I don't think it was quite right."

A piece of your lousy software, by the sound of it. Bey merely nodded and waited.

Manx sat silent for a few moments, and then said abruptly: "My visit to Earth, you know, is for a very specific reason. To see you and to ask for your help—as the Head of the Office of Form Control and Earth's leading expert on form-change theory and practice."

"You're a bit late. I'm not with that office any more."

"I know that is the case. I heard that you had ... resigned your position."

"No need to be diplomatic. I was fired."

The pale head bobbed. "In truth, I knew that also. You may be surprised to learn that from our point of view, your dismissal offers advantages."

"None from my point of view."

"It is my task to convince you otherwise." Leo Manx stretched upwards, his thin neck and hairless head craning like a turtle from the black supporting oval of the chair. "To do so, I must request your silence about what I am to tell you."

"Suppose I refuse to go along with that?" Bey saw the other man's discomfort. "Oh, hell, get on with it. I've spent my whole career not talking about things. I can do it for a while longer."

"Thank you. You will not regret it." Manx subsided in the chair. "Mr Wolf, there has arisen in the Outer System a problem so serious that all knowledge of it is given only on a need-to-know basis. In a few words, there has been a widespread breakdown in the performance of form-change equipment, to the point where the process is being undertaken only in cases of emergency, such as my own visit to Earth."

"Widespread? Not just a machine or two?"

"Hundreds of machines, with rates of malfunction that have been growing rapidly. A year ago, we could point to two or three cases of gross error in results. Today, we have case histories of thousands."

"Then it has to be a general software problem. You don't want me for that. There are others who know more and can give you better guidance."

Manx's eyes, startlingly round and hollow in the absence of eyebrows, looked away. "If you are perhaps thinking of Robert Capman . . . ?"

"I would, but he's on a long-term stellar mission. My suggestion is BEC themselves. Why not call them in?— they'll be as keen to sort this out as you are." Bey tried for an innocent expression. Here was as good a way as any of testing the honesty of the Cloudlander.

Manx looked pained. "We already approached the Biological Equipment Corporation. They sent a team of experts, who reviewed everything we could show them and declared that they could find no evidence of any problem. Unfortunately, we are not convinced that they conducted as thorough a review as one might wish. There has been a long-term disagreement with BEC, as to the proper amount of royalties the Outer System is accruing for the use of BEC's form-change hardware and software systems——"

"They say you stole their ideas, ignored their patents, and infringed their copyrights."

"Well, that is a little crudely put . . . but, yes, you have the gist of their argument." Manx smiled ruefully. "I see that our own security is less than we are inclined to believe."

"In a case like that it is—BEC will tell anyone on Earth who'll listen that the Outer System is robbing them blind."

"Which is certainly a—a——"

"Lie?"

"Exaggeration. A misrepresentation."

"You don't need to persuade me. I don't like monopolies, either, and BEC has one for the Inner System. But you said they did a review of 'everything we could show them.' Like to be more explicit?"

There was a raising of non-existent eyebrows. "You are a very perceptive man. There were a number of units that we could not and did not show to the BEC team."

"Pirated designs?"

"The Outer System prefers to think of them as independent developments. However, I believe it would have made little difference. The anomalous behaviour occurs with rather greater frequency in BEC's own equipment. Yet they insist that everything is working perfectly."

"Did your own engineers watch the BEC tests?"

"Yes. As BEC said, no anomalies were observed. As soon as they left, new peculiar forms were again produced." Manx began to push away the enfolding arms of the chair. "If you would be interested to see some of those forms, I have images here with me . . ."

"No. You'd be wasting your time."

"These forms are extremely strange."

"Dr. Manx, odd forms don't do anything for me. I've seen so many of those over the years, I doubt if you could surprise me." Bey stood up. "I accept that you have a nasty problem, but it's not one that would justify dragging me partway to Alpha Centauri. I lost my job, but I still like Earth. And I doubt if I could do anything to help you."

"How do you know that, without personal observation?"

"I've been around form control for a long time. As I said at the beginning, you have a software problem. The fact that BEC's team couldn't find it—or chose not to—makes no difference. Call 'em again, ask for Maria Sun. If anyone can solve it for you, she can."

Manx stood up too. "Mr. Wolf, it is my opinion that you underestimate both yourself and the difficulty of this problem. But I cannot change your mind about that, here on Earth. Rather allow me to introduce a new variable into the equation. While you were on the way here I asked for and read a copy of your dossier from the Office of Form Control. It is something that I ought to have done earlier. I learned more of your personal circumstances."

"You found out I'm going crazy."

"You are sick. If you know anything of the Outer System, you may know that we are advanced in the treatment of mental illness. That happens to be my own field. If you would agree to travel back with me—merely to observe the phenomena for yourself, for no more than a few days—I will devote my best efforts to your personal problem."

"Sorry. It's still negative." Bey headed for the door, but Leo Manx made a great effort and was there first.

"One more point, Mr. Wolf. And please excuse this importuning. You lived with Mary Walton for seven years. Is it possible that your reluctance to visit the Outer System arises from a fear that you may be obliged to interact with her there?"

Bey eased past the other man, trying not to touch him. "You're a conscientious and persistent man, Dr. Manx. I don't resent that—I respect you for it. I can't answer your question. Maybe I'm afraid I would meet Mary again. But in any case, I still refuse. Tell your superiors that I am honored to be considered."

"Yes, of course. But if by chance you should change your mind——" Manx was calling after Bey as he headed for the elevator. "I will be here on Earth for two more days! Call me, at any hour."

But Bey was already out of earshot. The final question about Mary had got to him more than it should. Was he over her, or wasn't he? Would he turn down a potentially fascinating problem simply because he might be forced to see Mary with the man she had chosen over him?

He was oblivious of the high-acceleration ride to the surface, oblivious of the evening crowds that pushed at him on the slideways. Manx's offer of dinner had never been realized, but in any case Bey had lost his appetite. He skipped dangerously across from high-speed to low-speed track, exited the slideway, and hurried into his apartment. He grabbed a projection cube at random from the file—they were all of Mary, it made little difference—and sat down to view it.

Predictably, it was one he hated to watch, but also one he had viewed again and again. Mary in an amateur musical, dressed in a long gown, bonnet, and parasol, and singing in the sweet, artificial little voice of a young girl. "Let him go, let him tarry, let him sink or let him swim. He doesn't care for me, and I don't care for him. He can go and find another, that I hope he will enjoy, for I'm going to marry a far nicer boy."

Bey felt his heart wither inside him as he watched. Nothing of her had faded; it hurt as much as ever. He was reaching to cut the cube when Mary Walton's demure figure rippled and darkened. A new scene was overlaid on the old and familiar one.

The Dancing Man. Twisting and tumbling across the image, red-clad limbs akimbo. He paused in the middle, nodded at Bey, and made a sing-song, questioning little speech that could almost be understood. Then he was away, skating backwards into the distance, head bobbing and hands waving cheerfully.

The Dancing Man—even here! In the middle of a sequence that Bey had recorded personally, four years ago. How could anyone possibly change that recording? Bey set the projection to the beginning, and forced himself to watch it through again. This time there was no Dancing Man. It was Mary all the way, to that intolerable final line when she set her parasol over her shoulder and waved goodbye.

Bey watched to the bitter end. Then he went across to the communications unit and called Leo Manx.

CHAPTER 4

*"All isolated systems become less orderly when
left to themselves." (This version of the
Second Law of Thermodynamics was offered by
Apollo Belvedere Smith, aged five, to explain
                why his room was in such a mess.)*

"There is one other thing you ought to decide before we
embark." Leo Manx was inspecting both his travelling
companion and Bey Wolf's luggage.

"Namely?"

"Do you want to spend time in a form-change tank on
the way out to the Cloud? If so, we must make sure that
the programs are available."

"You mean, switch to something more like your own
form, for physical comfort?" Bey shook his head. "I like
this form, and I know it tolerates low gravity and cold
pretty well."

"That was not the reason for my suggestion." Manx
took Bey's little travelling case and floated it one-handed
across to secure it in the cargo hold. "My concern is with
the response you may receive from Outer System citizens. It will be apparent to them that you are from Earth,
or at least from the Inner System. The two Federations
are not at war——"

"Yet."

"——but we are certainly locked in an economic strug-

244

gle over rights to the Kernel Ring. There have been skirmishes in the Halo. If you remain in your present form, I foresee some unpleasantness and rudeness when we arrive. You will hear yourself called a Snugger—a Sunhugger Imperialist; there will undoubtedly be sly remarks about your hairy skin."

"Same as you've been getting, when people here call you a bare-faced Cloudlander?" The other man's reaction was no more than a moment's twitch of the lip, but Bey was used to reading subtle signals. "Dr. Manx, if you got by on Earth without form-change, I can do the same in the Outer System. I'm used to criticism and sneaky comments."

"Actually, I went through a small form-change on the way here; a very minor adaptation—otherwise Earth gravity would have been too much for me. But it was quite different in my case. I knew I would be here only for a little while, until you accepted or rejected our plea." Manx caught Bey's expression, and realized he had made a mistake. "Of course, you have agreed to stay only long enough with us for a preliminary evaluation of the problem. I realise that. But I was hoping, if you find the situation intriguing enough, that you might prolong your stay. Not only for our sakes; for yours. If one has never visited the Outer System, there are many things to see and do."

"No sales pitch. If you're wrong, it's not worth it. If you're right, I can use a program when we get there."

"That is true."

"So what are we waiting for?"

Manx gestured out of the port. Bey suddenly realised that they were not waiting. Earth had disappeared, and they were already passing the Moon. The McAndrew inertialess drive had been switched on while they were talking, and they were accelerating away from the Sun at more than a hundred gees.

"Twelve days to cross-over point, then another twelve to the Opik Harvester," said Manx. "It is not the nearest Harvester to Sol, but it has a large number of form-change units on it. I have discussed our destination with my superiors, and we agree that it is a good place to begin."

"How far out?"

"Twenty-six thousand astronomical units—about four trillion kilometers."

Manx called a stylised three-dimensional figure onto the display screen. It was a representation of Sol-space geometry. Even with a logarithmic radial scale, the graphic occupied one full wall of the cabin. The Inner System, comprising everything out to Persephone, was crowded within a Sun-centred sphere of ten billion kilometer radius. The Halo reached out two hundred times as far, a diffuse torus within which the Kernel Ring sat as a well-defined narrow annulus. The Oort Cloud, home for the Outer System, was a vast sprawling spherical region, approaching the Halo on its inner limit, but seven times as large as its outer edge, stretching a third of the way to the nearest star.

Manx pointed to a cluster of color-coded habitats in the Outer System, and to the arrowed flight path that extended to them from the Earth-Moon environment. "The Opik Harvester is fairly near the inner edge of the Cloud, but a safe distance from the Kernel Ring. No danger of trouble from there. As you can see from our trajectory, we'll be flying rather close to the Ring itself in about nine days." He gave Bey a sideways glance. "I thought you might be personally interested in taking a look at that."

Bey was learning. Leo Manx's omissions—rarely accidental—were more informative than his speeches. Manx was too self-conscious or diplomatic to say some things himself. He preferred to leave logical loopholes, then answer questions.

"I have never been near the Kernel Ring," said Bey. "I assume you know that."

"Your background summary says as much."

"Then it should also show that I know little about Kerr-Newman black holes, and even less about how we use the kernels themselves as energy sources."

"That is indeed the case." Polite, and non-committal. Bey would have to dig deeper.

"So what makes you think I have any personal interest at all in looking at the Kernel Ring? Do you think you see a connection with my ... other problems?" Damn it, the habit was catching. He was getting as indirect as Manx. "I mean, with my hallucinations."

Instead of answering at once, Manx sat for a few moments, thinking. "That depends on the cause of those hallucinations," he said at last. "I hope that we will explore that subject together on this journey, when we have plenty of time. But answer me one question, if you will. When did your problems begin? Was it before or after Mary Walton left you?"

"Long after. Four months after."

"In that case, I do not believe that the Kernel Ring is connected with your hallucinations."

It was like pulling teeth. "But the Ring *is* connected with Mary?"

"Possibly. Probably." Manx was getting there, Bey could see the decision reflected in the expressions on the other man's face. "Mr Wolf, I deduce that in addition to knowing little about the Kernel Ring, you also are unfamiliar with customs in the Outer System. According to Colonel Hamming—whom I did not find to be a particularly sensitive person——"

"He's an asshole."

"A felicitous description. He told me Mary Walton left to 'run off to Cloudland with one of you guys', and the inference was that he was referring to a person from the Outer System, one that she met on a Lunar Cruise. Is that your own understanding of the situation?"

"It is."

"Did you ever meet this person?"

"Not a person. A man. No, I didn't meet him. If I had I'd probably have tried to cut him in two."

"So you are unfamiliar with his appearance? Now, if you will permit me a more personal question. You knew Mary Walton better than anyone else. Was she a woman impressed by appearances?—how a person looked, whether he was handsome?"

"I guess so." More stalling! Bey cursed his own reluctance to give straight answers. "Yes, she was. Too impressed. Looks mattered to Mary."

"Very well. You know what men from the Outer System look like. I suspect that I am a fairly typical example, and although I am quite happy with my own appearance"—Manx looked admiringly at his skinny body and bowed legs —'I know that I am far from the standards of beauty currently popular on Earth."

"That's irrelevant. Handsomeness is easy, all it takes is a little while in a form-change tank."

"Very true. *If* a person wishes to make such a change. I certainly did not, and you had a similar reaction when it came to modifying your own appearance to match an Outer System form. However, there is a more important point here. Although the man that Mary Walton ran off with *could* have picked an appearance that appealed to her, he would have had to do so *in advance* of meeting with her on that Lunar Cruise."

"I see where you're heading. You are questioning that he was from the Outer System?"

"More than that. Mr. Wolf, our citizens do not indulge in Lunar Cruises. To us, it would have as much attraction as a tour of Old City would offer the average Earth person."

"But some people might do it. Just to be different."

"They might." Manx looked away, refusing to meet Bey's eyes again. "But they did not. I have rather more information than I have so far revealed to you. Before I left our Earth Embassy, I checked all our visitors to Earth-Moon space for the previous four years. There was no one from the Outer System who went on a Lunar Cruise. Whoever Mary Walton met, he was not from our Federation."

"So where does that leave us?"

"With no more than a speculation. I have of course no direct evidence——"

"Talk, man! I can stand it."

"I do not think you will find your Mary in the Cloud, even if you plan to look for her there. The most likely person to have offered a false identification, and to be interested in Earth-Moon space as a possible source of energy needs, would be a renegade."

"You mean a rebel? An inhabitant of the Kernel Ring?"

"Precisely. The inhabitants of the Ring practise a curious co-existence. Rebel outposts are scattered here and there through its whole volume, side-by-side with peaceful settlers, energy prospectors, and free-space Podder colonies. The Ring admits every form of oddity, every human shape attainable by the form-change equipment. You should look there."

"For someone who works in the high-gravity environment around shielded kernels. Someone whose unmodified appearance is more like mine than yours."

"You follow my thoughts admirably." Manx moved the cursor on the display to delineate the annulus of the Kernel Ring. "Here. To conclude, it is my opinion that Mary Walton is not to be found anywhere in the Outer System. She is *here*. In the Halo, almost certainly somewhere in the Kernel Ring itself."

"Shacked up with a damned outlaw."

"I'm afraid so. A dangerous man, Mr. Wolf, who recognises the sovereignty of neither my Federation nor your own. A man who would not hesitate to kill either of us. Mr. Wolf! Do you hear me?"

Bey was no longer listening. As Manx had moved the cursor across the display, a familiar figure had appeared on top of it. He was sitting cross-legged, riding the little blue arrow and waving jauntily out at the two men. His song sounded a little different, but still just beyond comprehension.

The scarlet suit was brighter than ever. The expression on his grinning face was more than usually smug. Forget that hope, it said. It takes a lot more than a move to the Outer System to get rid of the Dancing Man.

CHAPTER 5

> *"Kernel* (def.): A Kerr-Newman black hole, i.e.
> a black hole that is both rotating and
> electrically charged. Kernels are found in nature
> only in the *Kernel Ring* (q.v.) between the
> Inner and Outer Systems. They range in mass
> from a hundred million to ten billion tons."
> —*Webster's New Worlds Dictionary*

At the end of the seventh day Manx began to push for a different approach. He had switched off his recorder and was glaring impatiently at Bey Wolf.

"I suppose you imagine that you are co-operating with me? You are not. I ask you for a full, detailed account of your relationship with Mary Walton, something I must have if I am to help you end your hallucinations. What do I get?" He tapped the recorder. "Monosyllables. Two or three sentence descriptions of complex interactions. Evasion. Obfuscation. Equivocation. Deliberately or not, you are prevaricating."

"I'm sorry. I don't like to talk about emotional matters. Particularly *those* emotional matters."

"Of course you don't. No one does, unless they have quite different mental problems. But if there's to be any progress you have to give me information. *Detail*. As much of it as you can. I perceive that you will not do so with simple question-and-answer techniques."

"So we're stuck?" Bey sounded more relieved than upset.

"No, we are not. With your permission, I want to put you into an enhanced recall status."

"That's illegal."

"Not in the Outer System. We have no statutes against self-incrimination."

"Barbaric."

"Perhaps we have less need of them. Stop trying to change the subject by inciting an argument. Will you allow me to induce an enhanced recall state, or will you not?"

Bey looked at him warily. "For how long?"

"If I could tell you that, I might find it unnecessary. A couple of days, maybe more."

"Then I'll miss the transit of the Kernel Ring you want me to see." It was a weak argument, and Bey knew it. Leo Manx was slow but persistent, like the turtle he sometimes resembled, and he would not give up easily.

"That crossing will occur tomorrow. Is it agreed, then? After we complete the transit we will move to enhanced recall technique. If the idea still makes you uncomfortable we can begin with direct reporting, then proceed to stimulated and dream sequences."

Bey nodded. At best it felt like a stay of execution.

The transit of the Kernel Ring was an anticlimax. Even with the highest magnification that the ship's sensors could provide, the Halo was no more than a scattering of misty dots of light. The unshielded kernels themselves gave off large amounts of energy, gigawatts for even the most massive and least active, but they radiated at wavelengths too short for the human eye to see. The shielded kernels were by design invisible. It was difficult to imagine people living in that emptiness; still less that it was the home of ruthless pirates, savages who might come boiling up from the darkness to take over cargo or passenger ships as they made their out-of-ecliptic transit from the Inner System to Cloudland. Least of all could

Bey imagine Mary, his lively, cosmopolitan Mary, enduring that waste of nothingness.

"You see with an Earthman's distorting perspective," said Manx, in answer to Bey's sceptical reaction. "To you, the Halo is nearly empty. To me, or to anyone from the Outer System, it is packed with life and energy."

"You use an odd definition of 'packed'."

"Do the calculation for yourself. There are millions or billions of people living in the Halo—we have no idea how many, since there is no central government there. Compare it with the Outer System. We are about fifty million people, and we know that we are grossly underpopulated. We will be for centuries. Naturally, we crowd together, most of us close to the Harvesters, but were it not for the help of our self-reproducing machines we could not exist. If we spread out evenly, each person in the Outer System would have a region sixty times as big as the whole of your Inner System to move around in. By comparison, the Halo is packed. It teems with life. Much too crowded for us."

Current accommodation allotment on Earth: 100 cubic meters per person. Bey thought of that, and wondered why the Outer and Inner System were arguing over rights to the Kernel Ring. From what Manx was saying, there was no way that the average Cloudlander would ever be comfortable with the "cramped" lifestyle in the Ring, and no way that the average Earth-dweller would be able to accept so much empty, frightening space.

"The argument is over energy—but surely there are more than enough kernels for everyone?"

"I wonder that myself," said Manx. "And there is an element of presumption that leaves me uncomfortable. Both the Inner System and the Outer System governments assume that they could if they wished displace the present rulers of the Kernel Ring. I am not sure that is the case. Have you heard of a leader called Ransome, and of Ransome's Hole?"

"Black Ransome? According to Earth's newscasts, he's just fiction."

"If they believe that, they have never left Earth. I

know of a half-dozen prospectors working the Halo who have lost cargo to Black Ransome. Some have lost ships also. It is a reasonable speculation that some have lost their lives, too, and are in no position to report anything. At any rate, true or not, the Outer System seethes with rumours about Ransome. Ships found empty and gutted, cargoes taken, crew and passengers ejected to empty space."

"If he's such a problem, why don't you send a force in to take care of him?"

Manx waved at the displays. "Find him, and maybe we could do it. His base is as much a mystery as he is. Ransome's Hole—or maybe it's really Ransome's *Hold*, everything about him is hearsay—is supposed to be somewhere in the Kernel Ring. But where? You're talking a volume of space thousands of times as big as the whole Inner System. And if we found him, I'm not sure any force that we sent in would win. Ransome's Hole is supposed to have its own defense system, able to handle anything we could throw at it. And he might have allies. The whole Halo is a melting-pot, the place that anyone can flee to if they find civilization intolerable."

"Or we find *them* intolerable." Bey bent to the high-resolution sensors with new interest. Was one of those spots of light, disappearing fast behind the speeding ship, some huge, well-armed base of rebel operations? And what else was down there, hidden in the darkness? Perhaps some lost colony of ancient doctrines, vanished from the rest of the System. "Home of lost causes, and forsaken beliefs, and unpopular names, and impossible loyalties." Who had said that? One of the Victorians.

"Black Ransome." Bey looked up. "Where did he come from, the Inner or the Outer System?"

"We don't even know that much. He must have plenty of energy, because he never takes the kernels from the ships. But where does he get his food supplies, or his other equipment? We just don't have answers to those questions."

The Kernel Ring was fading behind them. Leo Manx turned off the displays. Bey saw that he was holding the polished black cylinder of an enhancement recall unit, and smiling in what looked like anticipation.

"And we will find nothing about Ransome here, Mr. Wolf. We are past the region where the ship is in danger of attack. So we can now proceed to possibly more productive work. When you are ready . . ."

. . . I met her at an open-air historical event, seven years and four months ago, when there was an exhibit of old Earth animals. It was the first time they showed results of breeding back successfully beyond the Cretaceous, and the big extinct forms had attracted a lot of interest.

I say I met her, but that is at first an overstatement. I was in an overview booth, with half an eye open for illegal forms (not much chance of that; I hadn't seen one for years) when I saw her, though she was too far away for me to speak to her. But my eye picked her out at once.

No, it's not that I was attracted to Mary Walton at that point, not at all. I was *puzzled* by her. I had been in the Office of Form Control for more than half my life, and one thing that I had learned to do, whether I wanted to or not, was to monitor for anomalies. It was an unconscious act with me, and it's more than half the trick to spotting an illegal form.

In Mary's case, I knew there was something peculiar, though it certainly wasn't something illegal.

It was this. As you can see, I choose to hold my own appearance to about age thirty, but that's unusual on Earth. Most people like to look between twenty and twenty-five, with twenty-two the most popular age. Now, sometimes you will get older people who don't like that idea. They want to separate themselves from the real youngsters for some activities, and they spend at least part of their time in a form corresponding to age forty or fifty—even more, though anyone over sixty is very uncommon, unless they have other problems and drop the use of formchange treatments altogether. You saw the results of that when you picked me up in Old City.

Mary Walton was wearing the form of a woman

between forty-five and fifty, and dressed in the clothing style of a woman of that age; but I could tell from other indicators—eye movement, laughter, body posture—that she was actually a lot *younger* than she looked. It intrigued me. Why would anyone deliberately choose a form older than their true age?

While I was watching her, we had a minor problem with staffing, and I had to look elsewhere. But as soon as I could, I went to the place where I had last seen her, next to the big enclosure with the gorgosaurus in it. She was still there—trying to climb into the enclosure. If she had succeeded ... the animal was carnivorous, four metres tall, two tons in weight.

I arrived just in time to drag her clear. And to arrest her. And then to introduce myself.

She told me she was an actress, she was doing it for publicity. I suppose I knew, right from the first moment, that she was crazy. Insane, hopelessly unaware of reality.

It made no difference. Others will say that Mary was not conventionally attractive, that she deliberately chose to look exotic and a little peculiar. When she was living a part—she didn't act parts, she lived them—she might form-change to any age, and do anything she felt fitted the character. Some of them were strange, sometimes disgusting.

As I say, to me it made no difference. From the first moment she looked down at me from the fence, when I had hold of her leg and I was pulling her back by her long grey skirt, I was lost. I was spoiling her publicity plan, but she didn't look annoyed. She grinned down at me, with her head on one side and that ridiculous round grey hat with a feather in the side of it, and the blond curly hair pushing out underneath it—she was naturally fair, though she preferred parts that made her a brunette. And then she let herself go limp, and she came rolling off the fence in that old-fashioned grey cloth dress, and knocked me flat to the ground.

I was smitten even before I got up, and I knew it; but I wouldn't have done one thing about it. I have never been able to let people know how I feel. I have rationalised that, to the point where it does not usually bother me. Often, I insist it is a virtue. But not this time. I wanted Mary, but Mary was an unattainable prospect.

It wasn't just my inability to speak. I knew, even if she didn't, that I was three times her age. That alone should have made the whole thing impossible. Not for Mary. I didn't realise it at the time, but things like that made no difference at all to her. She was so much in her own world, and that world was so far from reality, age wasn't even a variable. When she did find out how old I was, she just said, "Well, that means I'll have at most fifty years of you, instead of a hundred."

How do you reply to something like that?

If you are a wise man, you don't even try. You grab the chance—it only comes once—and make the most of it.

That first day, I began to arrest her. She talked me out of it in about two minutes, and took me home to her apartment. I never left.

I had no idea at the time how sick in the head she was. That emerged little by little, as we became closer. Maybe it was a lot more obvious to others than to me. I always had the blinders on—I still do. When an old friend of mine, Park Green, came to visit from the Moon, we went to see one of Mary's performances. I asked him what he thought of it, and he shook his head, and said she was good, but he could see the skull beneath the skin. I hated him for that, and I never told Mary; but he was right.

That may have been the thing that limited her as an actress. She could play high drama, or artificial, mannered comedy, or broad farce—she was a wonderful comedienne, but she didn't much care for those parts. What she could not portray were simple people, because there was nothing simple inside her that she could build on. It limited her. She was always busy, always working, but in the end I know that she was disappointed with her reputation.

You know, I honestly believe that I was good for Mary. In our years together she never had to go for official treatment. There'd be times when she went non-linear, and when that happened I'd drop everything I was doing and stay with her constantly. And she'd come out of it. But those times became more and more frequent, and more and more severe.

When she suddenly told me, without a day's notice, that she was going off for a Lunar Cruise, I was delighted. Mary was always at her best when she had a new environment to learn, something fresh to challenge her. She was becoming more and more upset by crowds—an odd omen for an actress, but I didn't read it. The Moon would offer plenty of peace and change of pace.

She went. She called once, to say that she was not coming back, she was heading for the Outer System. And that was all.

I just about came apart.

Four months later, the Dancing Man appeared for the first time. And I came apart completely.

Bey lay back in his chair and looked up at Leo Manx. "Well?"

"Good." Manx was examining his records. "Very good."

"You have enough?"

"Goodness, no." Manx was incredulous. "This is a *start*—the first iteration. Now we can perhaps begin to learn something about you and your relationship with Mary. Give me another couple of days. Then it may be time to worry about your little dancing friend."

CHAPTER 6

"Entropy is missing information."
—*Ludwig Boltzmann*
"Entropy is information."—*Norbert Wiener*
"Entropy is leftovers."—*Apollo Belvedere Smith*

One quarter of the way to the edge of the Oort Cloud;
it did not sound too far. Call it 26,000 astronomical units,
and it became more substantial. Call it four trillion kilometers; it was then an inconceivable number, but no
more than a number.

To appreciate the distance from Earth to the Opik
Harvester it was necessary to have direct sensory inputs.
Bey Wolf looked back the way they had come and
searched for the Sun.

There it was. But it was the Sun diminished, Sol with
no discernible disc, Sol dwindled to the bright, brittle
point of Venus on a frosty Earth night.

"The element of fire is quite put out. The sun is lost,
and earth, and no man's wit, can well direct him where
to look for it." Bey, still staring back the way they had
come, took no comfort from the old words and longed
for the cosy familiarity of the Inner System. At his side,
Leo Manx was looking the other way, scanning the starfield ahead.

"Eh-hey! There we are! Ten more minutes, we'll be
home." He had already shed his loose travel suit in

258

favour of a pale yellow one-piece. His hairless arms and legs stuck out from it like the limbs of a gigantic and excited cricket. "There, Mr. Wolf. See it now? The Harvester!"

He spoke as of a first sighting, but he had already pointed out the Opik Harvester to Bey an hour before, as a dark spot occulting a tiny patch of stars. But now, as the clumsy bulk drifted closer, glimmering with feeble surface lights, his excitement was increasing.

Bey followed the pointing finger. For eyes conditioned by the constraints of gravity, the shape of the Harvester was difficult to comprehend. A dozen spheres clustered loosely to form a central grouping, but their coupling was done by the invisible bonds of electromagnetic fields, and the configuration constantly changed. Long, curving arms cantilevered away from the central nexus, reaching out to bridge a gulf that had no end. The final silver girders and antennae of those arms grew gradually thinner and less substantial, fading so slowly into void that their terminal points could not be seen.

According to Leo Manx, the big middle sphere was roughly twenty miles across. Bey could not verify that. It was impossible to gain any sense of scale from the Harvester's main features. The whole structure had been built by self-replicating machines of widely differing sizes, and designed to be run by them. Humans had been late arrivals, occupying the Harvesters only when the final step of life-support systems had been added.

The ship's McAndrew drive had been switched off two hours earlier, ending the signal silence introduced by the ionized plasma that propelled it. The communications unit had at once begun to scroll and chatter, urging Bey and Manx to join a meeting that was already in progress.

Manx, happy to be back in "decent" gravity, watched Bey's clumsy movements for a few seconds as they disembarked, then grabbed him by the arm. "Hold tight. You can practise later." He towed a weightless Bey along a succession of identical corridors, all unoccupied and showing no signs of human presence.

"Almost ninety thousand people," Manx said, to Bey's

question. "The Harvester is a major population center of the Outer System. About ten million service machines, I imagine, though no one keeps count. They make whatever new ones they decide they need, it has been that way since the first ones were sent here from the Inner System. I've sometimes wondered what the machines would have done if people had never arrived in the Cloud. Would they have eventually downed tools and quit, or would they have found some other justification for continuing to modify the Cloud? If there were no humans to use the biological products of the Harvesters, would the machines have found it necessary to invent us?"

To Bey's relief, they had reached a region of noticeable gravity. He was not too keen on the other implications of that—a shielded kernel had to be somewhere near, and that much pent energy made him uncomfortable. But it was nice to have an up and a down again, even if it were only a twentieth of a gee. He followed Leo Manx through a final door, on into a long room with a curved floor.

Three Cloudlanders were sitting at a little round table, each dressed in the uniform of a lemon-colored one-piece suit.

Wolf at once recognized the woman facing him. Given the frequency with which she appeared on Earth newscasts, it would be hard not to do so. Cinnabar Baker was one of the three most powerful people in the Outer System, and a scathing critic of everything that happened closer to the Sun than the inner edge of the Cloud. Her cheerful appearance belied her reputation. There was presumably the thin, gravity-intolerant skeleton of the Cloudlander within her, but in Baker's case it was well covered. She was a vast, smiling woman, maybe two hundred kilos in mass, with a flawless, pale skin. Her hair was thin and close-cropped, revealing the contours of a well-shaped and delicate-looking skull. The clear eyes and fine skin tone gave evidence of regular use of form-change equipment.

She stood up and held out a chubby, dimpled hand.

"Welcome to the Outer System. I am Cinnabar Baker. I'm responsible for the operation of all the Harvesters, including this one. Let me express my appreciation that you agreed to come here, and allow me to introduce you to some of my staff. Sylvia Fernald." She gestured at the woman on her left. "In charge of all software development and control theory in the Outer System. Next to her, Apollo Belvedere Smith—Aybee for short and for preference—my top science advisor and general gadfly. Leo Manx, senior psych administrator and Inner System specialist, you know already—probably all too well after your trip together from the Inner System."

"Behrooz Wolf," muttered Bey. It hardly seemed necessary. They knew who he was. How many hairy strangers were there on the Harvester, half a meter shorter than everyone else and with four times the muscles? Bey greeted the others, making his instinctive and immediate assessment of their ages, original appearance, and major form changes. There were anomalies, points to be thought about later, particularly in the case of Apollo Belvedere Smith, who was extra tall, rail-thin, and glowering angrily at Bey for no discernible reason. But for the moment Bey was pondering a more substantial question.

Cinnabar Baker was here, with three of the Cloud's scientists, technicians, and administrators, all apparently tops in their fields. They had been summoned to worry a technical problem of malfunctioning form-change equipment. Bey had come to know and like Leo Manx, with his quirky sense of humour and his shared interest in Earth history and literature. He felt that a perfect choice had been made, Manx was just the right combination of seniority, experience and intellect to work with Bey on form-change questions. But the others? It made more sense for Bey and Leo Manx to go straight to work. Why a top science advisor? Most of all, why Cinnabar Baker? She was far more senior than the problem justified.

Bey felt the stir of an old feeling, something that had been dormant for too long within him: suspicion; and with it, the *frisson* of powerful curiosity.

"Sylvia Fernald and Leo Manx will be your principal day-to-day contacts," Baker was saying. "If you find it necessary to travel through the System, one or both of them will accompany you. Aybee usually travels with me, and I have to be all over the place; but you will have first call. Any time you require him, he's at your service. That's enough, Aybee"—the man across the table had grunted his disapproval—"I told you the rules. Tell us what you need to know about our form-change programs, Mr. Wolf, and we will do our best to provide it."

Bey sat down between Leo Manx and Aybee Smith. He wanted to see more of the Harvester, but that could wait. It was time for a direct approach. "Naturally, I would like an overview of the problem you've been having with form-change equipment and programs. But that's not my first priority."

They were staring at him in surprise.

"I'd like to know what's going on here," he continued. "I don't think I have been given the full story. There are factors that have not been described to me." He caught Cinnabar Baker's quick look at Leo Manx, and the other's tiny shake of the head. "I must know what they are."

Apollo Belvedere Smith gave a grunt of approval. "Hey. I didn't want to bring you here, but mebbe you can do something useful after all." He turned to Baker. "Was I right, or was I right? He cottoned. I guess I should brief the Wolfman."

Cinnabar Baker shook her head. "You'll go too fast and leave too much out."

"Naw. If he's smart as he needs to be, he'll follow."

"Maybe. But it's still no. You can impress him with your brilliance later. I want Fernald to brief him. But before we begin." She stared straight at Bey, and he saw past the fat, friendly exterior. Cinnabar Baker was a person with drive to match her bulk, a woman who made up her mind in a hurry. "I won't ask you to pledge secrecy when you go back home, Behrooz Wolf," she went on. "Just don't talk about this while you're around here. We want to minimize alarm—panic, if you prefer that word. Now I'm starting to sound mysterious. Go on, Fernald, let's have it. Tell him what's been happening."

"Everything?"

"The whole story."

While they were talking, Bey had taken a closer look at Aybee Smith. His appearance suggested a man in his early twenties, but that of course meant little. Bey listened, looked, integrated posture, speech style, and the exchange between Aybee and Cinnabar Baker, and came up with a surprising conclusion: Apollo Belvedere Smith was a teenager, still under twenty. Yet he was Baker's top science adviser. Which meant he had to be at least half as smart as he seemed to think he was.

"Background first." Sylvia Fernald had moved around to face Bey. She was a good and logical briefer, and she began with a summary of what Bey had already heard in fair detail from Leo Manx. Three years ago there had been problems with form-change processes. Humans emerged from the tanks either with an incorrect final form, or in just the same state as when they went in. The problem had not attracted much interest at first, since a repeat of the form-change process would always lead to the desired result.

That had become less true in the past two years. Deviations became more pronounced, and repeat treatments often led to new anomalies. One year ago the first deaths had occurred in the form-change tanks. Every attempt to trace the problem had failed. The numbers of deaths and abnormalities were now growing exponentially.

Wolf was hearing little that was a surprise, and his main attention was concentrated on the speaker. Sylvia Fernald had chosen neither the walking skeleton of Leo Manx, nor the roly-poly bulk of Cinnabar Baker. She was slim, but not skinny, and incredibly ugly by Earth standards. She towered over Bey by a half-meter or more, with a gawky, angular build that seemed all spidery arms and legs. Like Baker, she wore her carroty-red hair short, swept way back from a high, pale forehead. But unlike the others at the table she had eyebrows, pale sandy arches that emphasized the size and brightness of her deep-set grey eyes and the sharp angle of her thin, jutting nose. Bey ignored the overall unpleasant impression, did his usual summation of variables, and decided she was on the young side of early middle age.

"How many cases, total?" he said, when she paused.

She hesitated, and looked at Baker who nodded. "Tell him."

"Nearly eighty thousand."

"My God. That's more than we've had on Earth in a century and a half."

"I know. And remember, that's out of a total population of fifty million, not your fifteen billion."

"And getting worse. Can you provide me with the rates of change?"

Sylvia Fernald nodded, after another quick look at Cinnabar Baker. "That's not the end of it, Mr. Wolf. I'm not an expert on the technology of the Inner System, but here our form-change systems, hardware and software, are the most delicate devices we have. They have to be shielded against interference, and there's triple redundancy and error-checking in every electronic signal."

Bey nodded. "Same on Earth. I'd be amazed if the procedures and the error-correcting codes are any different. I don't see how they could be. Form-change won't tolerate transmission errors. It's so delicate that an error rate of one bit in ten to the twelfth is enough to show. Nothing else comes close in sensitivity."

"Not on Earth, perhaps," said Cinnabar Baker. "But remember, here in the Outer System we are far more dependent on all kinds of feedback control systems. Go on, Fernald. The whole story."

"Three years ago we had our first problems with form-change processes. That was bad. But two years ago, other things began to go wrong. On a big scale. There are now billions of tons of hydrogen cyanide floating free near the edge of the Halo. The whole product line from the Kuiper Harvester went sour on us. It was supposed to produce aldehydes and alcohols from pre-biotic bodies in the Cloud, but the program went wrong, the automatic checks didn't work, and the first thing we knew was when a crewed surveyor reported anomalous spectral signatures."

"A year's production down the drain," said Baker. "And five years more work before we'll be able to clean it up."

"Another Harvester is producing the wrong materials," said Sylvia Fernald. "We caught that early, with no damage. We're busy now, checking the other thirty. We've also had signs of instability in a kernel control system; gigawatts of raw radiation if one of those got away. And oddest of all, nonsense reports have been coming in from our remote monitoring systems. They're scattered all over the System. Either our communications are generating batches of spurious signals, or space in the Outer System is filled with bizarre . . . things."

"Things?"

Aybee Smith produced a humourless laugh. "Yeah. Things. Tell him, Sylv."

"Visual phenomena." Sylvia Fernald was clearly uncomfortable with her own words. "Impossible events. I don't believe in them, myself, but the people who report them do."

"Come on, Sylv—you're stalling." Aybee Smith grinned fiercely at Bey. "How about a Space Dog—a blood-red hound running across Sagittarius, filling five degrees of the sky? It was reported from Spanish Station, on the other side of the Sun. Would you believe that?"

"No, I wouldn't." Bey looked at Cinnabar Baker, but her face was serious and she showed no sign of interrupting. "It's ridiculous."

"Right. So how about a flaming blue sword, down near the edge of the Halo? Or a rain of blood, sleeting across Orion. Or a great snake, wrapped around the Kernel Ring and swallowing its own tail?"

"How many people reported seeing these?"

"People?" Aybee Smith shook his head in disgust. "Wolfman, people are flaky. They'll see anything, or say they do. Look at you, you prove my point. You've been having visions, but they're right there inside your skull—

no one else sees 'em, right? Right. So if it was just *people*, I'd say the hell with it, they're all crazy—no offense—and who cares what they say they see. But this is different. These were *instrument* readings, not people babble. Sensors *recorded* this stuff. People only saw it later, when they looked at the files. We're talking serious here, not just crazy. You know what a lot of the people who've heard about this say? They don't say phenomena, they say *portents*. How do you like that?"

Bey was listening, but half his attention was elsewhere. Again, something was not adding up. It took a few seconds to recognise what it was, and turn again to Cinnabar Baker. "This has been going on for years?"

"More than two years. But getting worse, bit by bit. It sounds like nonsense, I know, but with everything else going on I have to take it seriously." She paused. "You're skeptical. I'm not surprised. But believe me, neither Sylvia Fernald nor Aybee is exaggerating or inventing."

"I do believe you. But I'm thinking we're still both playing games. Let me tell you something you may not care to hear." Wolf nodded at Leo Manx. "When he asked me to take a look at your form-change problems, I refused. Then an hour later I called him up, and agreed. So why did I change my mind? I'm not an idiot, even though you may think I act like one. Well, I left Earth because I knew that if I didn't, I'd be back in Old City in less than a week. I came to a place where I couldn't do that, even if I wanted to. I was going crazy there—maybe I'm still going crazy."

"I do not agree." Leo Manx sounded comfortingly confident.

"We'll see. Either way, I didn't feel I was cheating you. Crazy or not, I know form-change theory and practise as well as anyone. So I would get away from Earth, and maybe lose my hallucinations—you can dismiss them as nothing, but I couldn't. And maybe you would get help with your problem. That would be a fair exchange. Except that you haven't been honest with me. You're having trouble with form-change, sure, but now you're admitting your problem is much more general. *All* your signals and communications are screwed up. Form-change just happens to be unusually sensitive, signal distortions may show up there first."

"That is probably correct." Cinnabar Baker was not embarrassed.

"So now let's look at things from your point of view. I know form-change, but I sure as hell won't solve your other problems. You ought to have experts in bifurcation theory, in optimal control theory, in signal encoding and error correction, in catastrophe theory. Those are not my fields."

"I agree."

"So why don't you get the right people, people who already know the Outer System?"

"For this reason." Cinnabar Baker gestured to Aybee Smith, who took a thin card from his pocket and passed it to Bey. "Do you recognise any of those names, Mr. Wolf?"

Bey scanned it briefly, noting his own name half-way down. "I know two-thirds of them. You're certainly on the right track. The ones from the Inner System are top people. If the ones from here are comparable, you've got the best systems talent of the solar system on that list."

"I'm glad you agree with Aybee's judgement. He made the list, it's good to know he gets something right." Baker waited for Aybee Smith's indignant snort, then continued. "We tried to obtain the services of all those people. Every one."

"And they refused to help? I'm surprised, if you told them what you've just told me."

"No, Mr. Wolf." The real Cinnabar Baker was showing through, powerful and deadly serious. "They did not refuse. They had no opportunity to do so, because we had no chance to tell them. Of the twenty-seven names on that list, twelve are dead. Seven are hopelessly insane. And seven have disappeared. Our attempts to trace them, assisted when appropriate by officials of the Inner System, have all failed. That makes twenty-six. You, Mr. Wolf, are the twenty-seventh."

She stood up slowly, a massive and massively determined woman. "And now I am holding nothing back from you. You know what we know, except for the details. Do you agree with my view, that you have special motivation to work on and solve this problem?"

CHAPTER 7

"The emitted particles have a thermal spectrum corresponding to a temperature that increases rapidly as the mass of the black hole decreases. For a black hole with the mass of the Sun the temperature is only about a ten-millionth of a degree above absolute zero. The thermal radiation leaving a black hole with that temperature would be completely swamped by the general background level of radiation in the universe. On the other hand, a black hole with a mass of a billion tons would release energy at the rate of 6,000 megawatts, equivalent to the output of six large nuclear power plants."

—Stephen Hawking

The builders, caretakers, and first inhabitants of the Harvesters worked around the clock, without thought of rest. Bey Wolf was beginning to wonder if the human occupants were expected to follow the same schedule.

When the conference with Cinnabar Baker was over he had been settled into a huge but pleasant set of rooms complete with form-change unit and extended library access. Leo Manx, who took him there, pointed out that the quarters provided a fortieth of a gee sleeping environment. He obviously expected Bey to be delighted.

Bey, knowing that the source of the local gravitational field could only be a power kernel, no more than thirty meters below his feet, was not pleased. The triple shielding on a Kerr-Newman black hole had never failed—yet; but according to Sylvia Fernald, several in Cloudland had recently come close. At thirty meters, a few gigawatts of hard radiation wouldn't just kill him; it would dissolve him, melt his flesh from his bones before he knew what was happening.

Bey was tired by the journey and the novelty of the Harvester, and glutted with new information. He wanted to lie down for a while and digest what he had learned; but Leo Manx showed no signs of leaving.

"Sylvia Fernald and Aybee Smith will both be excellent colleagues," he said. He had stretched himself out on Bey's bed, just long enough for him, and closed his eyes. "But there are things about them that you should know before we begin. Aybee is extremely able, but a little immature."

A very comfortable bed, apparently. Bey coveted it. "He's just a kid."

"Exactly. Nineteen years old, but more knowledgeable and scientifically creative than anyone else in the Outer System. You may rely on him for science, but not for judgement."

"I'll remember. What about Sylvia Fernald?"

"She is more mature and also more complex. Her judgment on some of the subjects we discussed today may not be sound."

"Fifty-five years old?"

Manx lifted his head from the bed to stare at Wolf. "Fifty-six, as I recall. Are you able to do that with anyone?"

"I don't know. Probably. I've had lots of form-change experience. Why is she suspect?"

"You saw the list of names of people who died or disappeared. One of them, Paul Chu, was Sylvia's consort for many years. I believe they planned to become parents. But he vanished without trace six months ago, on a routine trip to the edge of the Halo."

"The Halo again."

"I know. I have had the same thought. But without evidence . . ."

"We'll have to look for evidence."

"Certainly." Manx lay silent, eyes closed, for another minute or two. He sighed. "You know, I was originally very doubtful about my trip to Earth; but it was a very good idea. Before I went, I always suspected that deep inside I was by nature an Earthman. Your history is so fascinating, and Earth is the origin of all the worthwhile cultures and arts. But not until I had made a journey there for myself did I realise that it was not for me. It was not home. *This* is home." He patted the bed and lapsed into another and longer silence.

"I think I'll have a sign made for that far wall," said Bey at last.

"Indeed?"

"Yes. It will say, 'If you have nothing to do, please don't do it here'."

Manx frowned and opened his eyes. "You wish for privacy?"

"I wish for sleep."

Manx sat up reluctantly. "Very well. Then I will leave. But I must mention one other matter of importance to you. I have completed my analysis of your own difficulties."

Fatigue changed to a tingle of anticipation. "The hallucinations? You think you can stop them?"

"No. On the contrary, I am sure I cannot. Because I am convinced that what you have been seeing are not the distorted constructs of your brain. They have been imposed from *without*."

"That's impossible. I've been in situations where I saw that red man, and there were other people watching the same broadcast. They saw nothing. I've seen him on a recorded program, too, then played the same program through a second time. He didn't reappear. And anyway, why would anyone *want* to make me crazy?"

"I don't know. However, I believe that if we can answer the first problem, of *method*, we will have gone far towards answering the second one, of intention. And an induced effect is a *technological* problem, not a psychological one. That offers us recourse. I propose to present the idea at once to Apollo Smith. If I know Aybee, it will intrigue him." He levered himself off the bed, sighed, and nodded to Bey. "And so to bed. Sleep well."

Which, of course, Leo Manx had now made out of the question. Bey turned off the light and lay on the bed (Manx had known what he was doing, it was extremely comfortable), but he no longer felt sleepy. *Induced effects.* He had considered that idea when the Dancing Man had first appeared, but he had dropped it for two good reasons: he could not see how it might be done, and he could not imagine why anyone would want to do it.

After five useless minutes, during which he again concluded that he knew of no way to turn Leo Manx's opinions to useful facts, Bey rose, dumped his clothes into the service hopper, and went through to the shower room. It was sinfully big, the size of a five-person apartment on Earth; no wonder Leo Manx had been crowded there. After a minute of juggling with unfamiliar controls, Bey ran the water as hot as he could stand, then accidentally switched it to an icy downpour. He jumped out of the spray with a scream and turned on the hot air.

As soon as he was dry he realized he had made another mistake. The only clothes offered by the dispenser were more of the pale yellow one-piece suits, too long and too narrow for his body. His own clothes had been eaten by the service hopper, and he could find no sign of shoes anywhere.

Finally he stuffed himself into one of the suits and managed to engage the fasteners. Looking at himself in the mirror was an unwise decision, but he suspected he was already as ugly as he could get by Cloudland standards. Bey left his quarters barefoot, and headed along a corridor that spiralled slowly away from the kernel. He had no idea where he was going, but he felt confident that he could find his way home. There was not likely to be another kernel in the interior of the Harvester, and as long as he followed the kernel's gravity gradients "up" and "down" he could not get lost.

After a few minutes of wandering he found himself in a broad accordion-pleated passage that was pouched and folded like the alimentary canal of some giant beast. That similarity went beyond appearances. Bey knew that the Harvesters prowled the Oort Cloud, seeking bodies high in volatiles and complex organic materials. Once found, these were ingested by the comet-sized maw of the Harvester, for transfer to the interior. They were heated with energy extracted from the power kernel, thawed, and dropped into the internal lake-sized vats, to be stirred and aerated by jets of carbon dioxide and oxygen. In that enzyme-seeded brew, the pre-biotic molecules of the fragments—porphyrins, carotenoids, polypeptides, and cellulose—were converted to edible fats, starches, sugars and proteins.

Bey stood by a viewing port and peered into a bubbling sea of pale yellow-green. Close by him, there was a shudder of moving machinery. A great valve had opened. Hundreds of thousands of tons of broth went streaming along helical cooling tubes, on the way to extraction of water, chlorophylls and yeasts. This batch was near its final stages. Most of the final product would be compressed, packaged into space-proof containers, and launched on the long journey to the Inner System. The Harvesters fed the population of the Cloud itself, but more important, their products were essential to the survival of everyone closer to the Sun. The same food products were the working capital that funded the outflow of technology and finished goods from the teeming Inner System.

And if there were a war, or an embargo? As Bey left that enormous production plant, he could not help wondering what would happen if the supply line failed. At first, nothing would be noticed at the destination. The payloads were transported to the Inner System at only a fraction of a gee acceleration, so they took a long time to get there. There would be food in the pipeline of the delivery system for at least ten years, even if the supply from the Harvesters was cut off today. But then the Inner System would be in real trouble—as much trouble as the Cloud would suffer, if the Inner System were one day to cut off the supply of power kernels, or to refuse to ship out manufactured goods. With such total inter-dependency of the two groups, any talk of war or of breakdown of commerce between them seemed ludicrous. And yet Bey knew that such talk was more and more common, more and more strident.

He had followed the local gravity vector downwards, and now he was almost back at his quarters. But the thought of the Kernel Ring led him to keep going, descending a steep staircase that dropped towards the kernel itself. Within fifteen meters he found himself on a black, seamless sphere, with no visible entry points. He was standing in a thirtieth of a gee field, on the first of the three kernel shields. Nothing organic would survive for a millisecond on the other side of it. Twenty meters or less beneath his feet was the kernel itself, a rapidly rotating black hole held in position using its own electric charge. This one would mass a couple of billion tons. It served as the power source for one whole sphere of the Harvester. Streams of subnuclear particles passed through the kernel's ergosphere, slightly slowed the kernel's rotation, and emerged with their own energy vastly increased.

The power provided by a kernel was large but finite. After maybe twenty years, its angular momentum and rotational energy would be depleted. A "spun-down" black hole with no rotation would continue to radiate according to the Hawking evaporative process, but that energy was far less controlled and useful. It was even a nuisance, since the monitor sensors within the shield needed multiple signal redundancy to assure error-free messages to the outside. A spent kernel was a useless kernel. It had to be "spun up" again to high angular momentum from some other source, or replaced by a new one from the Kernel Ring.

And if the Kernel Ring became inaccessible? Then the Cloudlanders would starve for energy, as surely as the

Inner System would starve for lack of Cloudland food supplies. And yet the Kernel Ring was the least controlled part of the whole System, and it was not clear who had the most rights to it. The Podders, the Halo's migrant spacefarers who lived within their spacesuits? Or maybe it was Black Ransome, waging war against both Cloudlanders and Sunhuggers from the mystery hideaway of Ransome's Hole.

Bey found the train of thought leading him again to Mary. Was she in the Kernel Ring, as Leo Manx insisted? Or was she to be found somewhere *here*, in the unthinkably big volume of the Cloud? If so, the Cloud's central library system might help him to locate her. Assuming that he wanted to.

"Since there's no help, come let us kiss and part. Nay, I have done, you get no more of me." Mary's last message had asked him not to look for her, but in typically Mary terms. She had left an opening for ambiguity. Bey turned to head back for the stairs, thinking that if he started to learn the library access system now he would never get to sleep.

He was so preoccupied with his thoughts that he almost walked into the three strangers.

There were two men and a woman. Wolf had time for no more than a quick look at them (again, no eyebrows, and suddenly that made sense; perspiration would not trickle down foreheads in zero gee). Then they were advancing on him.

"What the devil are you doing here?" The shorter of the men spoke loudly and angrily. He came close and glared down from his superior height.

"I'm sorry," began Bey. "I didn't know the kernel level was restricted territory. I was about to——"

"The kernel level!" The man turned to his companions. "Just like a Snugger, he doesn't understand what you say to him."

The woman stepped forward. "We're not talking about the kernel. You don't belong on the Harvester—or anywhere in our System. You get back to your own stinking kind."

The other man did not speak, but he stepped to Bey's side and jabbed him painfully in the ribs with a bony elbow. At the same moment the woman trod on Bey's bare instep with a hard-soled shoe.

"Hold it now——" Bey took a step backward. They were in a low-gee field, which favored the Cloudlanders, but Bey was sure that if he had to defend himself he could do it very well. He could break any of those thin limbs between his hands, and their feeble muscles had probably done as much as they could to hurt him. But he didn't want to fight back— not when he had no idea who or why. He lifted his arm as though to strike at the man in front of him, then instead lunged for the staircase.

He was all the way up before they had even turned to pursue. At the top he slammed the door in position and raced off along the corridor. On the threshold of his own quarters he ran into a tall figure coming out. Bey braked as hard as he could, but there was still contact. The man gave a grunt of surprise and went sailing away through the air, bouncing off the wall and then falling face-down across the bed.

"Hey! What the hell!"

Bey recognised the complaining voice. It was Apollo Belvedere Smith. He went across and helped him to sit up.

Aybee rubbed his midriff. "What's all that about?"

"I was going to ask you the same. I was running away from three of your people. I've no idea who they are, but they tried to start a fight."

"Oh, yeah. I came here to warn you not to leave your quarters. Close the door, Wolfman, and lock it."

"Why? What the devil's going on here?"

"You're the man they love to hate." Aybee stood up and began to wander around the room. "You didn't hear the newscast, right?"

"I've been looking at the inside of the Harvester."

"Yeah." Aybee was still scowling, but it was apparently his natural expression. "You know something, most people are real idiots."

"Not true. By definition, most people are average."

That earned a quick grin. "Y'know what I mean. They're animals. Last few days there's been more growling and scowling between government here and government in the Inner System than you'd believe. So in comes news a couple of hours ago from the far side of the Cloud. Bad deal. A whole Harvester destroyed, blown apart, thirty thousand people dead. Power plant went blooey. And newsword is that you Sunhuggers did it."

"Nonsense. The Inner System would never destroy a Harvester. We need that food."

"Hey, I never said I believed it, did I? It's like I said, people here are dumb. They see somebody looks like you"—Aybee paused to give Bey a detailed inspection, then shook his head and went on—"they hate him. You're not safe here now."

"That's Cinnabar Baker's problem. If she wants me to be useful, she'll have to find a way to give me working space."

The answering grin was even less pleasant than usual. "No worries. You'll get work space, Wolfman. The other thing on the news is just your line. Form-change foulups on the Sagdeyev Space Farm, a day from here. You and Sylv'll be heading there, see what you can sort out."

"You won't be going?" Bey wanted to know how important this was in Cinnabar Baker's mind.

"Don't think so. Not 'less you need me. Sylv can handle it. She's no dummy, and she's reliable. You'll like working with her."

It was probably the highest level of praise that Aybee offered to anyone. Bey nodded. "I have the same feeling. We'll get on together."

"Mind you, she's no good at *real* science. She comes to me for that."

"You're too modest."

"Mebbe I am." Aybee was examining Bey with a look of clinical curiosity. "Mind if I ask you a personal question?"

"Probably."

"Do you have hair like that all over? I mean, it must drive you crazy."

Bey held up his hand to show Aybee the open palm.

"OK. You know what I meant." Aybee grinned. "You think I'm a smart-ass, don't you?"

"Not at all. Fifty years ago, I was just like you. Brighter than fusion. I'm amazed how much smarter other people are these days."

"Senile decay?"

"Hang in for a little while. Your turn will come."

Aybee scowled. "Hey, Wolfman, don't say that. That's too true to be funny. Top mathematicians and physicists do their real stuff before they're twenty-five. After that they're just hacking. I've only got six years left, then it's all downhill for the next hundred years. How's it feel to be real old?"

"I'll let you know when I am."

"Sylv says you're pretty well along—after the meeting she got Manx to let her peek at your personal records. She's nosey. She tells me you been seeing things, and you don't know how you could have been fed 'em. And the Manxman thinks I could help. Tell me more."

"Not tonight, Josephine."

"Who?"

"Somebody even older than me." Bey advanced slowly on Aybee, "Shoo. You're leaving now. I'm going to throw you out—literally, if I have to. Catch me in the morning, I'll tell you all you want to know about me. Even how I grow hair."

"Sure." Aybee headed for the doorway. "I guess old people need lots of sleep."

"I guess we do." Bey closed and locked the door after him. If any more visitors were on their way tonight, they would have to break it down. He sat on the bed and considered Apollo Belvedere Smith.

Aybee was young, arrogant, opinionated, brash, and insensitive.

Bey liked him very much.

Part II

Part II

CHAPTER 8

Cinnabar Baker had no home, or perhaps she had thirty. Apartments were maintained for her use on every Harvester, identical in size, gravity, and furnishings. She travelled constantly, and spent at most ten days a year in each one.

She was said to have neither human intimates nor personal belongings. Turpin went with her everywhere, but he was not a possession. He was an old, cross-eyed crow with a big vocabulary and an absence of tail-feathers. When he was in a bad mood, which was often, he had the habit of tugging plumage out with his bill.

He was doing it now, and it was an unpleasant sight. Sylvia Fernald found it hard to take her eyes off him. The crow would pause occasionally to glare at her with rheumy, droop-lidded eyes, then go back to his self-destructive preening. He made no attempt to fly: instead he went waddling back and forth in a piratical roll all over the little round table in front of Sylvia, wings half open and muttering a bad-tempered parody of human speech. Sylvia tried to ignore Turpin and keep her attention on what Cinnabar Baker was saying. It wasn't easy. Sylvia had been asleep when the call came. She bit back a yawn, wondering how it was possible to be so nervous and yet so sleepy.

The latest summons had caught her by surprise, as had the earlier order, a week before, to attend the meeting with Wolf and help to brief him. She worked for Baker, that was undeniable, but the boss of the Harvesters had reached down past two intermediate levels of command to get to Fernald, and she had never offered any explanation.

This new call had been equally casual, as if there were nothing unusual in asking a junior staff member to come to a one-to-one meeting well after midnight. The big woman had been sitting cross-legged in the low-gee apartment when Sylvia arrived. She had exchanged the yellow uniform for a billowing cloud of pale-green spun material that left only her head and hands uncovered, and she seemed as fresh and alert as ever.

"Now let's think a bit more about Behrooz Wolf," she said, as though continuing a conversation already in progress. "We have Leo Manx's impressions, of course, and I have now heard from Aybee. But neither one is a close observer of what I might call inner states. You saw as much of Wolf as I did. What sort of man did you find in there?"

Sylvia had expected a discussion of Harvester control systems, or perhaps of form-change procedures. Her job did not include character assessments; but she could not tell that to Cinnabar Baker. And she was fairly sure that Baker could not be stalled with platitudes.

"Competent but complicated. I don't think I was ever sure what he was thinking."

"Nor was I." Baker smiled like the Gautama, and waited.

"He's obviously intelligent, but we knew that from his reputation. And I don't just mean for form-change theory. He saw that there were other matters involved here very quickly."

"Almost too quickly." Cinnabar Baker did not elaborate. Again she sat and waited.

"And he's obviously a sensitive type, too. I saw Leo Manx's reports on Wolf, and his relationship to Mary Walton." (And I can imagine how he felt when she left; but I won't say that to Cinnabar Baker.) "That means he's still very miserable, and thinks he's not getting much out of life. But he took a lot of interest in what we told him; so I suspect that although he *believes* he feels things strongly, his intellectual drives are more powerful than his emotional ones. He's like Aybee, he lives in a thought world more than a sense world. He wouldn't admit that, maybe he doesn't even know it. As for his other interests, it's hard to say anything. How does he spend his time when he's not at work?" "

While she was speaking, Sylvia found herself asking the same question about Cinnabar Baker. This apartment was tiny by Cloud standards, and minimally furnished. The walls were a uniform beige, unrelieved by pictures or other decorations, and there were no personal bits and pieces like the ones that filled Sylvia's own apartment to overflowing. Cinnabar Baker had a reputation for hard work. On the basis of the evidence, work was all she had.

"Did you find him attractive?" The question was so unexpected that Sylvia was not sure she had heard correctly.

"You mean, *physically* attractive?"

"Exactly."

"My God, no. He's absolutely *hideous*." Sylvia let that answer sit for a couple of seconds, then felt obliged to add, "I mean, I suppose it's not his fault, lots of people from the Inner System probably look like that. And he has an interesting mind, and I think he has a good sense of humour. But he's revolting looking, and of course he's very little, with those short stubby arms. And worst of all, he's . . . he's too . . ."

"Too?"

"Too *hairy*. I wouldn't be surprised if he's covered with hair all over him, like an ape, everywhere. Even on . . . Of course"—Sylvia suddenly became aware of how extreme she must sound—"I suppose he can't *help* any of that. Though with form-change equipment available . . ."

"I'm sorry you find him a little unattractive." Cinnabar Baker apparently had a great gift for understatement. She was reaching out to stroke the back of the crow standing in front of her, and looked down so that her eyes were hidden from Sylvia. "You see, I wish to make an unusual request of you. And since it's outside the usual range of duties, it has to be no more than an informal request."

"If I can do anything to help you, naturally I will." (The day had been crazy so far. Could it get any stranger?)

"Good. You know that you will be working closely with Behrooz Wolf, and travelling with him?"

"That's the plan."

"I want you to seek a relationship with him. A very close relationship."

"You mean—you want me to—surely you don't want me to—" Turpin chose that moment to give a long, gurgling laugh, like water flowing away down a drain, and Sylvia could not finish the sentence.

"I mean a psychological attachment," said Baker calmly. "If it turned out to be a physical relationship, so much the better. And I'll tell you why. Wolf was one of twenty-seven people we considered contacting to help us. He's the only one left, so we tend to say to ourselves, hey, he was really lucky. Maybe he *was* lucky. But maybe there's more than luck involved. Maybe Wolf knows more than he admits, and maybe there's a good reason why he didn't get wiped out with the rest. And some reason why he agreed to come here, after first refusing. If so, I need to know all that. Pillow-talk is better than truth drugs. If you could get close to him, persuade him to confide in you—"

"I can't do it!" Sylvia hadn't listened to anything past Baker's first sentence. "It's out of the question. I'll do most things, but that's too much to ask *anybody*."

"Maybe it is." Baker stopped stroking Turpin's back and fixed cool blue eyes on Sylvia. "I feel sure that the feeling is mutual. Wolf undoubtedly finds you no more desirable than you find him."

"I'm sure of it. You've seen Snugger women. Short and brown, all fat and hips and breasts. He must think I'm hideous. My God, I'm a half-meter taller than he is, at least. And miles too skinny for Earth taste. And anyway——"

"Anyway," said Turpin suddenly. "Anyway, anyway, in

for a penny-way." He took off with an excited flapping
of black wings, flew up and around in a lurching spiral,
and landed leering on Cinnabar Baker's shoulder.

"You underestimate the effects of prolonged personal
interaction," Baker was saying. She smiled. "In other
words, talking leads to touching. And beauty is easy. A
few hours in a form-change tank—not that I'm suggesting this, you understand—and you could be Wolf's
ideal of beauty."

"Never. I'm sorry, but I won't consider it. That's final."
Sylvia stood up. She should leave as soon as possible,
before Cinnabar Baker could try again to talk her into
something.

And so much for her own career as control specialist—
her now-blighted career. It had been ruined in the past
five minutes.

The last thought was the bitterest of all. When the
original summons had come from Cinnabar Baker, Sylvia
had been flattered and excited. The quality of her work
must have singled her out for special attention. She
would be assigned to the visitor from the Inner System
because she had unusual competence in form-change and
systems work.

Now it was clear that her professional skills had nothing to do with it. Her role was that of convenient female,
a lure set out to catch Bey Wolf. And now she had
refused? Cinnabar Baker might say she did not hold it
against her; but she would. Sylvia's career was in tatters.

"Please excuse me now." She looked at Baker, found
no words, and headed blindly for the door.

Cinnabar Baker watched her leave. As expected, Sylvia
Fernald had refused—vehemently. But the idea had
been planted. Now Sylvia would be unable to meet and
work with Behrooz Wolf, without also evaluating him at
some level as a prospective partner. And that was all
Baker had hoped to achieve.

"Hormones are everything, Turpin," she said to the
bird on her shoulder. "Brains are nice, and looks are
nice, and logic's even nicer; but hormones run the show.
For everyone, even for me and you. But we never know

it. I hope I wasn't too hard on Sylvia. Let's see if she'll change her mind when she knows him better."

The night's work was far from over. Humming softly to herself, Cinnabar Baker bent over the desk-top communications unit and reviewed the official statement she had prepared warning the Inner System about their interference in Outer System affairs. It would do. There were a couple of key words that could be stronger—"demand" instead of "request," and "intolerable" was better than "impermissible"—but they were easily fixed.

She approved it for release. Then she entered coded mode and requested a dedicated circuit for new, real-time communication. There was a moment's delay pending approval of heliocentric co-ordinates outside the usual network. That was cleared, using Baker's own authorization. The scrambling codes were assigned. Finally, on the outermost structures of the Harvester, the half-kilometer antenna turned its focused hyper-beam toward a destination deep in the Halo.

CHAPTER 9

'You can run, you can run, just as fast as you
can,
You'll never get away from the Negentropic Man.
        —crèche song of the Hoyle Harvester

Cloudland ships were easy to recognise: hydrocarbon hulls, bracing struts of carbon fiber, transparent polymer ports.

Necessity and Nature had set the rules. The bodies of the Oort Cloud provided a limited construction kit, little but the first eight elements of the periodic table. Metals were in particularly short supply. Rather than dragging those up the gravity gradient from the Inner System, the Cloudlander fabricating machines had learned to improvise. Less than one-tenth of a per cent of the ship that would carry Bey Wolf and Sylvia Fernald to the Sagdeyev Space Farm was metal, and that fraction would be reduced again in the new models.

Bey was trying to hold a conversation with Sylvia Fernald as they prepared to leave, but it was difficult going. Two days ago she had been friendly and at ease with him. He had known it and so had she. They were strangers, but they had hit it off together in the first few minutes, comfortable with each other's work style and attitude. He had been pleased at the prospect of working with Fernald—Sylvia, she had asked him to call her that before the first informal planning meeting ended. But today. . . .

Today he had been wringing words out of her, one by one: "This looks as though it will only hold two people. What about Leo Manx, Sylvia? I thought he was planning to come with us."

"He changed his mind." Her voice was expressionless. She was staring at the fine black hairs on his forearms, and refusing to look him in the eye.

Was *that* it? His appearance? When he had arrived at the Opik Harvester, Bey had been wearing the long-sleeved, long-legged style of the Inner System. Today he had adopted the scanty uniform of the Cloudlanders, and his physical differences were more apparent. The widespread use of form-change equipment had allowed Earth people to get used to pretty much anything. But the people he had seen here on the Harvester were all very similar, limited thin or fat variations on a single body type.

She had turned to check fuel and supply status, and was bending low over the panel. He moved closer to her, reaching out a muscular arm and stealthily comparing it with her pale, smooth limb. She sensed he was near her, and spun around.

"What are you doing?"

"Nothing." Bey wondered why he sounded guilty, and why her cheeks were flushed. If she stayed as jumpy as this for the whole trip, it was going to be an unpleasant twenty-four hours. The one accommodation shortage in Cloudland was found in their transit vessels. The McAndrew drive was fine, but the inertial and gravitational forces were balanced only in a small region on the ship's main axis. Bey and Sylvia would share that space, a cylindrical cabin about two meters across. Standoffishness would be hard. Sylvia herself was more than two meters tall.

They were making final preparations for departure, running a countdown together with awkward formality, when Aybee hurried in.

"Good. Thought mebbe I'd missed you."

"Four minutes more, you would have." Sylvia did a poor job of hiding her relief. "Are you coming with us?"

"No way." Aybee looked around the little cabin in disgust. "I need *space*, room to shine. You'd have to fold me double to get me in here. It'll be cosy enough with just you and the Wolfman."

The tense atmosphere went right by him. He was swinging a square satchel up from his side and opening the clasps. "Talked to old Leo again, and this time we got the problem right. First time, he asked me, how can you track down an input video signal that nobody else can see? I said, hey, I'll tell you five ways to do that, but I can't tell you which one's being used without more information."

"Three minutes," said Bey. "Or we'll have to start over with a new countdown."

"Loads of time." Aybee pulled from the satchel a thin rectangular box, a head-covering helmet, and a whole snake's nest of wires and electrodes. "Today, the Manxman tells me we had the problem wrong. He don't care *how* the signal gets in your head, he just wants to *see* it, know what it is drives you crazy. Different deal, right?— lot easier, because who cares if the signal came from outside, or if you made up the whole thing? The memory of it's tucked away somewhere in there"—he gestured at Bey's head—"so this gadget can pull it out for us."

Bey eyed the device without enthusiasm. It had a random and unfinished look. "You want me to put that thing over my head? How am I supposed to breathe?"

"Same as usual, in an' then out. There's air passages for that. Hey, loosen up. If I wanted to kill you, there's easier ways."

"Two minutes," cut in Sylvia Fernald. "Aybee, we should be in our chairs. You have to leave."

"Lots of time. Wolfman, don't you *want* to know how this works? It's dead good. See, you start thinking about what you saw—little red bogey-men, whatever. Those memories are stored away somewhere inside your head, scene-perfect. You never forget anything you experience, no one does, you just can't get at it, not in detail. So this takes your first-cut memory output, feeds it back to you, and asks if it's a perfect match. If not, it iterates the presentation until there *is* a match. My algorithm guarantees convergence. And all the time we're recording what we get. So at the end of a session, we've caught whatever you saw—even what you *thought* you saw, provided there's detail to it." He glared at Bey, who was packing the flexible helmet away into its case. "Hey, what kind of ungrateful bozo are you? I put a lot of work in that. Aren't you going to try it?"

"Are you saying it may not work?"

"Sure it'll work, sure as my name's Apollo Belvedere Smith."

"Then I'll use it when we're on the way to the Farm." Bey pointed at the countdown indicator. "See that? You can look at the results of your work in real-time if you don't get out of here in the next forty seconds. The hatch secures automatically thirty seconds before the drive comes on. You coming with us?"

"No way!" Aybee was jumping for the cabin exit. "Call back and tell us what you get. Leo Manx is itchy too." He was gone, but as the other two were moving to the bunks Aybee poked his head back in. "Hey. Wolfman. Did you really rough up those three people last night, before you ran into me?"

Bey was strapped in, clutching Aybee's satchel to his chest. "Just the opposite. I didn't touch them, but one had a go at my ribs, another trod on my foot. I could show you the bruise."

"Don't bother. You see one hairy leg, you've seen 'em all. But take a look at the news. They say you attacked them, without any warning. You're getting out of here just in time."

And so was Aybee. The two passengers heard the outer hatch close, no more than two seconds before the siren announced that the drive was being engaged.

Aybee's last minute delivery proved a blessing. Bey had attempted conversation with Sylvia again once they were on the way, but she was so obviously upset about something that after a few minutes he took out the flexible helmet, attached the electrodes, and placed the set over his head.

Aybee had not bothered with such details as operating instructions. Bey sat in darkness for a while, wondering if he had omitted to switch on. He was ready to remove the helmet, but he did not want to confront Sylvia's anxious face. If the device operated as advertised, he should be concentrating on the clearest memory he had of the Dancing Man. It was easy to bring into mind that tiny figure, coming into view from the left of the screen . . .

It was like form-change, but with one difference. In this case, the compulsion came from outside, not from within his own will. Bey was still conscious, but he had no control over anything. In his mind, the Dancing Man moved across the screen, paused, and moved again. *Dance, pause, adjust, reset, dance. Dance, pause, reset, dance.* On it went, again and again, each time so little different from the last that Bey could detect no change. *Dance, pause, adjust, reset.* He tried to count, while the act repeated forever, scores of times, hundreds of times, thousands of times. But he could not hold the number in his head. *Dance, pause, adjust, reset.* An endless, invariant procession of Dancing Men, capering one by one across his field of vision, twisting, turning, shuffling backwards out of view. They sawed deeper and deeper into his skull, through the protective meningeal sheath, carving into the tender folds of his brain, while he was screaming silently for release.

At last it came. The cycle was broken—with stunning abruptness. Bey shuddered back to consciousness, and found himself staring up at the frightened eyes of Sylvia Fernald. The helmet was in her hands.

"I'm sorry." She reached out as though to touch his forehead, then instantly jerked back. "I felt sure you were in trouble. You lay there for so long, and then you started to groan. I was afraid you might be in pain. Were things going wrong?"

Bey put his hands up to cover his eyes. The light had become much too bright, and he had a terrible headache.

"I'd say they were, but Aybee might not agree. I think he set the tolerances for convergence of his program too tight. I might have been days trying to reconstruct what I saw. Maybe I never would have got there. I could have been in that damned loop forever. Anyway, I'm all right now." He reached out and took her left hand in his, holding it tightly enough that her reflexive jerk did not free it. "I appreciate what you did, Sylvia. I could never have broken out of that on my own."

It was done on impulse, but suddenly it became an experiment. How would she react?

She allowed the contact for maybe half a second. Then she firmly pulled away and with her right hand reached across to press a switch on the side of the instrument. There was a click, and a brief buzz of sound. She waited a moment, then touched the front panel.

Bey stared at her. "You know how it works!"

"I looked at it long enough, while you were lying there. And I knew Aybee would keep it simple—he says he wants his work to be like the Cloudland Navy, designed by a genius to be run by idiots. I know which buttons to press, if that makes me an expert." She paused, her hand still before the flat front panel. "Would you like to see if you got anything? There's a playback feature, we could put it up on the display screen."

It was Bey's turn for anxiety. He wanted to know, didn't he? Surely he did, after all those months of worry? But he also felt uneasy, the same subliminal discomfort he had experienced when he learned that Mary was sending him a message from beyond the Moon.

"Well?" Sylvia Fernald was waiting, her long, slender finger poised now above a point on the panel.

The moving finger writes, and having writ, moves on, nor all thy piety nor wit, shall lure it back to cancel half a line ... Bey sensed himself on the brink of irreversible change, with that waiting finger as its agent. Old Omar the Tentmaker might be warning him. After months of accepting the Dancing Man as a harbinger of madness, perhaps Bey was about to discover darker possibilities. Knowledge might be more dreadful than ignorance.

He was very tired. His head was aching, worse than ever. His mind had turned to mush. And still he sat, unable to speak, unable to nod, and watched that poised digit.

"*Well*?" Sylvia was becoming impatient. And no wonder. What was wrong with him? He had to understand. Yet he found himself drifting off again into a half-trance, turning his thoughts away from the present . . .

Bey roused himself. Bad news or not, he *had* to know. He sat up, shivered, and nodded. "Run it."

The screen flickered, went dark, and slowly brightened. There was a splash of sharp colours, a kaleidoscope of overlaid images—red men running, dancing, leaping, sitting cross-legged, diving away, all overlaid one on another. Then the multiple exposures faded, and one picture emerged. It was as Bey remembered it, but now in clean and terrifying detail. The little man, the sharp-toothed grin, the strutting walk, the backward somersault, the jerky twitch of agile limbs. The magnetic eyes. The voice. There it was, the same sing-song voice, rising at the end of the sentence to frame a not-quite-intelligible question. Bey watched, listened, and was carried away into a dizzying resumption of the past. He reached out to play the sequence again. And again. The fourth time, Sylvia's hand was there first, pushing him away.

"No more. Not now." She had seen the expression in his eyes. Bey was far gone in his own fugue.

He sighed. "Aybee did it. He said he would. That was it, you know. Exactly."

"I know."

"I have to see it again." His hand was moving to hers, trying to push her aside. He had no strength in his arm.

"No. Later." She touched his forehead. As she suspected, it was hot and sweaty. "Bey, you have to sleep. It's been too much."

"I have to see it again. I have to *understand* it. You see, Sylvia, even now I don't understand." His voice was puzzled, a lost voice, but even as he spoke his eyes were closing. In less than thirty seconds he was sound asleep.

He was no threat now. Sylvia watched him for a few

minutes. His face was the countenance of the Inner System itself; dark, older, guarded. She reached out and moved him so that he could not see the display. He sighed in his sleep, but did not move from his new position.

She reset the audio input, so that she alone would receive it, and settled down to play the image sequence, over and over. It had meant something personal and disturbing to Bey Wolf, but to her it offered different and more practical mysteries. There had been hints to grasp at even in the first viewing.

She solved the first problem after four runs through Bey's reconstructed memory sequence. After another look at the controls, she made one adjustment and watched with satisfaction at what came onto the screen.

The second problem was not so easy. It depended on a dubious recollection from more than a year ago. Sylvia finally asked for help from the data base on the Space Farm, seven hours' travel ahead of them. They sent an image that confirmed her hunch. She settled down to wait for Bey to waken, watching his dark-complexioned face, wanting him to rest, but willing him to wake. She was itching to tell him.

He was asleep for almost six hours. As he woke, he at once turned and reached to turn on the display. She gripped his hand in both of hers.

"No. Bey, you don't need to."

He stared at her uncomprehendingly, still dazed with sleep.

"Watch," she said. She made the adjustment to Aybee's equipment, and started the playback.

The red man appeared, and still he was speaking. But now his sing-song words were clear.

*You can run, you can run, just as fast as you can,
But you'll never get away from the Negentropic
Man.*

And then, just before he danced away, off at the right side of the screen, he spoke again:

*Don't you worry, don't you fear, the Negentropic
Man is here!*

Bey sat open-mouthed. "What did you do?"

"Time-reversal, and slowed it down." She set out to
play it through again. "It was obvious. You'd have seen
it, once you'd watched it right through—objectively—a
few times. The movements didn't look right, too jerky,
and the intonation was wrong for normal speech. Playing it backwards, that's all it took to make the message
clear." She saw Bey's shake of the head. "What's
wrong?"

"It's *not* clear. Not to me. I understand what he's saying, and maybe Aybee knows how the trick was worked
to send me that signal. But what does it *mean?*"

"Negentropic?"

"That will do for a start. Negentropic. Negative
entropy? But that's just a word." Bey stood up. He
wanted to pace about, but there was not enough space
in the cabin to take more than two steps each way. After
a moment he sat down again and slapped at his knee
in frustration. "*Negentropic.* Why should somebody say
they're the Negentropic Man? Better yet, why would anybody send a message like that to *me?* I don't see how a
person can have negative entropy—I'm not even sure I
understand what entropy is. And I certainly have no idea
who's behind it all."

"But I do."

Sylvia's quiet answer caught Bey off-balance. He stared
at her. "How can you?"

"I recognised your Dancing Man. I had a suspicion
when I first saw him, but I wasn't sure. While you were
asleep I called ahead to tap into the Space Farm's data
base. And I found I was right."

"You mean he's somebody from the Outer System,
rather than the Inner System? He doesn't look anything
like a Cloudlander."

"He's not. And he's not a Sunhugger, either." Sylvia
was so caught up in her discovery that she forgot to

be cautious. She leaned across and gripped Bey's hand excitedly in hers. "Your Dancing Man isn't one of us. He lives in the Halo. He's famous, he's a rebel, and his name is Black Ransome."

CHAPTER 10

"Manx is on the way." Sylvia floated into the open bubble that looked out to the stars and secured herself next to Bey. "Flying a high-acceleration probe. He'll be here in twelve hours."

"He must be keen." Bey thought for a moment. "And cramped. The hi-probes are emergency equipment—the cabin's less than two meters across. He won't have room to turn."

"He'd better not try—it's a one-person ship, and Aybee says he's coming with him." Sylvia sounded quite cheerful at the thought. If she could survive the forced intimacy of her trip with Bey, she was prepared to let Aybee and Leo Manx suffer through their shorter travel time. "I told him what we found," she went on. "He can't wait to see it for himself."

They were at the Space Farm, and ready to disembark. Bey, accustomed to the formal (and protective) procedures for entry to Inner System ports, was baffled by the absence of quarantine. They had flown to a point near the central hub of the Farm, and been docked automatically without passing a checkpoint.

"Of course we were checked," said Sylvia, when Bey expressed his surprise. "The computer checked our ship's ID when we were still hours away."

"But if the wrong people were inside it—" began Bey. He stopped. Cloudland was so far from the Inner System in awareness of security measures, he could talk to Sylvia for ever but he doubted if she would fully understand him. Was this why a handful of rebels from the Kernel Ring could cause such chaos in the Cloud?

The failure to understand went both ways. Bey had been briefed on the Sagdeyev Space Farm, but somehow he had reduced it in his mind to a size that he could comprehend. A farm suggested solidity, intensive activity, compact production. The reality was so insubstantial that he felt they had arrived nowhere.

The farm was a mono molecular collection layer, two billion kilometers across. Its crop had been seeded hundreds of parsecs away and thousands of years ago, conceived in the fiery heat of supernovas and blown free by the same explosions. The harvest had drifted through space for millennia, borne on the winds of light pressure, until random galactic airs carried the precious atoms to the Cloud. Most of them would drift on until the end of the Universe, but a few would encounter and be held by the electrostatic charge of the collection layer. For them, aggregation could finally begin.

It was slow and selective work. The Farm was interested only in the heavy elements, metals and rare earths and noble gases. It winnowed billions of cubic kilometers of space to find their invisible traces.

The machines that monitored the farms needed no central processing facility. They could carry hundreds of tons of material with them, accumulating steadily until there was enough to ship to the Harvesters. The humans, frailer creatures, needed more. At the centre of the collection layer sat the habitation bubble, three hundred meters across. In it dwelt the score of people who had made the Farm their home. Two of those were now dead.

"Don't expect them to meet us," said Sylvia, as their ship docked at the outer edge of the bubble. "In fact, don't be surprised if we don't meet anyone in all our stay here. The Farmers avoid strangers, and that includes me as well as you. They know we're here, and they appreciate our help. They just don't want to see us."

"Suppose we need to talk with them about the form-change problems?"

"We'll probably do what they do themselves—use a

communications link." Sylvia led the way to the bubble interior, meandering along silent corridors that spiralled down through the concentric shells of the bubble. Everywhere was deserted, without even maintenance equipment. If Sylvia had not told Bey that there were people here, he would have believed the Farm to be derelict.

Sylvia was heading for the kernel at the centre of the bubble, but on their way they passed an area that was clearly an automated kitchen. Bey realised that he had not eaten since they left the Harvester. During the whole trip to the Farm he had been either unconscious, or too preoccupied to consider food. He paused. "Once we get to the form-change tanks we'll be in for a long session. Can we grab something here?" He was starving. He headed for the dispensing equipment without waiting for her answer, and placed an order. He did not bother to study the menu. Food in the Cloud was nothing like Earth fare, and he did not much care what he was given. When his dishes appeared he went across to the seating area and waited for Sylvia.

She was a long time coming. When she finally arrived she sat angled away from him. Her tray held a modest amount of food and a large beaker of straw-colored fluid. She stared at the liquid for a long time, then finally took a little sip, grimaced, and swallowed.

"Is it bad?" Bey lifted up a piece of food and sniffed it suspiciously. It looked like bread, and it smelled like bread. "Maybe we worked the machine wrong."

"No." Sylvia turned and gave an apologetic shake of her head. "The food is fine. The drink, too. But I've not eaten a meal with someone else for years. It's not a law or anything, but we don't do it, you know, except with a partner. Go ahead and eat, and please excuse my rudeness. I'll be used to this in a minute."

Not just hairy and unpopular; his habits were disgusting, too. Bey put down the bread he was holding. "I'm the one who should apologize. I knew Cloudland customs, but Leo Manx and I ate together all the time on the way to the Outer System. I didn't even think of it here."

"Leo was specially conditioned for the assignment. But really, it will be all right. It will. Watch me." She speared a yellow cube on her fork, squinted down at it in front of her nose, and put it stoically into her mouth. She chewed for a long time before she finally swallowed. "See! I did it."

After a moment Bey began to eat his own food. "Is it all right if we talk while we eat? Or would that be too much?"

"Of course. I would prefer it."

Bey nodded. So would he. The food was pretty terrible, bland and flavorless. *Good thing I couldn't order the meal I'd really have enjoyed*, he thought to himself. *Come to Earth, Sylvia, and let me introduce you to a broiled lobster.* "I wanted to ask you about Ransome," he said after a minute of silent chewing.

"I don't know all that much."

"But you knew enough to recognize him. Back in the Inner System, most people don't believe there is a Black Ransome. And Leo Manx told me that he's a mystery figure. If he's such an unknown quantity, I don't see how you could possibly have recognized him."

"Ah," Sylvia stopped eating and laid down her fork. She had managed only three small mouthfuls. "I wondered when you would get around to that. Did Leo tell you about my background?"

"A little."

"Paul Chu?"

"He did mention that. But only to say that you and Chu used to be partners, and he disappeared on a trip to the Kernel Ring. His ship was attacked, and he was taken prisoner."

"That's the official version, and I don't dispute it. But I don't believe it." Sylvia paused. She was not sure she wanted to talk about her personal history with Bey Wolf. She would rather talk than eat, but he might misunderstand her reasons.

"Paul and I lived together for nearly three years," she went on. "Most people who knew us thought it was permanent—I'm sure Leo thought that. But it wasn't. We argued like hell, all the time. If Paul were around now, I don't think we would be together."

"I heard from Leo Manx that you were planning to have children."

"No. That's Leo's wishful thinking. He's such a sympathetic type, he likes to think the best of people. He may have heard Paul and me talk about having children, a long time ago—but even when we were splitting up, we never disagreed in public."

"Why did you fight?"

"Not what you might think. Not sex. Politics. I'm sure you suspect I'm not friendly to Earth and the Inner System. I'm not. I believe that you are like parasites—and not even smart ones. You've failed the first test of a successful parasite: moderation. You wiped out parts of your own habitat—the passenger pigeon and the dodo and the whale and the gorilla and the elephant. Thanks to you, half the species on Earth have become extinct in less than a thousand years. Humans may be next."

"I agree, and I'm as sorry about it as you are." Bey looked at her earnest face. She was angry now, but that made her an easier companion. The cold, wary Sylvia was more difficult to deal with. "You sound pretty extreme about it."

"Extreme! Me? Bey Wolf, you don't understand. I'm a *moderate*. Everyone in the Cloud feels the way I do about Earth and the Inner System. We learn it when we're little children. But most of us would never do anything to harm the people of the Inner System. It's just a few fanatics, who want to go a lot further than general dislike. Paul was one. He *hated* the Inner System, and everything you stand for. One year before he disappeared, he joined an extremist group who talked seriously about starting a war between the Inner and Outer Systems. Paul told me their ideas, and asked me to join. I told him they were all crazy."

"We have people back on Earth who feel the same, but the other way round. They hate the idea that the Cloud controls food supplies. They want to crush Cloudland and control the Outer System. But they're all mad,

both sides. If we went to war with you, or cut off communications, it would be like men and women refusing to
have anything to do with each other. We could do it, but
our species would die out in a generation."

"Paul said it wouldn't work like that. After the collapse
of the Inner System, there could be a new start for everyone. But it would need a group that was all ready for
the takeover, with its own strong leader. He showed me
a secret piece of recruiting material. I decided that the
whole thing was crazy, and the leader—Ransome—was
craziest of all. But apparently he's terribly plausible and
charismatic. Paul thought Ransome was wonderful. He
said that Black Ransome had a secret weapon, something
that made sure he would win, even if he didn't have
many followers. I could see that people were following
Ransome's ideas, even though they were wild."

Sylvia had pushed her own plate away from her, but
she was watching intensely as Bey continued eating. He
found it disconcerting. There were odd undercurrents
flowing beneath this conversation, a sense that he was
performing some old, disgusting, and perversely erotic
rite, when all he was doing was eating a dreary piece of
synthetic protein.

"But then Paul disappeared," added Sylvia at last.
"And I feel sure he didn't die, and he wasn't captured.
He's somewhere in the Halo. Probably in the Kernel
Ring—he's an energy specialist. I think he's working for
Ransome. But I never found out what the 'secret weapon'
might be."

"Did you actually meet Ransome."

"Not in person. But I saw his video image when he
called with a message for Paul. He's your Dancing Man,
I'm quite sure of it."

"If he's the Dancing Man, I'll never forget him. It's
burned into my brain, exactly what he looks like and
sounds like. Do you know a way to reach him?"

"Not directly. He hides away in the Halo, but he has
more and more influence all through the Outer System."
Sylvia had taken another sip from her beaker. She was
peering at Bey's moving jaws, her grey eyes glistening.

He stopped eating. "I believe what you've told me, Sylvia, but it doesn't explain anything. I can accept the idea of Ransome as the leader of an organized terrorist group. I can even see how influential he might become in the Cloud. But I can't see why he would appear on a crazy message to *me*."

"Maybe he hopes to recruit you, too."

"That's ridiculous. For one thing, you don't recruit people by sending messages that drive them crazy and that they can't understand. For another, he has no idea who I am."

"Cinnabar Baker told me you are very famous, the top form-change theorist in the Inner and Outer System."

"That isn't enough to make anyone *famous*. Sylvia, Earth has lots of form-change specialists. I'm just one of them. You have to remember there are five hundred times as many people in the Inner System as there are out here."

"I know. If I had my way, we'd stay like that. Paul and I argued about this, too. He said the Cloud is underpopulated. I feel it's just right. We don't *need* more people. I don't think I could stand to live in the Inner System."

"Ransome probably feels the same way. Out here, he's a big bogey-man who's trying to start a war. He steals ships, he has a secret weapon, he kills people."

"But to some, like Paul Chu, he's a hero. Paul says he started out as a Podder. He tried to do development deals with the Inner and Outer Systems, and he only became a renegade when he was betrayed by both."

"Maybe he's good, and maybe he's bad. He's certainly famous here. But back on Earth he's just a bedtime story that people tell to their children. A lonely, mysterious outlaw, Captain Black Ransome, flying the Halo in a creaking, battered ship, solar sails tattered and decaying. He drifts silent and powered-down whenever there's a danger of discovery. He steals power, supplies, and volatiles wherever he can find them. He's the space version of the Flying Dutchman."

"Who is that?"

"An Earth legend. A man who sails Earth's oceans, endlessly seeking redemption. Deep water is his home. He never finds a landfall. He's not quite real, but he's very romantic. That's the way we think of Ransome, a combined myth and outlaw. If you suggested to someone from Earth that Ransome was trying to recruit me—a Sunhugger, a planet man who's only happy at the bottom of twenty miles of atmosphere—they'd say, well, they'd say that you were losing it. Crazy."

"*You*'re from Earth. Are you saying I'm crazy?"

Bey sighed. "Not crazy. Maybe a little strange and unpredictable. Come on, Sylvia, let's get moving. I want to see the Farm's form-change systems before Aybee and Leo arrive."

"I hope you'll find something. You know, Aybee looked at the failed form-changes on the Harvesters. He got nowhere, and he's awful smart."

"He certainly is."

"And he'll see this as a sort of contest, just the two of you. Do you think you can handle him?"

"I'll bet on it." Bey had finished eating. "I learned something a long time ago. My first boss wasn't a good scientist, and he had dozens of political fights with bright young people from the General Coordinators' office. They were mostly right, but he won, every time. I asked him how he did it. He pointed out the sign on his office wall." Bey allowed Sylvia to steer him out of the galley. "'Old age and treachery will defeat youth and skill,' he told me. It's one of the world's great truths. Aybee happens to be on the wrong side of the inequality."

CHAPTER 11

"Those are pearls that were his eyes;
Nothing of him that doth fade,
But doth suffer a sea-change
Into something rich and strange."
—William Shakespeare; Ariel's song, The Tempest

Behrooz Wolf was four trillion kilometers from home,
floating uncomfortably in free-fall in the territory of people who hated him, surrounded by a silence so total that
it hurt his ears. In that environment, the familiar technology of form-change was his lifeline.

Sylvia had led him to a chamber containing four
change tanks. Two of them were empty. The others contained the bodies of two dead Farmers. At Wolf's
request, they had been left untouched by their fellows
until he arrived at the Farm. He and Sylvia went at once
to the transparent ports and peered in.

She took one look and turned away. Bey heard the
sound of retching. He ignored it. He had seen too many
illegal and unsuccessful form-change experiments to
allow them to affect his stomach. He had work to do.

He rotated the two bodies using remote-handling
equipment, and examined their anomalies with the tank's
internal sensors. Both were originally male, and
according to the tanks' settings both had been using the
same program. The intended end-point was a form with

thickened epidermis, lowered metabolic rate, and eyes protected by translucent nictitating membranes. The men had been preparing for an extended mission outside, away from the Farm's main bubble. According to Sylvia, such missions were absolutely routine, and the form-change program that went with them had been used a thousand times.

Bey would not take her word for it. He intended to go over that program, instruction by instruction. But first he wanted to localise the problem area; and the only evidence for that was the end products in the tanks.

He studied the two corpses. Both men had experienced significant mass reduction—not called for by the program. The limbs had atrophied to stumps and their torsos had curled forward, to leave the overgrown head close to the swollen abdomen. Death had come when cramped and shrunken lungs would no longer permit breathing.

"Did you ever see forms like that before?" said Sylvia softly. She had herself under control, and was hovering just behind him.

He shook his head but did not speak. It would take a long time to explain that the final form was close to irrelevant. His diagnosis of program malfunctions was based on more subtle pointers: the presence of hypertrophied fingernails and toenails on the flipper-like appendages, the disappearance of eyelids, the milky, pearl-like luster of the membrane-covered eyes, the severe scoliosis of the spinal column. To someone familiar with form-change, they were signposts pointing to certain sections of program code.

Bey began to call program sections for review. His task was in principle very simple. The BEC computers used in purposive form-change converted a human's intended form to a series of bio-feedback commands that the brain would employ to direct change at the cellular level. Human and computer, working interactively, remolded the body until the intended form and actual form were identical, then the process ended. The chemical and physiological changes were continuously monitored, and any malfunction would halt the process and set emergency flags. The process could fail catastrophically in two ways: if the human in the tank did not wish to live; or if there were a major software problem.

Bey could rule out the idea of suicide. It resulted in death without any physical change except biological aging. That seemed to leave nothing but software failure, but he could see one other complication: this equipment had not been provided by BEC. It was a hardware clone, and the programs that went with it were pirated versions. There could be hardware/software mismatches, something that only BEC guaranteed against. His job with this set-up would be ten times as hard.

He began to examine a new section of code. Behind him, he was vaguely aware that Sylvia was leaving the room. That was a relief. She could not help, and she was a potential distraction.

Line by line, he followed the programmed interaction, tracking physical parameters (temperature, pulse rate, skin conductivity) and system variables (nutrient rates, ambient gas profile, electrical stimuli). He did not check those parameters against any equipment performance specifications. He did not need to. The region of stability was well mapped, and over the years he had learned the limits of tolerable excursion from standard values. All the programs in use as they were swapped in and out of the computer provided their own audit trail, together with chemical readings and brain activity indices. Reading and interpreting them was somewhere between an art and a science. It was something he had been doing for two thirds of his life.

He sat there for six hours in a total trance. If anyone had asked him if he were enjoying himself, he could not have given a truthful answer. He was not happy, he was not sad. All he knew was that there was nothing in life that he would rather be doing. And when he found the first anomalies, and began to piece together a picture, he could not have described the thrill. He had been provided with a precious broken ornament, shattered into a thousand pieces. He had to recreate it. As he fitted those fragments together, one by one, tentatively and painstakingly, he sensed the skeletal outline of a total pattern. That was exhilarating. But no matter what he did, the picture remained tantalizingly incomplete. And that was unbearably frustrating. Not all of the pieces had been provided. Parts of the code were not in the system at all.

He was roused by the sound of Sylvia Fernald's voice. She had entered the room with Aybee Smith and Leo Manx in tow. Bey turned and addressed his question to all three of them: "These form-change tanks aren't completely self-contained, the way the BEC units would be and should be. Where's the rest of the computation done?"

"That must be in the main computer system for the Farm," said Aybee at once. "It's a lot less expensive to do some of the analysis there. BEC and the other manufacturers rip you off bad. They overcharge you ten times for storage in their units. Is it a problem to use distributed computing? We do it a lot."

"It *shouldn't* be a problem. On the other hand . . ." Bey gestured into the port of the form-change tank. Aybee came close and stared in, frowning, for thirty seconds. Leo Manx couldn't take more than one horrified glance.

"I've checked the code, line by line," Bey went on. "And I'm convinced that the local programs here are working fine. It means that the problem has to be over in the main computer."

"Or in the communications lines," said Aybee.

"No." Bey shook his head, and suddenly felt his exhaustion. "Redundant transmission should correct for electronic noise in the signal. Even if that somehow weren't working, thermal noise or outside interference would give *random* errors. What we're seeing here is definitely not random change. It was closely calculated."

"But that makes it murder," protested Leo Manx.

Aybee gave him a fierce grin. "I guess that's exactly what the Wolfman is saying. And in that case, we'll have to meet with the Farmers." He waved aside Sylvia's objection. "Don't tell me, Fern, I know they won't want to do it. But for murder, they don't have a choice. You real sure about this, Wolf?"

"Positive."

"I mean, you wouldn't like me to check your results?"

"I'd love you to—or at least, I'd like to see you try. If you were really lucky and smart, that would take you about a month." Bey shook his head. "Aybee, it's not a question of your ability—but I *know* this stuff, inside and out. Believe me, it would take you a week just to rule out impossible combinations of the main variables. We don't have time for that. I'll take your first suggestion. Let's go meet with the Farmers. Right now."

"Hey, what about your Negentropic Man? That's what me and Leo came here for, not to look at dead things that make you puke."

"Plenty of time to look at that, too. We can do it while Sylvia talks to the Farmers." The interaction with Aybee was a fight with sharp weapons. The other was aggressive—and *smart*.

"More time than you think," added Leo. "The Farmers may not agree to meet with you, Mr. Wolf."

"They have to," insisted Aybee.

"With *us*, they have to," said Sylvia. "They might be able to refuse to meet somebody from the Inner System, and get away with it."

"Then don't tell 'em where he's from." Aybee sounded impatient. "You and Leo can sort that out. The Wolfman and me need to see the stuff from inside his skull. Right? Let's get at it."

CHAPTER 12

"I know more than Apollo
For oft when he lies sleeping,
I see the stars at bloody wars,
In the wounded welkin weeping."

                     —Tom o' Bedlam's song

"The Neg-en-trop-ic Man." Aybee dissected the word, saying it slowly and thoughtfully. "And there he goes."

He pressed the button. For the tenth time, the grinning figure in red danced away across the screen and waved his goodbye.

"Any ideas?" When it wasn't form-change theory, Bey was ready to admit that Aybee had the better chance of deciding what was going on. Sylvia might return at any moment, and Bey wanted to have a lot of his thinking done before he ever encountered a Farmer.

"Too many ideas." Aybee scowled at him. "It's not a well-posed problem."

"You don't think he means what he says?—that he's a man with negative entropy?"

"I'm sure he isn't. For a start, negative entropy has no physical meaning." Aybee made a rude noise at the display and turned it off. " 'Negentropic' just refers to something that decreases the entropy of a system. So a Negentropic Man ought to be a man who reduces entropy."

"But what exactly *is* entropy?" Leo Manx had been listening carefully, while the conversation made less and less sense to him. "Remember, I'm supposed to send a report back to Cinnabar Baker. I can't send her your gibberish about negentropy, she'd jump all over us."

"Hey, is it my fault if you're a dummy?" Aybee looked down his nose at Leo. "I'll give you a bunch of entropy definitions. You can pick any one you like. And don't blame me if you're wrong, because I sure as hell don't know how the word is being used here. Oldest use: entropy in *thermodynamics*. Entropy change was defined as the change in the heat in a system, divided by its temperature. Can a process involving heat transfer be run backwards? If not, the entropy of the system must increase. Rudolph Clausius knew that, nearly four hundred years ago. He pointed out that entropy tends to go on increasing in any closed system. If the universe is a closed system, its entropy must increase. So then the universe is running down to a state of minimum organisation, and we'll all end in uniform-temperature soup."

"But we're talking about a *man* here, not a universe."

"I know that, Leo. Hold on a minute, I'm getting there. Remember, this is complicated stuff. We don't want to make it so easy it's meaningless. Einstein said it right: things should be as simple as possible—but not simpler. Maybe our Negentropic Man has something to do with thermodynamic entropy, maybe not. Entropy number two: Ludwig Boltzmann found a *statistical* definition of entropy, in terms of the number of possible states of the atoms and molecules of a system. He showed that it produced the same value as the thermodynamic one, provided the system has a whole lot of possible states."

"How do we decide which definition we want?"

"We can't—not yet. We keep going, then we'll play pick and choose. Entropy number three: in *information theory*. Fifty years after Boltzmann, Claude Shannon wanted to know how much information a message channel could carry. He found it depended on a particular mathematical expression. The formula was the same as Boltzmann's entropy formula, except for a sign change, so Shannon called the thing he calculated the *entropy* of the transmitted signal. That confused the hell out of people. The information-theory entropy is a maximum when the information carried is as much as you can get with a given channel."

"Aybee, you're not helping. Three forms of entropy—and not one of them intelligible. Why don't people use clearly defined terms?"

"Hey, I understand them fine. We're lucky there's only four to pick from. Do you have any idea how many different things the word *conjugate* can mean in mathematics? One more to go. *Kernels* have entropy. Even a non-rotating kernel—a Schwarzschild black hole—has an entropy. Two hundred and fifty years ago, Jakob Bekenstein pointed out that the area of a kernel's event horizon can be *exactly* equated to an entropy for the black hole."

"But we have to pick one of your four definitions! Aybee, how can we possibly do it? They're all totally different."

"No. They sound it, but they all tie together through the right mathematics. The mathematics of ensembles, it's called. As for deciding which one we ought to be thinking about . . . don't ask me. Spin a coin. Thermodynamic entropy, statistical mechanics entropy, information theory entropy, kernel horizon entropy—which one is Wolfman's buddy talking about? We don't know. But there's more. Before you spin that coin, let me give you the other half of it. You see, the universe moves to higher values of thermodynamic entropy—that's Clausius, and the Second Law of Thermodynamics. But *life*—any life, from us to bacteria and single-celled plants, is different—"

Aybee was interrupted. Sylvia Fernald hurried into the room, grabbed his arm, and began to pull him at once towards the door. "They'll meet with us," she said. "But we have to do it right this minute, before they change their minds. Come on."

She led the way for Aybee and Leo, leaving Bey floundering along behind. The others were expert at moving in low gravity. He still rolled and yawed and missed handholds. He reached the chamber half a minute after the others, and looked around for the elusive Farmers.

The room was dark and divided in two by a wall of ribbed black glass. As Bey stepped forward, dim ceiling lights came on and the glass wall lightened to full transparency. On the other side of the partition, shrouded in white garments that left visible only dark pairs of eyes, two human figures became visible.

"Five minutes," said a deep, whispering voice. Cowls were pushed back, to reveal smooth skulls and nervous skeletal faces. "We promised at most five minutes."

"Did you see your people in the form-change tanks?" asked Bey at once.

"I did," said the taller figure. The deep voice was expressionless. "I found them."

"Were they alive?"

"Already dead. According to the temperature monitors, already cold. They must have been dead for at least a day."

"And no emergency signal was sent from the tanks?"

"Nothing. All indicators showed normal."

"Has anything like this happened before? Something maybe less extreme?"

There was a pause, while the two Farmers turned to look at each other. "Tell them," said the second figure. It was a woman.

"I think we must." The man turned back to Bey. "We had noticed some peculiarities. Nothing serious, nothing that was not corrected on a second attempt with the form-change equipment. We considered calling for help, but after a vote we decided against the intrusion. Our colleagues who died took part in and approved of the decision."

"You know when the problem began," said Bey rapidly. The two Farmers were beginning to move about uneasily. "Can you relate it to anything else that happened here on the Farm? Any visitor, any change in procedures?"

There was another pause—precious seconds of interview time slipping away. "The problems began six months ago," said the woman. "There have been no visitors to the Farm in more than a year. New form-change equipment was delivered to us at that time, but it performed perfectly for many months."

"How about unusual events? Did anything odd happen six months ago?"

"Nothing," answered the man. "There were automated deliveries to us, but that is usual. There were cargo shipments from here to the Harvester, as always."

"And there were—"

"No," interrupted the man. He reached out a hand, shielding the woman's eyes from the four visitors but being careful not to touch her.

"I must tell. Two of us are dead because we valued privacy above their lives. It must not happen again." The woman moved so that she could see Bey. Her voice was shaking. "Six months ago, some of us began to see things when we were out on the Farm. Apparitions. Things that could not be real."

The glass partition was beginning to darken, the lights to fade. "What were they?" asked Bey.

"Many things. Five days ago I saw a woman, many kilometers high and dressed all in red. She had long brown hair. Her clothes were the clothes of old Earth, and she carried a basket. She was striding across the collection layer, in ten-kilometer paces. She wore a white peaked bonnet, and beneath it her face was the face of a madwoman."

"A white bonnet, and a scarlet dress?" Bey jerked upright and reached out a hand. The partition was almost black. The ceiling lights were dim glows of red.

"No more," said the white-garbed man. His voice had risen in pitch and volume. "Our records will be available to you. You can see what came to the Farm during the last year, what was sent from it. You can read what our people saw. But there can be no more direct contact. Good luck."

"One more question," said Bey. He was moving urgently towards the black glass. "It's terribly important."

But the room was dark again. There was no sound from the other side of the wall.

When the deadly strike came, each visitor to the Sagdeyev Space Farm was in a different part of the habitation bubble. Officially, it was to allow them to eat alone. In practice, each had deliberately sought privacy.

Bey had been dumbstruck by the Farmer's last words, to the point where he was hardly thinking at all. A brown-haired female, dressed in scarlet, carrying a basket and with a white bonnet on her head; that was his Mary, Mary Walton, exactly as she had looked in *The Duchess of Malfi*. Bey had seen it in live performance five times, and in recording another dozen.

A coincidence of dress? If so, it was too improbable a coincidence for him to accept. But if *anyone* were to see such visions of Mary, it surely ought to have been Bey himself—not some reclusive Farmer, someone who had no idea what she was looking at. Bey sat with his head buzzing, too perplexed to feel hungry or thirsty. Somewhere on the periphery of his mind he knew that one of Aybee's comments on entropy was vitally important. Those ideas had to be integrated with the appearance of the Negentropic Man, and with elements of Bey's own knowledge of form-change theory. But that synthesis had to wait, until thoughts of Mary no longer obsessed him. The temptation to seek her was growing now, even though his idea that she was tied to events on the Farm was probably self-deluding.

Aybee Smith had not noticed that Bey was off in his own world, but it didn't take him long to realise that talking to Bey at the moment was a waste of time. Aybee went off to a terminal and tested the Farmers' offer. The final promise had been genuine; all the Farm records had been made available to the visitors. Aybee set out to make a chronology of every external interaction recorded in the previous year, and then to correlate that with the hallucinations and the anomalies in form-change performance. There were many hundreds of entries, but Aybee had lots of time. He never slept much, and if necessary he would plug along at the job for the next twenty-four hours. Like Bey, he relished intellectual challenge more than anything else in the world. He felt alert, fresh, excited and confident.

Leo Manx felt none of those. He had been awake for two full days. He had hoped to sleep on the trip to the Farm, but Aybee had insisted on coming along; and then he had hardly stopped talking through the whole journey. The hi-probe quarters were too cramped to hide away, and Aybee was too loud to ignore. He had gone on and on about signal processing and signal encoding until Leo was mentally numb. Bey's hallucinations, according to Aybee, must have been single-frame inserts, patched into a general signal, but coded specifically to his personal psychological profile and comlink. No one else would notice the signal, even if they were watching the same channel as Bey. And it would be simple to make the single-frame inserts self-erasing, so even if Bey tried to play them back on a recording, there would be no sign of them.

Now, at a time when Leo would have welcomed a nap, he couldn't get Aybee's last comments out of his head. He rubbed at his aching temples, and stared at the notes he had made.

"The entropy of the whole universe is increasing," Aybee had said. "But that doesn't mean that the entropy of everything in it must be increasing. In fact, life has the opposite effect. It increases regular structure—nonrandom phenomena—at the expense of disorder. Life is *always* negentropic. It reduces the entropy of everything that it comes into contact with. So *everybody*, and everything living, is negentropic in that sense."

"But the Second Law of Thermodynamics, the one you were quoting earlier—"

"—says that entropy tends to a maximum in a *closed, isolated* system. It tells you nothing about open systems, ones that exchange energy with others. That's us. We don't live in isolation. The Sun and the stars are constant sources of energy, and every living thing in the Solar System uses energy to create order at the expense of disorder. In the thermodynamic sense, you and me and the Wolfman and Fern are all negentropic."

"How about the other meanings of entropy? Do they make more sense for a Negentropic Man?"

"Considered in information theory, the information in a message decreases when the entropy of the signal becomes less. A noisy communications channel is negentropic, so far as the signal is concerned. If that's what the Negentropic Man does, we're not seeing signs of it. The reported random error rate for signals received in the Inner and Outer Systems doesn't seem to have changed at all. If it did, people would be getting jumbled, gibberish messages all the time. And if that had happened, I would have heard about it."

"And your fourth form of entropy?"

"That's associated with the power kernels. Any black hole has a temperature, an entropy, a mass, and maybe an electrical charge. If it's a kernel, a Kerr-Newman black hole, it also has rotational energy and a magnetic moment. And that's all it *can* have—no other physical variables are permitted. A kernel sends out random particles and radiation according to a process and a formula discovered a couple of centuries ago. What it emits only depends on the kernel's mass, charge, and spin. For a small black hole—billion-ton, say—the emitted energy is up in the gigawatt range. That's what the kernel shields are for, to stop that radiation. The entropy depends on the mass of the black hole, but I think we can rule out this one. If Wolf's Negentropic Man were dealing with kernels, he'd have to be a superman. Nobody could live for a second inside the shields. All you find in there are sensors, data links, and spin-up/spin-down equipment for energy storage and generation. Here." He had thrust a data cube into Manx's hand. "What I've been saying is all basic stuff. You'll find it explained there."

Leo had taken the cube. Sitting alone in an outer

chamber of the habitation bubble, he had played it through twice. It was beginning to make some sense, considered as a set of abstract statements. But it had little to do with the capering man who had haunted Behrooz Wolf. He peered at the cube, closed his eyes for a moment or two, and was asleep before he knew he was near to it. All thoughts of entropy vanished. He dreamed that he was far from here, again on Earth, again roaming the old Chehel-sotun temple in Isfahan. But this time he was in free-fall, unhampered by that crushing gravity. He could not have chosen a more welcome dream.

Sylvia Fernald had the most need for total privacy. She was talking to Cinnabar Baker through a hyperbeam link. It was voice-only, hugely expensive to operate, and there was still an annoying thirty-second line-delay before a reply could be received.

"You must return to the Harvester," Baker was saying. "All of you, and at once. There are developments here that dwarf the Space Farm's problems. How soon can you leave?"

"I'll have to go and tell the others." Sylvia replied immediately, but she could imagine Baker at the other end, chafing at the transmission delay. "So far as Leo and I are concerned, we can leave at once. But Aybee and Wolf are reviewing the Farm's data bases. That may take a while."

There was a pause that felt more like half an hour than half a minute. "You can't wait for that." It was the voice of command. "When you get back here, you'll understand why. Leave now, as soon as you can. I'll explain when you get here. One more thing: have you been able to get closer to Wolf?"

"Not in the way you mean." (But somehow I got turned on watching him eating. Would you call that progress?) Fortunately it was a voice-only link. Sylvia was sure her face would have betrayed her—maybe her voice was doing it, too. "I'll see what happens on the way back," she said. "But I'm not optimistic. I'm sure he finds me as revolting to look at as I find him. And Leo told me Wolf is still infatuated with a woman he left on Earth."

There was a final annoying delay. "He didn't leave her on Earth," said Cinnabar Baker at last. "She left him, to run off with somebody from the Halo. Big difference. Keep trying. Link ends."

New problems on the Harvester! What's happening to the solar system? It's one damned thing after another.

Sylvia hurried out of the room. She was heading for Bey's quarters in the higher gravity region of the habitation bubble when the impact occurred.

CHAPTER 13

No recording instruments on the Sagdeyev Space Farm survived the impact. The whole encounter had to be deduced from other evidence.

The object hit the southern hemisphere of the habitation bubble, close to the pole. It was a jagged brown chunk of the Primitive Solar Nebula, mostly methane and water-ice, and it massed about eighty million tons. With a relative velocity of a kilometer a second, it smashed clear through the bubble and emerged from the side of the northern hemisphere. It also missed by thirty meters a collision with the shields of the power kernel, and so failed to assure the immediate death of all humans on the Farm.

The momentum that the impact transferred to the habitation bubble did three things. It broke the bubble loose from the Farm's billion-kilometer collection layer. It left the bubble with a new velocity vector and a new orbit, sharply inclined to its old one. And it set the bubble spinning around the central power kernel as it caromed away into space.

Two thousand machines were left behind on the detached collection layer. After the first confusion they managed very well. The smarter ones herded the others into tight little groups, then settled down to wait for instructions or rescue. Whether that took place in one day or in one century made little difference. The smart machines knew enough to keep things under control for a long time. Not one of the two thousand was damaged.

The humans on the Farm were less lucky. Four of the Farmers were in chambers on the direct path of the intruding body. They died at once. Two others were left in airless rooms and could not reach suits. The rest of the Farmers followed the standard emergency procedure, and were into the lifeboat and clear of the bubble in less than a minute.

The visitors from the Harvester were both more and less fortunate. Their chambers were not on the main line of the collision, and the impact was felt at first as no more than a short-lived and violent jerk of acceleration. Leo Manx, Sylvia Fernald, and Aybee Smith did not know the emergency routines specific to the Farm, but they had been trained to react defensively. High acceleration of a habitation unit equalled disaster. They did not wait to see if the integrity of the bubble's outer hulls had been breached. As soon as they picked themselves up after the first shock of collision, they headed for the survival suits. They could live in them for at least twenty-four hours. Aybee had a mild concussion. Leo had five cracked ribs and a broken leg, but his deep-space training allowed him to override pain until he was safe in his suit.

Bey Wolf was in much deeper trouble. His room was closest to the line of destruction. Worse than that, he lacked the right reflexes. He knew there had been a major accident, but he had to attempt by thought what the others did by instinct.

He had been thrown head first and hard against the communications terminal. Drops of blood from deep cuts on his cheek and forehead were already drifting across the room when he came to full consciousness. His head was ringing, and he was nauseated. He wiped at his face with his shirt and staggered to the door. It was closed. Beyond it he heard a hiss of air, and he could feel the draught at the door's edge.

The sliding partition was tight-fitting, but not airtight. He had maybe a couple of minutes before the pressure dropped too low to be breathable. Just as bad, a faint plume of green gas was seeping *into* the room, and the slightest trace was enough to start him coughing. Wall refrigeration pipes must have ruptured. He might choke before he died of lack of air.

Suits. Where the devil were they kept? Bey hauled himself across to the storage units on the other side of the room. He jerked them open, one after another. Everything from chessboards to toothbrushes spilled out. No suit.

He caught another whiff of gas, coughed horribly, and mopped again at his bleeding face. What now? Where else might a suit be kept? Don't panic. *Think!*

He realised that if the data terminal were still working, it could tell him what he needed to know in a couple of seconds. He was moving across to it when the knock came on the door.

The sound was so unexpected that for a moment he did not react at all. Then he had a terrible thought. If someone out there in a suit were to try to come in . . .

"Don't touch the door." He shouted it, but already his voice sounded fainter in the thinning air. Asphyxiation would get him, not poison gas. He was aware of pain in his ears, and the cramping agony of trapped gas forced out of his intestines.

"Bey?" The cry from outside was muffled. It was Sylvia. "Bey, can you hear me?"

"Yes. Don't open the door."

"I know. Do you have a suit?"

"Can't find it."

"By the data terminal. In the foot locker."

He didn't waste air replying. The suit was there. But now he had to fight his way into it. He was growing dizzy, panting uselessly. He got his legs and arms in and pulled the suit up around the shoulders. But the helmet was too much. He concentrated all his attention on the smooth head unit, and managed to place it roughly in position. But he could not seal it. Anoxia was winning. The room was turning dark. At the edge of unconsciousness, Bey realised how much he wanted to live.

He was fighting the seals—and losing—when there was a crash behind him and a rush of escaping air. His lungs collapsed as the pressure dropped to zero. When

Sylvia arrived at his side he was almost unconscious, still groping single-mindedly at the helmet. She slapped it into position and turned the valve. The rush of air inside the suit began.

She bent to look into the faceplate. Bey's face was a mottled nightmare of fresh red blood and cyanotic blue skin. As she watched, the oxygen-starved look faded. The chest of the suit gave a series of shuddering heaves. Alive. Sylvia grabbed Bey's suited arm and began to drag him. She had come here at once, as soon as her suit was on, and she did not know the cause of the problem. Another crash or explosion might happen at any moment. Like any Cloudlander, she fled for the safety of open space.

The exit wound of the colliding chunk provided the widest and easiest way out. Sylvia and Bey accompanied a mass of flotsam, flying out into space with the last puff of internal air from the bubble.

Bey was unconscious. Sylvia, shaking with exhaustion, held him tightly and looked around them. The collection layer of the Farm had been left far behind. The surviving Farmers had moved their lifeboat close to the shattered bubble, and half a dozen of them were preparing to reenter through an airlock. They had a clear duty toward their missing fellows: rescue, or space burial.

Sylvia could see the ship that she and Bey had arrived on. It floated a few kilometers clear of the bubble, apparently undamaged, its warning beacons a red glow against the stars. She was not sure that she had the strength to get there. She set out, dragging Bey along with her. When she was nearly there she saw a suited figure jetting across to help her. It was Aybee.

"Leo?" she said.

"Inside. Banged up, but not too bad." Aybee took over and hauled Bey along behind him. "How's with the Wolfman here?"

"Hurt some." She was shivering. "He should be all right. Where's our other ship?"

Aybee waved his arm through a wide circle. "You tell me. The beacon's not working. I don't know how we'll ever find it."

As he passed Bey through the lock, Sylvia took a last look around. There was no sign of the ship that Aybee had arrived in. It was lost somewhere in the darkness, indistinguishable from a million other pieces of stellar flotsam.

She collapsed as she stepped out of the airlock. In the past twenty minutes she had forced her body all the way to its physical limits. Any more help for Bey Wolf would have to come from someone else.

Bey woke up three times.

Pain was the first stimulus. Someone was hurting his face, stabbing again and again at his cheek and forehead. "A bit crude," said a voice. "But it'll do. Couple more stitches, I'll be all done. You're a mess. You hearing me, Wolfman? No beauty prizes for you." The sharp pain came again, followed by a wash of icy fluid across his face. Bey grunted in protest, and drifted back to unconsciousness.

The second time was more alarming. And more painful. He woke, and tried to touch his throbbing left cheek. He couldn't do it. Something had him firmly held, unable to move. He began to struggle, to pull randomly against his restraints. He was too confused and dizzy to analyse what was happening, or why, but he fought like an animal, straining as hard as he could. It was futile. He was working against straps designed to hold a human body secure under a ten-gee acceleration. Exhausted after just a few seconds, he lapsed again to unquiet sleep.

Pain and consciousness came faster the third time, and with them—at last—vision. He was lying with his eyes open, staring at a woman's face. It was only inches away from him, pale and still. There was a tracery of blue veins on the temples, and the violet-black smudge of deadly fatigue below the closed eyes. He studied it, puzzled by its familiarity. Who was she? That rounded brow was well known to him. He tried to lift his arm to touch the delicate skull and the fine red hair. He could not do it. They were strapped side by side, lying on a single narrow bunk and securely held in position.

As he placed his fingers on the release mechanism of his harness, awareness returned. And with it, fear. He remembered. Violent impact. The panicky hunt for a suit. The fight for air. Sylvia's appearance at his side, just as that fight was lost.

He had a vague, surrealistic memory then of the nightmare ride through space, stars blurred points through a bloodstained visor.

"Sylvia!" She did not move.

Bey struggled free and sat up. He was again on the transit ship, and the McAndrew drive was on. They were moving with an indicated acceleration of a couple of hundred gees. He was lying in the same bunk with Sylvia Fernald. On the other bunk, strapped in and wrapped like a cocoon from neck to ankles, lay Leo Manx. As Bey straightened up, Leo's eyes rolled towards him.

"Where's Aybee?" said Bey.

"I don't know. But the last time I saw him he was all right." Leo turned his head, slowly and gingerly. "It is Sylvia I have been worrying about. I cannot move, and I cannot see her monitors. How is she?"

Bey scanned the condition sensors, supplementing that with his own touch to her cheek and forehead. "Out cold, but everything shows normal. What happened to her—and to you, too. And where's Aybee? And where are we heading?"

"Mr. Wolf, I am sure you can ask more questions than I can answer." Leo Manx's silky voice was gruffer. He was either in much pain, or terribly ill at ease. "I'll do my best. Sylvia Fernald made a supreme physical effort when she saved you, but it was too much for her. She collapsed as she reached the ship. At my suggestion and with the medical system's concurrence, Aybee extended her natural period of unconsciousness. She should sleep until we are close to the Marsden Harvester—our planned destination, where we should now find Cinnabar Baker. What was *not* my suggestion"—Leo Manx grimaced, with displeasure and then with pain—"was the idea that I would be bound here like an Egyptian mummy, unable to release myself. If you would be kind enough to free the harness . . ."

"What happened to you?"

"Broken ribs, and broken leg. Aybee exceeded his duties and his authority when he anaesthetized me, and then did this."

Bey moved to examine the telesensors for Leo Manx, spent a few seconds with the displays, and shook his head. "Sorry. The monitors agree with Aybee. You stay like that until it tells me something different. You should not move."

"Mr. Wolf, I assure you that I am quite able to—"

"Don't take my word for it. Try a deep breath." Bey watched as Manx tentatively inhaled, and gasped with pain. "Case closed. What about Aybee?"

Manx rolled his eyes toward the tiny console crowded against the cabin wall. Everything on the transit ships was a third of the usual size. "It was my expectation that he would be with us on this ship. Clearly, he is not. But according to the signal there, a message is waiting for us. I have been looking at the indicator for some time, but unfortunately I cannot reach it."

Bey went across to turn on the unit. As he did so he saw his own reflection in the display screen. Whatever Aybee's talents, plastic surgery was not one of them. Bey's face and forehead were criss-crossed with crude, ugly stitches, and the skin on his left cheek had been pulled down so far that the red socket of his eye was exposed. There was no chance that such a mess would heal cleanly. He would have to use one of the Cloudland form-change tanks. He switched on the set. Aybee's image showed no sign of either excitement or injury. He scowled out of the display like a bad-tempered baby. "I don't know which of you will be watching this, but hi. If it's you, Leo, I didn't lie to you. I intended to come along as well. But the ship was awful crowded once I had you in your bunks, and with those ribs I knew you wouldn't enjoy anybody cuddling up close to you, the way Sylv and the Wolfman were doing last time I saw 'em. So." He shrugged. "I had to change my mind. And

I haven't found any trace of the other ship. I'll look again, but if I'm delayed getting back there, don't be surprised. Here's a few things for you to chew on. First, the female Farmer we talked to. She's dead. We'll never get any more about that woman she saw walking on the collection layer. Second, the Farm can be saved, but the data banks are shot. So you should drop the idea that we can correlate the form-change problems with events on the Farm and the collection layer. I was doing that when the bubble was hit, and I'll tell you the only thing I'd noticed. The form-changes starting to go wrong coincided with a doubling of energy use on the Farm. That fact's for Wolf—you there, Wolfman?—and I hope you can make more out of it than I can. Bet you can't, though. Here's my last thought, and it's for anybody who wants it. From all I can tell, the bubble was hit by a Cloud fragment, one that was travelling unusually fast and from an unusual direction. Bad luck, you say?—except that the Farm had sky-scanning sensors, and the bubble had a standard response system. That fragment ought to have been given a little laser nudge when it was millions of kilometers away, and missed us by a nice margin."

He smiled from the screen, a humorless grin. "Now, I know what you're thinking, Leo. It's old paranoid Aybee, at it again. But try it on the Wolfman—he thinks more the way I do. And while he worries that, here's one more thing for you. The equipment that protected the Farm from space junk is the same type as we use on all the Harvesters. Foolproof, triple-tested, infallible. If the Farm can get hit, so can anything else. Nice thought, eh? Sweet dreams, you three. Think entropy."

The screen blanked. As it did so, the system alert inside the ship's cabin sounded its warning beep. They were close to crossover, the place where the ship rotated through 180 degrees and they changed from acceleration to deceleration. For that thirty seconds they needed to be strapped in.

Bey headed for the bunk, lying down again alongside Sylvia. As he did so, Leo Manx gave a gasp of irritation. "Mr. Wolf! Don't let it do that."

A spray syringe was creeping out of its holder above Manx, and quietly positioning itself close to his neck.

Bey paused from his strapping-in and checked the monitors. "Don't worry. It's only an anaesthetic. Apparently the robodoc thinks you're being too active."

"But I have no wish to go to sleep. Mr. Wolf. Stop it!"

"Sorry. Can't disobey doctor's orders." Bey lay back on the narrow bunk, squashed up next to Sylvia Fernald. He watched as the spray mist passed painlessly through Leo Manx's skin, and as the other man fell asleep in midprotest.

Bey liked Leo, and enjoyed talking to him. But at the moment he needed time to chew on what Aybee had said. If he had been allowed one guess as to something that might correlate with the deaths in the form-change tanks, he would have picked sabotage—something in the software on the Farm's central computer complex. That fitted the idea that feedback information was being tampered with, or supplied incorrectly. What he would never have picked, in a hundred guesses, was the Farm's total energy load. In fact, he could see no way that it *could* be involved.

He felt fully awake. His aches and pains were unpleasant, and there was a disturbing buzzing in his ears. But he could stand that. He lay back in the bunk, ready for a long, intense session of thought. By the time that he saw the anaesthetic syringe at his neck it was too late.

"Hey! No. I don't need—" Like Leo Manx, Bey fell asleep in mid-protest.

Bey had checked Sylvia's condition, and Leo Manx's, but not his own. He believed he was doing fine. The transit ship's computer disagreed. It knew that he should be safely asleep and resting, but it also understood that he was unlikely to obey a computer command. The machine had waited impatiently for crossover, knowing that Bey would then have to return to his bunk. Now, satisfied once more with the physical condition of all three passengers, the computer turned to other matters. At its direction the speeding ship passed through crossover point, and raced on for the second half of its journey to the Marsden Harvester.

The computer was justly proud of its performance. It encountered hardware problems so seldom that the automatic error-correcting codes were called on only a couple of times a year. Error checking and correction was completely automatic. No human realised it, but the ship's rate of signal error generation was less than a thousandth of that of the computers on the Marsden Harvester—and less than a millionth of the rate for the now-destroyed computer on the Sagdeyev Space Farm.

CHAPTER 14

"War is nothing more than the continuation of state policy by other means."
—Karl Von Clausewitz

"A thermonuclear war cannot be considered a continuation of politics by other means. It would be a means to universal suicide."
—Andrei Sakharov

Conflict between the Inner and Outer Systems was a battle between a cat and a kestrel, between a lion and an eagle. Each could hurt the other—perhaps fatally. But neither could possess the other's territory, nor rationally want to do so. Fifty million people might annihilate twenty billion, but they could never subjugate them. No sane Cloudlander desired to live crowded in to the Sun and the inner planets. And despite their enormous superiority in numbers, twenty billion could never control the sparse and infinitely dispersed inhabitants of the Cloud, constantly drifting outward, always farther from the Sun. No member of the United Space Federation could stand the cold, open space of the Cloud.

War was senseless. And yet war came creeping steadily closer. Its presence could be seen and felt, in the angry faces of people on the Harvesters, in the hoarding of food supplies and metals, in the false confidence and self-righteousness of the government speeches, and in the tense warning notes that flew between the Inner and Outer Systems.

Cinnabar Baker felt it better than anyone. She was officially responsible for the operation and maintenance of the Harvesters, but that position carried an additional duty as head of System Security. It made Baker, the most junior of the three people who ruled the Cloud, also the most powerful.

A couple of thousand staff members on her payroll sent back official reports from locations in the Cloud. Twice that number, scattered through the Inner System and the Halo, provided Baker's unofficial information network. If someone sneezed on Ceres, and that sneeze might mean bad news for the Cloud, Cinnabar Baker wanted to know about it.

Bey Wolf had watched the big woman in action, and asked himself, what makes Cinnabar run? The easy answer was the official one. She worked enormously hard directing the Harvesters, and that work gave her satisfaction. But the innermost depth of Cinnabar Baker, the invisible place where the ego is so delicate that a feather's touch will bruise it, lay elsewhere. She loved and cherished her secret security operation. The network was her eyes and ears. She would do anything to keep it in place. Yet even that was not her secret pride. When word drifted in through the grapevine of an impending disaster at the Sagdeyev Space Farm, she could not compromise her sources. There might be a chain of a dozen informants involved, each with his own unreliability quotient, and each with his own cover. Every one had to be protected. No details had been available, no statement of how or when an "accident" might be expected. Cinnabar Baker had a choice: she could ignore the rumblings of her own intelligence net, or she could recall Leo Manx and the others from important work.

She had chosen to send that urgent recall message, but the news of the Farm's destruction had not yet reached her. The Farmers were too reclusive a group to offer frequent messages. Silence was not significant. She

had no way of knowing that they were now struggling to
devise a makeshift communications link from the remains
of the old one.

Baker had the habit of returning to her office after
the evening meal, clearing her desk and starting again to
work as though it were the dawn of a new day. She had
arrived at the Marsden Harvester only that morning, but
now, at an hour when most humans were settling in for
their three or four hours of sleep, she was beginning to
sieve through the mass of print-outs of the day's incoming messages.

She had three types of informant. There were the ones
she had carefully planted over the years, reliable Cloudlanders who knew what she needed and who understood
how to screen important information from rumors and
rubbish. Baker took any inputs from them seriously.

The paid informants were another matter. Loyal to no
one, they tended to send her any old rubbish, hoping
that it might somehow be worth money. Their inputs had
to be looked at hard, and almost everything was dis-
carded or given little weight.

Then there were the revolutionaries. Small groups
within the Inner System were working for the overthrow
of their own government, and they were willing to form
alliances with the Outer System in order to do it. They
provided information free, and would be outraged at any
suggestion of payment. Cinnabar Baker worked with
them, and used their inputs. But she had no illusions
about their value. Most of her informants on Earth or
Mars preached the overthrow of the United Space Federation, but they would never live in the Cloud or the
Halo. Worse than that, they saw every event through the
distorting lens of their own paranoia.

Cinnabar Baker had inspected Bey Wolf very carefully
during their first meeting. Wolf's reputation for intelligence and insight was extremely high. But Leo Manx had
told of a self-destructive, hallucinating man, obsessed
with a former lover. That fitted the pattern of an Inner
System paranoid, one who might someday be converted
to form part of her recruited group of unpaid informants.

She had dropped that thought in the first fifteen minutes of their meeting. Wolf was too strong and too sceptical, too cold and analytical. He could not be manipulated in the usual ways.

But there were also unusual ways. At the end of that first meeting, Cinnabar Baker had set a high-priority trace on the whereabouts of Mary Walton. So far, she had two things. The first was a recent poor-quality photograph of Mary Walton standing with her arm around the waist of a stern-faced man. Even in that faded image, his eyes were the commanding orbs of a fanatic, blazing out of the picture. Scribbled on the back of the photograph were the co-ordinates of a location in the Kernel Ring, accompanied by a question mark.

Those co-ordinate strings had been noted as a place for future investigation, but not as a high-priority item. Baker had no idea how she might use any information on Mary Walton, but patience and foresight were two of her main strengths. She would never admit she was willing to work with anyone and anything to achieve her goals, but she would have found it hard to name a group she would reject.

Tonight there were ninety messages for her review. Half of them came from official news reports, the rest from her own network. With Turpin crooning on her shoulder, his black head bobbing or tucked away under one shabby wing, she set to work.

Outer System first—she was not naïve enough to believe that informants were needed only for the Inner System and the Halo. Most messages were simple statements of production or equipment problems. She skimmed through them, doing no more than confirm that the pattern of the past year was still present. The Outer System was going to hell. Navigation systems were failing, cargo transit vessels from the Inner System did not arrive, power systems were unstable or running close to failure, Harvesters failed their quality control tests, communications were suffering inexplicable glitches, and cargo packages that dropped Sol-ward from the Cloud were disappearing on the way. Aybee had done an analysis for her, and confirmed what she knew instinctively. What they were seeing was far outside the limits of statistical reasonableness.

In the mind of most of the Cloud's population, that left only one possibility: sabotage. And as the only instigator, the Inner System. Cinnabar Baker did not agree at all. She had her own ideas as to what was going on, and who was causing the trouble.

"But it's *how*, Turpin. How can Ransome affect all the control systems? That's the problem; and no one can help me with that."

The crow made a rattling noise like a set of bone dice being shaken, and stared at the sheets of paper with head to one side. "It's a bugger," it said solemnly.

"Indeed it is." Baker turned to the reports on the Inner System. The profile there had been slower to develop, lagging the pattern in the Cloud by a year or two. Now it was unmistakable to anyone who had watched events closely in both regions. It was the same story of inexplicable failure. Transit ships were disappearing, massive food shipments were failing to arrive on schedule, power supplies had become unreliable.

And the Inner System was reacting in a predictable way. They were blaming the Outer System. There was anger, and talk of sabotage, and threats of reprisals.

Cinnabar Baker could identify three people in the whole System who knew that the Inner and Outer Systems were not sabotaging each other. She was one. Her counterpart in the Inner System, a man whom she respected enormously but whom she had never met, was another. The third was the person who was causing all the trouble.

More and more, the lines of evidence converged on the Kernel Ring, and on the shadowy no-man's-land of Ransome's Hole. She was feeling her way towards its location, but her informants in the Ring had a habit of cutting off contact without warning. She had lost half a dozen in a few months. Her adversary seemed to know everything she did, as soon as she made up her mind to do it. She had looked unsuccessfully for the leak in her

own operations. She continued her efforts, assembling
fragments, pulsing her web of informants; but she was
still a long way from a set of co-ordinates for Ransome's
Hole.

And when she had them, what then? It was not clear
that a direct attack would succeed—or if it did, that the
sabotage would cease. Baker sighed and rubbed the poll
of Turpin, still quietly watching her flip the pages.

"Come on, crow. We've earned a break." She set down
the listings and wandered off towards the door, the bird
still gripping her shoulder. It was the middle of the quiet
period, and every rational person was asleep. Baker met
no one as she padded barefoot along half a mile of silent
corridor.

As she opened the crèche door, the sounds began.
Forty babies were crying, fifty more gulping and grunting
as they were fed by the machines. Three hundred others
were sleeping peacefully. The solitary human attendant
was lying down at the end of the room, eyes closed.

Cinnabar Baker did not wake him. She did not want
conversation. When she arrived at any Harvester, an
unheralded visit to its crèches was a high priority. To
her, it was the heart of the world. She had never found
a habitat where things were going well in the crèche,
and badly elsewhere.

She watched and listened for twenty minutes, walking
along the aisles and occasionally picking up and holding
one of the babies. They ranged in age from two days to
two months. One new-born had been placed in a form-
change tank for remedial work on a deformed limb.
Baker peered in through the transparent port and
checked the progress of the change. It was normal. She
made a mental note to return in three days to make sure
the outcome was satisfactory.

She checked the instruction monitors above each crib,
noting the frequency and duration of the parents' visits.
Finally she was satisfied. She stole away, rejuvenated,
ready for hours more of tedious work.

The government of the Inner System knew Cinnabar
Baker as a powerful, formidable woman. They would

have been little comforted to know that she happened
to be sterile. She was the biggest threat to their independence and way of life.

Perhaps they were right. But if so, it was only because
she could sense full-scale war looming closer and closer.
Cinnabar Baker saw herself as the secret mother of the
whole System. Her children could not be allowed to fight
each other, to kill each other. She would prevent that—
even if the whole System had to be under her control
before she could stop them.

To an inhabitant of Earth, all the Harvesters were the
same. They were remote, identical food factories, run by
soul-less machines and populated by a thin sprinkling of
people.

Bey was beginning to learn the truth. Each Harvester
was different, as different as the separate planets and
asteroids of the Inner System.

It had begun the moment they left the first airlock.
He had been swathed from head to foot in flowing hospital robes that left only his eyes showing, strapped to a
stretcher, and maneuvered swiftly inward from the surface. The sounds began in the first interior corridor. The
Opik Harvester had been eerily quiet, but this habitat
was filled with music, lush instrumental pieces that had
not been heard on Earth for centuries. Each concentric
set of chambers blended harmoniously into the next,
even though the same work was never played in both.

Bey looked for the source of the music. It was invisible, projectors hidden behind the luxuriant green plants
that climbed restlessly over walls and ceiling. He recognised them. They were an adaptation, a variant on the
free-space vacuum vines popular in the asteroid belt.

And then there were the people. The ones he had met
on the other Harvester had been furious—angry at the
Inner System in general, and at Bey in particular. They
resented his presence, enough to want to fight him.

The Marsden Harvester's population did not show
rage. They stank with fear. The people he saw as he was
hurried through the corridors gave him not a second

look. They were afraid, preoccupied with other matters, and most surprising of all, many of them were sick or deformed.

"I've never seen anything like it," said Sylvia, after they had moved past a group of agitated people. "This is the oldest of the Harvesters, and usually it's the most peaceful. They're all scared."

"They look terrible."

"They do." She turned to face him. "And so do you. Those cuts on your face are bleeding again. I'd take you right to the form-change tanks with Leo, but Cinnabar Baker wants to see you first."

"It's mutual." Bey had been brooding over one fact since he woke in the transit ship. According to Sylvia, it was Cinnabar Baker's order for an emergency departure from the Space Farm that had given Sylvia enough lead time to save them. "I have a question for Baker."

They had left the clean, open corridors of the Harvester's periphery, and were plunging on towards the center of the main sphere. This region had been built before mastery of construction without metals had been fully achieved. The vines were absent, and the chambers were shabby past hope of disguise. The walls sagged inward, the floor was wrinkled and blackened, and hair-like outgrowths of hydrocarbon filament blurred the clean outline of lighting units and ventilators. To Bey it was oddly comforting. It reminded him of Earth's familiar run-down cities.

Cinnabar Baker's apartment was the one point of constancy. It was identical to the bland chambers that she had occupied before, with plain furniture and drab beige walls. Turpin perched on the back of a chair, as dusty and dishevelled-looking as ever. The crow greeted the newcomers with a sinister muttering.

"Don't mind Turpin. He's been in a bad mood since we got here." Baker took a hard look at Sylvia, then at Bey's mangled face. She gestured to the grey chairs. "Ten minutes, Mr. Wolf, that's all I need. Then we'll get you to a form-change tank for remedial treatment—if you still want to go there."

"More problems?"

"And worse ones. Did you meet any people as you came here?"

"Dozens of them."

"So you know how they look. Do you know what's wrong with them?"

Bey shrugged. "Obviously, they're not using the form-change tanks. And some of the people I saw appeared old. They need treatment—soon."

"You didn't see the worst cases. The population of this Harvester has the highest average age of any group in the Outer System."

"Then you have an emergency. Some of the people I saw won't last more than a couple of weeks. Why won't they use the tanks?"

"They're afraid to." Baker passed a card across to Bey. "Those are the statistics for the performance of form-change equipment on this Harvester. I headed here as soon as I saw the figures. We're facing a ten per cent failure rate—many of them leading to death. Some of the units are going wrong three-quarters of the time, and the results are hideous. People won't go near a tank, and it's hard to blame them." She frowned at Bey. "Mr. Wolf, why are you smiling? There is nothing funny in this."

"Sorry." What Bey was feeling was not humor. It was relief. "If I was smiling, it's because I can finally do something to justify my presence."

"Do you know what's wrong?"

"Not yet. But I will in a few days." Now both women were staring at him in perplexity. He realised that a smile on his stitched and battered face must be a gruesome sight.

"What we faced before were intermittent faults," he went on. "One-in-a-million faults. That kind are almost impossible to track down. You can set up test procedures, and observe for years, but you may never run across anything wrong while you're actually watching. Now we're in a different situation. I can set up monitors on a few tanks, and be sure I'll find something on at least one of them in a reasonable time. Give me a day or two."

"Can you correct the problem?" Baker's face showed her own relief. "I know it's early to ask that, but we need to tell people something."

"If I can find it, I can fix it. And I'm pretty sure I'll find it."

"How?" Sylvia looked at Baker. "I don't want to be the pessimist, but we have to know how he does it. Bey has to go into a form-change tank himself in a little while."

She was *worried* about him. Bey Wolf's surprise was genuine. He had lived with form-change equipment for so long, it had never occurred to him that someday he might die with it. In this one area he was completely confident. "I'll tell you just what I'm going to do. It's no big mystery, and once you understand it, you can do it, too. I'm sure the form-change problems are software, not hardware—we established that on the Space Farm. We'll use a diagnostic program that exits the form-change program after every major step, and performs a status check. When we find a software inconsistency, we run a ferret routine to trace it back to the block of instructions that produced it."

"Is it easy?"

"It's routine. It's exactly what BEC does when they are testing a radically new form. I'll show you how it's done. But before we do *that*"—Sylvia was standing up— "I have a request."

Cinnabar Baker nodded politely. Bey knew that she would have preferred him to get right down to work on the form-change process.

"You sent Sylvia an urgent message, telling us all to leave the Farm," he said. "Why did you do that? If it was just to get me back here to look at form-change problems, why drag Aybee and Leo Manx back, too? They still had things to do on the Farm."

"Mr. Wolf, if you ever tire of the Inner System, there is a position for you in the Cloud." Cinnabar Baker nodded slowly. "You are very astute. I had a warning—a tip-off—that something bad was going to happen to the Farm. The Farmers themselves would ignore any request to leave, but it would have been criminal to leave the four of you there without warning."

"You were told that we were all in danger?"

"No. I was warned on your behalf, specifically. It was my conclusion that you were all at risk."

"Who told you? I suppose that you have a network of your own—people who serve as your informants, pass on to you rumors and gossip."

Sylvia looked uneasy at his comment, but Baker nodded again, her manner relaxed. "I do. Naturally, it is not something that we advertise."

"Does it work both ways—to *spread* information and questions through the System, as well as collecting answers?"

"Only too well." Baker paused for a moment, looking around her. "It may be happening now. I am not the only one who uses informers. Secret information leaks from my office so quickly that others often seem to know it before my own staff."

"That's fine. I want something spread as widely as possible, and I want it spread as a rumor."

"It can be done. What is it, Mr. Wolf?"

"I want you to get out the word that I was killed in the accident on the Sagdeyev Space Farm."

"Easy enough to do. But why do you want it?"

"Protective paranoia. Someone was after me when I was on Earth, trying to drive me crazy. I think they were still after me on the Farm—it's a self-indulgent idea, that someone would arrange to destroy the whole Farm just to get me. But I believe it, and I think you do. If they know I'm here and still working for you, they'll keep trying. The safest person is a dead man."

"Dead man," repeated Turpin in a sepulchral whisper. "Dead man." He walked along the back of the chair and peered at Wolf with bright, beady eyes.

"Very well." Baker nodded, but Bey could see the doubt on her face. Was she continuing his own train of thought? If it were improbable that someone was seeking to end Bey's life or destroy his sanity, their continued failure was even more improbable. He had been too

lucky. And it opened again the question as to why he
was worth killing—or worth saving.

In his dog days at the Office of Form Control, Bey
had sometimes thought of the detection of illegal forms
as a vast game of chess. In that game he was the master
player, one who controlled the movement of people and
equipment on a giant board that spanned the space from
Mercury to Pluto. It was a game that he had never lost.

Now another game was being played, on a much bigger board and with higher stakes. This was a battle over
a territory that ranged from the Sun to the edge of the
Cloud, one that stretched a quarter of the way to the
stars, a new game that was spreading panic and anger
and threat of total war through the whole System. And
this time, Bey himself was nothing more than a pawn.

CHAPTER 15

"A Kerr-Newman black hole, or kernel, charged and rotating, is a highly dynamic object. The rotational contribution to its mass-energy can be extracted (or added to) using the Penrose process, and the kernel's own electric charge can be used to hold it in position, or to control its movement from place to place. Thus, such black holes are "live"; they can provide energy to or remove energy from their surroundings, in a controllable way, and they can be placed at any desired location. They are power kernels.

A Schwarzschild black hole is a kernel that is neither charged nor rotating. It is a kernel in a debased and limiting form, a spherically symmetrical object that has lost all electric charge and rotational energy. It is "dead," in the sense that one cannot extract from it in a controllable way any of its mass-energy. Unless it is "spun up" (i.e. given rotational energy using the Penrose process) it is not useful for power production.

The Schwarzschild black hole is not, however, totally inert. Like any other kernel, it gives off particles and radiation from its hidden interior according to the Hawking evaporative

process, at a rate depending only on its mass (smaller black holes emit more strongly than larger ones). However, the pattern of this emission is predictable only in overall statistical terms. All events and processes occurring within a certain region about the center of any black hole, whether of Schwarzschild or Kerr-Newman type, are unknowable. The interior of the black hole within this "event horizon" constitutes, in some sense, a separate universe from ours."
    —from the 2011 centennial Festschrift volume, compiled in celebration of John Archibald Wheeler's one hundredth birthday.

Aybee was in trouble. He was smart enough to know it, and smart enough to realize he was unlikely to get out in a hurry.

His decision to remain on the ruined Farm had been perfectly reasonable. There was too little space for him on the transit ship; Leo and the others were in the competent hands of the ship's emergency medical system; and Aybee himself was not urgently needed back on the Harvesters. His offer to help the Farmers had been politely—and predictably—refused. While they were maneuvering the habitation bubble back into contact with the collection layer, Aybee switched to a long-duration suit and went hunting.

He had two items he particularly wanted to find among the thousands of bits of debris created in the collision. One was the ship he had arrived in. It would almost certainly need repairs, but it might be his quickest way home when he was ready to leave.

With the help of the suit's microwave sensors he found it in the first twelve hours. It was floating a couple of thousand kilometers from the collection layer, with a small relative velocity. Aybee tagged it with a tracking beacon and went on to the harder part of his search.

The central computer of the Farm had been on the direct line of impact. Not even a trace of it was left. But there must have been backup storage for its records. It was in a region of the bubble that had been smashed open by the impact but not totally destroyed. Somewhere in the mess around the Farm Aybee hoped to find the secondary storage cube. It would be small, no bigger than his fist, and he had no illusions about how hard it would be to find it.

With so much debris of all shapes and sizes, the only hope of identification was through the data cube's reflectance spectrum. He selected the spectral signature for a data cube, set up a spatial survey for it, and settled down to wait. While the scan was being performed, he finally had time to look around him.

And to gasp.

If he had been less busy, he might have noticed it hours earlier. A dark oblong stretched across a quarter of the sky, hiding the bright starfield. He cut in his low-light sensors, and saw it at once as a massive cargo craft, drifting closer with unlit ports and with drive off. It was the type used to carry food shipments from the Cloud to the Inner System, a low-acceleration ellipsoidal hull over a kilometer long and six hundred meters across. It felt close enough to touch.

Aybee did not consider for one moment that it might be a rescue vessel. The approaching shape was too dark and lifeless. He floated himself across to a tangle of ruined cabin furniture and set himself in the middle of it.

The hulk approached within two hundred meters of the battered habitation bubble. A dark port opened, and a file of suited figures emerged. Their suits were bulky, ending in a characteristic flared and massive lower section. That solid base contained low and high thrust jets, power supply, food, air, and water recycling systems, medical facilities, exercise units and communications equipment. At the wearer's command, the flared bottom would open out to a thin-walled twenty-meter sphere, or couple with one or more other suits to form a common living volume.

Only one group used suits like that. Podders!

But these were Podders many billions of kilometers away from their usual haunts in the Halo. They were entering the dim-lit habitation bubble now, passing to the interior through the gaping hole near the South Pole. The bubble was on emergency power, but it was still far brighter than the dark cargo ship.

What was it doing here? It was inconceivable to Aybee that there was anything valuable left on the Farm, even including the machines and metals on the collection layer. And the Podders were showing no interest in those.

While he watched, another port in the cargo vessel began to dilate. This one was huge, an opening nearly forty meters across in the end of the ship nearest to the bubble. He stared at it, waiting for something to emerge.

It was completely free of the ship before he knew it was there, and then he did not see it. All he saw was a circling array of electromagnets. At their center sat a moving sphere of blackness, drifting slowly under their control towards the habitation bubble.

It was a kernel, totally shielded by electromagnetic baffles. At the center of that dark sphere sat a tiny, billion ton, Kerr-Newman black hole, its fierce sleet of radiation and particles balked and turned back on itself by the triple shields. The kernel had been halted. It hovered, stationary with respect to the bubble, and waited. The bubble's own main port was opening. Finally a second sphere of aching black emerged from the gaping port, its position controlled by surrounding electromagnets.

Aybee watched in amazement as the two drifting spheres changed places. The shielded kernel from the Farm finally vanished into the cargo hull, and after a few minutes the new kernel was jockeyed into place by the bubble's port. It was nudged on down, into the interior.

Aybee was bursting with curiosity. He nestled down into the tangle of space junk surrounding him, and inched the whole assembly gently forward until he could see into the bubble's open port. He peered out through the mess of shattered furniture.

The kernel was replacing the one that had been removed. Aybee had noted the status of the Farm's power kernel when he and Leo Manx had arrived. It had abundant rotational energy and was nowhere near depletion. There was no sense in replacing it—unless the Podders needed power, and were swapping the kernel from the bubble for a dead one from their cargo ship.

It was a simple matter to test that idea. One look at the new kernel's optical scalars would tell Aybee what was happening, and that was a one-minute job if he were next to its outer shield.

The port was closing, and now the Podders were leaving, one by one. As the final suited figure disappeared silently into the cargo hulk, Aybee headed for the bubble.

That was the exact point where Bey Wolf would have put his hand on Aybee's shoulder, told him to wait a moment, and asked a basic question. Where were the Farmers? But Bey was billions of kilometers away. Aybee left his shelter of ramshackle cabin furniture, and headed into the bubble along the gaping exit wound of the earlier impact.

The Farmers and their servant machines had accomplished wonders. Already the bubble's interior had been cleared of broken fittings. Makeshift bulkheads had stabilized the atmosphere of the interior and set up a new system of corridors that provided access to the habitable part of the bubble.

Aybee drifted down toward the bubble's center. The new kernel had been established there, in place of the original one. It had plenty of available energy—according to Aybee's recollection, almost exactly as much as the old one. The mystery was greater than ever. Why swap two identical kernels for each other?

He headed up a narrow stairway that would take him away from the kernel, and towards the bubble's outer surface. At that moment he learned that the Podders had not left permanently. Three of them waited in a tight group by an exit duct, while a fourth one was leading a group of three Farmers out of the bubble at gunpoint.

Aybee ducked back into the shelter of the stairway and reviewed his options. He could wait, hoping that the Podders were finally done and were all leaving. Or he could take more positive action, heading out through the entrance wound created by the impact of the ice fragment.

The disadvantages of both ideas were easy to catalog. His hiding-place was completely exposed to anyone who wandered by, and the way down to the kernel was a blind end. If the Podders wanted to be sure they had all the Farmers, they would not overlook the surface of the kernel shields. On the other hand, he had no idea what might be waiting in the other direction. The Podders had first entered the bubble there, and some of them could be there again.

Bey Wolf would have waited. He was a great believer in putting off decisions, which he dignified as "keeping open all his options."

Aybee couldn't do that; he had too nervous a nature. After at most a minute he was hugging the side of the tunnel and creeping away towards the surface of the bubble. He was careful to look at the way ahead, and turn every few seconds to make sure that he was safely out of sight of the four Podders behind him. He was doing that at the exact moment when a fifth Podder, also looking the other way, emerged from a narrow gap in the wall and ran right into him.

The suited figure didn't bother to speak. He waved the gun he was holding at Aybee, and gestured him forward.

Aybee could take a hint. He nodded, and moved off along the tunnel towards the outer surface. The radio silence he had been observing earlier now seemed pointless. Aybee scanned for the frequency the Podders were using and turned his suit to transmission.

"What are you going to do with me?"

The figure behind him grunted with surprise. Aybee realised it was a woman. "I thought you people didn't talk to anybody," she said. "None of your buddies said a word."

She thinks I'm a Farmer. But if I play that part too well, she won't tell me anything.

Aybee grunted. "We don't talk much. But this is an emergency."

"Don't talk much, and don't listen much either." The Podder sounded disgusted. "I'm not going through all that spiel again. Do as you're told, and don't give us any trouble, and you'll be well treated. If you start cutting up, you'll find you're six to a cell."

The ultimate threat for a Farmer. Aybee didn't like the sound of it too much himself. He still had memories of the cramped trip to the Sagdeyev Space Farm with Leo Manx.

"Where are you taking me?"

"Are you deaf? Wait a minute." She moved around in front of Aybee and peered in through his faceplate. "I haven't seen you before. We didn't get you the first time through. Where were you?"

"Outside."

"And you came back in?" The Podder gestured him forward again. "Well, now I've seen everything. You were safe out in space, and you came back in. How dumb can you get?"

Aybee had three good reasons not to answer. First, he assumed it was a rhetorical question. Second, he had to agree in this case with the Podder's implied comment on his brains. He had been safe outside, and all he needed to do was wait for the Podders' ship to go away. Then he could have spent the next month inside the bubble, if that was what he felt like doing.

And third, he didn't need to fish for more information about the Podders' immediate plans for him. He could guess them. They were close to the great hulk of the cargo ship, and a hatch was gaping open. With the woman close behind, Aybee drifted on into the gloomy interior. He wondered how long it would be before anyone on the Harvesters even noticed he was missing.

CHAPTER 16

"She did corrupt frail nature with some bribe,
To shrink mine arm up like a withered shrub,
To make an envious mountain on my back
Where sits deformity to mock my body;
To shape my limbs of an unequal size,
To disproportion me in every part ..."
—William Shakespeare; Henry VI, Part 3

Every emergence was different.

Bey came out of this one dry-mouthed, wobble-legged, and furious. He knew the form-change process better than anyone. He could tell when parameters had been changed from their original settings, even when he was the subject, and this time he knew he had been through a lot more than simple tissue restoration.

The door of the tank sprang open, and he looked out. Sylvia Fernald was sitting by the control board, staring at him.

He roared with rage, a horrible squeal of unfamiliar vocal cords. "What the hell have you been doing to me?" The ionic balance of his body was still adjusting, and the chemical rush of anger was strong enough to propel him forward out of the tank in one movement. "Don't try to lie, you've been meddling and you know it."

"You call it meddling when somebody tries to help you?" She stood her ground. "I've just saved you. You'd

349

have been cut to bits as soon as people in the Harvester knew you were here. No one from Earth is safe now."

"I can look after myself." Bey tried to gesture in anger, but his fist would not close. His body felt terrible, a bad size, a distorted shape. "A form-change like that—you could have killed me."

"I studied the change very carefully. It's a standard type of form for the Outer System."

"I didn't need a change."

"*Wrong!* You need a change. More than a change— you need a damned *keeper*. I've had it with you, and I don't care what Baker wants." Sylvia stood up. "You're an idiot, Bey Wolf, you know that? You come out here, an Earther, and you think you're God's gift to the Cloud." She gripped him hard by the arm, and pulled him along the room. He stumbled after her, still too weak to give more than token resistance. She halted by the door at the end of the room. "Take a look there. What do you see?"

Bey found himself in front of a full-length mirror. He was facing a nightmare, naked and thin as a skeleton, tall and stooped as a praying mantis. All the muscles had gone from his arms and legs, leaving ugly tendons and sticks of bone that ended in taloned hands and feet. His ribcage jutted like parchment drawn over a dry wooden frame. The hair was gone from his head and body, and his browless eyes glared demented out of hollow sockets. His hairless genitals looked vulnerable and ridiculous. He stood frozen, his skull-head mouth gaping open.

"What do you see?" She had gone on shouting at him, but he had not even heard her. "What do you see?"

"You did this to me!" He shook his arm loose. "You're insane. You've turned me into a monster. I've got to get back in the tank, make this right again."

"No!" She stood in front of him, blocking his movement, and he realised how tall he had become. They were suddenly eye to eye. "It's time you learned something, Behrooz Wolf—if you're still able to learn anything at all. I don't know what you see, but I'll tell you what

I see, and it's the way everyone thinks in the Outer System."

She stepped back, and swept him from head to toe with a searing glance. As his anger had calmed, hers had grown. "I see a passable-looking man for the first time since I met you. A man I would be pleased to know, a man whose company I might even enjoy. Not a damned monkey. Not a squat, hairy toad. Not a hirsute, jowly, sun-sucking *midget* that no normal woman would be seen dead with. And *yes*, I did it to you. And *no*, I'm not sorry I did it. I sat by that damned tank for a hundred straight hours, to make sure nothing was going wrong with the change I keyed in. And *yes*, I knew what I was doing. And *no*, I don't expect you to appreciate it. You're too graceless, too selfish, too self-obsessed, too wrapped up in your self-superior idea that anything from the Inner System has to be good and right." She was screaming at him. "So damn you, Bey Wolf, if you want to get back into that tank, go ahead. I won't stop you. And I won't interfere when the people on the Harvester grab you and spill your guts."

Bey's body chemistry change was complete, and his condition was stabilising. He was beginning to feel almost normal, but he also knew that the mood swings might be far from over. He stared fascinated at his image in the mirror, and shook his head. "I look like a form-change *failure*. Those legs—you actually *programmed* for those legs?"

"They're great legs."

"They're revolting. Look at them! Too short, too white, too bowed." He turned to face her. "You're serious, aren't you? You think I should thank you for this."

"You should go down on your knees and kiss my hand. My God, I was doing you a favor." She had stopped shouting at him. "You're supposed to have brains. Use them. You asked Cinnabar Baker to announce that you had been killed on the Space Farm, so you could explore the problem without people knowing who you were. How well would that have held up, when people saw you? You *had* to change. I suppose you thought that you'd blend right in with the rest of us, with your ridiculous Earth body."

"All right. But why didn't you warn me?"

"Would you have agreed to this body if I had?"

"Never." Now that he was not angry, Bey was feeling a bit guilty. She had sat by the tank for days, looking after him, and he could see how pale and tired she was. "But do you blame me for feeling that way? Would you have let me change *you*, so you look like an Earth woman?"

"Don't be disgusting."

"Well, then. But I'll admit it, you're right about one thing, and I want to apologize for shouting at you. It's an odd thought, but in this stick-insect body I *will* be less noticeable here." Bey took another look at his reflection and grabbed for a robe by the door. It was suitably long and full—when he had it on he could see nothing but his hands and head. "That's better. I'd rather not see myself. But I still wish in some ways I could get back in the tank. I don't seem to be *done*."

"Are you feeling sick?"

"Not exactly. But I'm certainly feeling a bit Plantagenetish."

"A bit *what*?"

"You know. Or if you don't, you should." Bey held the robe tight around him, stood up as straight as he was able, and declaimed:

" 'Deformed, unfinished, sent before my time, into this breathing world scarce half made up, and that so lamely and unfashionable, that dogs bark at me as I halt by them.' Richard the Third. One of my all-time heroes."

She stared at him. Finally she laughed. "My God, Leo was right. You *are* insane. You're worse than Aybee. Totally crazy."

Bey considered her statement. He was a bit light-headed, definitely that; but it wasn't his strongest feeling. "More like totally starving. Whatever you did to me, it left me hollow. Can I get some food?"

"We can try. And you'll have your big test. We'll see

if you can pass—as a Cloudlander. Here, wait a minute." Bey was all ready to head out of the door. "You'll never pass in that outfit."

"You all seem to dress the same. There must be a uniform near."

"Wrong again." Sylvia gestured at her own grey suit. "I'm still just the way we came off the ship, but I wouldn't dream of mixing with other people here like this—or in the old uniform. You seem to think all the Harvesters are the same. They're not alike, any two of them, in either their layout or their people. This Harvester is super fashion-conscious. Nobody here would be seen dead in those yellow suits we wore on the Opik Harvester. If we want to be inconspicuous, we have to follow local ways. Come with me. It's right next door."

The room she led him to had rack after rack of clothing, gaudy, varied, and extreme. Bey hesitated, then shrugged. "I've no idea. You know how to make me blend in. Pick something."

Within two minutes she had selected a pair of skin tight peacock-blue suits with matching footwear and tall egg-shaped hats. They seemed designed to make Bey look even taller and thinner, and were in his opinion the most ridiculous outfits he had ever seen.

He stared in disbelief at his reflection. "We can't go out in public like this. Everyone in the Harvester will laugh at us."

"They won't even notice. Not in this Harvester."

"But the people we saw as we came in from the ship didn't look like this."

"They were maintenance and operations crews. In uniform. You wouldn't know them if you saw them off-duty."

Bey started for the door, then paused for a last look in the mirror. "Are you *sure*?"

"Trust me. You look quite handsome." Sylvia tucked her arm in his, and led the way. "Remember, until you get the hang of that body in low-gee, you let me set the pace. Pretend we're a couple. Don't talk much at first, and if you don't know how to move, just let me drag you along."

They set off along a mysterious zigzag of corridors and stairways. Bey knew he was lost within one minute; in ten minutes, he knew why the Cloudlanders had picked their preferred forms. He was shaped just right for a low-gee environment. He could pivot his top-heavy body around its center of mass, and use his long arms to control the direction of his movement, unhindered by excess muscle or fat. Even the air somehow smelled better now, but whether that was his new physiology or his imagination he could not tell.

The hall they came to was crowded for a room on a Harvester. Bey's initial worry, that this was too public a first appearance for his new body, vanished when he saw the general behavior. A peculiar sense of panic and excitement filled the air. No one took any notice of him and Sylvia. A couple of hundred noisy people were milling around a dais at one end, and as Bey looked at them he felt reassured. He was one of the most conservatively dressed. Pink sequinned pantaloons and curved-toe slippers competed and clashed with scarlet tunics and glittering black hose. Earth-taste was non-existent.

At a gesture from Sylvia, Bey slipped into an eating cubicle at the back of the room. Sylvia in the next cubicle was out of sight unless she stood up to look over the partition, and one-way glass in the front wall allowed both of them to see the rest of the hall. Most of the crowd was clustered around a scarecrow of a man with a blue skullcap, a long white robe, and a mask that covered the lower half of his face.

"You have a choice!" He had a muffled, booming voice, echoing from the room's bare white walls. "I can *give* you a choice. If you do not like the idea of form-change, if you do not care to face the terror of the tanks, *there are other ways.* Ancient secrets, the mysteries of Earth's antiquity, means of treating illness that do not depend on the use of form-change tanks."

"Nothing good comes from Earth!" The shout came from somewhere in the throng of people.

"From today's Earth, you are right." The man on the platform turned to that part of the crowd. "I think we ought to destroy Earth, and all the Inner System." There was a roar of approval from the crowd. "But that does not mean that the knowledge of old Earth is useless. All our ancestors once lived there! I have learned Earth's old secrets."

Bey spoke to Sylvia, busy ordering food in her cubicle from the table server. "What's he talking about?"

"I was going to ask you the same thing. He said something about knowledge coming from ancient Earth."

"The distilled wisdom of long-dead ages," the booming voice was continuing. "Three hundred years ago, the knowledge that I possess was tightly held by a small group of people. When form-change came in, the need for their skills disappeared. They lost their power. Their special learning vanished. But not for ever! By intense research, I and my assistants have repossessed those lost skills. We are the New Aesculapians." He held up two clear bottles, one filled with a cloudy green liquid and the other filled with small white spheres. "Whatever your ailment, we can help you! One of these will be the answer."

"Oh, my God." Bey had been chewing on a bland yellow wedge of material that Sylvia had ordered. Now he almost choked, and spoke with his mouth full. "I never thought I'd see this."

"What is he offering?"

"Pills and potions. Panaceas. He's saying he's a doctor!"

"You mean a—a *physician*?" Sylvia groped for the old word. "There are no such people in the Cloud."

"Nor on Earth, any more—there haven't been for two hundred years. I didn't think there ever would be again, anywhere." Bey was ecstatic. "Before purposive form-change was developed, there were thousands of them. They were enormously powerful, just like a priesthood. Those clothes and masks he's wearing were their robes. I wonder he isn't spouting the Hippocratic Oath and writing prescriptions."

"Writing *what*?"

"Purchase approval for chemicals. They used to treat diseases with chemicals, you know—and with surgery, too."

"Surgery. Isn't that *cutting*—"

"Right. Cutting people open. Before it was outlawed, they were allowed to do that. I hope he's not proposing it here."

The white-coated man was being mobbed with people, shouting out their problems. He had been joined by half a dozen acolytes, who were beginning to hand out phials and packages. Sylvia opened the door of her cubicle and stepped out. "I have to tell Cinnabar Baker about this. We can't allow it."

"No." Bey came out quickly to grab her sleeve and restrain her. "First we get samples, have them analyzed. I'll bet they're totally harmless. Come on."

They had not finished eating, but the food and drink had been enough to produce another mood change. Bey was getting a little sleepy, and extremely cheerful. He began to make his way towards the center of the crowd. Sylvia caught up with him and pushed in front. "Not you. I'll do it. I can move easier than you. You stay right there."

She eeled into the mass of people, and returned a couple of minutes later with a bottle in one hand and a packet in the other. She held them up triumphantly, but just before she reached Bey she halted and her expression changed. She was looking right past him.

"Here comes your real test." She leaned close and spoke rapidly. "If you pass this one, you're home free."

Bey slowly turned. Heading towards them across the room was a smiling woman dressed in a cloudy dress of flaming pink. "Sylvia! I had no idea you were here."

"I just arrived." Sylvia squeezed the woman's hands in both of hers, then stepped back. "Andromeda, this is Behrooz. He's also visiting the Harvester. Bey, this is an old friend of mine, Andromeda Diconis. We studied optimal control theory together, many years ago."

"Too many. But Sylvia was always better at it than I was. That's why I'm here, in my boring little job, while Sylvia roves the System." The woman had taken Bey by the hand, and was giving him a head-to-toe stare. Her glittering blue eyes and full mouth held an odd and unreadable expression. "Very nice clothes you have—you *both* have. Perfectly matched. What are you doing here?"

"Behrooz works on communications equipment," said Sylvia, before Bey could speak. "He's an expert on it."

"We can certainly use some of those here. Where are you from, Behrooz?"

"The Opik Harvester."

"Ah. Such a dull place—I would never want to live there. And you are a communications *expert*? How impressive." Andromeda Diconis was still holding Bey's hand, but it was Sylvia that she spoke to next. "I'm sure he is an expert on many things. But my dear Sylvia, whatever happened to your other friend? What was his name, Paul?"

"Paul Chu. I suppose you didn't hear. He disappeared on a mission to the Halo."

"Oh, yes, now you mention it I did hear that. But I thought he came back. Someone here said they'd seen him, just a week or two ago. Anyway, we don't want to talk about *him*, do we?" Andromeda finally released Bey's hand and reached up to straighten his collar. Her fingers ran over the hollow of his throat. "Not when you've been able to make new friends, Sylvia. And very attractive friends, too. I'll tell you what, I'm going to stay here and have something to eat. Would you and Behrooz"—Bey earned a dazzling smile—"like to wait for me, and then we can all go to the concert along the corridor?"

Sylvia placed her hand firmly on Bey's arm. "Not today. We've just eaten, and Bey has had a very hard day. He needs to rest now."

"I'm sure he does. I'm sure you *both* do. But it's wonderful to see you again, Sylvia, and I'll call you tomorrow." She reached forward and stroked Bey's forearm. "And I really look forward to seeing you again, Behrooz. Once you're properly *rested*."

Bey tried to smile and nod, but Sylvia was already towing him off towards the exit. He waved to Andromeda Diconis, and received a blown kiss in return.

"What's the hurry?" he said, as soon as they were out of earshot. "Was I making her suspicious?"

"Not in the slightest." Sylvia's manner was a mixture of pleasure and irritation. "You passed perfectly. Couldn't you tell? She'd never have acted that way if she thought for one moment that you were from the Inner System. She's the perfect Cloudlander, looks down on everything inside the Kernel Ring. But Andromeda was all ready to eat you for breakfast."

"If I was passing perfectly, why drag me away?" Bey rather liked the idea of being eaten for breakfast by Andromeda.

"Because Andromeda has to think that I'm jealous— the way she would be. She thinks she understands our relationship exactly, and that's the best thing that could have happened. Andromeda's a total bitch, but she took you at face value, as a Cloudlander. And she's the universe's greatest gossip. Give her a day or two, and everyone will know that I have a new companion, a man from the Opik Harvester."

"Isn't that dangerous? They may want to meet me."

"She'll tell people that I'm jealous of you, and want to keep you all to myself. It's a perfect reason to let us stay private while you work. But that's something we'll worry about tomorrow."

"Uh-uh." He yawned. " 'Tomorrow, and tomorrow and tomorrow.' Great word. Great speech. Hmmm."

Sylvia had noticed the change in Bey since leaving Andromeda Diconis. Another common after-effect of a long session in the tanks was hitting him. He was on a high, but fast running out of adrenalin and energy. The surprise of waking in a strangely different form and the stimulus of the new surroundings had been enough to give him a lift for the past few hours, but that was fading.

"Come on. Before you fall asleep in the corridors." It had been a convenient excuse to leave Andromeda, but it was true enough. Bey Wolf would need a good rest before he was fit to work on the Marsden Harvester's form-change problems.

She led him away toward his assigned quarters. Bey didn't speak, and by the time they arrived his eyes were closing. Sylvia steered him to a bunk. He was asleep before she could add another word. After a few moments she gently removed the bright blue clothes and the extravagant hat, and secured him in the bunk with loose straps. He would become used to low-gee sleeping soon enough, but he might be disoriented when he first woke.

He lay flat on his back. Sylvia looked over the sleeping body with approval. "Pretty good job I did with you, Behrooz Wolf, if I say it myself. Andromeda was fascinated, and she's a connoisseur. 'Very attractive friends,' eh? We'll have to fight to keep her away from you."

Sylvia frowned, remembering another of Andromeda's comments. Someone on this Harvester had seen Paul Chu, recently. Even if it were no more than a bit of gossip, Sylvia needed to follow up on it. Cinnabar Baker had pointed out the problem. When you talked of war and sabotage, all roads seemed to lead to the Kernel Ring; but no roads led to Black Ransome, or to Ransome's Hole. Unless she could track the lead to Paul, and he could provide the pathway.

She started for the door, then paused. She mustn't go back to the hall too soon. Andromeda had her own ideas about what Sylvia and Bey were doing at the moment, and Sylvia wanted to keep that idea intact.

She forced herself to wait for almost two hours, thinking hard and watching the steady rise and fall of Bey's bony chest; at last she headed for the concert hall.

The lights had dimmed automatically. Bey lay in darkness, listened to the faint hissing of the air ventilators, and wondered what had wakened him. He was almost in free-fall, floating with only the imperceptible tether of a pair of retaining straps. And he was not ready to wake. He felt groggy with sleep, so tired that it was an impossible effort to open his eyes.

"Bey!" The voice came again. It was no more than a whisper, but it jerked him at once to thrilling wakefulness. It was a sound to rouse Bey from the dead.

He opened his eyes. The projection system in the corner had switched itself on, and revealed the interior of a dark room. In the center of that open space, her face illuminated by the faint gleam of a single red spotlight, sat Mary Walton.

"Bey!" The soft call came again.

"Mary. Where are you?"

"Don't try to answer me, Bey. This message was pre-recorded, so I can't hear what you're saying. It is triggered when you respond to your name and open your eyes."

She was as hauntingly attractive and as crazy-looking as ever. Bey even recognised her outfit. It was the one she had worn when she played Titania, a long, russet gown that should have been dowdy but which glowed with fairy tints of warm light. He had last seen it locked in a closet of his Earth apartment. Her voice was even more familiar, as wonderful as ever, the smoky, husky murmur that made Bey hear sexual overtones even in her comic speeches.

"I don't want you hurt, Bey," she went on. "I've already saved you many times, back on Earth and on the Space Farm; but I don't know how many more times I can do it. You have to stop what you're doing, leave the Harvesters, get back to Earth."

"How did you know where I am?" Bey responded automatically, forgetting that she could not hear him.

"You are being used, you know, by the Outer System." She had not paused. "It's not your problem, but they'll try and make it yours. The Outer System is going to break down, more and more, and if you try to stop it, it will kill you. Say no to Cinnabar Baker, whatever she suggests. When Sylvia Fernald tries to sleep with you— she will, if she hasn't already—remember that she's doing it as part of her job. You are nothing to those people." Mary raised her hand. On her middle finger glowed a huge kernel ruby, the rarest gemstone in the System. "It may be over between us, Bey, but don't ever forget that I'm fond of you. I saved you, when the messages were making all the others die or go mad. Give me credit for that. Goodbye now, and please take care. Sleep well."

She waved. The projection unit's image slowly faded, until after twenty seconds Bey could see nothing but the ghostly glimmer of the kernel ruby. Finally, that too was gone. The sleeping chamber was again in perfect darkness.

Bey was sweating hard, and his heart was pounding. He was filled with a mixture of excitement and amazement. Mary's final words had been a grim joke—he would not sleep now, not for hours. He loosened the straps that had held him snugly in position and walked across to the projection unit. It should hold a recorded copy of that whole message.

The recording storage was completely blank. Naturally. Bey was not even surprised any more. After the Negentropic Man, after the projected images that were filling the Outer System, and Mary's ability to leave a message for him wherever she apparently chose, no other anomaly of the communications system could be ruled out. It was all impossible.

But one impossibility throbbed in his head harder and harder, the longer he thought about it. If Mary knew where he was, then perhaps she could find a way to send a message; but *how*, in a total region of space so large that the whole Inner System was no more than a dot at its center, did she *know where he was*?

She had known of his trip to the Sagdeyev Space Farm. She had learned of his return. She had tracked him to these quarters within a few hours of his arrival there. How? How did she know?

He would *never* get to sleep. *Never, never, never, never, never*. With that single word resounding in his head, he went drifting irresistibly towards the slumber of total exhaustion.

And it was in those final moments, swimming down towards new unconsciousness, that Bey had a first inkling as to how Mary knew what was happening so quickly. He tried to catch the thought, to study it, but it was too late.

He was asleep.

CHAPTER 17

Aybee had a problem. He wanted his captors to think he was from the Space Farm, not a representative of the Cloud's central government. On the other hand, he could not afford to meet any other Farmers. They would know at once that he was not one of them, and they would have no reason to hide the fact from the Podders.

For the moment at least he seemed safe. There were plenty of Podders visible near the lock of the cargo vessel, easily recognized from their suits, but he could see no sign of Farmers. Steered along by the woman behind him, Aybee went drifting on into the interior. From the outside, the ship had been an inert, lifeless hulk, a derelict abandoned in the early days of Cloud colonization. Within, the airless enclosure was filled with activity.

Aybee looked around him with a professional eye. They had entered through one of the ship's forward ports. The outer hull arched away from them, a great curved span of carbon fiber sheet with strengthening beams of hardened polymers. From the inside it seemed much more than six hundred meters wide. There was enough interior space here for whole cities, complete with everything from food and power production to swimming-pools and games fields. But there were signs that the ship was more than a simple colony.

The first giveaway was the bracing struts and massive electric cables. They ran through the whole interior, and there was no reason to have them unless the ship had to withstand acceleration. Aybee did a quick mental calculation, and decided that the mechanical and electromagnetic stiffening was consistent with about a two-gee thrust.

That at once told him something else. At two gees, the ship was over a year's run away from the Podders' natural home in the Halo. There had to be some way of moving people and materials faster than that. Aybee looked again around the cluttered and dimly lit cargo shell, and saw the expected equipment far away near the outer wall. A high-acceleration ship hung there, McAndrew drive off. From the design, it would allow up to three hundred gees before the gravitational and inertial accelerations were in balance. Aybee studied that ship very closely. With it, the Marsden Harvester was only twenty-four hours away.

The second oddity was the presence of transparent internal partitions and numerous internal airlocks. Cargo hulls were rarely pressurized, and the Podders had no interest in living within an atmosphere. Their suits were all the air supply they cared to have. So who wanted parts of the ship to be air-filled, and where were they?

Finally, there were the kernels. Aybee could see a dozen places where the local spherical structure implied housings for shielded kernels. That suggested a monstrous power demand. One kernel would be sufficient for normal operations of a volume this size, even if it were a full-scale colony ship. The alternative explanation, that the kernels were being used for some other purpose, made no sense without more data.

Aybee turned back to the woman behind him. Inside the ship, she had put her gun away.

"What are you going to do to me?"

"Just keep going. You'll find out in a few minutes." She relented. "Don't worry. We don't kill people without a good reason."

But we do kill people with a good reason? Aybee wondered what a good reason was. Trying to escape? Lying about your identity? Being a spy for the Outer System government?

They were entering a new section of the ship, passing

through an interior lock into an enclosure with opaque walls. Aybee heard the hiss of air, and looked questioningly at the woman.

She nodded. "Transition point. Here's where I leave you. Get out of your suit and go through the inner lock." She switched to some other transmission frequency, had a conversation that Aybee could not follow as he was removing his suit, and gestured him forward. "Move it unless you like to breathe vacuum. I'll be exhausting this lock again in thirty seconds."

Aybee had been worried when he took off his suit, because underneath it he wasn't dressed like any of the Farmers that he had seen. But apparently the Podders were no experts on Space Farm attire, and certainly the woman did not give his clothes a second glance. He went on through.

A man and a woman were waiting for him on the other side of the lock, facing him across a curved table.

More mystery. Neither one of them had the stunted form and compact build preferred by Podders, or the elongated shape of a Cloudlander. Aybee was in about a twentieth of a gee field, which suggested that the room must be close to a kernel. Both the people in front of him appeared comfortable with that, which meant they were not likely to be from the Inner System.

The woman gestured him to a seat opposite her. She had black hair, black skin, and a wary look in her eye. "Leila tells us that you talk," she said. "Good. That's a nice change from your buddies."

Aybee sat down, hunching low in the chair. "All right, so I know how to talk. What happens to me now?"

"That depends on you. I don't suppose you know any physics?"

"I know a bit." It was no time to act insulted.

The other two people looked at each other. By this time Aybee had decided what they were. They had the build of Inner System inhabitants, but not the Sunhugger look. Both of them hailed from farther out, and yet both of them were used to gravity. That meant the Kernel Ring, living in close proximity to shielded kernels.

"We'll test that in a little while," said the man. Aybee noticed that he was wearing a kernel ruby in his shoulder epaulet. "D'you know maths too?"

"Some." There was a fine line to be walked here. Too much knowledge might be as dangerous as too little.

"Then if you know an adequate amount, you'll have a choice. Either you can go to a Halo development project, a long way from here, and work with no one but a few of the other Farmers and a lot of machines. That's what all your friends will be doing, helping to build a new Farm—the Halo is short of metals, too. Or if you're really willing to work with people, we have a more interesting prospect to offer you."

"I don't like the sound of no Farm. I've had it with Farms. Tell me about the other thing."

"Not yet." The woman was looking at him suspiciously. "First, we want to hear *you* talk, and make sure you can say more than a few phrases. You can start by telling us why you're different from the rest of the Farmers. They haven't said ten words between them."

Nasty question. If he seemed too different from the other Farmers, these people would wonder why. If he were too similar, he'd be sent out to the edge of nowhere and spend the rest of his life building a collector to sieve stray atoms from nothing.

If you have to lie, make the lies little ones. "I was the interface," he said at last. "With people from the Harvesters. When engineers came to the Farm, *somebody* had to work with them. We all had a psych profile run. I looked like the best choice. So I got special training. I sorta liked it, wanted to do it more. Mebbe even get a job away from the Farm."

The man nodded, but the woman leaned forward and stared Aybee in the eye. Her own eyes, glowing brown with a yellow center to the iris, gave her a definitely feral appearance. She had the dedicated face of a fanatic. "Did you interface with the group that came to the Space Farm from the Opik Harvester," she said, "just a couple of days ago?"

"Yeah." Aybee did not even blink. "They insisted on

a face to face with us. I met 'em, four of 'em. My special training came in real useful."

"How long were you with them?"

"Not long. Ten minutes, mebbe. I been wondering what happened to 'em since the impact. Were they all killed?"

"Why do you care?"

"Dunno. Guess I wondered if they were here, too. They're like me, don't mind working with other people. *Are* they here?"

"No. They went back where they came from. We saw their ship leaving."

Aybee hid his relief. But the woman was suspicious again. "Why do you care about them? Never mind, I'll accept that you talk. It seems to me maybe you talk a little too well. I don't know how you could stand it on the Space Farm."

"Let's give him the test," said the man. "If he's lying about what he knows, we don't have to waste more time talking."

The woman shrugged, and slid two sheets of paper across the table to Aybee. "Write your answers right there if you want to," she said. "Or say them out loud to us. We don't care."

"I'd rather write. If you have something I can write with." Aybee had seen the first page of questions, and he had a new worry. If the test were all like this, he needed time to think. He was being asked things so elementary that he wasn't sure how much ignorance he should feign. For what these people had in mind, ought he to know Newton's laws of motion and Maxwell's equations and the classical definitions of entropy? Almost certainly. But how about Price's theorem and spinors and Killing vectors? They were on the list, too, along with Newman-Penrose constants and Petrov classification. He had written papers on each of these, but he didn't want anyone here to suspect that. The questions themselves were also a tantalizing hint as to the work he might be expected to do. He would certainly be working with kernels.

He took the pen they gave him, and carefully wrote out his answers. Two wrong out of each ten. That ought to be about right.

Aybee could see the irony of it. For half his life he had been trying to do well on stupid tests; now he had to do just well enough to be accepted but badly enough to be plausible.

He handed back the sheets, and for the first time in his life sweated while he waited for test results. The man was reading his answers, and his expression was guarded.

At last he looked up. "Did you work with the kernel on the Space Farm?"

"Some. Part of my job, to check power use and rotational state. Learned how to measure the optical scalars. That was all."

"You're not afraid to go near a kernel?"

"Not if the shields are in good working order."

"I'll second that." The man flipped the pages casually onto the table. He turned to the woman. "What do you think, Gudrun? It's your decision."

She nodded. "Do you work hard?"

At last, a question that Aybee could answer comfortably. "You bet. Harder than anyone I know. Try me."

"I guess we will. You have to know one more thing, before you say yes or no. If you join us, you'll have a chance to become a full part of our group. We have big plans, but we're few in numbers. That means wonderful opportunities. But many people do not understand the importance of our goals. Once you join us, you'll be considered a rebel by the Outer System. Now let me ask you directly. Do you want the assignment?"

"I think so." Aybee nodded his head slowly. He had to appear interested, but cautious. "The Outer System never did nothing for me. I never asked to be out on the Farm. Guess I'd like to know more about your deal, though, before I'm sure."

"Fair enough." For the first time the woman smiled, and held out her hand. "You're on for a trial run. I'm Gudrun. This is Jason. What's your name?"

Spacehooks. What's my name? Better pick somebody

real. Aybee groped for the name of his first instructor in calculus. "Karl Lyman."

"Welcome to the program, Karl. Are you tired?"

"Nothing special."

"Then let's go and eat." She saw his expression and laughed. "I don't mean *with* me. Don't worry, we know what people are like in the Outer System. You can have your own cubicle, you won't have to look at anybody taking meals. But I want to find out a bit more about you, and tell you what you'll be doing." She gave him another look, but this one was of a shared secret. "I liked your answers to that test, and I think maybe you were wasting your time on the Farm. You may be able to go a lot farther with us than you realize."

As they stood up she moved to his side and looked up at him. "One thing, though. You're too tall for this place. We don't even have a bed to fit you. When you've started work, Karl, we'll give you a spell in a form-change tank and cut you down to size."

Aybee put on a worried frown. "D'yer think it's safe? I mean, we've had bad trouble with form-change equipment on the Farm. Bad stuff coming out of it. Suppose yours don't work right either?"

Gudrun and Jason exchanged a quick look. "Don't worry your head about that," said the man. "That's something we can guarantee—absolutely. You'll have no trouble with our form-change equipment."

They led the way on into the interior of the ship. Aybee, following close behind, pondered that final remark. Gudrun and Jason, whoever they were working for, had plenty of confidence and conviction. They acted as though they had a direct pipeline to the secrets of the universe. Could they deliver safe form-change operation, though, where the whole Outer System was failing?

Aybee wondered if he had become an instant convert to their fanaticism. Somehow, he was sure they could deliver what they promised.

Part III

Part III

CHAPTER 18

"So when this world's compounded union breaks,
Time ends, and to old Chaos all things turn."
—*Christopher Marlowe*

Bey Wolf had inherited a good stubborn streak from his German father, and a subtle and suspicious mind from his Persian mother. Both parts of the combination were needed now. He was stuck in the middle of a rank impossibility.

He had analysed 157 defective form-change runs. They ranged from minor flaws too subtle to be detected in outward appearance, to grotesque end-forms that could never have survived in any environment known to Bey. Every one was different; but in one way, all were alike. The ferret routines that he had introduced into the purposive form-change programs confirmed that there had been systematic modifications to whole sections of code; they pointed always to the same impossible blind alley. The changes were no accident. They were so complicated, they must be generated by a computer—but in a place where no computer capability existed on the Harvester.

He swore, and grumbled, and grunted to himself. His work had gone on obsessively for several days, broken only by hurried meals and occasional naps. He had not washed or changed his clothes. He was surrounded by empty disposable plates and cups, listings, diagnostic trace routines, system flow diagrams, and his own scribbled notes and questions. Paper was everywhere, sprawling across the floor and over every available surface.

Bey was totally frustrated and oddly content. No one on the Harvester could help him, and he did not want help. He wanted to solve this *himself*. He did not admit it, but intense concentration was also a form of therapy. He wanted to keep the disturbing thought of Mary Walton's visitation out of his head.

Sylvia Fernald had stopped by a couple of times in the first day of work. She had watched his efforts sympathetically, spoken to him, and left when it was clear that his mind was elsewhere. On the third day Leo Manx had also appeared. He came to the door of the room several times, stared in disgust at the mess, and hobbled away. The wounds he had received on the Space Farm were not yet fully healed, but he was in no apparent discomfort.

When Leo came by for the fourth time, he stayed, standing silent in the doorway and puzzling over a blue folder that he had brought with him. Bey Wolf ignored him, until a final and irrefutable statistical analysis came back on the display screen. At that point he swore at length, switched off the unit, and turned to the other man.

"That does it. I know exactly *what* happened—and I've no idea how."

Manx looked up from his own musings. "If you've discovered anything useful, you're making more progress than I am. What have you found? Cinnabar Baker will want to know."

Wolf waved his arm at the sea of listings covering the floor around them. "I have output trace listings of everything. Do you know how the Harvester computer system works?"

Manx frowned at the question. "Well, I feel sure it's a straightforward distributed system. There's computing capacity and major storage in a couple of hundred nodes located at different points in the Harvester, and local storage with limited compute power at a few hundred more. Everything is tied together through a fiber communications system. It's exactly like the integrated computer system on the other Harvesters—or in your own Office of Form Control, back on Earth."

"My ex-office. So there's nothing unusual about the arrangement?"

"Of course not." Manx had stepped gingerly into the middle of the paper jungle, and was now carefully collecting the listings into neat piles. "Bey, you must have known all this days ago—you couldn't generate these message traces without knowing."

"I thought I did." Wolf grabbed an elaborate schematic. "The general structure is shown here. I took this, and I began to search for places in the system where spurious coding sequences could be introduced to modify the form-change programs. Watch now."

He switched on the wall-sized display screen. "I've color-coded this. You need to know what they mean. The blue network is the overall connection plan for the distributed computer system. The red nodes show where we have data storage, green ones show computer elements. Purple dots are sensors—data collection points for the computer system. Orange dots are form-change tanks. They have some of their own storage and computer power, but they rely on the master system for some data and computation. Understood?"

"Perfectly. I hope there's a point to all this."

"There is. Just watch. I spent days working it out. You're going to see my ferret routines, chasing down all the places where false code might have come into the system. We'll do just one case now, for a form-change anomaly they had in the resource control office of this Harvester. Watch the moving yellow tracer." Bey entered the command, and leaned back in his chair.

For a moment or two, the display was static. Then a fine yellow line appeared at one of the orange dots, and crawled across the screen. It reached a green node, divided there, and two yellow daughter traces continued on their way to a red element of the schematic. ("Picking up data from two different banks," said Bey. "That happens a lot.") The yellow lines crept onwards, reaching new computer nodes, sometimes branching, sometimes terminating there. After thirty seconds a complete tree structure had been established, starting at a single form-change tank and spreading across half the screen.

"That's one complete form-change operation," said Bey.

"It's too complicated. I can't follow that structure."

"Nor could I, without help. The central controller used whatever computer power happened to be available— that's why you see so many green nodes in use. It's a horrible mess. Now, I'm going to add the other hundred and fifty-six cases, all at once. You'd expect the picture to become even worse, impossibly complicated."

"It's impossibly complicated already."

"I agree. But it simplifies. Watch." Bey entered a new command. The whole screen lit up with a tracery of moving yellow lines. They each began at a form-change tank, and branched and zigzagged across the display. Thirty seconds later the screen steadied. Leo Manx shook his head. Lines were everywhere, a tangled mass of knotted interconnections, convoluted and horribly interwoven.

"I hope you don't expect me to read anything useful out of that."

"With a little help you will." Bey was busy again at the terminal. "I agree, it still looks like a gigantic mess. So I wrote another program to help sort it out. I asked for a statistical analysis of the places that each branching set *ended*. That would tell me how often form changes were using a particular data storage bank, or a particular computer. If one storage area or computer were receiving unusually heavy use, that would be a good place to do some trouble-shooting. Take a look at what I found. The program flags every terminating node that occurs more than two sigma away from the mean for all nodes."

A couple of dozen points on the screen began to blink.

Leo Manx stared at them blankly. "Very interesting," he said after a few seconds.

"You're wrong. It *is* interesting—once you look at those nodes more closely." Bey stood up and went to the wall display. "Some end at computer elements, some end at data banks. Very reasonable. But what about this one?"

He was pointing at a flashing purple point on the screen.

"What about it?"

"Leo, remember the color code. Purple. That means it's a *sensor*—a place that collects data for the computer system."

"That's not surprising. There are sensors on each form-change tank."

"True. Not surprising—*if* this were a sensor associated with a form-change tank. It would be collecting physical readings from the tank, and using those in the programs. But this sensor should have nothing to do with a form-change process. And *every* form-change anomaly has a branch that ends there. That sensor was involved *every single time* we had a form-change problem."

Manx had stood up, and was craning to see the blinking point next to Bey's finger. "I don't know which sensor that is. Are you sure it's not a form-change monitor?"

"I checked it a dozen times. It's not. So I decided that it had to be a signal coming from *outside* the Harvester, maybe something we were picking up on beamed data from an external antenna. It's not that, either."

"Don't keep telling me what it *isn't*." Leo Manx was losing his usual courtly politeness. "We have to check this directly. Which sensor is it?"

"I'll tell you, but you're not going to like the answer." Bey tapped the display. "That sensor is inside the Harvester, but it's in the hardest place of all to check. It monitors the radiation level from the Harvester's kernel, and that means it's sitting where we can't get at it. *Inside* the kernel shields."

Leo was shaking his head. "You're suggesting that somebody put a computer and a data storage unit in there? It couldn't happen. Nothing but hardened sensors can operate inside the shields—even the remote-handling machines that manipulate the kernels don't have programs."

"I know. But I'm convinced there's *something* there, inside the shield. Some information source, some chaos-generator for the form-change process. It's the 'negentropic' influence again—spurious information that's the source of disruption for the whole system."

"But the other problems we've had were nothing to do with form-change!"

"We've gone past form-change now, Leo. Form-change just happens to be highly sensitive to signal control sequences. Problems show up there first. But what I've found takes us into kernel control theory, and that's a different game. I don't know enough about Kerr-Newman black holes to decide what's going on. That's why I've been waiting for Aybee to get back from the Sagdeyev Space Farm."

"Then you might have to wait a long time. He's not there."

"But he's on the way back, isn't he?"

"I'm afraid not." Leo Manx retreated to a cleared area of the floor and sat down cross-legged. "Before I came here I was with Cinnabar Baker. She'd just had a report from a repair and maintenance crew who had reached the Farm. Apparently it's totally deserted. No Farmers, no Aybee."

"More mechanical trouble?"

"No signs of that. The bubble was half-way repaired, reasonably habitable. But deserted. It was just as though everyone had decided to down tools at the same time, and leave. We have no idea why they went, or where they went. Or even *how* they went. Baker says that no transit vessel was missing. All they took with them were their suits. There was no sign of new violence."

"So it could be worse. Aybee's probably safe. And he's a survival type." Bey left the screen and flopped down untidily on a pile of output listings. He was almost at home in his new body, but the odd center of mass offered occasional surprises. "But it's very bad for me. I don't know who else to ask."

"We have other experts on the kernels."

"Not like Aybee. I need someone who thinks round corners." Suddenly, Bey's labors were catching up with him. He was exhausted.

"And so do I." For the first time, Leo Manx held up his own blue folder. "That's why I came to you. You've got your problems, I've got mine. Aybee got me started on this before we left the Farm. I need him as much as you do. But he told me to talk to you if he wasn't there—I don't know if you cherish the notion, but Aybee suggests that you and he think about things the same way."

"He's wrong." Bey made no attempt to take the proffered folder. He was still staring moodily at the display screen. "Aybee's smarter than I am, but he makes me feel a thousand years old. I don't have his childlike faith. If I can't solve my own problems, I'm sure I can't solve anybody else's."

It was a dismissive comment; at that point Leo Manx was supposed to stand up and leave. Instead he inched forward along the floor and placed the folder open on Bey's knees.

"The Negentropic Man," he said. Bey looked down at him, then shook his head.

"Where he came from," went on Manx. "What he means. Aybee listed four ways of thinking about entropy: thermodynamic entropy, statistical mechanics entropy, information theory entropy, and kernel entropy. But he couldn't suggest which meaning was appropriate."

"Nor can I."

"That's all right. I don't want to ask you about that." Manx lifted one sheet from the folder. "Aybee suggested that if we want to make progress we ought to examine the exact time when your hallucinations occurred. I've made a list of everything that you told me when we were in transit from the Inner System. Now I'd like to make sure it's complete."

Bey stared gloomily at the list. He knew what Leo was

doing: exactly what he would have done himself with a reluctant partner. Bait him with something he was interested in, reel him in slowly, and hope that after a few minutes you could drag him far enough to be useful.

Well, what the hell. It was a game two could play, and Bey had gone as far as he could in the form-change tracking without allowing time for his ideas to sort themselves out.

"You only want to hear about my seeing the Negentropic Man? You know that Sylvia is sure he's Black Ransome?"

"I know. We have only her word for it. Isn't the Negentropic Man the only person you saw in your hallucinations?"

"He was, until a few days ago." Wolf did not look up. Now that he was into it, he wasn't sure he wanted to tell anyone at all about Mary's strange visit. It felt remote and improbable. Even the day after it happened, he had become half convinced that he had dreamed the whole episode. "I saw Mary Walton," he said at last. "After I came out of the change tank."

"You mean—saw her in person?"

"No. A recorded message, left in my sleeping quarters."

"And you didn't tell Sylvia, or Cinnabar Baker?"

"No." Bey hesitated for a moment, evaluating the risk. He decided that he had to trust *somebody*—they couldn't all be spies. "Leo, I had a reason why I didn't talk about this. We have an information leak here. We arrived from the Space Farm just a few weeks ago. No one knew we were coming, no one even knew we had survived the 'accident' there. No messages were sent out from here *after* we arrived, saying we were here. I know, because I checked the message center myself. And yet, as soon as I went to my sleeping quarters, a planted recorded message from Mary Walton was waiting for me. Leo, until I was taken to those quarters, I didn't know *myself* where I would be sleeping."

"So that's why you didn't talk about it to me, or Sylvia Fernald, or Cinnabar Baker?" Manx was full of an

unfocused energy that made his arms and legs jerk like
a puppet's. "Bey, I know you're not used to Outer System
ways, and I know where you're heading. But it's crazy.
Those are terribly serious charges that you're making,
and it's just as well you told this only to me. I can absolutely assure you that Sylvia and Cinnabar are not providing information leaks."

"Not *intentional* ones, maybe. But think back, Leo.
Somebody seemed to know we were going to the Farm
almost before we set out. Somebody knew we were here
the moment we arrived."

"Then it must be somebody on the Harvester staff."

"On two different Harvesters? We left the Opik Harvester, we came back here to the Marsden Harvester.
Are you suggesting that there are *two* leaks, both close
to Cinnabar Baker, one on each Harvester?"

"Then who? I hope you don't think that I——"

"There's an old Earth saying: 'Everyone's suspect but
me and thee; and I'm none too sure of thee.' " I thought
about you. But I don't see how it could be. When we
arrived here you were in pretty bad shape, and you went
straight to the tank for remedial form-change work. You
weren't conscious until after this happened."

"Your faith in me is touching. I wonder why you're
telling me now."

The bait was taken. Now to reel in the line. Slowly.
"Because I need your help, Leo. And I want your word
that you won't pass this on to anyone, unless we've discussed it first. And I mean *anyone*."

"Not Sylvia? Not even Baker?"

"*Especially* not Baker. Can't you see that if we're logical, her office is the only place where the leaks can start?
Don't tell her anything, unless it's at a meeting that I've
arranged, in a place I arrange. I think we should talk to
Sylvia and see how she responds to the idea of a spy in
our group. Will you come with me, right now, and do
it?"

"Under one condition." Manx took back his blue folder
and looked at it in a puzzled way. Somehow the whole
conversation had headed off in an unintended direction.

"Anything reasonable."

"Then you take a shower first. I don't want Sylvia or anyone else we meet to think that smell is coming from me."

"Is this the Leo Manx who dragged me out of Old City? All right. If you insist. Let's go."

Later, Bey would describe the shower as a wasted effort. As soon as he was scrubbed clean and dressed in clean clothing to Leo Manx's satisfaction, they headed for Sylvia's quarters.

But she was not there. No one knew where she was, or when she would be back. Twelve hours earlier, Sylvia Fernald had requisitioned a high-gee transit ship. She had headed inward, towards the edge of the Halo, travelling fast and travelling alone. She had told no one her mission, and no one on the Harvester seemed to know her destination.

CHAPTER 19

"Stone walls do not a prison make,
Nor iron bars a cage."
                              —Richard Lovelace
"—but empty space does a pretty good job of
it."
                              —Apollo Belvedere (Aybee) Smith

The training schedule was rigorous but reasonable. Four hours of theory in the morning; a food break at which all the trainees were expected to eat together, and to discuss what they had learned; four hours of practical work in the afternoon; and then the evening free, but with enough reading, interactive education sessions and quizzes to fill at least another six hours before sleeping.

It was scheduled to continue for seven weeks. Aybee kept his head down for the first couple of days, watched what the others were doing, and tried to fall nicely in the middle of the group when it came to tests and answering questions. That wasn't so easy. The rest of the trainees were a miserable, mismatched set who had apparently been dragged in from random sources. In Aybee's not-so-humble opinion, none of them had the least idea of any kind of science, and a couple of them acted positively half-witted. They offered bizarre answers to the simplest mathematical questions—Aybee couldn't figure out how they came up with such odd replies.

On the third day he made his first request. He was not used to eating food with other people; it would be a lot less strain if he were allowed to take the midday break alone. Could he get permission?

Gudrun looked doubtful, but she agreed. There were twenty-four trainees, and Aybee's absence would not make much difference to the discussions. "Remember, Karl," she added, "if you hurt your progress because you can't talk to others while what you've learned is fresh in your mind, you'll have no one but yourself to blame. If the reason you're doing this is that you find the work difficult and you're embarrassed to talk with the others, come and see me. I'll arrange personal coaching for you."

Aybee/Karl nodded politely. He had gained an hour. The morning classes so far were routine general relativity material, three centuries old, and he didn't need to discuss that with anyone. More than that, he didn't want to. The big danger was that he would reveal how much he knew about the subject.

The evening work was a joke. He didn't need to do the reading, and he could handle all the rest of the assignments in the middle of the day. His next request to Gudrun was a little more risky. He handed in a perfect test, which he was usually careful to avoid doing, and went to see Gudrun that afternoon.

She beamed as he came in the door. "Well! Smart Karl. You don't seem to be harmed by missing the midday sessions."

"Hope not." Aybee had the horrible feeling that he was her favorite trainee. She always looked at him in a special way. "But I'm not used to high gravity. Not like the Farm. I sleep bad here. Wake up a lot in the middle of the night. If I'm all done with my work an' that happens, could I look round the ship?"

Danger signs. Her smile vanished, and she was staring at him suspiciously. "Look at *what* in the ship, Karl?"

"Dunno. Whatever." He waved his arm vaguely around them. "Power supplies, maintenance shops. Anything."

"Oh, that shouldn't be a problem. But only if you still

do well enough in your training. Let's see how you perform in the next few days."

She wasn't worried about security—she was worried that he would take too much time wandering around and flunk! Aybee made less deliberate mistakes on the tests, and three days later he had his permission. He was fascinated to see what was off-limits: armories, main drives, and the areas where the suits and transit ships were kept. It made good sense for them to keep him out of those until they were absolutely sure about his loyalties. It was also no big loss. So long as they were steaming along to nowhere, Aybee didn't like the idea of leaving the ship until he knew exactly where he was.

There was one big unexpected freedom. He would be allowed to go to the kernels, and do what he liked there. Gudrun must have decided that he wasn't interested in suicide by fiddling with a power kernel and blowing up the whole ship. It also tended to confirm what she had said at their first meeting. When the training course was over he would be working with the kernels.

The first night he had his permission to wander, he couldn't use it. A formal evening meeting was scheduled for all the trainees. After a special dinner which Aybee did not eat, they were subjected to a four-hour session of live and recorded speeches, slogans and arm-waving.

Gudrun stood up and offered her version of System history. Between the millstones of the Inner and Outer System, the inhabitants of the Halo had been crushed for over a century. The Kernel Ring was a borderland, a dangerous region of scattered high-density bodies. As a result, all the travellers from Sunhugger territory bypassed it on their journeys outward. They were quite willing to exploit its energy supplies, but none of the wealth generated from the Kernel Ring's resources was ever returned to it. That was unjust and intolerable. Finally, it was going to change. The balance of power had shifted. The Halo had a born leader, and the Revolution had begun.

Jason came next, and he was worse. The Outer System is composed of oppressive tyrants! The Inner System is decadent! It supports an idle and growing population by the efforts of our people! Both Federations deserve to fall! You are all part of a great reform that will achieve those ends—and soon!

Aybee hid his yawns, but he noticed that the other trainees were lapping it up. Gudrun, Jason, and the handful of other permanent crew of the ship knew how to whip up enthusiasm. They had enough for everybody. Gudrun stood up again for another statement. A special announcement would be made on the ship in a few days, reporting an event that was truly extraordinary. All training would be interrupted when it happened, and everyone would have two days free. The group cheered.

Aybee cheered as loudly as anyone, and wondered if propaganda had a cumulative effect. If so, he'd have to find a way to escape before his own brain was softened.

Escape seemed harder and harder. All the access points to suits, transit ships, and weapons were guarded not by humans, which would have been bad, but by machines; Roguards that didn't sleep, couldn't be distracted, and couldn't be persuaded. Aybee decided that he needed some radically new approach. The next night, he set out to prowl the ship.

He had no illusions about the size of the task that faced him. The ship was small compared with the central sphere of a Harvester, but it was still huge. With a length of two kilometers, and a diameter of six hundred meters, the ship he was on now had enough internal volume to house a couple of million people on Earth—or one or two Space Farmers. Podders and the rebels of the Kernel Ring sat somewhere between those two extremes, but Aybee could not guess at the ship's internal structure from the limited regions he had seen in training.

Fortunately, he did not need to. Overall ship schematics were held in a central data bank, and he had been studying them in the evenings for over a week. There were half a dozen blank spots in the plans, which he assumed corresponded to regions of special privacy, but all the rest of the ship was there.

As an experiment, he headed outward towards the surface. The ship had been built to carry cargo, and so all the internal bulkheads and corridors were a later addition. The whole habitat interior had an unfinished and neglected look to it. Mildewed partitions were warped and grimy, and at central communications nodes, masses of cables and fiber lines festooned the walls and ceilings.

Aybee wandered on, committing everything he saw to memory. If the need ever arose he wanted to be able to run through the ship blindfold.

No one questioned him, no one stopped him. In a few minutes he was at an observation port, peering through the outer shell of the hull to the stars beyond. He could tell from the positions of the constellations that the ship was heading sunward, but that was all he was able to deduce. He watched quietly for ten minutes. There were no signs of other manmade vessels out there, or of natural bodies of the Outer System.

When he finally moved on, easing his way along the hull towards the nearest airlock, a Roguard appeared at his side before he had gone fifty meters. It seemed to ignore him, but it moved as he did and ignored his questions and commands. Twenty meters before he reached the lock, it passed silently in front of him and extended a broad polymer net to block his path.

Aybee didn't try to talk to it. The machine was too stupid for logic. Instead, he turned to head away from the surface. When he was forty meters from the ship's hull the machine dropped behind. He turned to look, and it was disappearing through a service aperture. Aybee did not go back. If he did, he was sure that it or its sister Roguard would be there again to balk his progress towards the airlocks. Instead he headed on down the gravity gradient for the nearest kernel, two hundred meters away.

In the corridors he encountered a couple of dozen maintenance machines and three humans. The machines offered him friendly greetings. The humans, each two feet shorter than Aybee, said not a word. They hardly looked at him, and seemed preoccupied with their own worries.

Was it his trainee's uniform, which made him so much lower in status than anyone else on the ship that they would not even talk to him? If so, that was fine with Aybee. He travelled on, along a dirty passageway coated with the grime of a decade's neglect. Somehow the controller of the cleaning machines seemed to have lost this narrow alley from its memory.

He passed down a narrow final stair, just wide enough for his skinny body, and he was there. The shielded kernel was not the one that had been removed from the Space Farm. This one was a monster. Even at the outer shield's thirty meter radius, Aybee judged that he was standing in a field of over a twentieth of a gee. That put the kernel mass at nearly eight billion tons. It must have been found near the middle of the *Zirkelloch*, the circular singularity that formed the center of the Kernel Ring.

That did not mean it was particularly useful as a controllable power source. If it were a slowly rotating kernel, approximately a Schwarzchild black hole, it was useless for anything except raw heat.

Was this one rotating?

Aybee fixed his eyes on one point on the ceiling and crouched low. No doubt about it, this kernel was both massive and rotating extremely rapidly. He could feel the inertial dragging as the kernel's spin rotated the reference frame along with it, tilting the local vertical.

He turned his attention to the controls. Most of them were already familiar to him. There were a dozen superconducting electromagnets, holding the charged kernel firmly at the center of its spherical shields. They appeared standard, no different from systems that Aybee had seen in dozens of other energy generation facilities.

There was the energy-extraction mechanism itself, clearly identifiable by its plasma injection units. This system was unusually finely calibrated, allowing far smaller changes to the kernel's rotational energy than any that Aybee had seen before; but that was an easy technological refinement, within the power of any kernel user. It was not clear why anyone would *want* to do it.

The first sign of real oddity came in the sensor leads. They were ten times as big as Aybee expected, suggesting a high signal-carrying capacity, and they ran to a substantial computer sitting right on the outer shield.

A computer to do what?

Inside the shield, the spinning black hole of the kernel was sending out a seething stream of radiation and particles. That random energy emission was a nuisance, and the shields were a necessity to reflect it back on itself. At the same time, the sensors monitoring the outward flood within the shields allowed the mass, charge, and angular momentum of the kernel to be measured to one part in a trillion.

Aybee crouched on the dull black surface of the outer shield, staring at the computer and its connecting cables for a long time. He would have loved to follow those optic bundles a meter or so further, beyond the shields. It was impossible. There were hatches for robot access, but he would not survive a moment inside the shields.

He stood up, puzzled, and stared thoughtfully at the sensor leads for a few minutes. When he finally wandered through the corridors back to his own quarters, his head was whirling with ideas and conjectures. He had theories, but no way to test them. What he needed was a long spell of quiet thought.

What he found, when he arrived at his room, was Gudrun. She was sitting on his bed. She had abandoned her silver-blue uniform and badged cap for a brief black exercise suit and purple skin makeup. Gudrun nodded at him and patted the bed next to her.

Aybee eyed her uneasily, and remained standing. "I was just taking a look round."

"I know. Sit down, Karl."

He placed himself at the far end of the bed. "I'm doing all right, aren't I?" He cleared his throat. "I mean, no problem with my work?"

"Just the opposite." She inched along closer to him. "Karl, you've been doing well, but I'm convinced you could do a lot better. Some of your answers on the tests are so concise and clear, they're better than anything in the training manuals. I'm using them as reference material. Where do you get them from?"

Aybee swore internally and shrugged. "Dunno. I just write what I think of."

"If you can think that way consistently, there's more in your future than a job as a maintenance engineer. I want to do something special with you."

"What do you mean?" Aybee didn't like the look in her eye.

"I want to take you to meet the big boss—the head of the whole Revolution and Movement. We have his orders to sift for unusual potential, and report it to Headquarters." She misread his concern. "Don't worry, I wouldn't send you there alone. We'd go together, just you and me, on one of the special high-acceleration transit ships. I'd be your sponsor."

"When?" The training course had five more weeks to run.

"In a couple of days. Jason and the other assistants can handle the training course easily enough. It's five days' travel from here to Headquarters in the new ship, but we wouldn't waste the time. You have a lot to learn. I'd give you personal coaching and special training." Gudrun had moved Aybee all the way to the end of the bed, and he couldn't retreat further. Her golden-brown eyes were gleaming. She took his hands in hers, and stared at him possessively. "And we still haven't done that form-change, have we?—the one that we talked about when you signed on. You're still too tall for comfort. We'll work on that. There might be some spare time for a form-change on the journey, too. I want to make you look more like one of us—less like a Cloudlander." She squeezed his hands. "What do you say, Karl? It's a one-time opportunity."

Five days confined to a high-gee transit cabin with Gudrun. Five days of "personal coaching" and "special training." What did that include? He had horrible suspicions. Aybee avoided her gaze, but she was very close. Everywhere he looked he saw nothing but bare flesh, plump thighs, arms and shoulders and breasts.

"Well, Karl, what do you say?" She was whispering, close to his cheek.

Aybee closed his eyes in horror. *Do I have a choice?*

He took a deep breath. Look at it this way, Apollo Belvedere Smith: you go to Headquarters, and the chances of finding out if your ideas are right are a hell of a lot better there than they are here. Whatever happens on the journey, you can handle it. So say yes quick, before you decide you can't stand the idea.

He nodded, eyes still closed. "It sounds ... wonderful."

He felt Gudrun's hand on his thigh. "I'll make sure that it is," she said. "We'll leave tomorrow. I'll put a form-change tank and size reduction programs on the ship, too. You can use them as much as you want to. But you'd better get some rest now, Karl. You need your rest."

"Yeah." Aybee swallowed. "I think I do."

She was moving slowly away from him. He could breathe again. He looked at her red lips and half-open mouth. She seemed ready to eat him.

Just make sure the form-change tank and size-reduction program is there, Gudrun. I'll use 'em, all right. In fact, if this trip is anything like I imagine, I'll use 'em over and over. I'm going to arrive at Headquarters as a two-foot midget.

CHAPTER 20

"I disapprove of every conspiracy of which I am not a part."

—Cinnabar Baker

Sylvia Fernald had agonized over the decision for a long time. Who should be told what she was planning to do, and how much should they be told?

On the one hand, her attempt to contact Paul Chu was in no sense an official mission. She had not been ordered to do it, or even asked to think about it. On the other hand, Bey Wolf and Aybee Smith believed that the rebels were behind the technical malfunctions in the Inner and Outer System, and they agreed with Cinnabar Baker that the rebels' end objective might be to instigate an all-out war between the other two parties. If that were the case, and if Paul were part of the rebel group, a dialogue with him was supremely important. Sylvia knew of no one else who might be able to open that dialogue. Paul had always been secretive and mistrustful, but he would talk to Sylvia.

Wouldn't he? They had been very close, but in the final months she had never known what Paul was thinking, or even what he was doing. But surely he would at least *talk* to her—they had been partners for more than three years. On the other hand, if he were now a rebel himself, she ought not to be talking to him, and if she did meet with him she should not tell anyone she was doing it.

Sylvia wondered and worried, and at last settled for a compromise. Since she would be using a Cloudland ship in her travels, someone in government had to know and approve it. But the fewer people who knew, the less the danger that her mission would be leaked to others.

Sylvia looked at her options: Leo Manx was a good man, but pedantic in approach and (much more dangerous) apt to gossip. Bey Wolf would not talk, but he would probably try to stop her. Aybee, her first choice, was off who-knew-where, and all her other close friends in the Harvesters would be overwhelmed by the implied responsibility. They would feel a compulsion to tell their superiors—who might then tell anyone.

In the end, Sylvia called Cinnabar Baker directly and asked for a private meeting. If the information were likely to end with Baker, it might as well begin there.

The other woman asked her—typically—to come to her quarters that same day, but at one o'clock in the morning. Sylvia spent the next twelve hours making final preparations for her departure, and rehearsing what she was going to say to Baker. When she finally entered the bare-walled apartment, she forgot about her prepared speech.

Cinnabar Baker looked terrible. She had lost fifty or sixty pounds, and her grey-toned skin was lined and pouchy. From time to time she rubbed at her eyes, wheezed deep in her chest, and produced a rumbling cough. Turpin sat blinking on her shoulder. Each time she coughed, the bedraggled crow provided an impressive imitation of the sound. He must have had plenty of time to practice.

"I know." Baker saw Sylvia's dismay. "Don't tell me I look like hell, and don't worry. It's not permanent. I've been overworking, and everyone here is scared to let me near the form-change machines for a remedial session. The machines are so messed up, people are afraid I'll turn into a pumpkin. What can I do for you? We have ten minutes."

Sylvia jumped into her description of how she had found a trail that should lead to Paul Chu. Half her explanation proved unnecessary—Cinnabar Baker knew more about the relationship with Chu than Sylvia dreamed. Baker waved her on past that, then listened in a silence broken only by her coughs and hoarse breathing.

At the end of it she sniffed and pinched the end of her nose between her fingers. "I've heard your reports, and the ones from Leo Manx. Do you agree with him, that the rebels are behind Bey Wolf's problems with the 'Negentropic Man?' "

"I think so."

"You've saved Wolf's life at least once, probably twice. Do you know what the ancient Chinese, back on Earth, used to say if you saved a man from drowning?"

Sylvia shook her head in confusion. Cinnabar Baker had lost her.

"They would say you are then responsible for the welfare of that man, for the whole rest of his life. Let me ask you, how much of what you're proposing to do is for the sake of the Outer System? And how much are you doing it to help with Wolf's personal problems?"

The suggestion floored Sylvia.

She had acted to save Bey on the transit ship and on the Space Farm without thinking for a moment about her own motives. She would have done as much for anyone. And as for sitting beside the form-change tank while Bey Wolf was in it . . .

"Don't bother to answer that." Cinnabar Baker was moving on. Sylvia had been there more than ten minutes. "Tell me this instead. You're proposing to leave at once. What's the hurry? Why not wait a few more days?"

"More days?" repeated Turpin.

Sylvia shook her head. "I daren't. Paul Chu is at that location to perform a facility conversion, adding a low-gee drive—probably to a cometary fragment. That means he'll be working alone except for machines. We'll be able to talk freely. But that will last only another couple of weeks, then he'll be leaving. I don't know where he'll be going next."

"Does he know anything about this?"

"Not a thing. I didn't suggest to *anyone* that I might try to visit him. You're the only person who knows I'm even thinking of it." She saw the slow nod of Cinnabar Baker's head. "You will approve it, then?"

Baker grunted. "Fernald, I never did like Paul Chu. I remember him, and I don't believe he'll do one thing to help you." She held up her hand. "But before you begin to argue, let me tell you I'm going to approve your request. You ought to have this job for a day. You'd approve *anything* that might give you a toehold on our problems. The Cloud's technology is all going to hell, people daren't go near the form-change machines, we've been receiving communications from some of the other Harvesters that suggest the populations there have all gone crazy, and I just had a report from the other side of the Cloud about a bad accident on another of the Space Farms. To top that off, one of our inbound cargo ships was destroyed yesterday, and the Sunhuggers are blaming *us* for it—saying we blew up one of our own vessels!"

She sighed. "All right. You've heard enough of that. Of course I'll approve it. Go do it, and use my authority if you need it to get your ship. But one other thing"— Sylvia was standing up—"this has to be a two-way street. You won't tell anyone where you're going. And I won't tell anyone, not even the Inner Council, what you are trying to do. If you get into hot water, I'll have to disown you. I'll even deny that you had my permission for a transit ship. We have a firm policy, you see, we don't deal with the rebels in any circumstances. Understood?"

Sylvia bit her lip, then nodded. "All right."

Cinnabar Baker reached out and took her hand in an unexpected gesture. "We never had a meeting tonight, Fernald, and you leave by the other exit. I have another group of people waiting outside. Good luck, and good hunting. You'll be a long way from home."

"From home," echoed Turpin hoarsely. The crow wagged his head. "Way from home."

That had been eight days ago. Eight days of silence and solitude. Sylvia had maintained strict communications blackout all through the journey, even when the ship's drive was inactive and it was easy to send or receive signals.

But now, as she slowed to approach her final destination and the rendezvous was only a few minutes away, her nervousness increased. The urge to send some kind of message back to Cinnabar Baker grew stronger. Sylvia had been provided with an ephemeris for a body in an orbit skirting the outer part of the Kernel Ring, and told that Paul Chu should be there. But the positional data had come with an admonition to strict secrecy, and nothing else. She had not been told the nature of the object to which she was travelling, or whether it was large or small, manmade or natural, a colony or a military base. She had *assumed* a cometary fragment—why else would he be installing an add-on drive unit—but suppose that was wrong?

Well, she would know soon enough. At last, the body was visible. From a distance of five kilometers, it was like an irregular, granular egg, shining by internal lights. Sylvia turned the high-magnification sensors onto it. She was confused and her nervousness had increased. The object was about three hundred meters long, too small to be a Harvester, a colony, or a cargo ship, and the wrong shape for a transit vessel. That fitted with the idea of a small comet nucleus, still rich in volatiles. Yet the pattern of ports and lights implied an inhabited body, and two docking ports and airlocks were clearly visible on the surface.

If it were a natural body, then it was one that had already seen some internal tunnelling and modifications. The newly installed drive unit was easily recognised, gleaming at the thicker end of the lumpy body.

Delay would not help, and she had not come all this way for nothing. Sylvia was already in her suit. She allowed the transit ship to dock itself gently against the bigger port, opened the cabin, and went straight to the lock.

It was open, contrary to standard safety regulations. And the *inner* lock was open, too, which meant that the interior of the body was airless. If Paul Chu were inside, he was either wearing a suit, or he was a corpse. Sylvia noticed how loud her own breath sounded in the helmet. She set her suit receiver to perform a frequency sweep and passed on through the inner airlock.

The first chamber had been carved from the water ice and carbon-dioxide ice of the cometary interior, and it was clearly intended as a workshop and equipment maintenance facility. There were plenty of signs that it had been recently inhabited, with cutting torches still attached to their fuel bottles in a toolshop chamber, and an electrical generator in stand-by mode. Three or four construction machines were waiting patiently against one of the walls. Sylvia regarded them with irritation. They were obsolete models by Cloud standards. If they had been made just a little bit smarter, she could have asked them what was going on. As it was, they had been designed with a specialized vocabulary and understood nothing but mechanical construction tasks. If no one came along to give instructions, they would wait contentedly for a million years.

She passed on through a sliding partition, deeper into the interior. The scan on received signals had produced nothing, so she switched to an all-frequency broadcast. "Paul Chu. This is Sylvia." Her suit repeated the message automatically, over and over, and listened for any reply.

She had reached the temporary living quarters built by the machines near the center of the body. He was not here, but there were many signs of his recent occupancy. That was definitely his computer link, the one he had used for ten years. No Cloudlander, no matter how long he was away from the Outer System, would ever leave metal objects strewn so casually around, unless he knew he would be coming back soon, or he had been forced to leave in a great hurry.

Or dead, said her mind insistently.

She pushed away the thought. Perhaps Paul was somewhere on the other side of the body, or perhaps he had
been temporarily called away.

But called away to what? And to where? She had seen
no sign of other bodies in her approach, and her suit
radio had an effective range of many thousands of
kilometers.

Then suppose that he didn't *want* to meet her, and
was hiding away to avoid an encounter? That thought
rejected itself. How could he be hiding, when he had no
idea that she was even on the way here? He thought she
was back in the Outer System.

Almost against her will, Sylvia set out to explore the
desolate interior. Sometime, far in the past, this had been
a human home for a long period. There were kitchens,
bedrooms, even chambers set up for entertainment and
for exercise. Those rooms held harnesses, and stretch
bars, and workout machines, each with dials to measure
effort level and progress. But over all the equipment and
instruments lay a thin layer of sublimed ice. No one had
touched anything here for years, maybe for decades.

In less than half an hour, she was convinced that there
was no one anywhere on the hollowed-out comet. She
was alone. And only a few moments later she felt a
strange vibration beneath her feet, and sensed a slight
pressure on the front of her suit. She knew at once what
was happening. The airlocks had been closed on the
body's surface, and the interior was filling with air.

She set off, hurriedly retracing her steps towards the
lock through which she had first entered. When she was
halfway there a flicker of movement appeared at the end
of a corridor.

"Paul?" She paused, her hand on the wall of the corridor. "Paul Chu? Is that you, Paul? Who is there?"

The corridor now supported a full atmosphere, and
her voice went echoing along the narrow passageway.
There was no reply, but suddenly a little machine came
scuttling into view and moved towards her. Three meters
away it paused. Sylvia was thrilled to see it. Unlike the

others that she had seen, this one she recognised as a
very advanced model, one that was scarcely out of the
development labs. It was a GA machine, a General Assistance model that would perform hundreds of tasks with
vocal direction and little human supervision. If it had to,
it could fly her home in her own transit ship.

"What's been happening here?" She advanced on it
confidently. No machine would harm her—no machine
could harm her, except by accident. "Where are the people? Is Paul Chu here?"

It said nothing. The arrays of detectors on the front
of the machine had tilted her way, and there was no
doubt that it was aware of her presence. But when she
was within a couple of paces, it began to back away. A
second machine of the same design had appeared at the
end of the corridor, and advanced to stand next to the
first.

"Come on." Sylvia was becoming impatient. "I want
answers. Don't pretend you can't understand me, I know
you're a lot too smart for that. What's been going on in
this place?"

From a circular aperture at its base, the second
machine suddenly extruded a pair of long, rubbery arms.
Before Sylvia could retreat they had moved forward to
circle her ankles.

"Hey! Let go of me!"

It took no notice, and now arms from the first machine
came forward to wrap around her forearms and her waist.
She was gently lifted off her feet and held in mid-air.
Both machines moved in unison along the corridor, holding Sylvia as delicately but as firmly as an armed bomb.

"There is no problem." The first machine finally spoke,
in a voice that Sylvia recognised at once. It sounded just
like Paul Chu. "We will be going on a journey. You will
be quite safe. One moment."

While Sylvia struggled as hard as she could, yet
another pair of arms appeared to check the closure of
her suit helmet.

"What do you mean, a journey? Damn you, let go of

me. Take me to see Paul Chu. *I order you to release me.*"

That *had* to work. No machine could hold a human against her will, unless it was to save life.

"We cannot do that." The voice was suitably regretful and apologetic. "We cannot set you free; not yet. But we can take you to Paul Chu's present location. Maybe you will see him there."

"When?" They were already in the lock, and there was a hiss of escaping air.

"When we reach our destination. Ten days' journey from here."

They were outside, drifting along in a glimmer of starlight. The second machine had stayed behind at the lock, so now she was held only by her arms and waist. Sylvia saw a new shape in front of her, a small ellipsoidal object only twenty meters long. It was like no ship she had ever seen. "We can't fly in that." She spoke into her suit radio, offering what should have been for a machine the ultimate threat. "If you make me fly in that, it will *kill* me."

"Not so." The machine sounded shocked, but it did not even pause. "Otherwise, of course, we would never permit it. Ten days will quickly pass. Perhaps when we are on the way you would like to play chess with me? We will be alone."

"I hate chess!"

As Sylvia was carried into the ship she had a final unhappy thought. She had given Cinnabar Baker the coordinates of this destination, and felt pleased with her foresight. But how much use would that information be, wherever she was ten days from now?

CHAPTER 21

"Any sufficiently advanced technology is indistinguishable from magic."

—Arthur C. Clarke

Aybee had seen many transit ships during his wanderings through the Outer System. The design was standard. It differed only in detail whether the fabrication was done at the Vulcan Nexus, whispering its way across the surface of the Sun, or out in the Dry Tortugas, wandering the remote and ill-defined perimeter of the Oort Cloud.

Every transit ship had a thick disc of dense matter on the front end. Every one also had a passenger cabin that could slide back or forward along the two-hundred meter central spike jutting out behind the mass plate. The McAndrew vacuum energy drive sat at the plate's outer edge. The whole assembly looked like an axle with only one wheel attached.

It was a shock to be taken by Gudrun to the front of the ship, and be shown a smooth, spikeless ellipsoid just twenty meters long.

Aybee stared at it like the audience at a magic show, waiting for the missing bluebird to appear. "Where's the rest of it?"

"There is no more." Gudrun laughed. She was bubbling with excitement. "I told you, Karl, the surprises are just beginning. This is the ship for our journey. It arrived from Headquarters two days ago."

Aybee made a complete circuit of the outside. The ovoid had a smooth glassy hull, polished and unmarked. He could see his own distorted reflection in the convex surface. That alone was sufficient to make it out of place in the dingy and grimy environment of the old cargo ship. It was as new as its surroundings were old. Odder yet, it showed no sign of a drive mechanism. There was nowhere to attach the massive disc that balanced gravity and acceleration, and the clear ports suggested that at least half of the internal space was passenger quarters.

As a supposed trainee, Aybee couldn't tell Gudrun what he was thinking; which was, either this supposed ship was a total hoax, and would go nowhere—or there were whole realms of physics unknown to the best minds in the Inner and Outer Systems.

Instead he said, "Who built it?"

"Headquarters. It's very new and very fast. The old ships took weeks to get to Headquarters—it's over six hundred billion kilometers. We'll be there in five days!"

"What's the acceleration?"

"That's not relevant. This works on a new principle. They are making more of them, but today there are only a handful of others like this ship."

But there ought to be none *like it.* Aybee did the instant mental conversion, five days for six hundred billion kilometers meant about five hundred gees. Then he at once ignored his own answer. The range calculation made sense only if the ship performed like a transit ship, with an acceleration phase, a crossover, and a deceleration. There was no reason for that assumption. If the ship were as new as it seemed, Headquarters could be on the other side of the galaxy. Aybee had no idea how it could function. At the moment he didn't even know what questions to ask.

"How is it powered?" he said at last. "With a kernel?"

That was fishing. The transit ships used the McAndrew vacuum drive, not kernels.

"No. But apparently it has a low-mass kernel at the centre."

Curiouser and curiouser. Even a small kernel was a

few hundred million tons. Why accelerate that mass, if you didn't need it?

They went aboard, and Aybee's confusion performed a quantum jump to a higher level state. The internal living space on the ship was ten times what he had expected. There was too little space for any reasonable power supply, engines, or drive mechanism.

In the back of his mind Aybee had already decided that a new and first-rate intellect must have arisen in the rebel communities of the Kernel Ring. That was the only way to explain something as radically different as the new ship. But once inside and looking around him he was forced to drop even that idea. Too many things were new and unfamiliar. Out of a dozen different internal systems, he could identify and explain maybe half of them. And those few hinted at something that Aybee had been groping his way towards for the past four years, a new landscape just beyond the horizon.

Aybee had a clear image of current science, of its peaks and valleys and grey clouded areas where theory failed. Technology advanced constantly, but it depended on models of the physical world that were often centuries old. It advanced by ignoring the foggy regions, those places where deep understanding had not been achieved and where the subtle paradoxes lurked. Aybee had charted those anomalies. It was shocking to find the misty curtain suddenly blown aside, and a new world shining forth in full-blown glory.

Gudrun had no such worries. She sat down confidently at the control board and began to follow the simple sequence of instructions provided by the panel's prompting. The new ship did not seem to amaze her, but Aybee recalled the description of the Outer System Navy: a system designed by a genius to be run by idiots. And when he thought of the level of genius needed to come up with a whole system so different from anything he had ever seen, his skin crawled with excitement.

Five days. That's how long he would have, to explore everything and find out how it all worked. Aybee had been dreading so long a trip with Gudrun, but now he wished the travel duration were double. His usable time would almost certainly be less than five days. Gudrun would insist on talking—or worse—for part of it, and she also wanted him in a form-change tank, to waste more precious hours.

Even while she was finishing the command sequence to move them out of the cargo hulk and on their way, Aybee was thinking hard. What he needed was a complete reversal of roles: Gudrun absent, and Aybee free to explore the ship. How could he manage it?

Cinnabar Baker would have solved that problem in a moment. With stakes so high, Gudrun had to be out of action for the duration of the journey. One blow would do it; then the disposal of a corpse, or the confinement of an injured body to the medical unit.

Aybee had plenty of brain-power. The idea that Gudrun could be killed or injured occurred to him at once. She had finished the control sequence, and now she was with the communications unit. As she crouched before the panel with the headset shielding any of his actions, he picked up a heavy data storage case and moved to stand directly behind her. It would take only a moment, a single strike to the unprotected skull.

Now!

Aybee stared the possibility full in the face—and blinked. For the first time in his life, he was forced to face one of his own limitations: he was not particularly fond of Gudrun, but regardless of logic and motivation he could not harm her physically.

He put down the case and stared at her in total frustration. At the same moment, she swivelled round in her chair to look up into his face. Her expression was curious, somewhere between cold and startled. Aybee could visualise a five-dimensional knotted manifold and manipulate its topology in his head, but he could not read that human countenance. If he had, he would have recognized a look of fear.

"I've been in touch with Headquarters," Gudrun said after a few moments. "I said we'll be on our way any moment now."

Aybee nodded. It hardly seemed like a universe-shattering revelation.

"And I'm afraid we can't do the things we'd planned," she hurried on. "There have been changes. I have urgent work to do on the journey, so you'll have to occupy yourself as best you can. Don't come in here."

Without another word she went through to the aft part of the cabin and slid the door closed. Any child could see that something had happened to upset her very much.

But if Aybee were a child, he was the little boy who had suddenly been given the run of the candy store. He stared after Gudrun for all of ten seconds, until he heard a high-pitched whirring sound from somewhere beneath his feet. A new mechanism had come into operation.

Aybee felt no acceleration, but he suspected he might be hearing the drive. It was easy enough to test the idea. The McAndrew propulsion system produced a faint sparkle of eldritch light as high-speed particles collided with the occasional hydrogen atoms of free space. He went across to the port and peered out.

And gasped. There was no pinpoint twinkle of drive interactions. Instead, the whole star field had been replaced by a tangled rainbow of color, rippling across his field of view.

From that moment, Aybee forgot all about Gudrun for many hours.

CHAPTER 22

"*I often wonder what the vintners buy*
One half so precious as the goods they sell."
—Omay Khayyam

Behrooz Wolf claimed to have no conscience. He denied having brains. What he had in place of both, he said, was a little voice that whispered in his ear, urging him to take actions that his natural indolence discouraged.

It was doing it now, interfering with his work. What he *wanted* to do was solve the mystery of the demon of form-change, that impossible chimaera that could live in the radiative inferno inside a kernel shield and send a stream of misdirection through the computer system to the rest of the Harvester. (And if it could do it to form-change, it could do it to everything else. It was the key to wholesale delusions, impossible sensor messages. Even the Negentropic Man himself, and Mary's visitation, and failed mass detection systems—*something* had allowed that cometary fragment to crash undetected into the Sagdeyev Space Farm.)

That's what he *wanted* to do, work on technical problems. So why was he wandering the interior of the Marsden Harvester, seeking a woman whose last name he had not at first remembered?

It could only be the dreams; persistent, chaotic images that came in the middle of deep sleep. He saw flashes of

Mary in indescribable danger, of vague menace creeping towards her. He heard cries of fear and pleas for help.

Or was it *Sylvia* that he saw? The visions blurred and faded as he watched, one face flowing into another. And were they dreams, or were they messages, like the first one he had received from Mary? When he woke he was never sure what he had experienced. All that remained was the feeling of urgency.

Bey wandered on. He was looking for Andromeda, but Andromeda who? Leo Manx had never heard of her. Bey went to the central data bank and asked for a complete listing of all the Andromedas—Diconis, that was the name he had been groping for; but the computer offered only a general location within the Harvester. She was a woman with no permanent partner and no particular job. Bey started with the dining area where they had met, and widened his sphere of search from there.

His new form had a stamina level inferior to his Earth body. After seven hours of roaming the Harvester's corridors, asking for a woman that everyone seemed to know and no one was able to locate, he was wilting. He needed food. He gave up his search, headed for the nearest dining area—and found Andromeda Diconis.

He dropped the idea of food and filled a jug with purple-red wine when he saw her. This was a meeting he did not expect to enjoy (*so why was he doing it?*). She was alone, dressed in a cleverly cut garment that suggested body curves where there were none. He had to hurry, since she was carrying a tray of food and about to enter a dining cubicle. He grabbed his jug and a cup, hurried that way, and crowded in after her.

She gave him a first amazed stare, then a gasp of pleased recognition. "Why—Behrooz. What a nice surprise."

"I have to talk to you."

"But I'm about to eat." She gestured to the tray in front of her. "You'll have to wait until I've finished. Unless"—her face turned pink, but her eyes were gleaming before they looked away from his—"unless you were thinking of staying here while I do it."

"Sure. Here, we'll share this." Bey placed the wine on the table between them and heard her gasp. He might be getting into more than he realized.

Andromeda was looking around her, checking that no one else had seen Bey enter the cubicle. "Wait a minute." Her voice was breathless, and she quickly set the table controls to make all the walls opaque. "There— if you are sure you really want to?"

"I do. I'm sure." Bey picked up the flagon and poured wine. He did not think Andromeda was a woman who did favors for nothing. Who was it said that Paris was worth a mass? One of the Henrys. Well, Sylvia was worth more than that. According to his estimates, she had saved his life at least twice. And she had sat for days by the tank when he went into form-change, to make sure nothing bad happened there. Sylvia was worth it, whatever it took. Bey followed his instincts, picked up his cup of wine, and drained it.

Andromeda had taken a spoonful of a clear soup, but she was hesitating with it poised in front of her mouth, watching him drink. Bey stared right at her, not letting her off the hook. After a moment she gave a little shiver, pursed her lips, and sipped in a determined way. She swallowed, blushed, and said, "I hope you don't think I'm like this all the time. I mean, I'm really a very respectable woman."

"I know. Sylvia says you're the tops." Bey gulped more wine, and watched Andromeda lean forward and lick her lips. Her nipples were pushing against the indigo fabric of her dress. He was even getting excited himself. Maybe the Cloudlanders knew something that Earth people had never learned about the serious business of eating. Bey struggled to keep his mind on the job at hand. "She says the two of you go way back together. You were big buddies until she set up with Paul Chu."

"We were." Andromeda swallowed another lascivious spoonful of soup. "I was very disappointed when that happened. I mean, he was *nothing*. Little, and fat, and full of strange ideas."

Lady, that was me two weeks ago. Bey leaned across,

poured a full glass for Andromeda, drank deep from his
own glass, and nodded agreeably. He had not eaten for
a long time, and the alcohol was pumping straight
through to his bloodstream. Andromeda was beginning
to look much more attractive. "I don't know why she
started to hang out with him." He leaned forward.
"Wasn't he part of some religious group?"

"Not *religion*. Revolution." She gave Bey another
knowing look, waited to be sure he was watching, and
took a deliberate swallow of wine. Her face was flushed
and her lower lip swollen. "He was into revolution, and
Borderland politics, and all that rubbish. I don't know
how much she told you about the two of them, but they
were an item for a long time. I think she still has the
hots for him. I don't know what she told you, but in my
opinion she hasn't got him out of her system."

"Was she asking about him?" The question was overly
direct, but Andromeda was too preoccupied to notice.
She was sitting with a forkful of food poised in front of
her. Not until Bey fixed his eyes on her again did she
slowly place it in her mouth, pull the food free with her
white teeth, and chew steadily while he watched. The
pulse in the hollow of her throat was throbbing.

"She was asking." Andromeda finally swallowed and
put down her fork. "She was asking about him, and I
told her how I thought she could get in touch with him."

"You *know* that?"

"I'm fairly sure I do. He was here secretly, but he
wanted certain people to be able to reach him. I know
who they are."

"And you could tell me?"

"Well, not immediately." Andromeda licked her lips
again. "It would take time to find them. But we could
look together."

Bey knew what was coming. " 'There's a divinity that
shapes our ends,' Andromeda, 'rough-hew them how we
will.' "

"I'm sorry?"

"Shapes our ends." Lord. He'd had far too much to
drink (but too much for *what*?)

Andromeda laughed. "You're such a *strange* person—
not at all the way you look. If you want to search, I can
tell you where we should start." She moved closer to
Bey. She had lost all interest in eating. "I have their
names and locations—but not with me. Back in my private quarters. We'd have to go there. If you want to."

She paused, and was looking at him enquiringly.

With a wild surmise. Silent, upon a peak in Darien.
Lord, he *was* drunk.

"Well, Bey." She had stopped smiling. "Do you want
to?"

" 'Being your slave, what should I do but tend upon
the hours and times of your desire?' "

"What?"

"I mean, let's go. Now. To your place. I want to."

"Mm. Are you *sure?*" Now she was playing hard to
get. "I mean, what about Sylvia?"

" 'I have been faithful to thee, Cynara, in my fashion.' "
I mean Sylvia, I mean Mary, *for God's sake.*

"What?"

"I mean, I'm quite sure. Can't wait. Let's go." Bey
lurched to his feet, clutching the half-full flagon of wine.
She was out there somewhere, in the featureless gulf of
the Outer System. He was going to find her. If he had
to lay his body down to do it, that was part of the game.
Whatever it took, he was going to find her. But not quite
yet.

Leo Manx stared at him in disbelief. "Let me get this
straight. You're leaving tomorrow for these co-ordinates."
He tapped the sheet he was holding. "In the wilderness.
And you don't want me to come with you. I'll second
that. You don't want to tell the Harvester controllers
where you're going. All right, if you say so. But what are
you hoping to accomplish?"

Leo Manx was a good listener. He proved it now, while
Bey outlined his ideas. At the wilder moments, Leo muttered to himself but did not interrupt. "How are you
proposing to prove all this?" he said at last.

"I'm going to bring one back. A live one." Bey was

white-faced, exhausted, and somewhere between stoned and hung over. Four days of wine, drugs, and Andromeda Diconis was not an experience for the faint-hearted. They had wandered the Harvester together from one end to the other. Andromeda believed in stimulation rather than sleep. If he survived, Bey wanted to see her again. He had to know where she got her energy. "But if I don't make it back," he went on, "there has to be at least one person who knows exactly where I'm heading and what I think is going on. That's you."

"But how am I ever going to persuade Cinnabar Baker that what you're doing makes sense?"

"You don't start with Cinnabar. You *end* with her, and only if I don't come back and there's absolutely no other alternative. I told you the danger. Did you do what I asked you to?"

"As much as I could. Have you ever tried to brief your boss, without telling her what's going on?"

"A hundred times. It's the first rule of self-preservation. Do you have them in a safe place?"

"The co-ordinates? Sure I do. But you realise those co-ordinates are almost certainly *not* the location of Ransome's Hole? They're too far out of the Kernel Ring."

"I know. But they're the only starting point I have, and I feel sure Sylvia went there. I'm leaving now. If everything goes to hell, you know what to do. Give me thirty days, then if you don't hear from me assume I'm dead and gone."

He was ready to go, but Leo Manx stopped him. "Bey, you tell me you need thirty days before I panic, and you're not frantic now about Aybee. So why don't you give as much breathing room to Sylvia? Maybe she's working her own agenda. You could ruin it for her."

Leo deserved an answer, but Bey didn't have one. All he had was that small voice again, whispering in his ear. It said that Aybee might be fine, and Bey might be fine, but Sylvia was in trouble. Or was it telling him that he owed more to her than he did Aybee, and so he had to worry more about her?

Bey couldn't turn off that voice, but he could sometimes

see through its strategies. He was in a hurry to leave, but not perhaps for the obvious reason. If he found Sylvia, she might lead him to Paul Chu. And Paul Chu might lead to Black Ransome. And Black Ransome was the Negentropic Man, that grinning, dancing figure who had driven Bey near insanity and forced him to leave Earth. *That* was who Bey was after. Wasn't it?

Maybe. The inner voice insisted on the last word. You want to get even with Black Ransome, I can believe that. And you want to solve the mystery of the kernels, which begins and ends with Black Ransome. But aren't we conveniently forgetting one other little thing? If you find Black Ransome at the end of the trail, who else may you find with him? And what will gallant Bey Wolf do then?

CHAPTER 23

"Time to worry, time to fear,
The Negentropic Man is here."
—*crèche song of the Halley Harvester*

Aybee Smith was a helpless prisoner, boxed up in a ship with a woman who would not talk to him, racing towards an unknown destination, heading for a meeting with people who were sworn enemies of everything that Aybee's own civilisation stood for.

Any logical person would have been worried sick about his own future. And logic ruled Aybee's whole life. He loved logic, he lived by logic. And yet he did not give any of those worries a single thought. He was busy with something far more important.

The ship was a treasure-box of mysteries. Beginning with the puzzle of the drive mechanism (no high-density balancing plate, and no acceleration forces) he had listed twenty-seven devices that required some new technology—or, beyond mere technology, some new physical principle!

With a mental clock ticking always in his mind (*five days!—too little time*) Aybee had foregone the luxury of sleep or rest. No matter what they did to him at his destination, he could sleep when he arrived there; today the exploration of the ship was his only goal.

Gudrun appeared from her locked quarters only for a

few minutes twice a day, when she found it necessary to use the ship's single galley. Aybee was eating randomly, snatching food when he could bear the interruption to his work. He and Gudrun met in the galley only once. She avoided his eyes and did not speak. He didn't even notice. A new insight had occurred to him, a possible basis for the ship's garbage disposal unit, which somehow removed the mass from the ship but did not eject it to open space.

While she prepared her meal, and fled, he sat motionless and gawped at the blank wall. Aybee worked in his head. He only transcribed results when everything was complete. So far, he had written nothing.

He had performed a taxonomy of those twenty-seven anomalies, placing them neatly into four major categories. Thus:

(1) inertial versus gravitational mass; half a dozen devices on the ship, including all its positional and navigation systems, could be explained very well in one simple theory—*if* Aybee were willing to abandon the Principle of Equivalence. He wasn't. He would give up his virginity first.

(2) heat into motion; another set of devices on the ship made sense only if heat could be converted *perfectly* to other forms of mechanical energy; in other words, if Aybee were willing to give up the Second Law of Thermodynamics.

The Negentropic Man again! In a closed system (and what was more closed than the ship?) Aybee was asked to admit an entity that would decrease entropy. He remembered Maxwell's Demon, that tiny imp who was supposed to sit in a container sorting molecules. The fast-moving ones would be allowed to pass in one direction, only slow-moving molecules in the opposite one. Maxwell's Demon had been introduced in 1874, but Szilard had banished it completely in 1928. Hadn't he?

Aybee wasn't sure any more. But he certainly didn't want to give up the Second Law of Thermodynamics. Eddington's words were graven in his memory:

"The law that entropy always increases—the second law of thermodynamics—holds, I think, the supreme position among the laws of nature. If someone points out to you that your pet theory of the universe is in disagreement with Maxwell's equations, then so much the worse for Maxwell's equations. If it is found to be contradicted by observation, well, these experimentalists do bungle things sometimes. But if your theory is found to be against the second law of thermodynamics I can give you no hope; there is nothing for it but to collapse in deepest humiliation."

Aybee agreed with that. Wholeheartedly.

(3) force-field aberrations. By the end of the third day, Aybee had devised an alternative theory which explained how the drive might work; but it involved the introduction of a new type of force, similar to the ancient and long-discredited concept of "hypercharge." Aybee shrank from such *ad hoc* leaps into darkness. *"Hypotheses non fingo"*—"I don't make new assumptions." If that had been good enough for Isaac Newton, it was good enough for Aybee.

(4) information from nothing. All the rest of the ship would work fine—if only it were possible to create information from random noise! Chaos to signal, that was all Aybee needed. The ship's communication system seemed to *depend* on that impossible capability. Could he accept it? Aybee knew exactly where it would lead him, and he didn't like it. He would again need a way in which entropy could be decreased. It was the Negentropic Man, popping up again in a different but equally unappetizing form. Aybee hated the whole idea.

Five days flew by. The approach to their destination was an irritating distraction, but finally a necessary one. Aybee would not stop thinking about the physical problems—he *could* not stop thinking—but at least he would have an obligatory break from it.

One hour before arrival, Gudrun appeared grim-faced from her cabin and moved at once to the communications terminal. She was wearing a space-suit, and it was clear that she was very nervous. But her feelings were not obvious enough to break through Aybee's shield of obsessions. He went on working, until the very moment when the ship docked and the lock began to open. Then it was not Gudrun's voice that brought him out of his reverie, it was the clatter of metal from within the lock itself.

"There he is!" Gudrun had run to the opening and squeezed through it. She turned to point back inside. "That's Karl Lyman. Be careful—he's dangerous!"

The airlock on the ship, like its passenger quarters, was far bigger than on an ordinary transit vessel. Aybee stared into it, and saw to his amazement that it was crammed with armed men, all in full space attire and squeezed tightly together. There were eight or nine of them; to a Cloudlander, that many people in one place was a major gathering. Gudrun had pushed into their midst. As he watched, all the weapons lifted to point straight at him.

"Into your suit," said an uncompromising voice. "If you have an explanation, you can give it later."

It was not a time to argue. One shot from any of those weapons would pierce the average hull. Aybee had a suit on and was ready to go in less than thirty seconds. He nodded as he closed the final seal. The outer lock opened, and air hissed out into vacuum. One of the guns lifted and gestured. "Outside."

One step behind Gudrun, Aybee moved on through the lock. It had been three days since he last looked out of an observation port, and now he stared around with keen interest. The strange rainbow aurora had vanished, presumably disappearing when the drive went off, and the familiar starfield was all around. The Sun was visible off to his right, noticeably more brilliant than it had been when the journey began. Aybee made a quick assessment of its apparent magnitude, and decided that they were somewhere on the outer edge of the Kernel Ring.

The ship had docked on the perimeter of a structure that was no more than a minor way station, a long skeletal framework of struts with clamps to hold ships in position and massive tanks for fusion fuels. The group moved to a little pinnace propelled by a high-thrust mirror-matter engine. Their real destination was a few kilometers sunward, a dull darkness whose size and shape could only be assessed from stray glints of sunlight splintering off external ports and antennas.

The body was roughly spherical, perhaps five kilometers across. Aybee stared at it with the greatest interest. If he were unworried, it was not that he was confident of his own fate. He was simply unable to drag his mind away from the new physical universe suggested by the ship he had arrived in. If he had any emotion, it was anticipation; whatever he had seen in transit, there would be greater marvels here, where the transit ship had been built.

Aybee did a quick analysis. The sphere ahead might be a source of ships, but it was not itself a ship. It was also the size and shape of a cargo hulk, but it was not being used for cargo. There were no signs of a drive mechanism, and there could be none, since the delicate spikes and silvery filaments of exterior antennas were incompatible with accelerated motion. They were no stronger than tinsel, and would be crushed and deformed by the slightest of body forces.

It could be a colony, like the Outer System's free drifters; or it might be a converted factory, originally dedicated to the production of a particular line of goods.

Aybee abandoned speculation. They were moving to a huge airlock built into the hull's convex surface, and already several of the party had their hands ready to break suit seals. Aybee waited. If anyone attempted to breathe vacuum, he would not be the first. He was amused to note that Gudrun had positioned herself as far away from him as possible, at the opposite side of the lock. The escort had apparently formed their own conclusions about Aybee's threat to them. No one held a gun at the ready, and half of them didn't even bother to look at him.

The inner lock opened. The group moved quietly forward into a large, bare chamber, with a flat floor and a local gravity field that varied irregularly from one point to the next. To Aybee, that suggested the resultant vector from many kernels, scattered through the interior of the body and each adding its own field component.

The man in front halted and turned around. At his gesture, Aybee removed his own suit with the rest. For the first time he could assess their physical appearance. Most of them had the short, stocky build that he associated with the Inner System and the Kernel Ring, but two were long and lean, as much Cloudlanders as anyone that Aybee had ever seen. They were probably not recent arrivals, either, since they were not dressed in Outer System style; their arms and legs stuck wildly out of clothes far too small for them.

Gudrun was staring at him in fear and horror. Aybee felt tempted to go across, wiggle his fingers in his ears, and see if she screamed. What was she expecting? Someone to appear in a puff of smoke and carry her off to hell?

Instead he nodded amiably to the others in the group. "Well." They all stared at him. "You got me. What happens now?"

"That depends on you." The speaker was a black-haired man with dark skin and a thickset build. Aybee recognized the voice as the one that had been ordering him around. "I was told to get you here, that's all. If Gudrun is right"—the man spoke as someone who already knew her well—"then you're in trouble. We don't like spies here. If you're innocent, you'll have to prove it."

"Guilty until proved innocent. Nice. Where's here?"

Several of the men stirred uneasily at Aybee's question. "Got a bit of a nerve, haven't you?" said the stocky man. "What did you tell him, Gudrun?"

"Nothing." She was defensive. "At least, not very much. I thought until we were on the ship that he was just a new trainee that we captured on the Sagdeyev Space Farm. How was I supposed to know he's a Cloudland spy?"

That produced another reaction from the rest of them, and a couple of guns were again pointed at Aybee.

"I don't think you want to believe this," he said. "But I'm not a spy, and I've never been one."

"He's lying!" Gudrun's face was flushed with anger. "He even gave me a false name. He says he's Karl Lyman, but his real name is Smith—Apollo Belvedere Smith."

That shocked Aybee more than he wanted to admit. He could see how he might have revealed by his actions that he was not from the Space Farm, or that some other Farmer might have said he was not part of that group. But how could anyone know his real name? Unless he had taken to talking in his sleep, he had never mentioned his name since the accident back on the Farm.

"*Is* that your name?" asked one of the tall, thin escorts. "Because if it is, then, man, you're in deep trouble." He turned to the rest of them without waiting to hear Aybee's answer. "There's an Apollo Belvedere Smith who works for Outer Systems headquarters. High up, staff position. So if this is him, he's definitely a spy, and we have to——"

"I tell you, I'm not a spy." Aybee cut him off before the other could finish. "I'm a *scientist*——"

"He's lying!" shouted Gudrun. "He's no scientist. He lied to me."

"He did," said a quiet new voice from behind the group. "And yet, oddly enough, he is not lying now. He is telling the exact truth."

Everyone spun around. A small, lightly built man had stepped into the chamber through its open inner door. He was dressed in a tight-fitting suit of rusty black, and on his head he wore a peaked cap of the same sable tone. His face was fine-boned and pale, with an odd little smile on the thin lips, but that expression was belied and dominated by the eyes. There was no smile there, only a dark and piercing look that demanded and held attention.

Aybee found his attention drawn to those eyes. It took an amazing effort to look away. He heard Gudrun gasp. She at least had not been expecting the new arrival. But she must be less surprised than Aybee himself. For although the dress was quite different, and the teeth no longer incongruously blackened, Aybee recognised the man standing in front of them. It was the Negentropic Man, just as he had danced and capered through Bey Wolf's tormented memories.

The newcomer stepped forward, and the others moved aside to make a corridor. Right in front of Aybee, the man stopped and looked up. Aybee was a head and a half taller. The thin grin widened.

"As you said, Apollo Belvedere Smith, there was no lie. You are a scientist, and Cinnabar Baker thinks you are the best in the System." He held out his hand. "Let me welcome you here, and let me introduce myself."

"That's not necessary." Aybee took the outstretched hand, and decided it was time to do more than just deny everything. He had to establish independence. "I know where I am. This is Ransome's Hole. And you are Black Ransome."

If Aybee had expected a shocked response, he was to be disappointed. The other man frowned, just a little, and gave Aybee's hand a dry, firm shake. "I'm Ransome, true enough. Some call me Black Ransome, although that is not my name. And some call this Ransome's Hole, too, though I would never do so." The smile returned, warm and embracing. "I'm going to welcome you here, whether you want it or not. You've come a long way, and we must talk. You may be very valuable to us. Come on."

Aybee had apparently been switched in status from prisoner and spy to welcome guest. Gudrun gasped, but there was no murmur of dissent from anyone. The force of Ransome's personality was too strong to brook argument. Instead, the group of people moved to leave a clear path to the door. He turned and left, confident that Aybee would follow.

That annoyed Aybee. So Ransome was to lead, and he was supposed to trot along behind like some pet animal? No way.

He left the chamber just behind Ransome, and tagged along until they were out of sight of the other group. But then he paused and looked all around him. Ransome went on and was almost out of sight in the curving corridor, heading deeper into the sphere along a spiral path whose field in less than fifty meters fluctuated from almost zero gee to a thirtieth of Earth-gravity. The floor turned in the same space through 180 degrees. In any other structure, Aybee would have known just how to interpret that. The path must wind its way past two shielded kernels, one below the "floor," the other, forty meters further on, above the "ceiling"—which had become the floor.

That was the only logical explanation, but Aybee's new experiences on the transit ship had taught him to mistrust preconceived ideas. He slowed his pace and hunted backwards and forwards, seeking a point of maximum field in the corridor floor. If he were now close to a kernel, he would feel an inertial dragging.

He went down on his hands and knees and put his head close to the floor, moving it slowly about. While he was in that position he saw a pair of black-clad legs standing a few feet in front of him.

"If you're going to travel all the way like that," said Ransome's calm voice, "it will take you a long time and I won't wait. I'll send one of the machines back here to show you the way. It *is* a kernel down there, you know. What else did you think it might be?"

Aybee stood up. He was still young enough to hate looking like a fool more than anything in the world. For the rest of the journey through the interior of Ransome's Hole, he trudged grumpily along right behind Ransome.

In a few minutes they came to the end of the corridor and passed through into a great hemispherical chamber, furnished to a level of luxury that Aybee had never seen. Glittering silver sculptures of human and animal figures were everywhere. The domed ceiling housed a huge sprinkler system, able to deliver anything from a fine mist of rain to a total deluge. Fruit trees and flowering vines, trained in elaborate espaliers along walls and trellises, grew beneath in disciplined variety. At the center of the chamber stood its most spectacular feature. A forty-meter globe of greenish water was held in position by the gravitational field of the kernel at its center, and brilliantly colored fish were swimming within it. Fronds of weed and branched coral grew down on the kernel's outer shield, and an external lighting system created ever-varying patterns of light and dark within the clouded interior.

Aybee goggled. No one had anything like that in the Outer System, not even the three General Co-ordinators.

Ransome had caught his expression. The shorter man shrugged. "Not for me, Aybee Smith. That isn't my taste at all." He sounded amused and tolerant, far from the fanatic rebel promised by his reputation. The ogre of the Kernel Ring was easy company, lulling you to relax and listen to him.

"But sometimes you have to do these things, don't you?" Ransome went on. "For the sake of the less scientific. Stick around here for a while, and you'll see worse. Maybe you should think of this as my version of the Hanging Gardens of Babylon."

The what of what? Aybee decided to look it up when he had a chance. Meanwhile, he could not help changing his mind about Black Ransome. The man was treating him like an equal rather than a prisoner, and given the other's reputation and authority, that had to be flattering.

"Now this *is* my own taste," said Ransome. "A person can really work here." He led the way through a gleaming door of white metal, on into a sparsely furnished room about eight meters by six. A long desk, half-covered with random piles of data cubes, stood against one wall. Half a dozen displays were mounted above it, on plain beige walls that carried unobtrusive light fixtures, the biggest holograph projectors Aybee had ever seen, and no decorations of any kind. Elaborate computer consoles were built into the surface of the desk itself.

Ransome sat down on one of three easy chairs and gestured to another one. Now that they had arrived, he seemed in no mood to speak. There was a long, uncomfortable pause, with Aybee standing waiting and Ransome staring blank-eyed at the wall.

At last Aybee tucked himself into a chair. They had been made for Ransome's convenience, not for a tall

Cloudlander, and his knees came up near his chin. "So I blew it," he said. The personal failure had been troubling him since they first reached Ransome's Hole. "Mind telling me how?"

Ransome raised dark eyebrows questioningly, but still he did not speak.

"I mean, my *name*," added Aybee. "Gudrun knew it, and you knew it. But I told her I was Karl Lyman when she found me on the Space Farm, and nobody did a chromosomal ID check on me. You shouldn't have had any idea I was lying. So I must have done something dumb. I'd just like to know what it was."

Ransome shook his head. "You demean yourself, Aybee Smith. It was not your failure. Watch." He nodded to one of the displays and played briefly with the miniature console set into the arm of his chair.

The screen glowed. Aybee had half-expected to see the result of some unsuspected test, conducted on the Space Farm, or perhaps on the dark cargo hulk. Instead, a color image appeared. It was Sylvia Fernald, seen full face. After the flicker of a fast audio search, her image steadied and began to speak.

"We thought Aybee would have been here long ago," she was saying. "Now it looks as though he was captured along with the others. Do you have any idea where they were taken?"

"Not yet." The voice was Cinnabar Baker's, and as the field of view on the display scrolled across and down, Aybee realised that he must be viewing the scene through her eyes.

"I hope he has the sense to lie low until we can trace him," said Sylvia, from outside the field of view.

"If we ever can," said Baker. "We have no clues so far. If he's still alive—we're not sure of that—he could have been taken anywhere in the System." Now the screen showed the main display in Baker's own office. It held a listing of the names and physical description of all personnel of the Space Farm, plus Aybee's own personal data.

"You know Aybee," said Sylvia. She appeared again in

the picture. "If he is alive, he'll be looking for a chance to get away——"

"——as I'm sure you were," said Ransome. He cut off the display and Sylvia vanished. "But once we knew you had not left the Sagdeyev Farm with the others, we could identify you from your description and take special precautions."

Aybee was still staring at the blank screen. "That was in Baker's private apartment. It was seen through her own eyes!"

"Indeed." Ransome leaned back comfortably in his chair. "Aybee Smith, you are surprised. You should not be. My resources for the collection of information through the whole System—even within the Coordinator's private apartment—are unmatched. Cinnabar Baker keeps no secrets from me. I know every word that is said, in every one of her meetings. If you want more proof of that, I can easily provide it. I have been aware of your own existence and of your potential for more than three years. Had I realised that you were with Behrooz Wolf on the Space Farm, I would have prevented the accident there."

"Could you have stopped it?"

"With ease. I controlled the whole destiny of the Sagdeyev Farm, from form-change units to matter detection systems. But before we come to something so specific, let us be general. You are a young man, and you are fascinated by science. Let me ask you, do you have equal interest in politics?"

The tone in Ransome's voice was still casual and detached, but Aybee detected a heightened level of interest. He shook his head. "Politics isn't for me. I leave that sort of stuff to people like Baker."

"Ah. To be young. You will change as you grow older. If you do not know politics, do you know the theory of dissipative systems far from equilibrium?"

"I know all the classical work, Onsager and Prigogine and Helmut. And I've followed what Borsten has been doing on iterated function spaces in the past few years." The abrupt turn in the conversation was baffling, but

Aybee was on familiar ground. Maybe they were going to talk about science at last.

"In that case you will readily follow what I am about to tell you, even if you at first have trouble accepting it." Ransome's eyes were like magnets, drawing Aybee's attention against his will. "I can demonstrate to you that the whole civilization of the solar system is on the brink of massive change—total and irreversible change. I know this, and soon everyone will know it. In the language of dissipative systems, we now stand at a bifurcation point, at a singular moment on the time line. As you know, this bifurcation implies an instability. In such situations, the future of a large system can be controlled by small forces. I have such a force at my disposal!—the same force that guarantees we occupy a singular point in time. But before the new system can emerge, the old order must crumble and fade. The process has begun; you have seen the signs, in the general breakdown of the Outer System. From its ruins, we will create the new order. Today's divisions into Inner System, Halo, and Outer System, will disappear. There will be a central government, a single point of power and control. It will be here, under my control. My office will become the center of the solar system." He leaned forward towards Aybee, eyes dark and hypnotic. "The program to accomplish this is well advanced. But in certain scientific areas I need help. You are well equipped to provide it, and I can guarantee that you will find the work totally fascinating. And think of the prospect. You will help to define the future! You will help to *create* the future. What could compare with that?"

He paused and looked at Aybee expectantly. His voice had never risen a decibel, always completely thoughtful and reasonable. But in terms of its persuasive power, it was like a triumphant shout.

Aybee struggled to resist the feeling of enthusiasm and well-being that was flooding through him. He had always been a loner, never one to join any movement, and now some small corner of his brain was fighting back. But it *was* a small corner—most of him was in there cheering for Ransome.

He forced himself to think again about his journey to Ransome's Hole. He wanted to hear about the new scientific advances that made the little ovoid ship possible. If Ransome were the genius behind those developments, Aybee had to hear the theory—all the theory. Instead he was listening to a man talk about politics. Was it conceivable that the scientific genius and the would-be emperor were the same person? Aybee knew very well the sacrifices and the demands on time and energy called for by great scientific advances. He was prepared to meet those demands, but could anyone combine such a life with an attempt to take over the solar system? Surely not.

Aybee felt the flood of enthusiasm giving way to rational thought. He knew it was no time to argue with Ransome. Instead he nodded slowly and said, "What you are telling me is fascinating. I'd like to hear more."

He was not surprised when Ransome accepted his apparent conversion. The other man projected so powerfully, he was probably amazed by anyone who did not become his follower on first exposure.

Ransome stood up, so warm and friendly and convincing that Aybee began to have second thoughts about his motives. "You have much to learn, Aybee Smith. To the few thousand people already devoted to my cause—yes, we are still spread that thin—I am their only scientific expert. They see me as their prophet, and as the source of all the new technology. But there is a limit to what one man can do, and I have no more than scratched the surface of the possible. That has been enough to allow us to begin the reorganization of the System. You will help me to take our work much further. When you are ready, we will go to the laboratories. You can begin work there as soon as you like. The facilities are the finest that we can provide."

He paused and frowned. "Of course," he added mildly, "there are certain precautions taken for such sensitive work. As you will appreciate, it would be intolerable if word of our plans and discoveries were to leak prema-

turely to the Inner or the Outer System." He smiled.
"The monitor systems are automatic, and beyond my
control. Attempted escape would unfortunately and inevi-
tably lead to your capture, perhaps to your death. Now,
shall we proceed?"

CHAPTER 24

"Mary, Mary, quite contrary
How does your garden grow?
With spinor fields, and kernel shields,
And pretty men all in a row."
—crèche song of the Opik Harvester

The self-reproducing machines that alone made possible the rapid development of the Oort Cloud had never been so important in the Inner System. Fifteen billion humans were quite self-reproducing enough. Bey Wolf, accustomed all his life to human limits on work habits and energy levels, had not yet made his adjustment. He knew in the abstract what a group of machines could do, but their actual performance still amazed him. And they never seemed to stop work, even when Bey could see nothing useful to be done.

The odd logic of that had been explained by Leo Manx on their original trip out to the Cloud. "It's actually more economical of resources to keep them working," he said. "You see, if they're *not* working they're programmed to make more copies of themselves. And that takes more materials."

"But why not just switch them off?" said Bey.

Manx shook his head. "They're designed for continuous use. If you don't want them to decline in performance, you have to keep them busy."

Typical Outer System design philosophy, but Bey was now looking at a good example of what Manx had meant. Sylvia Fernald had approached this same destination and found the darkness and silence of a mausoleum. To Bey, near to rendezvous just seven days later, it seemed inevitable that the body had looked then much as it did now, gaudy, bustling with activity, ablaze with internal lights. Half a dozen ships lay in the docks, and the irregular egg-like outline of the surface was blurred and softened by a tangle of free-space vines, tilting their silver and black webs to drink in the miser's dole of radiation from distant Sol. The idea that the whole body had been dark and deserted as recently as two days ago never occurred to Bey.

Its small size was a surprise. In the Inner System, a few hundred sets of orbital elements covered everything significant. The vast majority of planetoids were uninhabited, and likely to remain so except for mining operators. Travel to any of the interesting destinations took one to a body at least ten kilometers across, with an associated population center. There would be thousands of people there, at minimum, if not the billions of Earth, the hundreds of millions of Mars, or the tens of millions of Europa and Ceres.

That Sylvia would come so far, to arrive at a body with a handful of people, was perplexing to Bey. However, it might also make his own task easier. He was seeking Sylvia, but beyond that he had another motive. He sought the trail that would lead him onward, to the right location in the Kernel Ring and the Negentropic Man himself. Whatever lay here, this was an improbable end point for Sylvia's own travels.

There was little point in trying for an inconspicuous arrival. Space radar systems would have marked his progress and projected his arrival time when he was millions of kilometers away. Bey ignored the manual controls and allowed the docking to proceed automatically. He did not put on a suit. He was not being over-confident, nor was he a fatalist. Any dangers would derive from humanity rather than Nature, and they would call for intelligence, not speed or strength.

The lock opened. He drifted through, and found himself in the middle of a fairy tale. The interior of the body had been converted into a single chamber, hundreds of meters across. Its vaulted walls were painted in red and white and gold, and vast murals reached up to the domed ceiling. Unencumbered by gravity, needle spires and slender minarets rose bright from the outer surface next to Bey, and lacy filaments arched between them.

He looked instinctively for signs of a kernel, and headed for it right across the central chamber. No matter that he had spent much of the past week brooding on the impossible possibility of a demon inside a kernel shield, some indestructible, pachydermous, and unimaginable end product of infinite form-change that would bask and bathe in the radiation sleet within the shields. Never mind that thought. There would be a local gravity field near a kernel, and he yearned for it, even if it were a weak one—Earth habits died hard.

As he approached the outer kernel shield he was struck by a shocking thought. In his fascination at the sights within the lock, he had missed a central mystery. He could see almost the whole of the body's interior; and although a dozen machines were visible, there was no sign of another human being. Had he come all this way, on a wild chase that would end on a deserted pleasure sphere? He knew such things existed, created as the hideaways of wealthy and reclusive individuals of the Outer System. They were maintained by their service machines, patiently awaiting the arrival of their owners, and for ninety-nine days out of a hundred they were uninhabited. If no one at all were here, his journey would have been a complete waste of time and effort.

Down on the kernel's shield Bey saw another oddity. Amid a riot of free-growing plants, a little bower had been created there, using a woven thicket of plaited vegetation to form a living roof and walls. The sight gave him an irrational shiver of premonition along his spine.

"Sylvia?" His voice was unsteady. Logically, he had no

idea what came next; but the dark recesses of his hind-brain knew it already. He floated on down towards the kernel's shield. "Sylvia," he repeated. "Are you there?"

A sudden giggle came from the inside of the bower, and a curly-haired head peeked out past the tangled leaves. "Bey? Oh, my word. What have you done to yourself?" The laugh came again, this time full-throated. " *'Bottom, thou art translated.'* You're so long and thin—and no hair! I knew it, you let them put you in one of your horrible form-change machines." It was Mary, moving out to meet him and filling his arms. "Oh, Bey, you're here at last. It's so good to see you again."

The questions had tumbled through Bey's head, one after another. How had Mary known he was coming—how had *anyone* known he was coming? That information was supposed to be a close secret. Why was Mary here? Where was Sylvia? Mary had recognized him instantly, despite his changed form, but how had she been able to do that?

He thought everything, and at first asked nothing. Mary was a drug that had lost none of its strength. She still ran through his veins. He felt light-headed with unreality.

"Right here," she was saying. Bey found himself led by the hand into the little bower, and seated on a rustic bench fabricated to resemble aged and knotted wood.

It was typical of Mary that she felt no need to explain anything, and just as typical that she wore a costume equally alien to both the Inner and Outer Systems. Her print dress of faded dark-purple flowers on a pale grey background belonged to another century. It fitted perfectly with the bower, and with the woven basket hanging over the end of the bench. She was wearing a hint of flower perfume, light and fresh.

Mary was playing a part—but which one?

"How did you know I was coming here?" Bey forced himself to ask that question, and at the same moment had a suspicion of the answer. He had told Leo Manx to tell no one—but did Leo have that much self-control?

All it might have taken was one short conversation with Cinnabar Baker, and for Leo telling Baker was still second nature.

Mary was smiling at him as sunnily and possessively as if they had never parted. He thought for a moment that she had ignored his question, but then she said, "It's just as well for you that I learned you were heading this way, and better yet that no one else saw the message before I could take care of it. Otherwise you'd have found an armed guard waiting instead of me." She snuggled against him, and laughed when she found that her head now touched not his shoulder but half-way down his chest. "Oh, Bey, I've been taking good care of you. I changed all the messages that were going to you. If it weren't for me, you'd have been dead or crazy long since."

Bey had learned long ago that Mary didn't lie. If her answers failed to match the real world, that was only because her perceptions of reality were so often awry. She had been protecting him—or at least she believed she had.

"What happened to Sylvia Fernald? She was supposed to be here." He was rewarded with a frown of disapproval.

"I know all about her. The two of you have really nothing in common."

"That's not true." Bey half agreed with Mary, but he felt the perverse need to defend Sylvia. "We have lots in common. She's educated. She saved my life—twice. We get on well together, and she's a—a nice, kind woman," he ended lamely.

" 'Be she meeker, kinder than, Turtle-dove or pelican, If she be not so to me, What care I how kind she be?' They used to be *your* lines, Bey. Have you changed that much?"

"I came here to find her, Mary."

"I know. And I came here to stop you searching any more. I know where she is, and she's safe enough. But you don't want to go looking for her. It might put you in danger."

"From whom?"

Mary shook her head. Bey knew exactly what she meant. She would not lie, but she would refuse to speak. They had slipped into the old relationship, just as though Mary had left Earth no more than an hour ago.

"I won't stop looking," he went on, "There's more at stake here than me or Sylvia. The whole system is coming unglued. That has to be stopped."

She turned her head and looked up into his face. "The same old Bey. Saving the world. You ought to know better. You worked half your life for that stupid Office of Form Control, and what reward did you get at the end? They threw you out, with never even a thank-you."

"They had a good reason."

"You haven't changed at all, have you? Still honour and glory and once-more-unto-the-breach-dear-friends." She rubbed her hand across his chest. "Bey, if only you could stop living in the past and the future, and live in the present for a little bit, you'd have so much more fun."

If anyone in the universe lived in the present, it was Mary. The signal was clear and tempting. Bey heard all his internal voices shouting at once to justify the action. "A few hours delay can't make any difference" . . . "Mary will become your ally, and she can take you straight to Sylvia" . . . "Mary scorned now would be your bitterest enemy" . . . "You've been away from each other far too long" . . . "All the time you thought she had forgotten you, she was *protecting* you" . . . "Live in the present" . . .

Bey turned and leaned down towards Mary's waiting face. Her eyes had closed.

But where has Mary been all this time? And what has she been doing? Amid all the clamor of emotions, that single questioning whisper in Bey's mind was drowned out completely. It didn't stand a chance.

A few hours had stretched into a day, and then into two and three. It was a long time before Bey saw a possible approach to the problem.

Mary was immune to all forms of logic. He had known

that for years. It was maddening, but it was also part of her charm, and it meant that she would be unmoved by any rational reason for taking Bey back with her to the Kernel Ring, and (ultimately) to Black Ransome. Kernel-demons and form-change anomalies and System-wide hallucinations meant nothing to her. Another motive was needed, something that went deeper than logic; Bey had lain awake for hours trying to think of one, and returned again and again to a single question. Why had Mary come to meet him here, secretly? She was apparently not trying to capture him, and she had made it clear that she did not intend him to stay with her permanently.

He thought he had the answer. Mary had come for personal reassurance. She knew he had travelled a vast distance in pursuit of Sylvia Fernald. Mary hated to give up any man. The idea that she had been superseded by Sylvia, so that she could no longer move Bey to her whim, was intolerable. She wanted to show that she still owned him, and could still control him.

Bey looked at the sleeping form stretched out next to him. So far, the demonstration must be to her satisfaction. Now he had to make use of the same fact.

The most difficult thing was to be casual and convincing enough. Mary did not lie, but she had a sixth sense that told her when others were doing it to her. The best way was to make her feel that any decision was her idea.

Bey dropped the first word while Mary was showing him around the elaborate new gardens that the machines had built under her direction in a single day. It was in answer to Mary's complaint that he was too bony now to lie next to in comfort, and it took the form of a vague comment on his part that the standards of beauty for women were very different in the Inner and Outer Systems.

"For the Cloudlanders, curves are out," he added. "And yet that doesn't mean that a Cloudlander will be unattractive to somebody from the Inner System—or that a Sunhugger disgusts somebody from the Cloud."

Mary had not reacted to the comment, but Bey knew she had registered it. He waited. It was hard to keep his own mental processes under control. Emotion and real affection for Mary competed with his long-term logical plan, and Bey knew from experience that logic could lose.

Later in the day Mary was studying a recording of one of her own old performances, as Polly Peachum in *The Beggar's Opera*. She remarked how good she had looked as a redhead.

Bey agreed enthusiastically. "My favourite hair color. As a matter of fact, naturally red hair—" He paused, and went silent. Mary also said nothing. Sylvia had red hair.

They watched the performance together. When Macheath was looking at Polly and Lucy Lockit, and singing, "How happy could I be with either, were t'other dear charmer away," Bey knew that Mary was watching him from the corner of her eye.

She was preoccupied for the rest of the day. Late in the evening she suddenly asked him if he and Sylvia Fernald had been lovers.

"Of course not!" Bey sat up. "You've seen her, you know how tall and gawky and strange she is. And she has a long-time partner of her own, back in the Cloud, so she wouldn't look at anyone else. And did you know, when I arrived at the Opik Harvester she said that I looked like a hairy little monkey? To her, I'm totally hideous. . . ."

Bey went on with his protests just a little too long. He did not need to point out to Mary that his own appearance had changed considerably since the arrival at the Harvester, to a form much more pleasing to Sylvia Fernald's tastes. On matters like this, Mary's instincts reached a conclusion ten times as fast as any logic.

The next morning, Mary was very quiet. At midday, she casually announced that she would be returning to the Kernel Ring. If Bey wanted to take the risk, he could accompany Mary. Did he want to go? If he did, he ought to get ready.

Bey accepted, equally casual. However, he did not feel satisfied with the way the conversation had gone. He had achieved his objective, but his little inside voice would not keep quiet. Too easy, it said, much too easy. When a difficult goal is achieved with no effort, it's time to be suspicious. You want to get to the Kernel Ring? Sure—and maybe someone else wants you there, too.

CHAPTER 25

"In Ransome's Hole you'll lose your soul
(We won't come to find you).
With Ransome's breath you'll meet your death
(The Dancing Man's behind you).
Ransome takes one,
*   Ransome breaks one,*
*   Out—goes—you."*
               —crèche song of the Marsden Harvester

Bey had been wrong. He might be the only person who would ever know it, but still he hated the idea.

Back on the Sagdeyev Space Farm, he and Aybee Smith had agreed to differ. Aybee felt that a life without surprises was no fun. Bey agreed; but he pointed out that ninety-nine of any hundred conceivable surprises were unpleasant ones. That was why he tried to analyse *all* outcomes of a situation, rather than just the one he liked best. Aybee agreed—in principle; but he pointed out in turn that complete prediction was impossible in anything but abstract theory; the cussedness of the real world promised that the actual outcome would be unanticipated. Bey agreed; but he suggested that *any* chance of successful prediction was better than no chance. Aybee nodded. Honor was satisfied, and they moved on to other subjects.

Bey truly believed what he had told Aybee. When he

set out to follow Sylvia Fernald into the depths of the Halo, he had foreseen and analyzed four scenarios. One, the search might reach a dead end, and he would return to the Harvester. Two, he might find Sylvia, but she would have discovered nothing useful and already be at her own point of frustration, so they would *both* go back. Three, Bey might be captured and detained before he found Sylvia or reached Ransome's Hole. Fourth, he might be captured after he reached the Kernel Ring.

The idea that he would find *Mary*, rather than Sylvia, at that first location was so preposterous that it had not been in his thoughts at all.

So Aybee had been right. Bey allowed himself the luxury of a moment's irritation; then he inspected the ship that Mary had arrived in.

His reaction to it was not so strong as Aybee's. He had done little space travel, and although he knew that the ship was radically different in appearance from the ones he was used to, he didn't realise how much new science had to be in it. He also had many other things on his mind. With Mary at her sunniest, most affectionate, and most demanding, he had little time to worry about spacecraft. She was in a holiday mood. If she thought for a moment that she was taking Bey toward danger, it didn't show in her manner.

She complained only at the end, when the ship neared its destination in the central annulus of the Kernel Ring. "We're *crawling*. Why do we always have to go so *slow* when we're nearly there?"

"Safety requirement," replied the hollow voice of the ship's main computer. "Proceed with caution. Danger zone."

The computer was treating the region with great respect. They were picking their way through the maze of debris, unshielded kernels and high-density fragments that littered the central part of the Kernel Ring. Those shards were the relics of a catastrophe four billion years ago, when a toroidal region of space-time had suffered gravitational collapse and spewed high-mass elements towards the Sun. Life on Earth owed its existence to the event, but that was of no interest to the computer. Like Mary, it too lived in the present. Today this location housed the freaks of the solar system. Here were collapsed objects invisible to deep radar and massive enough to destroy a ship, side by side with co-rotating kernel pairs whose signals played havoc with navigation systems.

Bey had never been here before, but he knew the place's reputation. The Kernel Ring had been left undeveloped for a good reason. A thousand ships had been lost in the early days, before transit vessels to the Outer System learned to fly high above the ecliptic.

Danger, said the small voice in his ear. *Danger*. Ninety-nine of any hundred conceivable surprises are unpleasant ones. But the shiver in Bey's spine was not fear. It was excitement. Ransome's Hole was visible now; or rather, it was invisible, a dark occulting disc against the continuous starfield. And it was *big*, big enough to contain anything: armies, weapons, factories, cities, monsters and treasures and mysteries unguessed at. Bey stared at nothing, and was stirred by emotions he had not felt for years. He was in the past again, pursuing illegal serpent forms into the black depths of Old City. He was eager to begin, wondering if and how he would survive. The same ineffable force was now quickening his pulse, drawing him on, tugging him down into danger.

While he was watching, brief flashes of blue-white fire sparkled on the black disc. He recognised them. Short-range drive units. Five small vessels were heading out towards them.

Bey glanced at Mary. She frowned, shook her head, and said, "Not my doing." But she did not seem too surprised.

Within a couple of minutes the five had been joined by others. Surrounded by an escort of a dozen pinnaces, the ship drifted to a docking and attached to a lock. The hatch swung wide, and Bey followed Mary out.

A dozen armed soldiers were waiting, their weapons raised and ready. Two paces to their rear stood a short, black-clad man with folded arms. His face was thin, with prominent bones, a sharp nose, and a trace of a self-confident smile. Bey stared at those piercing eyes, and after a few seconds the unmoving features before him seemed to shift and flow, re-assembling themselves like an optical illusion to a different and familiar pattern.

The Dancing Man—the *Negentropic* Man; without the clown-like scarlet suit and black filed teeth, but unmistakably the same in face, body, and movement. Bey shivered. That face and burning eyes brought frightening memories from the edge of death and madness.

"Full house," said the Negentropic Man. He stepped forward, still flanked by his guards, and nodded approvingly at Bey. "I am Ransome. I have been curious to meet you for a long time, Mr Wolf. When a man or woman refuses to commit suicide or to become insane, no matter what the external pressure, that person is of interest to me. And here you are, in my home." He turned, and his wave took in the whole habitat. "You see how obliging the universe can be. If I had originally set out to lure you here, I might well have failed. But by allowing you to sail freely with the winds of space, you arrive even before I am ready for you."

Ransome placed his arm possessively around Mary's waist. She did not resist, but she gave Bey a strange, uncertain look.

"So you have me. What happens now?" said Bey. He had seen eyes like that three times before in a human head, but none of their owners was living.

"For the moment, nothing." Ransome was disconcertingly at ease. "I have unfinished business with two of your friends, and then a couple of other things to take care of. You will have to bear with your own company for a little while. Later you and I must talk. I feel sure that we are going to be working together." Ransome gave Bey a dismissive, self-confident little nod, and turned to go. Mary followed without a word.

"Mary!" Bey called after her as the guards moved to separate him from them. He received a brief glance in return from lowered brows, then he was being hustled away. The guards escorted him deep into the habitat's interior, and finally stopped at an oval door. They ushered him through without comment and left at once, but as they went a bulky machine took up guard position at the entrance.

How long was the "little while" that he would be on his own? Ransome's joking tone suggested it might be quite some time. Bey turned in the doorway and stepped close to the Roguard. It stood solidly blocking his path.

"Allow me to pass. That is an order."

"The order cannot be obeyed." The voice was soft-toned and polite. "Egress is prohibited. You lack authorization."

"Who has authorization?"

"You do not have authorization to receive information on authorizations."

Bey retreated. He had not expected a useful answer, so he was not much disappointed. He went to sit at the table in the little dining area, and pondered his situation.

Against the initial odds—and suspiciously easily—he had found his way to Ransome's Hole. He was in the middle of the enemy stronghold, unarmed, surrounded by guards, held prisoner by a probable megalomaniac with the power to destroy the solar system; now he had to decide what to do next.

What *could* he do?

After a few minutes he stood up and made a leisurely and thorough survey of the living quarters. They were perfectly adequate for a stay (voluntary or otherwise) of weeks, months, or even years. The walls, floor and ceiling were white, seamless and solid. There was a comfortable-looking bed, a large and well-equipped washroom, a full food-production facility, a small computer with its own recreational and educational data bases, and even a small exercise unit that included simple form-conditioning. Notably absent was any type of communications equipment, audio or video.

Bey went to the little form-conditioning unit, turned it on, and reviewed its capabilities. It was the simplest and cheapest of the commercially packaged form-change systems. The options it offered were minimal. They included monitoring and feedback for standard muscle tone improvements, routines for minor physical repair such as sprains and bruises, and a couple of low-gee/high-gee conversion modules; that seemed to be all.

Bey opened the cover and checked the telemetry inputs and internal storage. It was a BEC unit, completely self-contained, and the hardware was standard and quite powerful. That meant the weaknesses were in the software. The programs that came with the unit lacked all the more substantial form-change functions—it did not even permit eye adjustments, which Bey had needed for near-sightedness since he was a teenager.

What was he supposed to do when everything began to look fuzzy? Squint, or make himself eyeglasses? He closed the cover of the unit in disgust. On Earth no one had used anything so primitive for over a hundred years.

Bey went once more to the open door, and this time tried to walk directly through it. The waiting Roguard again blocked him. He put his hand onto the machine's exterior, estimating its strength and sensitivity. It did not move.

"How long will I remain here?"

"That information is unavailable." There was a pause, then the machine added: "It will be no longer than two years, since the food supply has been set for such a period."

"Two years! That's terrific news."

"Thank you."

Bey closed the door in the Roguard's face, went to the bed and stretched out on it. He should have known better than to waste his time talking. No machine of that type could recognise sarcasm.

He closed his eyes, but he had no thought of sleeping. There was a job to do here, and it was a big one. The first step was a rough time estimate. How long would it need for development and testing, and then how long for the process itself to be completed? If the answers came out too high, he might as well relax and forget the whole idea.

Within ten minutes Bey had a first estimate. Five weeks, total, if he worked day and night. That was far

too long. He had to cut it somehow by a factor of at
least three. It was time for something rough and ready
and less than perfection. The logic flow and accompa-
nying condensed code for an alternative approach began
to take shape in his head.

The next estimate came out at two weeks. Still too
long, and he had taken all the legitimate speed-up steps.
Now it was time for desperate measures. He had to begin
accepting higher physical risks.

Bey lay on the bed for another four hours. At last he
sat up, ready to start. As he did his last-minute preparations, it occurred to him that he had one unexpected
asset. Ironically, the wild card in his favour was the Negentropic Man himself.

In his lectures to the beginning class at the Office of
Form Control, Bey Wolf used an analogy: "Purposive
form-change is a *process*, a tight interaction of life-support machinery and real time computer code." The display on the wall behind him provided a flow diagram,
bewildering in its complexity. "There's a typical sample
up on the screen—a straightforward one, as a matter of
fact. By the time you get out of here, that will seem
simple and familiar. But knowing how to read one of
those schematics won't be enough to protect you. To be
useful in this office, you have to see *beyond* the detail,
to grasp a whole form-change picture in one swoop."

The wall display changed, to show an old-fashioned
map, bright with colours and dotted with fanciful illustra-
tions. "Each form-change is a journey, from a defined
starting point to a defined end point. But those journeys
all cross a part of the great ocean of form-change. Some
areas of that ocean have been explored completely, and
all commercial form-change programs navigate within
that charted region. But beyond the safe waters lies a
wilderness, unmapped and unknown. And *dangerous*.
Never forget that.

"Everyone who tries a radically new form-change
experiment is embarking on a trip through the unknown.
And when you work in this office, you often have to

follow the route of the pioneers, across those perilous waters.

"Now, we can't provide an infallible pilot across that unknown sea. No one can. But what we *can* do is teach you what to look for. You'll learn to recognize—and avoid—the shoals and reefs of form-change, the whirlpools and undertows. You'll always design your programs to follow the safe, smooth trade routes. . . ."

Sound advice.

But the lessons of the classroom had not been designed for desperate emergencies.

Bey sealed the lid of the tank, stared at the control sequences, and prepared for coming agonies. With this degree of uncertainty, anything might happen. He was using change sequences that he had never employed before—never *heard of* before. They ignored his own teachings, driving an accelerated program that skirted the reefs, risked the whirlpools, ran the gauntlet of lee shores. It was a guarantee of discomfort and danger, of disaster.

He entered the final command.

The first few minutes were the familiar touch of sensors and catheters, followed by the flicker and swirling rainbow of colors and sounds. Bio-feedback was beginning, no different from what it had been a thousand times. Soon it would by-pass his eyes and ears, to establish direct brain contact. A dozen steps flickered by in a few minutes, the standard preliminary tests as the form-change machine confirmed the parameters of his body.

And then . . . the change.

He sensed a ripple of command, a cold and alien touch through all his being. Strange discomfort touched him—entered him—became a pain that grew as rapidly and irresistibly as a wind-blown fire, until it burned in every cell. His body shook in surprised agony.

Wrong, totally wrong. Stop it now, while you can.

He thrust away the panic response that rose from the base of his brain. The pain was to be expected, the result of too-rapid change. The shortcuts *were* wrong, but that was by his own design—shape-change achieved by deformation and

muscular contraction, not by slow and careful rebuilding
of body structure. It was a perversion of true form-
change. He tried to stay calm, as his body's core temperature climbed over twenty degrees. Chemical reactions
were running at ten times the normal speed, but still he
could understand and follow the processes.

And then pain passed a new threshold, and logic failed.
. . . *he was stretched on a rack, seared by internal
flames. His body was melting, twitching and writhing
against the control straps. A thick layer of mucus
squeezed from his skin. Catheter pumps doubled their
rate of chemical transfer.*

A new change came, more basic and more deadly.
. . . *heart pounding an irregular rhythm. Heart stopping. A moment of supreme agony, heart lifeless, a stone
in his chest. Lungs collapsed. Kidneys and bowels and
bladder, frozen in their action. Blood congealing.*

The form-change machine had taken over completely.
Only his brain was left, directing the purposive form-
change.

The fatal form-change. This change should take weeks,
not days. He had underestimated the pain, misjudged
the danger. No one could endure such change-speed, it
would kill him.

Heartless, lungless, he could neither groan nor scream.
He had made a choice, and now he was paying the price.
Even with the machine's help, body parameters were
uncontrollable. A dozen times, the monitors in the form-
change unit flared their warning signs. Chemical concen-
trations were wildly far from equilibrium, ion balances
at fatal levels, synapses firing spastically out of sequence.
He had lost awareness of his surroundings. The semi-
conscious body in the tank shuddered and writhed,
enduring rates of adaptation beyond all rational limits.

Slow down. Slow down. Reverse the process. Every
organ, every cell, screamed for relief. And relief was possible. With purposive form-change, the will of the subject
always played a central part. The urge to retreat became
irresistible.

Stop now, stop now. The fear was no longer deep in

his brain. It was rampant surges of pain and terror, invading every hiding-place of will and resolve.

Stop. Stop now. He fought against the urge to end it, but the torment was too great. He was in terminal agony, hearing the whimper of protest from every cell. The limit of endurance had arrived, had passed. Pain intensified, sharpened, rose to levels that defied belief. . . .

No more. Give in, or die.

And as that thought took firm possession of his mind, the pressure eased.

He sagged in the retaining straps of the tank, unable to move. Every nerve of mind and body was aflame. He sucked the pain deep inside him, grinning in triumph. He could hear his heartbeat.

It was over. No matter what came next, he had won this stage. He had the right final form; he knew it without looking. His tortured body had been cast up, twisted and misshapen, on a strange shore—and it was the destination he had chosen!

Bey Wolf had crossed the form-change ocean.

Part IV

CHAPTER 26

Live with a man for years—and then discover that you know nothing at all about him!

Sylvia had been convinced that at the very least Paul would listen to what she had to say. She had clung to that thought, all through the long journey and docking at Ransome's Hole, and then on through a maze of corridors and slideways that took her and her Roguards deep into the habitat interior. And finally, face to face with him, she realized her mistake.

"It was very foolish for you to come here." His expression was cold, and he stared through her as though she didn't exist. He was wearing the same drab uniform as all the others she had seen in Ransome's Hole.

"Paul, I had to. Terrible things have been happening in the Cloud. Thousands of people have died, and all the time——"

"A mistake, and a total waste of time." He turned to the machines standing beside her. "Take her to living quarters K-1-25, Level four."

"Paul!"

But he was already turning, refusing to look her way. "You had your chance to work with us," he said coldly, as he walked out. "Ransome is a once-in-a-millennium genius, the best hope for the solar system. You wouldn't help when we needed it. Why should anyone listen to you, now when we don't need help?"

And then he was gone. Sylvia tried to run after him, and found the Roguards blocking her way. She pushed at them angrily, taking out her frustration on the resilient plastic. Endless weeks of travel to seek Paul Chu's ear—and then dismissed in one minute, without any sign that the two of them had once been lovers and close friends!

It was such an anticlimax, Sylvia was ready to burst with frustration. The machines were moving her back the way they had come, holding her lightly with their jointed arms. She fought them at first, but it was pointless. The gentle touch disguised their strength, but they could apply many tons of force with each flexible limb.

After ten more minutes of slideway travel they brought her to an open door, and guided her through it. As it slid closed behind her she spun around and cursed the silent machines.

"Helps your feelings," said a familiar and cynical voice from behind her. "Don't do much good, though. Better save your breath."

She turned. "Aybee! How in Eden did you get here?"

"Long tale—a long and a sad tale, as old Lewie C. puts it. Turns out Ransome doesn't trust me quite as much as I thought." Aybee Smith was sitting cross-legged across a high table, long limbs dangling to each side. "Wait just a minute. I already did this two days ago, but let's make sure nothing has changed." He hopped off the table and circled the room, peering at ventilator grilles and under and on all free surfaces. Finally he nodded. "I'm pretty sure we're safe to talk. No monitoring—or if there is, I can't find it."

He pointed to a chair and returned to sit again on the table. "All right, Sylv, let's play catch up. Who first?"

His scowling face had made Sylvia feel better already. She described everything that had happened since she left the ruined Space Farm, then heard of Aybee's own zigzag passage from there to Ransome's Hole.

"At least you had no choice," she said. "I'm the stupid one—I set out looking for trouble. And now the whole system's ready to be blown apart, and neither of us can do a thing."

"Not right now. But every day I'm here, I learn more about what makes this place tick." Aybee was prowling the perimeter of the chamber. "They shouldn't have put us together, and they ought to be monitoring us. Ransome is over-confident."

"Over-confident! Right, and with plenty to be overconfident about. We're in a mess. I don't know why you're looking so pleased with yourself."

"Because we finally have a chance to learn what's screwing up the solar system." Aybee squatted down and wrapped his arms around his crossed legs. "I'll tell you one good thing your friend the Wolfman told me, when we were on the Space Farm. He says, you solve problems by getting into the *middle* of 'em. When we were out on the Harvesters we were sitting on the outside edge of things. We only felt Black Ransome's effect at third hand. Now we're right at the heart of his power."

"And we're totally powerless! Aybee, even if we got out of these rooms, I'm not sure we could do anything. Ransome controls everything. We couldn't get a message to Bey Wolf or Cinnabar Baker."

"We might get one to the Wolfman, but it wouldn't help. Last time I saw Ransome he told me Wolf is here, too. He pointed out how convenient it was, all three of us coming to him."

"Bey's in Ransome's Hole? However did he find his way?"

"Same as you and me, I'll bet—a little bad luck and a big lump of stupidity. He came here on one of the super-fast ships, same as I did. Ransome is hoping to make Wolf a convert to his cause, like he's trying to convert me. You, too, if you let him."

"Then Baker's our only hope. Aybee, you're the smart one. You have to find a way to let her know where we are."

He was shaking his head. "Sorry, Sylv. It's worse than that. When you said Ransome controls everything you were closer than you realised. He controls Cinnabar Baker."

"Never! The Cloud is her whole life. She'd never sell out to Ransome."

"That's what I'd have said, two weeks ago. But Ransome *showed* me. When you get to meet with him he'll show you, too. He has direct transmissions of meetings from inside Baker's personal quarters. Secret papers and interviews, too, from the Opik and Marsden Harvesters. She must be running a portable recorder during her important meetings, and transmitting 'em here by sealed hyperbeam."

"Aybee, I think you're crazy. But if you happen to be right it's an absolute disaster. You tell me that, and still you don't think that Ransome has everything under his control?"

"Maybe he does—for the moment. But he can't have corrupted every person in the Outer System. And he's been winning for too long. It's time for *our* run of luck."

"Aybee, if I said anything like that you'd tell me it's statistical gibberish. According to Paul Chu—damn that man—Ransome has been winning because he's a genius. Are you going to disagree with that, too?"

"Funny you should say that." Aybee stood up and stretched. "I do disagree. I came to Ransome's Hole in a hell of a ship, too advanced to be believed. New drive, new nav system, new technology all over it. First thing I asked when I got here, who's the genius? Ransome, everybody says, all the ideas come from him. He's the one."

"But you think not?" Sylvia knew Aybee's weaknesses, and evaluating the abilities of others was not one of them.

"Hell, I *know* not. Ransome can snow most people here with physics, maybe all of them. He knows a lot, and he talks a great line. But he's not the real thing."

"How do you know that?"

Aybee gave her a sinister smile. "Because, Sylv, I *am* the real thing. Take it from one who knows, Black Ransome didn't invent that new drive and that new ship. He says he's the Negentropic Man, and something's sure feeding bad information to the Cloud's control systems. But Ransome's not the genius who dreamed up the entropy reduction and signal generation system. No way."

"Then who *is* the inventor? Are you saying Ransome

has some super-genius working for him here? And how does the entropy reduction system work?"

"I was afraid you'd ask me that." Aybee smiled more horribly than ever. "You see, Sylv, I don't have the answers. But let me loose for a day or two in this place—and I'll get 'em."

"Oh, Aybee." Sylvia slumped down on the chair. "I don't believe in giving up, but be a realist. We'll never get out of here. Black Ransome may not be your super-genius, but he's certainly smart enough not to trust us."

"Speak of the devil." Aybee gestured behind Sylvia. The door had opened, and standing there was Ransome himself, as cold-eyed and commanding as he had been when Sylvia saw that first video message for Paul Chu. He was unarmed and wearing a simple black tunic. His face was pale and showed signs of some unusual strain.

Ransome nodded to Aybee and Sylvia. Behind him stood two of the Roguards. For twenty seconds no one moved.

"You will come with me," said Ransome at last. And then, to the machines, "These two people are now in my personal custody. You are relieved of guard duties until I return them here."

"Where are you taking us?" Sylvia didn't like the tone in Ransome's voice. There was a strident edge to it that suggested a man under enormous pressures.

"Wait and see." Ransome lifted his arm and pointed to Aybee. "You first, in front of her. I'll be right behind you."

"Sure." Aybee stepped easily through the door, with a nod at the waiting machines. "Don't wait up for us, we might be back late. Where do you want me to walk, Ransome? You're the one who knows where we are going."

"Follow the gravity vector. Always up."

They started along the left-hand corridor, heading away from the nearest kernels. In forty yards they had reached the first branch, and passed a group of armed humans. Everyone nodded respectfully at Ransome and moved to allow the trio to pass on to another segment of passageway. Aybee walked on until he came to a spherical chamber and another fork in the path.

He paused and turned again to Ransome. "I don't know which one of these leads outward. Take your pick."

"Left. Keep going." The voice was gruff, and Aybee could see beads of sweat on the other man's face. They moved slowly forward, to a curved part of the corridor screened both ahead and behind them. An open door leading to an empty maintenance chamber stood on the right-hand side.

"Through there." Ransome nodded his head. "Both of you."

Aybee tensed himself as he went through. Sylvia was between him and Ransome—if he turned now to grapple with him, would she be able to get out of the way fast enough?

He had to try. He was spinning around, reaching out his long arms, when the man behind him groaned and sagged forward against the inner wall of the room.

"Aybee! Get him!" Aybee heard Sylvia's shout, but Ransome had fallen forward. His torso flexed itself, then straightened in a painful stretching movement that dropped it to the floor and jerked it two meters into the room.

"Close the door. Keep watch for people," said an agonized voice. "I can't hold any longer."

Then Ransome was twitching on the smooth floor, while Aybee and Sylvia looked on in astonishment.

"Ransome. Are you all right?" Sylvia was crouching down next to him.

"Ransome may be fine." The voice was down to a whisper. "But I'm Bey Wolf. Help me, Sylvia. I need five minutes clear."

The body was jerking into violent spasm. The contorted face that looked up at Sylvia was still Black Ransome's, but at the back of the pained eyes she saw something else. "Bey! Is it really you? What's happening?"

The body had uncurled to full extension. Now it looked nine inches longer. The torso shivered. "I did what I told—my classes at Office of Form Control—never to do. Most stupid and dangerous thing in the world. Accelerated form-change, badly defined end-form—programmed from scratch—no chance to do parametric variations. I'm outside—region of stability. Size reduction through muscular contraction. Only have partial muscle control." Ransome's face worked to a twisted smile. "Five minutes more."

"Hey, Wolfman, take your time." Aybee had looked out along the corridor, and now he slid the door closed. "We're safe here. I'll watch this. Sylv, see if you can help."

"Don't touch me. I'm getting there." An internal crisis had passed, and the twists and jerks in Bey/Ransome's body were easing. "Aybee, you seem to know your way—around this place. How far—from the main communications center?"

"Half a kilometer. Back along the corridor, and then head out towards the periphery. The place will be guarded, though, and it's not far from Ransome's own quarters. Ransome might be there."

"I don't think so—I think he's been off-habitat. Anyway, we have to take the risk. I have maybe—one hour, before I have to get back to a tank. This form's a *disaster*." Bey was grunting with pain and effort, forcing his body back to the shorter, more compact shape of Black Ransome. "We should be able to get into the com centre. No one here argues with Ransome—not even the Roguards. They told me how to find you without a question. Help me up, Sylvia."

"You look terrible. Take more time."

"We don't have time. We've got to get to the communications center and send a message to the Cloud, saying where we are, before Ransome shows up again. Or someone does a random chromosomal check on me. Or I fall apart. Once the coordinates of this place are known, it doesn't matter so much if we're captured again. Right. Any time."

The tics and twitches were subsiding, and the face had again smoothed to the pale, decisive countenance of

Black Ransome. With Aybee leading the way and Sylvia ready to support Bey if he needed it, they walked quietly on through the habitat and then made a turn outwards. The twisting corridors were deserted, allowing Bey to pause and rest along the way. During the final fifty yards Sylvia felt her face tighten with anticipation and tension, and was sure she would be noticed. But the guards at the entrance to the communications facility merely stiffened to attention, stepped back a pace, and saluted as the three passed. Bey/Ransome stood on the threshold and looked around. The center was empty. He nodded back casually to the guards and closed the door.

"That's the most dangerous part over, at least for the moment." Bey sighed and moved across to the hyperbeam unit. "I knew just what Ransome looked like, even how he moved and sounded—I saw more than enough of the Negentropic Man—but I didn't know his speech patterns, or the way he greets people."

"Bey, we got troubles you don't even know about." Aybee held out a hand to prevent him from touching the hyperbeam communication console. "It's not safe to send a message to the Cloud—Ransome has Cinnabar Baker in his pocket. I've seen messages from her."

Bey shook his head and turned on the communications set. "It's not news to me, I suspected as much. I didn't like the idea when I had it myself, but I knew there was a leak—and I didn't see how it could be anybody but Baker."

"But if we can't trust her, who can we trust?" said Sylvia.

"We don't trust anyone. We send the message everywhere, spray it across the Inner and Outer Systems. Aybee, can you take over all the communications channels?"

"For a general broadcast?" Aybee glared at the panel for a few seconds, then slowly nodded. "Guess so. Takes a few minutes to set it up—and if I grab 'em all, we'll be noticed. I'll have to push a hundred other users right off the system. Everyone in Ransome's Hole will head this way."

"That's a different worry. Get the com system ready. Sylvia and I will work on the message."

"Give me five. Make me a formatted data set, all ready to send." Aybee bent over the panel and began to work. After a few minutes he swore and looked up. "Problem. System's not set up for general broadcast."

"Can't you jury-rig?" Bey could hear the sound of his own voice changing, and his hands were starting to tremble. He didn't have long to get to a form-change tank.

"I can. But I'll have to sit here and baby it. It's a low-data rate, too—I'm going to need half an hour's transmission. But as soon as we start, this whole habitat will start to buzz."

"Agreed." Bey stood up. "Sylvia, you can finish the message. We want everyone in the System to know that Ransome is the cause of control and communications breakdown. Tell them the location data for Ransome's Hole, what he's been doing, all you know about him. Ask help from anyone who can give it. Say we need a hundred ships or a thousand, from anywhere in the System, and while you're at it add a note saying that there's a leak in Cinnabar Baker's office. If it's Baker herself, that takes care of it. If not, she'll do something fast. And you, Aybee, as soon as you're ready, grab the outgoing circuits and send the message."

"What about you?" Sylvia had stood up when Bey did, supporting him as he swayed to his feet.

"I've got to guarantee Aybee his thirty minutes. Hold the fort here. Don't try to leave, even if you finish sending the message. Just lie low until I get back."

"Bey, you look terrible." Sylvia could feel his arm trembling. "I ought to come with you."

"No. You couldn't help me, and sending that message is top priority. Get it ready, then help Aybee to send it."

"What are you going to do?"

Bey gave her a wan smile. "I wish I knew. Don't worry, I'll think of something. Aybee, take a ten-second break and tell me how to get to Ransome's personal quarters. Maybe I can cut off our trouble there, right at the top."

Aybee nodded, paused for a moment, then rattled off

a series of directions. Then he at once bent back to his control panel. It was Sylvia who watched unhappily as Bey blundered towards the door. He still resembled Ransome in general appearance, but now his body language was subtly wrong. His movements had become jerky, with violent and random twitches of muscle in his arms and legs.

Sylvia kept silent and forced herself to watch him go. Bey thought he had another half-hour before he was forced to find a form-change tank. She suspected that was irrelevant. Long before that, Bey would be unable to pass as Black Ransome to anyone with eyes or ears.

CHAPTER 27

"God does not play dice."

—*Albert Einstein*

"God not only plays dice, but also sometimes throws them where they cannot be seen."

—*Stephen Hawking*

"God knows what God does."

—*Apollo Belvedere Smith*

There was silence in the communications center for five minutes after Bey left. Sylvia had quickly completed the formatted message and defined a directory reference for it, but then she was reluctant to speak and break Aybee's concentration. He was setting up the master sequence that would take over in one swoop every outgoing message circuit in Ransome's Hole, and it was important to provide no hint of that intention until the moment came for override.

Finally he glanced across to Sylvia and nodded. "Ready as I'll ever be. Where's the message?"

"I put it into a restricted access bank for safety—so no one can take a peek by accident."

"Right idea. Password?"

" 'LUCKY.' "

"Yeah. Let's hope." Aybee entered the final call sequence and sat back in his chair. There was a moment's pause, then a flicker of lights across the full display. He

457

nodded. "OK. We're in business. Now the fun starts—people are being bounced off com circuits all over the habitat."

"Will they know the command came from here?"

"Dunno. Probably. I couldn't see any way to stop it—but I did my best to make 'em freeze. I slapped Ransome's name on everything, so it looks like he's the one grabbing circuits." He stood up. "Keep your eye on that read-out. If it goes to zero, yell. It means I'll have to take over. We'll be all done when it hits two eighty. Then we can release the channels."

"What are you going to do?"

"Still don't know. Bey said, lie low, but we don't want to just sit here. We need to be useful." Aybee went to the door, opened it a fraction, and peered out. At once he drew back and allowed the door to close.

"What's wrong?"

"Guys outside. Four of 'em."

"Heading this way?"

"No. Not even looking. Just standing there. Bey's doing, for a bet. He sent 'em here to stop anybody getting *in*. But it means we're stuck." Aybee stared around the communications center, then walked across to a horizontal trap-door set in the curved floor. He lifted it and peered through.

"That won't help." Sylvia had followed his actions. "There's only a kernel down there. The door just gives access to the outside of the shields. You won't be able to get out that way."

"I know. I just want to take a look. I've been itching to get close to a live kernel ever since I arrived here." He paused with the trapdoor half open. "How's that counter?"

"Up to one seventy."

"Going smooth. Let me take a little peek here." Aybee lay down with his head through the opening of the trapdoor. "It's a live one all right. Whopping cable for the sensors. Big junction box, too—just like it was on the Space Farm's kernel." He craned further into the opening, wriggling his body forward across the floor until only his hips and legs were visible to Sylvia. "*And* its own computer console." His voice was muffled. "Seems like there's a direct link from the kernel sensors to the habitat's central computer. Now why do that, unless . . ." Another eighteen inches of Aybee disappeared through the trapdoor.

The count in front of Sylvia had been climbing steadily. It finally reached 280 and froze there, lights blinking softly. A "MESSAGE COMPLETE" indicator flashed on. She released all the com circuits, and walked across to the trapdoor. She tapped Aybee on the thigh.

"What's up?" His body twisted round so he could look at her.

"Nothing bad, but we're all done with the message. If you want to go down there, you'll find it easier feet first." She waited as he turned, and followed him down the narrow ladder until they were both standing on the outer shield of a kernel. Sylvia stared down at the black, polished surface.

"How do you know this is an active kernel?"

Aybee pointed. "There's the control unit for angular momentum. I've checked a bunch of 'em, this last couple of weeks. Most of them aren't connected to spin-up/spin-down systems, so they're not ready as energy sources or energy storage. Matter of fact, I'm not sure just what they *are* doing." He paused. "This is a live one, though. Hooked up and active and ready to roll."

The kernel's control panel was a compact unit sitting on the curved shield surface. Aybee squatted down by it. "So far, so good. Want first crack at it?"

"I wouldn't know where to start. But if you know a way to tell what's inside the shields, you can check what Bey suggested to me when we were working on the message. He thinks there's some new form-change product in there, something that can survive near a kernel. He tried to scan the shield interior back on the Marsden Harvester, looking for something unusual, but he didn't find a thing. He wasn't sure he was doing it right, though. Leo Manx told him to ask you, because this is your line of work. But you were off having fun on the Space Farm."

"Yeah. Had a great time there. Real pleasure trip."
Aybee was already at the control panel, staring vacantly
at its complicated console. "This layout's a strange one
for a power kernel console. Too many functions. *And* it's
directly linked with the habitat's central computer."

"Can you scan the interior?"

"Dunno." Aybee listed the control function menu and
studied that for a few seconds. "Guess I can. Only thing
inside the kernel shield—apart from the kernel—should
be the radiation monitors. I'll use them to do an interior
scan, and output it to the screen. We'll pick up an image
of anything inside the shields. But I'll bet my butt that
we don't find anything in there."

He turned on the display and set the interior monitors
to perform a slow scan within the innermost kernel
shield. The kernel itself, pouring out gigawatts of radiation and particles, appeared as a tiny, intense point of
light on the monitor. The triple shields, reflecting back
that sleet of energy, showed on the same monitor as a
softer, continuous glow.

They both stared at the screen, waiting in vain for any
anomalous pattern. When the scan had finished Sylvia
shook her head. "That does Bey in. He was sure there
had to be something inside. What now?"

"We gotta use pure logic." Aybee was back at the
controls. "One: there's an information source inside the
kernel shields. Two: there's nothing inside the shield but
the kernel. Therefore—nice clean syllogism—*the kernel
must be the information source*. I've been skirting that
for weeks, wondering if I'm off my head—but no one
would let me get near a kernel and find out!"

"Aybee, let's not get too ridiculous. A kernel is a *power*
source. It isn't an *information* source. And how can
there be anything inside a kernel? It's only billionths
of a centimeter across. And even if there were anything
inside, it couldn't ever get a message out. A kernel is
a black hole!"

Aybee was shaking his head and changing the scale on
the output display. He had zoomed into the area around
the kernel itself. "Come off it, Sylv. Black holes stopped

being black in the nineteen seventies, two hundred and fifty years ago! Hell, you know that—why else do you need shields? You know black holes pump out particles and radiation. Every kernel has its own radiation temperature and its own entropy. Maybe its own *signal*."

"But it's too small! You couldn't possibly pack a signal generator in such a tiny volume."

"We don't know how much space there is *inside*, or what the inside of a kernel is like—no idea at all. The interior has its own geometry, its own space-time signature, probably its own physical laws. Hell, people have been saying for centuries that the inside of a black hole is a 'separate universe,' but we never bother to think through the *implication* of that. If the inside of each kernel is a separate universe, *anything* could be in there—including somebody capable of communication."

"Somebody? You mean something *alive*? How did it get in there?"

"Hey, you'd better define life for me. If you mean something capable of generating non-random signals, then yeah, I mean *alive*. As for how it got there—it's been in there all along."

"But *how*? And what could something inside a kernel possibly want to say?"

"One question at a time, Sylv. Do you want to find out what's going on, or do you want to run a debate? Remember, thermodynamics only tells what's happening on *average* for a kernel's radiation. It doesn't say what gets emitted at any particular moment—so let's take a look at this." Aybee turned on a second screen. "We don't see a thing when we just monitor the total radiation output of the kernel, because the average level is so high. But I can display the time-variation of the radiation—the deviation from the average. See that fluctuation? Now it could be a *signal*. Information, coming from the kernel—from nowhere. Just what Bey was looking for, as bad inputs to the form-change process. And I'll bet this could be responsible for breakdown of communications, all through the system. Don't forget there are active kernels in all the important places, everywhere from the Harvesters to the

Space Farms. It could be the cause of the snake wrapped around the Kernel Ring, the giant woman walking across the Space Farm collector, flaming blue swords, giant red space-hounds—you name it."

Sylvia was studying the rise and fall of the radiation pattern. "But it doesn't *look* like a signal. It's like pure noise."

"A perfectly efficient signal looks like noise—until you know the rules." Aybee was tracing the circuits leading from the kernel monitors. "Before the signal can be interpreted, it needs to be *decoded*. And that's where the computer systems must come in. See, this signal is fed as an input data stream to the computer—the central computer for Ransome's Hole. Let's have a look at what the computer thinks it is seeing. It starts by—uh-oh." He was staring at a new signal on the screen.

"What's wrong?"

"Bad news for Bey." The alert signal vanished and was replaced by a flashing message. "While I was playing with the com system, I took a precaution. I set up a priority interrupt for information about Ransome." Aybee was frowning at the screen. "According to this, Ransome is in two places at once on the habitat. I asked for positional fixes, but all I get as an answer is 'NO DEFINED LOCATION.' Bey might run into the real Ransome."

"Can you do anything about it?"

"Not one thing. We don't even know where he is."

"Then we have to keep going." Sylvia was more intrigued than she had realized. "Let's find out what we've got here. What's the next step?"

Aybee did not answer for a minute or two, then he marked a point on the screen with the cursor. "See that trace? It says there's a program on the main computer system, one designed as an interface with this kernel. It ought to be the code/decode algorithm. We can try it. You stay right here, Sylv, and tell me what happens. I'll go to the upper console and execute that module."

Aybee scampered back up the ladder, leaving Sylvia to wonder what they were hoping to accomplish. It was difficult to see how fiddling with kernels could help them to escape from Ransome's Hole. But it was hard to stop Aybee when he had the bit between his teeth—and now she didn't want to stop any more than he did.

The lighting in the kernel shield chamber was poor, and Sylvia was forced to lean close to see the miniature control display. For another minute or two there was nothing to claim her attention. Then she noticed that the spin-up/spin-down mechanism on the kernel had suddenly been brought into action. It was adding and subtracting tiny bursts of angular momentum, far too little to make sense as power supplies.

"Are you doing that?" she called out.

"Doing what?" Aybee's head appeared at the trapdoor.

"Spin up and spin down. But just little changes. Now it's stopped."

"I've been entering a question about kernel operation. But it shouldn't cause kernel spin change." Aybee was suddenly gone again. "How about that?" called his voice from above.

"Yes. It's doing it again. And now I'm seeing a change in the kernel radiation pattern. What's causing it?"

"I'm not sure, but I've got ideas. Hey!" His voice rose half an octave. "Did you just poke something down there? Touch the sensor leads, maybe?"

"I'm nowhere near them."

"Well, I'm getting something wild on the display here. Come up and look at this."

Sylvia hurried up the stairs and went across to Aybee at the console. The display was flickering with random lights. While they watched it moved suddenly to a distorted pattern of letters. Sylvia gaped as the screen steadied and an intelligible message began to scroll in.

QUERY . . . QUERY . . . QUERY: ARE YOU READY TO RECEIVE?

"Ready," said Aybee, and added softly to Sylvia, "Let's hope we are."

MESSAGE TRANSFER: DEGREE OF TRANSMITTED SIGNAL REDUNDANCY HAS BEEN REDUCED. ENCODING ENTROPY PER UNIT NOW DIFFERENT FROM ALL PREVIOUS

RECEIVED COMMUNICATIONS. DEDUCE PRESENCE OF NEW SIGNAL-GENERATOR IN SENDING SYSTEM. QUERY: WHO ARE YOU?

Aybee blinked and stared at the panel. After a moment he shrugged. "My name is Aybee Smith." His voice was suddenly husky and uncertain, and there was a moment's pause before the vocoder could make the adaptation and a transcript of his words appeared on the display screen. "I am special assistant to Cinnabar Baker, General Coordinator of the Outer System. I have with me Sylvia Fernald, responsible for control systems in the Cloud. Hey. More to the point. Query: Who the hell are *YOU*?"

CHAPTER 28

*"... he felt for the first time the dull and angry
helplessness which is the first warning stroke
of the triumph of mutability. Like the poisoned
Athulf in the Fool's Tragedy, he could have
cried, 'Oh, I am changing, changing, fearfully
changing.'"*

— Dorothy L. Sayers

The interior of Ransome's Hole reminded Bey of some
great, cluttered warehouse. Scattered through it, seem-
ingly at random, were hundreds of kernels, each enough
to power a structure twice the total size. The minute
singularities were distributed through the whole structure, held in position by electromagnetic harnesses and
floating within their triple spherical shields.

With no other masses to provide gravity, the kernels
defined the whole internal field of the habitat. Corridors
curled and twisted, following the local horizontal; free-
hanging cables snaked their anfractuous and eye-dis-
turbing paths across open spaces, bending to follow invisible equipotentials. The floor of a corridor could veer
through a right angle in thirty meters, and still provide
a constant-gravity environment.

In Bey's present condition the journey through the
interior was one episode in a surrealistic nightmare. The
spiralling geometry around him matched perfectly the

reeling condition inside his own head. He concentrated his attention on following Aybee's instructions, and staggered forward. Fortunately the interior tunnels were almost deserted. He was beginning to hope that he would reach Ransome's quarters unseen when he saw ahead of him an armed group of four security officers. Two of them were facing his way. There was no way he could now avoid their attention, and in any case he knew no other way to his destination.

Bey put all his strength into standing upright and walking smoothly forward. When he was five paces from the group he gave them a curt nod. "Busy?"

"No, sir." The reply was prompt and respectful. "Not particularly."

"Good. There's an important message going out from Com Central, and I don't want anything to disturb it. I want you to go there and make sure there are no interruptions until I return."

It sounded feeble—*he* sounded feeble. But all he saw was a deferential nodding of heads. As the men moved past him, Bey risked his luck one more time. He reached out to take the hand weapon from the last man's belt. "Let me borrow this. I'll return it to you."

He had gone too far—he was sure of it. But the man did no more than nod, say, "Yes, sir," and hurry along after the others.

Bey stood without moving until they were all out of sight, then allowed himself to sag against the wall of the corridor. Standing erect and talking had been an enormous drain on his energy. He took one step forward, and felt in mid-pace a shock through his whole body. It was an internal vibration, a tremor of catabolism from every muscle and every nerve. Some inner barrier to destructive change had suddenly crumbled.

He set his mind on the turn in the corridor, twenty meters further on, and thought of nothing beyond that point. He took one step. His body responded reluctantly and imprecisely to his will; but it moved. Another. One more. One more . . .

He was at the turn. How long had it taken? The next

goal was ... what? A change in color of the corridor, thirty paces away. He had to get to that, there was nothing beyond that. Another step, and then another.

He guided himself along the wall with one outstretched hand. There at last. His eyes sought out and recorded the next objective.

One more effort—twenty steps. Surely he could do that much?

And then one more. Don't think, just move.

On the final approach to Ransome's personal quarters, Bey caught sight of his own reflection in a silvered wall panel. He thought at first that he was facing a distorting mirror. His limbs hung stiff and awkward from his body, his eyes started bloodshot from their sockets, and there was a grey, pasty look to his face. He tried Ransome's confident and commanding smile, and it was a madman's leer.

He stepped closer to the shining surface. It was perfectly smooth and flat, producing no hint of distortion. And the closer he came, the less he looked anything like Black Ransome. He stretched his arms wide and flexed his shoulders. There was the click and crack of frozen joints. His muscles were on fire, and every sign of mobility was leaving him. More and more, he was a poorly made, ungainly scarecrow, hung on a misshapen frame. He staggered on.

He had been prepared to bluff, lie or fight his way into Ransome's quarters. Now he was sure that he had passed the point where he had the strength to do any of those. Fortunately they were unnecessary. Perhaps Ransome was so confident of his own power to command loyalty that he scorned protection, or perhaps this area was protected only when Ransome was there; whatever the reason, Bey was able to pass unchallenged through the entrance.

Aybee had told him about the rococo style of the first chamber, with its great water-globe filled with exotic fish. Otherwise, Bey would have added that to his growing list of hallucinations. He went on, towards the inner suite of rooms. He had no idea how much time had gone by since he left Sylvia and Aybee. They needed every minute he could give them. In the back of his mind he still held an unvoiced hope: if somehow he could capture or neutralize Ransome himself, the chance of escape from Ransome's Hole still existed. He knew they could not wait for reinforcements. That would take weeks, even with an instant response to Aybee's signal from the fastest ships of the Inner or Outer Systems.

At the door of the inner chambers he hesitated for a moment. Surely the message would have been completed. In any case, he dared not wait. He could feel the changes coursing through every part of his body. His long training allowed him to compensate for some of them, but he was close to the limits.

The weapon he was holding was set at lethal level. He raised it, opened the door, and stepped through. And saw, no more than six meters from him, not Ransome but Mary.

Typically, she had ignored the standard dress code of Ransome's Hole. She was wearing a dress of russet velvet, with puffed shoulders and a choke collar, and on her head she wore a broad-brimmed green hat. She turned slowly at the sound of the sliding door, an imperious look on her face.

Mary was certainly playing a part—but which one? None that Bey recognized. He lowered the gun, so that it was no longer trained on her midriff. Mary ignored it anyway. She moved right in front of him and reached out to put her hands on his chest.

"Bey!" (So much for the idea that he still resembled Ransome.) "My poor sweet, what happened to you?"

"Where is Ransome?" His voice was failing, curdled in his throat.

"Bey, what are you *doing* here? I wanted to come and see you last week, but I was told you were no longer on the habitat. When did you get back?"

"I never left. Where is Ransome?"

"My poor love." Mary was holding him away from her and inspecting him closely, touching beneath his eyes with a gentle finger. Bey realized for the first time that he was crying. "I don't know what you've been doing to yourself, but I know what you have to do next. You look so sick. We've got to get you to a form-change tank— right this minute."

"Soon. Not yet. Where's Ransome?"

"Bey, you shouldn't even be thinking of Ransome in your condition." She was supporting him, holding him close. "You're shivering all over. I have to look after you."

"Where is Ransome?"

"I don't—" began Mary. She was interrupted.

"If you are so interested in my whereabouts, Mr. Wolf, you might at least look at me." The casual voice came from Bey's left, from a shadowed part of the room. He jerked to face in that direction. Ransome was standing there. As Bey raised the gun, the black-clad figure took two steps forward.

"No closer," said Bey. "This is on maximum setting."

"So it is. How very unfriendly." Ransome sounded as calm and rational as ever. "Come now, Mr. Wolf, can we not dispense with these posturings of violence? We are both civilised men, and we have much to talk about."

"Not true. You're a murderer. We have nothing to talk about."

"Let me persuade you otherwise. Do you realise, Mr. Wolf, that this is the third time that I have underestimated you? Really unforgivable on my part. But it makes me more convinced than ever of your value to my operations. You could do wonders for our security systems."

"I'll do nothing for you." Bey waved the gun at Ransome. He was feeling increasingly dizzy and unable to talk. "Move back."

"You will feel differently, once you understand my mission." Ransome moved another step closer to Bey. "You regard the two of us somehow as 'enemies,' people on opposing sides of an argument. But we are not. You will surely admit that you owe no allegiance to the Inner System—they dismissed you after a lifetime's work. As for the Outer System, those people have nothing in common with you. You and I can work together very well. So why not be practical? The old order of the Solar

System no longer applies. It will soon be gone for ever. Put away that gun and sit down. It is more dangerous to you than it is to me. And you and I must talk."

"I'm past talking."

"No, listen to him, Bey." Mary clutched his arm, but she did not try to interfere with his aim. "He's right. I've followed the reports from the Inner System. It's a total mess there."

"Sure. Because he"—Bey tried to gesture at Ransome, and found his arm taking on a spastic movement of its own—"has been doing his best to *make* it a mess. Can't you see, Mary, he's the *cause* of all the trouble?" Bey waved his arm again at Ransome. "I don't have the time or taste for talking to you. Get back up against that wall."

"Don't be silly, Mr. Wolf." Ransome advanced another step. "You escaped from your quarters. An unusual achievement, and one that I am quite willing to recognize. But beyond that you are powerless to influence events. You are in desperate physical shape, and you do not seem to understand reality. I can have a hundred people here to overpower you in a few minutes. So put away that gun."

"Get back! Last warning."

But Ransome was still coming forward, still smiling. And Bey was at the end of his own strength.

It was now or never. With shaking hands he pointed the gun squarely at Ransome's head, groaned, and fired.

There was the usual dazzling flash of blue. Bey sagged against the wall. Ransome had given him no choice—too many lives depended on stopping the man—but Bey was sick at what he had done. Would Mary forgive him, understand that he had to do it?

As the Cherenkov radiation pattern died away, Bey raised his head. Unbelievably, Ransome was still moving. He had walked right through a high-intensity beam. Impossible!

Cherenkov fringes appeared. As Bey watched, Ransome's face turned yellow and began to bubble. The skin evaporated in bursting pockets of light, exposing the wall behind as their color swirls faded.

The bubbles of Ransome's face were bursting in Bey's own brain. He dropped the gun and sagged against Mary. "Field interference effects—a holograph!"

"Of course." The image of Ransome was beginning to fade, and only his voice seemed to hover clear in the air. "How else could I appear to you when I am far away? And what a simpleton you must be, Wolf, if you imagine that I would not have taken precautions against both death and discovery!"

Ransome's uniform was becoming transparent. His smile showed a black mouth, black teeth, as he turned to face Mary. "Leave this idiot now. He deserves to die. And from the look of it he hasn't long to wait."

He glared at Bey and shook his head rebukingly, his face filled with contempt.

"I'm afraid I sadly overestimated you, Wolf. You're a fool, no more intelligent than any of the others. Did you seriously believe that I would expose myself to possible death, when my life's work is unfinished? If you had agreed to co-operate, I could have saved you. But you tried to kill me—and that means your own death. Your life is finished. For me, and what I am going to do, it is just beginning."

"No." Bey's throat was tightening. He had little time for more words. "You're crazy, Ransome. You're the one who doesn't know reality. *You* are finished. A message was sent from here a few minutes ago. All circuits, to the Inner and Outer Systems. People know where you are, what you are, how many your actions have killed. You're done for, Ransome, even if you don't admit it. No matter where you run to, where you hide, you'll be found and caught and brought to trial."

The image of Ransome's face flared with anger and astonishment. "That was a truly intolerable act. And quite a futile one. I am not finished—I have scarcely started! And I have tools available to me beyond your imagining. I would say, wait and see, but you will not live long enough for that. Die now, Wolf, your time is over."

Was it true? Did Ransome have more secret fortresses, other resources? Bey did not know, and he could no longer attempt analysis. If there were to be new battles with Ransome, others would have to fight them.

Black Ransome. The air around Ransome was turning black now. Or was it Bey's own failing consciousness?

"Leave this ignorant fool, Mary, and follow me," said a curt voice. And then even the dark shadow was gone.

Bey struggled to stand upright, to lean away from Mary. She was staring at him, holding him, her eyes wide and her face close to his.

"Bey! Can you hear me?"

Grim, grinning king. Ransome is gone, Ransome is gone. His head was dissolved, faded to black. *Fade far away, dissolve, and quite forget* ... Bey tried to nod, failed, felt his legs lose all their strength.

"Bey!" The voice was Mary, his Mary, infinitely sorrowful and far away. "I'm here." He could no longer see her. He tried to grip her hand, but as he did so all feelings withered from his fingertips.

Mary, dressed in white and strewing flowers. (*"There's rosemary, that's for remembrance."*) As he watched she grew, thinned, paled, became Sylvia, frowned at him in disapproval. *Too little, Bey Wolf, too hairy. Hideous.* Without warning her features flowed, became those of Andromeda Diconis. Her lower lip was full, her face flushed with passion, her red hair—red hair?—Mary's hair, Mary's husky voice saying, "There's beggary in the love that can be reckoned," a pale face beneath flowing dark hair and an elaborate headdress. He had seen *that* costume before, many times.

Bey's mind was a chaos of quantum states, transitions without warning or control, words and fragmented images interwined.

I am dying, Egypt, dying; only I here importune death awhile, until of many thousand kisses the poor last I lay upon thy lips. He heard Mary speaking in his mind, saw again the cotton robe, the dark coiled hair, the tall headdress, fought against her grasp. But you're not dying, Mary. I'm the one that's dying. *I have a rendezvous with death, at midnight on some flaming hill.* But that's not quite right, I'm remembering wrong. And this isn't Earth.

I'm dying here, far from Earth. *Far from eve and morning, and yon twelve-winded sky.*

I was always sure that I would die on Earth. In the evening, at the end of some perfect summer's day. *Sunset and evening star, and one clear call for me.*

He felt Mary's arms tightening around him, holding him in the world. Then that sensation too was going. In the end there was nothing left, nothing to hold on to. The whole universe was blinking out of existence.

"Thy hand, great Anarch, lets the curtain fall, And universal darkness buries all."

Bey was gone.

CHAPTER 29

"Nothing endures but change."

—*Heraclitus*

Bey had fought hard against it, but the pressure was at last irresistible. He was driven up, reluctantly up; up to life, up to consciousness, up to discomfort, up as firmly and finally as a cork in a tidal wave.

He washed ashore to wakefulness, and for a while he lay with his eyes closed, rejecting the world. But he could not block out the sounds. Close to him was a clogged, asthmatic wheeze, the rattling breath of a human being close to death.

After two minutes Bey could stand it no longer. He allowed his eyes to open, and at once came fully awake.

Perched on the open door of the form-change tank, no more than fifteen centimeters from his face, stood Turpin. The crow's head was tilted to one side and its beady black eyes glared unblinkingly at Bey. It again produced a dreadful groaning wheeze, and followed it with a gurgling cough.

That was echoed by a more distant throat-clearing. Three meters beyond Turpin sat Leo Manx, his face angry and reproachful. When he saw that Bey's eyes were open he nodded. "At last. Good. I will inform the others."

He stood up and hurried out, before Bey could ask the first of his dozens of questions.

Perhaps it was just as well. Bey could not speak. He leaned forward in the tank, and coughed his lungs clear of dark, clotted phlegm as Turpin shuffled out of the way with a squawk of rage.

By the time that he could breathe, Manx was back with Aybee.

Aybee stared at the spotted floor in front of Bey. "You got me here to see that? Gross, Leo. Extremely gross."

Bey ended a final coughing fit. "How long? How long was I—" He ran out of air.

But he already had some idea of the answer. A trip from the Outer System took weeks. If he and Leo were in the same room, a long time had passed. Even before he saw Leo, Bey knew that he had been in the tank for an extended session. He could feel it, in the mutability of every cell.

"Thirty-six days." Aybee looked accusingly at Bey. "Sleeping your head off, Wolfman. *And* you missed all the fun."

"You were in desperate shape," said Manx. "The form-change that you did ... unmonitored ... most ill-advised——"

"I know. I'm supposed to be dead. You caught Ransome?"

"No." Leo Manx was still looking annoyed. "He got clear away. We have no idea where he went, where he is, what he's doing. Naturally, we're still looking."

"Mary?" Bey's wind had gone again, and he was wheezing. He suddenly realised where Turpin had found the inspiration for that tortured breathing.

"She's here." Aybee paused, then caught the next question in Bey's look. "On Ransome's Hole, I mean. We're still on the habitat." He grinned. "Us and more people than I ever wanted to see in my life. Everybody you ever heard of is here."

"Answering our message?"

"Yeah—and another one I sent a bit later. That one pulled 'em here in droves. Sylvia's about ready to go into hiding. Hey, can you walk better than you talk? If so, you can see for yourself why things are running wild."

"I can walk." Bey considered the prospect. "Maybe."

"Then let's do it. You have to see this for yourself."

Bey stood up, almost toppled over, and realised as he did so that he was back in his old Earth shape. "How the devil . . ."

"Mary Walton," said Aybee. "She didn't really know how to do it, but when you collapsed she grabbed you and stuffed you any-old-how into a form-change tank. Set you up short and hairy—the way she knew best. Just in time, too. Sylvia saw the monitors when she got there. Five more minutes, you'd have been fertilizer."

"That's what I feel like." Bey slowly followed Aybee out of the room, allowing his body to drift along in the low gravity. So Mary was here, and so was Sylvia. Between them they had dragged him back from the edge.

He was glad to be alive. But no one else seemed too pleased.

"What's making Leo so angry?"

"He was locked up for a week. He blames you." Aybee was leading the way into the central communications area. "Cinnabar's even madder. Sit down there."

Bey looked slowly around him. He had sat in this chair before. He remembered coming here with Sylvia and Aybee—just. He must have been far gone.

"Why are they mad?"

"They'll tell you." Aybee wasn't listening. He was at the console, long body tight with excitement. "Lock in and hold onto your skull. We're going online." He spoke into the vocoder. "RINI connect. Identification: Apollo Belvedere Smith. Reference: Anomalous signal generation, defined in session 302. Query: What is status?"

He turned to Bey. "Takes a few seconds. Far as I can see, that's for encoding and decoding at this end. Their replies are instantaneous. Someday we'll know how."

"*Whose* replies?"

Before Bey could get an answer the screen was filling. The words on it echoed through the lock into Bey's ears.

THIS ACCESS POINT CONTINUES. ALL OTHER SIGNAL GENERATION TERMINATED *no equiva-*

lent. QUERY: STATUS OF ANGULAR MOMENTUM CHANGES?

"Computer still can't translate times," said Aybee to Bey. "That's what 'no equivalent' probably means. I'm wondering if the Rinis *have* times in our sense. If not, this next bit won't mean much to them, either." He said to the vocoder: "All angular momentum changes for identified kernels will cease in three more days. Query: Can you confirm we have complete list?"

LIST CONFIRMED. REQUEST INFORMATION ON ALL OTHER KERNELS, MASS, CHARGE, ANGULAR MOMENTUM, *no equivalent*, LOCATION YOUR REFERENCE FRAME.

"We will provide. Request that the following message be sent to access point 073. Transfer message begins. 'Cinnabar Baker leaving Ransome's Hole in four hours. Expect arrival at Brouwer Harvester nine days from now.' Transfer message ends."

DESIRED TRANSMISSION PERFORMED. REQUEST: CONTINUED TRANSFER SHOULD PROCEED FROM GENERAL DATA BANKS.

"We will provide all the general data banks." Aybee grimaced at Bey. "Want to say anything? All right, let's cut it. Request: Session end."

SESSION END.

"Offline." Aybee turned away from the vocoder, grinning with mad satisfaction.

"What the hell was that all about?" Bey was feeling angry, but he recognized it as one of the mood swings that accompanied emergence from the tanks. "I assume you're willing to tell me."

"Sure. Just a minute." Aybee set up a control sequence. "Got to give them the data—they want the general system data bank sent through, it's a hell of a job. Going to take months." He leaned back. "You had it half-right, you see. The source of spurious information that was screwing up form-change and everything else is inside the kernel shields."

"But not a changed form, the way I thought it had to be?"

"No. It's something inside the kernels themselves. It—or they—sends out the standard radiation stream, but it's modulated to carry messages. It's your source of negative entropy."

Aybee spoke casually, but he couldn't hide his excitement. From anyone else, Bey wouldn't even have listened. With Aybee, he had to take it seriously. "You know that what you're saying sounds impossible."

"Sure does. That's why it's so interesting. Wolfman, I keep telling the Co-ordinators, but they still can't grasp the importance of this. Nor could Ransome. Even though he was using the Rinis for his own purposes, he missed the real point."

"He was the one who discovered this?"

"Not proven. Somebody in the Kernel Ring stumbled across it, but I'll bet it wasn't Ransome himself. They were spinning-up and spinning-down kernels. Routine stuff, the usual energy storage and extraction. But the things inside one of the kernels could detect the change in angular momentum. They hated it, it affected their inertial reference frames. But they're *smart*. They figured out the cause, and modulated the radiation emission in reply—sent a signal, in effect. After that it was a straight programming job at this end, signal encode and decode. The trick was to spot first that it *was* a signal."

"*Inside* the kernel." Bey stared down at the floor. A billion ton kernel had an event horizon only a few billionths of a nanometer across. The ultimate hidden signal source. "They call themselves 'Rinis'?"

"No. They don't call themselves anything at all, far as I can tell. That's the code name I gave them. The computer answer to anything I asked at first seemed to be R I N I—'Received Information Not Interpretable'—so I stuck 'em with it. I'm getting better at questions now, though."

"Who are they, Aybee?"

"Can't give you one answer. Everybody asks me, but I say it's too early for that sort of question. Intelligent, sure. Smarter than us, could be. A species, maybe. But it's more like they're a new universe. A whole cosmos.

I'm not ready to worry that. I'm still getting my head around a bit of their science. They gave Ransome a bundle of things—new drives, new communications—but there's a lot more than he realized. We're going to get some wild theories out of this."

"They're more advanced than we are?"

"Yeah." Aybee paused. "Or maybe I mean maybe. I don't know how to compare. If I wanted to talk fancy like Leo, I'd say it's like their science is *orthogonal* to ours. They move along a completely different axis of understanding. It's easy to use their ideas, and hell to understand 'em. I'm still having trouble with the basics. Like, are the Rinis a single entity, or a finite—or an infinite—number of entities? That sounds weird, but from what I can see of their counting it's based on non-denumerable sets instead of integers."

"They can't be a single entity. There has to be at least three of them."

"Why?"

"Because I've seen that many kernels putting out false form-change information."

"That would be true if each kernel was totally separate. We used to think that, now I'm sure it's wrong. The kernels—at least the kernels involving the Rinis——"

"Isn't that all of them?"

"No. That's why Ransome had to switch kernels on the Space Farm. He wanted to get one of his special kernels out when it had done its job. But the Rini kernels are connected somehow. What's known by one is known by all of them. At once, no matter how far away. That's what brought so many ships here. I sent a message saying I might have a system for instantaneous communication, across any distance."

"But if they all connect, they're only one object."

"Not to us. We think they're separate objects. But to *them*, their space could still be singly connected. It's like Flatland. To a being living in two dimensions, on a flat floor, each leg of a chair meets the floor separately, and must be a separate object. That's the way the kernels seem to us. But in a higher-dimensional world—their world—they are all connected, all parts of one chain."

"But then you shouldn't be able to supply energy and angular momentum to each kernel separately."

"Why not? You can paint one leg of a chair." Aybee turned to Bey. "Hey, I'm glad you're back in circulation. I've been wanting talks like this for weeks, but nobody seems to care. Cinnabar and Leo and the rest of 'em are all too busy running around talking politics and stopping wars, and there's all this really good stuff needs looking at. Do you know how the drive the Rinis gave Ransome works?"

"No. But it can wait until tomorrow." Bey stood up. "I'm tired now. Don't bother to get up, I can make it out of here on my own."

He was being sarcastic. Aybee had shown no sign of moving. In fact, as soon as Bey said he was leaving Aybee nodded and turned the computer on again.

Bey's own feelings were more complicated. Everything that Aybee said was fascinating, but Bey was getting tired. More than that, he was restless, to the point where sleep was out of the question. Without any conscious plan he set out to follow a familiar path, drifting along the corridors that led from the communications center to Ransome's private quarters.

When he opened the door he thought that the outer chamber was unoccupied. Then he noticed Sylvia Fernald standing around by the side of the great water globe, staring in at the fish. Next to her was Cinnabar Baker, even thinner than when Bey had last seen her.

They had their backs turned, but Baker somehow sensed his approach and swung around. When she recognised him she produced a sound somewhere between a snort and a laugh. "At last. I've waited a month to be rude to you."

"You and Leo both." Bey wasn't getting the praise he had expected. You'd think that when somebody nearly killed himself, to make sure an important message got out . . . "I guess you weren't the information leak out of the Harvesters."

"Of course I wasn't. But I had quite a time proving it. You made it sound as though the only ones who could be leaking information to Ransome were me or Leo—and then you ruled out Leo."

"That's the way it looked. It had to be somebody close to you, and it had to be someone who moved with you from one Harvester to another. And Leo and Aybee were away with us on the Space Farm."

"True."

"So that means—"

But Cinnabar Baker had spun around and was heading for the door. "Figure it out," she said over her shoulder. "Or if you can't, Sylvia can tell you about it."

Bey stared after her. "She is *mad*. I wouldn't want to argue with her when she's like that."

"She's been furious for weeks. I've never seen her so angry. But not at you. At Ransome. He did the unforgivable thing."

"Worse than trying to take over the System?"

"Much worse, if you're Cinnabar Baker." Sylvia sat down on a long bench by the side of the water globe and patted the seat next to her. "Sit down, before you fall down. You look exhausted."

"What did Ransome do?"

"Baker wouldn't have minded as much if he had done it to her, personally. But Ransome's people got hold of *Turpin*. They put an audio-visual tap into his head. Everything the crow saw and heard was transmitted straight to Ransome; and Baker never went anywhere without Turpin—he even slept in her bedroom. She realized what was happening when she saw the viewing angle of some of the shots. Worst of all, the tap hurt, and the feed for it made poor old Turpin nearly blind and deaf. When Baker found that out she wanted to wring Ransome's neck with her own hands."

"Where is he?"

"We don't know yet. But we'll track him down."

"I'm not sure of that." Bey finally sat down next to Sylvia. He had become used to being tall, and it was disconcerting to find that his head again came only to her shoulder. His hands were feeling numb, and he rubbed them together. "Ransome was clever enough to make a bolt-hole for himself. He's still as charismatic as ever, and he'll always be able to draw people to him."

"I know. Paul thinks Ransome makes the sun shine. But next time he tries anything we'll be ready. Ransome's finished, but he doesn't know it yet. I almost feel sorry for him. Mary told me——"

"Where is she? I wanted to thank the two of you for saving me."

Sylvia looked at him and put her hand gently on his shoulder. "She didn't leave a message, Bey? She said she would."

"I didn't check."

"I'm sorry. Mary left Ransome's Hole. Yesterday, and secretly. I knew she was going to do it, and I suppose I should have tried to stop her. But I didn't. She's going to look for Ransome, wherever he is."

The numb feeling was spreading from his hands through his whole body. Mary had gone. Left him again. He accepted the fact instantly. It was something he had sensed when he entered the chamber and did not find her.

"That's terrible." He took a deep breath. "I thought she really loved me."

"She does, she always will. She told me that, and she had no reason to lie."

"But she prefers Ransome."

"She didn't say that. But she said that Ransome needs her more than you do."

"How can she possibly think that?"

"The last time I talked to Mary, she told me to ask you something."

"She seems to have told you an awful lot."

"She did. But here's her question. Before Bey tells you his heart is broken, she said, ask him this: of all the things that have happened to him since he left Earth, which has been the most exciting and satisfying? And ask him to *think* before he answers."

"The most exciting——"

"You're not doing what Mary asked. Think first."

"I *am* thinking."

And he was. *The most exciting.* Was it looking out of the ship, for his first sight of a Harvester ... or the strange, perverse pleasure of the first meal with Sylvia ... the satisfaction when he learned that the Dancing Man was not a dream of his own unstable mind ... the Space Farm rescue ... the giddy time with Andromeda Diconis, sampling the pleasure centres of a hedonistic habitat ... the thrill of Mary's voice where he had never expected it. Making love to her. Or ... a memory flooded in, total and satiating. Bright yellow tracers ran again in his mind.

"It was when——" He paused, then the words were wrung out of him, reluctantly, one at a time. "It was when I was looking for the reason for the wrong form-changes. And when I realized that the source of the problems must be inside the kernel shields. But I could never describe that feeling to anyone. And there's no way that Mary could have known it."

"Of course not. She doesn't think that way. She didn't know about the form-changes, and she didn't know about the Rinis. But she sensed what *sort* of answer you had to give, if you were truthful. Because she understands you, very well. Don't you see it, Bey?" Sylvia put her arms around him. "Mary needs to be needed. When *you* needed her, she saved you—even when you were still back on Earth and didn't *know* you needed her. Ransome wanted to cause chaos and stir up trouble between the Inner and Outer Systems. He knew that form-change equipment would be more sensitive than anything else to the Rini effects on information flow, so trouble would show up there first. Anyone who might understand what was happening had to be dead, insane, or converted, and it seemed easier to drive you crazy than to kill or convert you. But Mary found out what he was doing. She scrambled their signals, so that the images you received were distorted and less effective."

"They were almost too much."

"But they weren't. You stayed sane. She would have

taken any risk for you. And Ransome needs her now and she'll take risks for him. You *want* Mary—but Ransome *needs* her."

"I almost died for Mary, back on Earth."

"Did you? Leo told me that you had the Dream Machine on a medium setting—low enough to break out of it when you decided you wanted to."

Bey stared mindlessly into the great water globe. A small, red-throated fish had come drifting lazily towards them and was poised at the curved transparent wall. It stared goggle-eyed at the two humans, looking at the universe beyond the barrier. That had been Bey, before he came out here. Tucked away in his own little fishbowl, safe and warm below a blanket of atmosphere. *Earth.* Suddenly he had a great longing to be back there, to see blue sky and drifting clouds.

"I'm going back, Sylvia. My job here is finished. The Rinis are interesting, and they're going to change our whole universe, but they will be Aybee's lifework, not mine."

"I know." Sylvia was still holding Bey. "Aybee's going to miss you. He'd never say it, but you're his idol, you know."

"Hard luck for Aybee."

"He could do a lot worse. Mary told me one other thing. She said that when you met her out in the Halo you talked a lot about me. She didn't speculate why, but I think you were trying to make her bring you here."

"I was. It was the only way I could think of to do it. I wanted to make her jealous, so she would want to bring me along and see I preferred her to you. I don't mean that I *do* prefer her to you, but . . ."

Sylvia was shaking her head. "Bey, when I hear you say things like that I wonder if you know anything about women at all. If Mary had been the least jealous, or thought for a moment that you were interested in me, the last thing she'd do is encourage a meeting."

"But that's exactly what she did."

"Do you need it written out for you? You didn't talk

Mary into bringing you with her to Ransome's Hole—she was intending to do that all along!"

"But you said there was no way she would——"

"Not so you could see if you liked Mary better than me." Sylvia's voice was warm. "You hairy, self-centered little ape. Mary did it for *her* purposes, not yours. She wanted to see if she liked you better than Ransome. But after she heard you talk about me, she said she felt less guilty about leaving to follow him."

Bey sat for a few seconds in silence, staring into the blue-green depths of the water. He was feeling tired, but not the slightest bit heartbroken. Even the revelation of Mary's motives didn't upset him.

"I'm a total idiot, you know," he said at last.

"We're all idiots."

"I'm the worst. I thought I was being so clever with Mary. I'm going back, Sylvia. Back to Earth, back to something I'm good at. To the Office of Form Control again, if they'll have me. But I'm really going to miss you and Aybee and Leo. I'm even going to miss Cinnabar and old Turpin, but I'll miss you most of all. Would you come and visit me—see the Inner System for yourself?"

"Among all those little, hairy, Sunhuggers?" He knew it, she was laughing at him. "What do you think I am?"

"I think you're a big, heartless skeleton that pretends to be a woman. Earth's not as bad as you think. I think you'd like it. Will you do it? Come and visit?"

"I'm not sure." She ran her finger along the hair on his wrist and refused to look at him. "No promises. But we'll see."

Bey nodded. It was all the answer he could expect, but it was enough.

He looked again into the water globe. The little red-throated fish was up against the wall, and it was still staring out at him. It had no eyelids, but Bey felt sure that it was trying to wink.

GRAND ADVENTURE
IN GAME-BASED UNIVERSES

With these exciting novels set
in bestselling game universes,
Baen brings you synchronicity at its
best. We believe that familiarity with
either the novel or the game will
intensify enjoyment of the other.
All novels are the only authorized
fiction based on these games and
are published by permission.

THE BARD'S TALE™

Join the Dark Elf Naitachal and his apprentices in
bardic magic as they explore the mysteries of the
world of The Bard's Tale.

Castle of Deception
by Mercedes Lackey & Josepha Sherman
72125-9 * 320 pages * $5.99 _____

Fortress of Frost and Fire
by Mercedes Lackey & Ru Emerson
72162-3 * 304 pages * $5.99 _____

Prison of Souls
by Mercedes Lackey & Mark Shepherd
72193-3 * 352 pages * $5.99 _____

And watch for **Gates of Chaos** by Josepha Sherman
coming in May 1994!

POUL ANDERSON

Poul Anderson is one of the most honored authors of our time. He has won seven Hugo Awards, three Nebula Awards, and the Gandalf Award for Achievement in Fantasy, among others. His most popular series include the Polesotechnic League/Terran Empire tales and the Time Patrol series. Here are fine books by Poul Anderson available through Baen Books:

If not available at your local bookstore, you can order all of Poul Anderson's books listed above with this order form. Check your choices and send the combined cover price/s to: Baen Books, Dept. BA, P.O. Box 1403, Riverdale, NY 10471.

Name _____

Address _____

City _____ State _____ Zip _____

JOHN DALMAS

He's done it all!

John Dalmas has just about done it all—parachute infantryman, army medic, stevedore, merchant seaman, logger, smokejumper, administrative forester, farm worker, creamery worker, technical writer, free-lance editor—and his experience is reflected in his writing. His marvelous sense of nature and wilderness combined with his high-tech world view involves the reader with his very real characters. For lovers of fast-paced action-adventures!